W9-DHG-399

SUNFLOWER

By Rebecca West

Fiction

The Return of the Soldier
The Judge
Harriet Hume: A London Fantasy
War Nurse: The True Story of a Woman Who Lived,
Loved and Suffered on the Western Front
The Harsh Voice: Four Short Novels
The Thinking Reed
The Fountain Overflows
The Birds Fall Down
This Red Night
Cousin Rosamund

Non-fiction

Henry James
The Strange Necessity: Essays and Reviews
Ending in Earnest: A Literary Log
St. Augustine
Black Lamb and Grey Falcon: A Journey
through Yugoslavia
The Meaning of Treason
The Meaning of Treason, revised edition
A Train of Powder
The Court and the Castle: some treatments of a
recurrent theme
The Young Rebecca
1900

Books with David Low

Lions and Lambs
The Modern 'Rake's Progress'

SUNFLOWER

REBECCA WEST

First published by Virago Press Limited 1986
41 William IV Street, London WC2N 4DB

Copyright © the Estate of Rebecca West 1986
Copyright Afterword © Victoria Glendinning 1986

All rights reserved

British Library Cataloguing in Publication Data
West Rebecca
Sunflower.
Rn: Cicily Fairfield Andrews   I. Title
823'.912[F]   PR6045.E8

ISBN 0-86068-719-8

Typeset by Goodfellow & Egan, Cambridge
and printed in Finland by
Werner Söderström Oy,
a member of Finnprint

The jacket painting is reproduced
by kind permission of
Matsuoka Museum of Art, Tokyo

To my friend
G.B. Stern

I

SHE never could understand machinery. So when the chauffeur tried to explain what was so seriously the matter with the automobile that it would take a whole two hours to repair, she cut him short and said, 'Never mind, Harrowby. Accidents will happen, and anyway it's much nicer than travelling by train.' She noticed a look of real perturbation round his nice eyes, and was puzzled till a flash of comprehension came to her, and she hastily explained, 'Oh, it's all right about my being late. I'm not expecting – anyone.' But she did wish Essington would not get so angry when she was late that the servants noticed. It wasn't her dignity she was thinking of; she was too tired to think of that. But it dug away her defences. For if nobody else knew how he behaved, then when she woke in the middle of the night and felt like a trapped rat she could pretend that things weren't so bad, she could say to herself, 'I expect I imagine most of it. For he's awfully fond of me, really. He can't get on without me. Look how he always wants me to go away with him for his holidays. Yes, I'm silly, that's what I am.' But if other people knew about it she couldn't fool herself, and had to go on feeling like a trapped rat.

She shivered, and said, 'Well, I suppose I can't go on sitting here if

1

you're going to do all that to her. I'll go for a walk,' and stepped out of the automobile. The garage yard was full of the clear light of May, and it was a pleasanter place than most of its kind, for it had evidently been an old livery-stable and its walks were of mellow red brick, patterned with streaks of moss and golden patches like freckles where time and sunshine had toasted away the surface. In the end wall was an archway barred by an iron gate, through which one could see a green country garden that was as much orchard as garden, with fruit trees standing in grass too long and strong for a lawn, and rows of rhubarb. It made her think of the orchards round Chiswick when she was a little girl. They had been so pretty; and she had had time to look at them, for then her days had been too empty as now they were too full. She was glad that this breakdown which gave her an hour to herself had happened in this little market town, where there were orchards.

'Harrowby,' she asked, 'didn't we pass a pretty place with water, just before we came into the town?'

'Yes, Miss, a kind of big pond it was, with lily pools. A gentleman's estate left to the district for a park, I should say it was. There were seats. About three quarters of a mile back, it was.'

'Oh, dear! That's too far. I'd have to walk a mile and a half in all. I suppose I won't have time. And it was so pretty. It seems as if one never could do anything one wanted, doesn't it?' She felt like crying. Nowadays she was all to pieces.

'But you said, Miss, that you hadn't got to hurry. And I could run you back to town in an hour and a half from here. This is Packbury, you know. I should go if I were you, Miss. It'll do you good.'

It was all right. There was really no reason at all why she should not go. It was simply that she was so unused to liberty, so seldom free from the leash that jerked her back to heel whenever she was doing anything she enjoyed, that she felt at a loss when she was on her own. She pulled herself together and said gaily, 'All right. I'll come back here. Don't try to fetch me, for I'll take a footpath if I can.' She hadn't been on a footpath for years. He tuned up his engine and took the car, calling over his shoulder, 'Never known you have an hour to yourself before, Miss!' She smiled and waved her hand, and turned towards the street. She meant to buy some fruit and chocolate, and eat it sitting by the pond.

But a young man in overalls, the man Harrowby had been talking to about the car, stopped her. 'I'm proud to have your car in my garage, Miss Fassendyll.'

2

She did so want to buy that fruit and get away by herself to the pretty place. But she had to pause and look pleased, since he meant to be kind. 'Oh, that's very nice of you. Fancy your knowing me!'

'Well, who wouldn't? My wife –' he gave a broad, shy smile, 'she'll be real sorry she isn't down to see you, she's laid up just now. Some people say she could pass herself off as you any day. Quite a joke it is among our friends.'

'Isn't that interesting! I do wish I'd seen her. But I expect she's far nicer than me really. Tell her I'm ever so sorry I didn't see her, won't you?'

'I will, Miss. I can't tell you how disappointed she'll be, for you're her favourite actress. When we were passing through London last year on our honeymoon we went and saw you. She wouldn't hear of going and seeing anybody else. "I want to see Miss Sybil Fassendyll," she said, and that was that. Rosalind you were.'

'Oh, was I!' She sighed. 'The papers said I was awful.'

'We thought it was lovely. Never enjoyed an evening at the theatre more, particularly considering it was Shakespeare. I suppose there's a lot of jealousy and that to account for what they write in the papers.'

'No, I don't think it's that. They're kind, most people. I didn't know anybody when I started, and look how they've let me get on. But sometimes it's hard to understand what they want you to do . . .' Her eyes wandered vacantly round the yard. She became absorbed in contemplation of this mystery which nowadays was constantly vexing her, as to what the art of living could possibly be. One went on to the stage properly dressed and made up as the character and said the words as they would be said in real life. How could there be anything more to it? Yet it seemed, from the way that people went on, as if there was. She wished this man would not go on forever standing between her and oranges, and the pretty place with water, and rest. Apart from making her think of uncomfortable things he was horrid with his flat, smug, deliberate voice, his characterless, genteel phrases, and his peculiarly wide smile, which showed a gold-crowned tooth in his lower jaw. But there he stood in her path, quite undislodgeable, slowly turning a spanner in his hand, and smiling fixedly and over-broadly. She looked away again, and a spike of white lilac, thrusting above the tortoiseshell reds and golds of the wall, caught her wandering eye. Absently she said, 'You've got a nice place here. It looks old, too.'

3

'As old as you can think, Miss,' he said, still turning the spanner, still smiling. 'This was the stable yard of the White-Faced Stag Inn before it was burned down, and nobody knows how old that was. Queen Elizabeth slept there, anyway.' It seemed that he must be about to stop, for the pause was long, but he did not. 'We had an awful job to get the place right. Had to take up all the old cobblestones, for one thing.'

'Isn't that a shame! I always think they look so pretty.'

His smile grew broader. 'That's just what my wife says. But you wouldn't like to drive into a garage all bumpitty-bumpitty, would you?' He laughed tenderly, as if something in that feeling about the cobblestones struck him as very comic and lovable; labouring the point ridiculously. Then he began to tell her interminably how much it had cost to set the place in order, how he had spent every penny of his gratuity on it, to which she said wearily, remembering the cloud-marbled surface of that pond, 'Well, I hope you're doing well now.'

In a moment during which she nearly groaned aloud, he did not reply. Then he muttered, 'Well, we were able to get married on it a year ago,' and looked at her with shining eyes and a smile that was not fixed at all but trembled on the tide of a deep feeling. He opened his mouth, and closed it. He had ceased to turn the spanner in his hand, and was holding it away from him stiffly, exhibitingly, like a priest holding a reliquary; it might have been the symbol of something sacred that he possessed and wanted to tell her about and could not because he was overcome by reverence. It came to her suddenly, for she was clever about people though she could get the hang of nothing else, that he had been telling her all these dreary things about the cost of removing cobblestones and the price of petrol-pumps because they were part of a story that he knew to be wonderful; and from a kind of glow of love about him, that was as real and perceptible as might have been the flush of rage or the pallor of despair, she knew that he was right and that the story was really wonderful. This man and this woman were in love, and it was lasting though they had got each other; they were living a marvellous life. This aroused in her feelings not only of happy sympathy but of partisanship, for she had been accustomed though not resigned to a world where everything – politics, business, the arts and sciences – were esteemed above life. 'Why do they make such a fuss about Shakespeare because of "Romeo and Juliet"? It's more wonderful to *be* "Romeo and Juliet", like these people, than just to write it down,' she thought contentiously while

4

she smiled into the man's blindish, radiant gaze, and cried, 'Isn't that lovely! Isn't that lovely!' She felt a little guilty, because she used what they had taught her about modulating her voice to help herself to sound really glad. It seemed to her – and the thought was painful, as if dwelling upon it would force her to the realisation of some immense loss – that had they both been inarticulate they might have found it easier to understand each other. For it was not as if she were wholly articulate. That would have been all right. But though they had taught her to say a lot of things, these were chiefly passwords that made possible entrance into restricted circles, like saying 'gehl' instead of 'gurl', so that rather than widen her power of communicating with her fellow-beings they had narrowed it. 'I've been muckered about,' she thought resentfully. It was a sign of the general incalculable queerness of things that her clear, rounded sentences and definite gestures should proceed from a condition that was not at all satisfying, while the completion of this man who was happy with his wife expressed itself in these broken, inadequate, stockish mutterings. 'You see,' he was saying, 'I had to have enough and a bit more, for she came from a good home, a very good home. Much better people than me she comes from . . .'

'Yes, yes, I know what you mean,' she nodded sagely.

He began again to turn the spanner in his hand, looking down at it. 'It's a queer thing you should have come like this. It's always been something remarkable like, you being so like my wife. We've often talked about it.' He spoke with great gravity, and she understood why. She could not have found it out for herself, it was a little too difficult for her. But it had been explained to her by Essington, in one of those rare moments when he stood back and looked at her and thought about her, instead of just crying out for her with closed eyes, utterly dependent and quite uninterested in how she might be, like a very young baby with its mother. One night after dinner he had been very kind and happy, she could not at first think why, till she remembered that it was from no more substantial cause than a walk along the Row, tender and melancholy and achingly contenting, with the pale coin of dead leaves spinning down the aisles of dark wet earth, under trees that were but bare tracery, as if the year, crazed with her losses, were playing pitch and toss with her last wealth in a ruined church, and the blue mist above the Serpentine making it look like the place where the dead of London might go the night they die and linger, wistful but too drowsy to be afraid; while the warm lights came out in the houses

5

overlooking the park and one remembered that one was not dead, and that at home there would be toast. They had hurried home, skipping when there was nobody about because the cold air was working on them like wine, and had muffins for tea, and she had played Farnaby and Purcell to him on the pianola all evening, and there had been a perfect little dinner with a pheasant that was just right. It showed how really good he was, and how sweet, that it was only simple things like that which made him happy. His successes did not; it was part of his tryingness that he would come back from all his big political meetings in an itching fury of self-loathing, as if he had looked down into the abyss of vanity and hypocrisy and intellectual dishonesty that engulfs those who believe the people when it praises them. But that night he had been very happy. He had made her sit on the little stool at his feet in front of the wood fire, and had actually asked her about her work, which as a rule he resentfully ignored in the same spirit that an old-fashioned housewife ignores the follower who prevents her servant from giving all her time and energy to her domestic duties. She went to her desk and brought out some photographs that she had been wanting to show him for some days, but had not dared to because he had been going through one of his bad times. Two girls, one a mill-girl in Oldham, the other the manageress of a sweet-shop in Huddersfield, had spent what must have been a lot of money to them on being photographed in the poses of her own best-known portraits, and they had sent her their own photographs and the ones they had copied with long letters exultantly pointing out the closeness of the resemblance, and asked her to sign her own, so that they could put them together in the same frame for their sweethearts. 'Isn't it funny,' she had wondered, 'that anybody should be proud of being like somebody else? Wouldn't you think everyone would want to be just like themselves? It's so modest of the poor things.'

Essington had taken the photographs, though he did not look at them for more than a second. Nowadays it seemed as if hardly anything concerning personality could hold his attention; he cared only for thick books, for interminable talks about ideas that would go on being true if the human body had no flesh on its bones, if trees were not green in summer, if there were no such thing in the world as sound. It made him terribly difficult to amuse in the times when his brain was tired and he had to rest from work. But he looked down at her, as she sat on the stool at his feet, for quite a long time. When he spoke his china blue eyes were wet. 'It's because you're one of the two or three people in every century, Sunflower, that are more than what they are. You're supposed to be the most beautiful woman in the world –' 'Isn't it funny!' she had interjected, 'They never notice that my nose isn't straight.' At that he gravely felt her nose all the way from the bridge to the tip, and said he thought that it was straight enough, and told her that, whether she truly was or not, the people liked to think of her as the most beautiful woman in the world; and that they liked too how she had risen to her acclamation out of nothing, for everybody knew that only a month before her famous appearance in 'Farandole' she had been serving in a stationer's shop in Chiswick High Street. Indeed, she contained within herself two of the great legendary figures that man has invented everywhere and in all times: Venus and Cinderella. And they were not – he bade her remember – invented idly. They fed desires that must be fed if man is not to lose heart and die. For Venus promises him that there shall be absolute beauty in this world, that the universe shall bring forth perfection which shall make its imperfection a little thing, lightly to be borne; and Cinderella promises him that this harsh order of things which is life may be only temporary and subject to reversal at any time, so that the mighty may be put down from their seats and those of low degree exalted. These things are not understood by the people, but they are felt by them. The mill-girl in Oldham, the sweet-shop girl in Huddersfield, believing themselves to be like Sybil Fassendyll, obscurely know themselves to be by that resemblance related to some system which proved Oldham and Huddersfield a dream, and the waking a fair one. And their sweethearts, obscurely too but more intensely, because only the most passionate egoist can love himself as one loves others, rejoiced in that conviction. 'Think of it, Sunflower! There's a cotton operative in Oldham, a railway clerk in Huddersfield, who feels like a pious Catholic in the Middle Ages who fell in love with a woman who was like some miracle-working Madonna, just because his girl is like you . . .'

And Essington had been right. This little man, with his shy, flickering, devout smile and the solemn, ritualistic movement of his hands as they turned and turned that spanner, was plainly thinking of the resemblance between his wife and her as proof of some imminent sacredness. It was astonishing that Essington, the brilliant and important Essington, whom only the jealous denied to have the greatest mind in the world, who with an almost vicious fastidiousness desired to know as little as possible of all those minds that were not nearly equal to his,

7

should have known the heart of a stupid, flat-spoken little man who kept a garage in Packbury! It showed the power of love. He understood this lover because he himself loved her. Ecstasy shook her. She wished that they could all four be standing here in this yard within the red-gold walls, a group of kindly, friendly lovers, she, Essington, this little man who had so much in his heart, and his wife whom she conceived as a younger, lovelier sister of her own, with a nose that was quite straight . . .

There interrupted the happy grazing of her mind one of those sudden, splintering, ripping noises that are apt to break out whenever there are men in overalls. She clapped her hands over her ears and spun round protestingly, because her nerves were so broken that any loud noise made the tears stand in her eyes, and she had so greatly liked the quietness in which she had been standing with the little man. A mechanic was breaking open a large packing-case just inside the garage, with an immense appearance of gusto, and flinging himself upon the crust-coloured boards, tearing off strips of sallow sacking, releasing innumerable shavings to the mercy of the draughts. She marvelled at the way that men did not mind noise, till it struck her that she herself had not minded noise before she was with Essington, and that as a rule single girls could bear what troubles their ears brought them with calmness. 'They wear one down,' she muttered, and drooped; for if they wore one down, well, one had to be worn down. But she was diverted from that sad strain of thought by the nature of the object which was being disclosed by the mechanic's onslaught. It was a perambulator, a new and really prodigious perambulator. Its navy blue body was varnished till it was glossy as water sliding to a weir; its spokes gleamed with the sober but even brightness of the very best japanning, and there were foppishly white rubber tyres; the experienced eye could note that the leather hood was the kind that really washes and does not crack. 'C-springs, stops, a safety-chain and all!' she breathed, 'A really nice one!' She knew a great deal about prams. It had been part of her duty at the stationer's shop in Chiswick High Street to take out baby Doris in her pram every afternoon. That one had not had ball-bearings. This one had. Somebody wouldn't have to break her back pushing the thing when there was bad weather. With that nasty cheap thing the Jenningses had, into which it was a shame to put a pretty little dear like baby Doris, she had often halted in front of baby-carriage shops and gazed enviously at the really nice ones in the windows, and indeed had indulged in dreams of buying the most expensive one on her own account some day, for she had then never doubted but that her future would hold a pram. Oddly enough, as it had turned out, that future was to hold nearly every other kind of manufactured article – telephones, Rolls-Royces, fitted dressing-cases, Paris-to-London aeroplanes, there didn't seem any limit to what she might buy or use – but never a pram. Yet say what you like, there was something nice about a good pram, about this one, for instance, as the man wheeled it off the floor of its case and on to the concrete, where it stood quivering as Essington's greyhounds sometimes did, evidently so resilient that it would run nicely over the bumps, so stable that it would not overturn too easily. 'I don't say it mightn't be better finished,' she pronounced, 'I don't suppose it's one of Hitchings', but I do say it's well-built and handy . . .'

In the midst of these technical musings a wonder, an exciting wonder, struck her. Whose pram was it anyway? Was that why the little man's wife could not come down and see her? She imagined the girl who was like her sitting waiting upstairs at one of those windows that overlooked the garage, behind those nice clean Nottingham lace curtains. That must be lovely. One would not have to keep on worrying about trying to make oneself cleverer, because one was doing what was recognised as a whole-time job. Everybody in the house, particularly one's man, would be thinking of one with kindly concern; there would not be that awful feeling of having to keep up to scratch, of having to win approbation that would be coldly withheld if one's performance was not good enough. One would be able to sit there resting, waiting, obtaining that peaceful entertainment which animals must know out of the accidents of substances near at hand: pressing the paint blisters on the sun-scorched edges of the shutter, putting one's eye close to the flaw in the pane and watching how it made the red-gold wall and the surmounting spike of lilac waver as if they were deep under an uncoloured, viscous sea. But the poor young thing had still that awful agony to go through. She shuddered, for like people of almost any age, she hated to think of anyone younger than herself in pain; it perpetually seems to us, whether we are twenty or thirty or forty or fifty, that it is only just in the last two or three months that we have learned how harsh this business of life is and armoured ourselves against it, and we cannot bear to think of mere tender youngsters (as we were before the few months) having to face this dreadful knowledge and assume that armour, which is not light. Oh, poor young thing, poor young thing . . .

9

Perhaps, however, the baby had come already. But the little man would have told her if it had. No, he need not. He might have kept it to the very last, then it would be mentioned casually, lest the Fates should hear and guess how well things were going with him and his wife and do something to spoil it all. She often used to feel like that when she first lived with Essington. But she did wish the little man would say it out now, because if that pram really did belong to him and not to a neighbour it made it all the lovelier that he was so much in love with his wife, since he must have seen her looking ugly and had to look after her. She must know that before she went back to town. It was something to hang on to, knowing that even if you were not happy other people were. She must say something that would lead up to it, though of course he would not tell her if it had not happened. It was only rich smart people who talked about babies before they were born; she had turned scarlet when she first heard them at it. Pondering what she could say that would help him to tell her if he wanted to and not press him to if he didn't, she looked into the distance; and met the eyes of four people who were standing beside a small yellow car.

Nice manners they had, staring at a person like that. They might think that though a person was on the stage that wasn't to say that they liked being treated off the stage as if they were a waxwork. She was always slow of thought, and never slower than when she was forced to suspect that the world was not kind, but the look of them made her apprehensive, for though they were all smiling as they looked at her there was a kind of grease on the surface of their gaze, a kind of scum of squalid feeling . . .

And at her elbow the mechanic said, 'Beg pardon, Mr Pantridge, but that party with the yellow Morris-Cowley was asking if Lord Essington lived in the neighbourhood. I've never heard of him being round here, have you?'

'No, not a bit of it,' said the little man. 'His place is down Cookham way. Some of us went over from Reading Hospital first time I was wounded. His wife gave us tea. A very nice lady she was. Tell 'em they're dreaming. What do they want to know for? Got a cousin who does his lordship's lamps?' He was annoyed at being interrupted, and immediately went on telling her about his wife's eldest brother, who had done so well in the war that he got a commission.

Her jaw dropped. She stared at the four, wondering how they could do such a thing. When startling things happened to her she always became a child again at the impact and felt as if she had no previous

10

experience of the sort. For a moment these people seemed to her as prodigious as gnomes and giants; and then noting the cheap, smart make of the women's clothes, the excessive something about the men's skirted overcoats, the common look they had of trying to look not better but worse than they really were, a kind of aspirant unpurity, she wearily placed them as members of a type she had encountered hundreds of times before. 'What we want to know' cads, they were. One saw them sometimes at the Embassy Club; they did not belong to it, but men who had to be nice to them because of business took them for a treat and they sat about staring at the people, bobbing forward suddenly to ask who they were, and getting pop-eyed if they had asked about anybody who was divorced or kept. A blush began to sweep over her face, her neck, her breasts, which had begun to smart since she realised that they were thinking of her as a sexual being. These men she thought would have liked to buy all the women in the world, but the money hadn't run to it. These women would have liked to be bought by all the men in the world, but they hadn't found their way in to the market. So they dreamed beastly dreams of the world as they would have liked it to be, men and women all sticking together like jujubes in a box, and to make them more solidly satisfying they pretended that they were real things that happened to real people. It was they who said that Connie Maddox had had a black baby; who said that Lettie Aylmer, who was straight, had had an affair with the Duke of Victoria, so that when she got engaged to young Lennie Isaacs his people, who minded, being Jews, were horrid to her for quite a long time. And God knew what they had said about her; what they were saying about her at this very minute. In pain, for she was silly and never got used to this sort of thing, she stared across at them to see what they were saying. It would be something new and lying, for the true thing, about Essington, was too old to amuse. They were sniggering together, with pleased moist smiles under noses wrinkled with disgust, like horrid children talking of a nasty secret. There wasn't any knowing what they might be saying, she said to herself again and again, lest when she stopped she should maybe know what they were saying.

When the little man had paused in his story of how well his wife's eldest brother had done in the war, she put out her hand and said, 'I must go. I promised to call back somewhere we passed on the road . . .'

He was a very nice little man. Though he would plainly have liked

11

the bright presence of the patron saint of his family imagination to be for ever in his yard, he let her go at once. 'Well, it's been very kind of you to let me talk to you like this. Eh, my wife will be vexed she couldn't see you. I wonder . . . I wonder . . .'

Ah, he was not going to let her go, after all. But there was evidently something he quite dreadfully wanted.

'What is it? You were going to say –'

'I wonder if you'd just wait one second while I get my wife's photograph. It was taken just after we were married. We thought of sending it to you at the time, it was so like, but we didn't have the nerve. She would be so pleased if you'd seen it . . .'

The poor darling. If the girl was waiting upstairs this might help to pass the time for her. She smiled unsteadily. The tears in her eyes were incommoding her. Those awful people would not go away. 'Of course. I'd love to see it.'

It would be all right if he asked her to come into his house. But he did not. He thought of doing so, she could see, for his eyes went to the green side-door and then back to her, but was checked by some thought. Doubtless there was a tyrannous nurse installed there already who was capturing the house for her fuss and litter of preparation and resented visitors. She gave him a little encouraging smile, as if she quite liked waiting in the yard; and he left her.

•

Well, the yard was still full of pleasantness. One ought to think of that. There was still the May sunshine, and the red, gold-freckled walls; there was the spike of white lilac, now bobbing springily under some bird-gymnastics executed lower down on its bough: there was the iron gate, and the homely orchard garden. But in that direction she did not dare to look, because they were standing there. What was the use of trying to think of pleasant things when they were standing there! People couldn't have been taught right when they were young if they could do a thing like that. They were just blatantly gaping, with one man fiddling with a suitcase on the carrier as an excuse for delay that would not have taken in a cat. It was Essington's theory which he had constantly and irritably impressed on her that she ought not to mind this sort of thing, that indeed it was impossible that she could sincerely mind it; but that did not at the moment seem to be true. She tried to imagine what would be thought about it by those people who

12

in her mind were most remote from him, most unlike him in that vein of unfriendliness to her and all her instincts which ran like a dark vein through his love for her; by Rettie Adamson, a girl she was at school with whom she used to walk with on the Monkey's Parade in Chiswick High Street, and Olga Hammond, who used to dress next to her when she was in 'Farandole'. She had really loved both of them, but of course she hadn't been able to keep up with them. Either of them, put in her place, would have gained some satisfaction by reflecting on her superiority in looks over the two women who were tormenting her. She tried to brave it out that way. They certainly were a couple of miseries and no mistake, with their umbrella legs and their Palais-de-danse faces. Now she was all right: she was five foot eight and every bit of her measured what it ought to; her hair was real gold, lay it against a sovereign and it didn't look so bad; lots of people thought she was the most beautiful woman in the world; if she was turned into a statue they could put her into a museum without getting an artist to alter her. But coldly she realised this would not do. She was as far away from Rettie and Olga as Essington was, though not in the same direction: and in that position, which she felt to be very lonely, she knew that her immense physical conspicuousness made her situation far worse. She could not quite see how; but there gleamed deep in her mind a picture of herself as a vast naked torso, but not of stone, of living, flushing flesh, fallen helpless on its side in some public place of ruins like the Forum in Rome, with ant-droves of tourists passing incessantly round her quickly, inquisitively, too close. Sometimes it was hot, and dry winds swung against her weakly like a tired arm, flung dust on her, and dropped again; and tourists crowding along in the shadow of her limbs put up their sweaty hands to experience her texture and stroked the grit into her flesh. Sometimes it was wet, and her groins were runnelled with thick shining ropes of water; and the tourists, going quicker than ever, rushed along her flanks and pricked them with the spokes of their umbrellas.

The queer things one thinks of! And there sounded in her ears the tones that somehow had something to do with this picture, of Mr Thursby Jingal, who writes the Spy-Glass in the *Daily Show*. It was last week that he had said to her, 'There are people who are News. Not because of anything they do, not because of anything they are. But just because they're News.' She had objected. 'But so is every leading actress, isn't she?' And he had answered, 'No. Nina Purefoy is a leading actress of far higher standard than yourself. But she isn't

13

News. You know as well as I do that Lillah Plumptre is almost as beautiful as you are. But she isn't News. And – er – social things have nothing to do with it. Betty Packhard has had – er – a very interesting life. But she isn't News. It's something all of itself. And you've got it. You had it when you were a little girl doing your little five minutes in 'Farandole' and drawing your five pounds. Even in those days if you went into the Carlton with a young fellow and had a bite and Nina was sitting there after the most colossal first night in history and Lillah was looking as glorious as Helen of Troy, and Betty was there with her diamonds and her Duke, it would be your pink hat and green gloves that the Spy-Glass would notice. I tell you, you're News . . .' His tones had been creamily congratulatory. But being News was like living under a glass bell, a transparent prison, in whose walls the normal light of day was changed to heat that made every incident of one's life grow to an unnatural size, an unnatural sappiness . . .'

The bird that had been bobbing on the lilac-bough whirred and shot itself up into the sunshine. It must be fun to be able to fire oneself off like a gun and be the gun, to press the trigger and be the bullet; and such fun to bounce and bounce in the thin bright upper air among the pretty dustless treetops. Well, one could swim and dive. Really, this was a good world. It would be all right if one was brave. It was cowardly of her to mind that the people were talking about her and Essington, because it was true. If she had not been willing to stand by what she did she might not have done it. But, oh, why couldn't Essington have married her, and made it not true any more? Now he was out of politics he could have afforded to let Lady Essington divorce him. But it was wrong of her to think of that, for there was a principle involved; though she was not quite sure what it could be. It could not be disbelief in the institution of marriage, for he always did his formal entertaining at Lady Essington's house and in lots of ways he seemed to feel that a wife ought to be better treated than someone you live with. There was that time when he had made her cancel her rooms at the hotel she always went to at Cannes because Lady Essington had suddenly made up her mind to go there. She was quite sure, however, that there was some sort of principle involved. It might just be that one had a right to do what one likes. But it could hardly be that, for being stared at by beasts was exactly what she did not like doing. Nevertheless, though the principle continued to elude her, she never doubted but that it existed. Her failure to perceive it she ascribed without question to her own incapacity; for she well knew that always when she tried to make a generalisation out of the abundant and confused facts of life she found herself in the position of the people in a comic advertisement of meat extract that she had once seen: one earnest worker was holding up a bull while another tried to press it with a shoe horn into a small bottle which dangled on one of its hooves like a glass boxing-glove. She never hoped to confine the great bull life in her minute and brittle mind. But Essington was different. His mind was as large as life. He would know this principle. Mildly she marvelled at his greatness, and at his queer kind vagary in loving her, who was so stupid; and reflecting that anyway all this was irrelevant, since the point was that what these people were saying was true, and she must therefore not mind them saying it, she lifted her head and faced them.

That defence went at once. She had to look away and droop her head. For from the grease that floated on these people's gaze she perceived that what they were saying was not true. It was probably a lie about her and some man that she had never seen; if by chance it stuck to the facts close enough to give her Essington as a lover it lied in making them live a beastly sort of life together. Drinking, and rowdy parties, and all the kind of things that come into some people's minds when they think of legs, though goodness knows why, for legs are just legs. That was downright funny. She didn't drink at all; and Essington drank nothing at lunch and only weak whisky-and-soda with his dinner. They didn't give parties. Essington hardly liked anybody. And she didn't go out to parties much now; she had so often had to break engagements because he turned up unexpectedly that now she hardly liked to accept invitations. Sometimes, indeed nearly always when she was not rehearsing, he would tell her that he would come to her during the day, but that he could not say at what hour; and then she could go out only for a little while at a time, nervous dashes into the park with one eye on a watch, and come back to sit about alone, for he hated to find people out when he came. There was nothing at all to do then. One could not do any housework, with all the servants about; and being beautiful one must not sew, for that brings on the little fine lines round the eyes which are the beginning of the end. There was the pianola, of course, but music did not interest her very much; and there were books, but she was stupid. Sometimes, sitting in the quiet rooms, she used to think that though she had a nice house and pretty things and all the flowers she wanted, she did not have as amusing a time as her mother had had at 69 Tyndrum Road, Chiswick. She had

had a horrid little house and not very much money, but there was always a lot doing, what with cooking and running up clothes on the sewing machine and talking to the milkman and the neighbours and going round to Aunt Bessie and Aunt Polly and doing the shopping. Shopping on Saturday night was particularly exciting, with the naphtha flares burning outside the shops in the High Street, and all one's friends bumping by with their stuffed string bags, all very jolly and amiable with the joy of buying things. That was a hard life: but this was a dull one. What was she saying? She had forgotten that it was all right when Essington did at last come, so great, so cleverly, so childishly dependent on her, even after ten years. He would drop his face into the curve of her neck and shoulder and rub his face against her warm flesh like a baby or a puppy . . . 'Let's go to bed quite early. I am so tired. I couldn't sleep at that damned house. Sunflower, let me lie up close to you . . .'

Of course there was that for them to think nastily about. Essington did do that to her. But why in the name of goodness did people get so worked up about that? When one came to think of it, which one hardly ever did, there was so little in it, either way. It was no use pretending it was such a marvellous thing, because it wasn't, at least not for women. Those women over there could have all she'd ever had of it, as far as she cared. But they ought to know better, being women. It wasn't so very bad either. It was odd rather than really horrid, like giving a man a queer kind of medicine. And, anyway, however you looked at it surely she had been good. There had never been anybody but Essington, though there might have been. There might have been. It seemed to her, as she remembered the chief among those there might have been, that a cold wind had breathed into the yard through the iron gate. Those fools were giggling about her because they thought she was bad; but it was rather her fault that she was too good. Wouldn't it have been better for her to have been bad and given Marty Lomax what he wanted? Then, though he would have died just the same, he would not have died crying out against her cruelty. She knew people said that you ought not to let a man do that to you unless you were married to him, and that anyway if you had to break that rule you must never, never let two men do it; yet when she remembered his thin voice saying over and over again, 'I want Sunflower. I love Sunflower,' she felt a chill of guilt, as if she were a nurse who out of malice had failed to dress a patient's wound and stop a deathly bleeding, an unnatural mother who had withheld food from her weak child. Surely nothing really mattered except being kind. She wondered achingly how she could have refused anything to anybody who was so lovely to look at as Marty. There never can have been anybody much lovelier. He must have been a most beautiful baby, for when you looked closely at his hair you saw that it looked drab only because it was clipped so short, and it was really bright gold. And he had such nice grey eyes, which were so purely smiling light that they came out white in all his photographs. And he was so tall, yet as pretty in his movements as a polo-pony. Besides, just as the sight of a clergyman always reminds one of a church and religion, so the sight of Marty always reminded one of something, though one could not say exactly of what, except that it was warm and pleasant and yet so unsettling that one wanted to run out into the open air and not come back.

She found herself thinking of Francis Pitt. That always happened when she thought of Marty, now that he was dead, and it was odd. She couldn't guess why the image of a man she had known very well should invariably recall and be immediately wiped out by the image of a man who was not at all like him and whom she had only seen once, and that quite a long time ago. It must be six or seven years now, for it was during the war. She had gone to the office of a charity to see the secretary about a matinée, and since the lift was out of order she had had to walk upstairs. As she stopped on a landing and looked at the names on the wall directory to see if it was here the office was, a little man with hair the colour of a fox and a very big mouth ran very quickly downstairs from the floor above. He paused and looked at her out of queer grey eyes which were the colour of bad weather, with extreme appreciation and utter lack of interest. It was plain that he cared for women, for he looked at her as a sailor looks at a ship, but everything in him was absorbed in anticipation of something he was going to do. With her mouth a little open, because what he did seemed to be charged with significance, like the movements of a really great actor, she noted the dead halt at which his feeling for beauty made him come to a stop in front of her, and the springy vehemence with which his eagerness for what he was going to do made him pull himself together, strike his gloved hand with the other glove as if that were a spurring signal, and race on down the stairs. She leaned against the wall, listening to his quick footfalls, that were as explicit as laughter. When the sound changed and she knew he had come to the hall she went to the banisters and leaned over, but there was nothing

17

to be seen. In the silence she stood and turned over the thought of him in her mind. No doubt what she had noticed about the dramatic effect of the two contrasting movements – the sudden halt, the sudden racing spurt – would come in useful some day in some part that she had to play. She reminded herself that she must think more of her work. Many people found complete happiness in their work. Then she went on to the office, which was on the next floor, and they told her that she had just missed meeting the chairman of the committee, Francis Pitt, the Australian millionaire. She was glad at that, for if they had met he might have felt bound to stop and talk to her out of politeness, and that would have distracted him from full enjoyment of his happiness. He had been so happy! The recollection of it always gave her a curious fluttering, laughing feeling. Sometimes it came to her when she was sitting learning a part, and she had to get up and walk about the room, rubbing her hands which then felt as if they were charged with electricity. It had come to her hardly at all while she was seeing Marty, but it had come to her often since his death and she was glad. That the man who had been so happy still existed somewhere was proof that the tomb had not taken all youth to itself, that other things survived besides those which did not challenge death by being over-much alive; which was what one thought sometimes, when one was tired.

She had remembered a man stopping and looking at her on a landing and then running past her down the stairs. That was all. Why should she feel as if some veiled figure had raised a rod and struck what it was her religion to pretend a rock, and drawn a hollow sound? Suddenly she found herself admitting that everything was wrong with this situation in particular, with her situation in general, and that there was no way of thinking it into being right. If Essington really loved her he would not put her into a position which made horrid people giggle at her and make up ugly stories; and she was always suffering things from him which it was not bearable that she should suffer from a man who did not really love her. But all that was nothing beside the central falsity of her life, which she could not put into words, which she could not grasp with her mind, because she was so stupid, but which appalled her. She saw a vast desert. The words bankruptcy, starvation, crashed through her mind. The trapped rat feeling that came to her often in the night came on now in spite of the sunshine, which indeed it dimmed; and she wanted to run and run and run. But she could not do that, any more than she could ever do anything she wanted to do, because the horrid people were still looking at her and would go away and say that they had seen her drunk, if she did anything odd; and the good little man was coming towards her with the photograph.

She took it in her hand, which was now clammy and shaking, and breathed: 'Oh! . . . Isn't she lovely!'

Of course it was far lovelier than if the girl had been lovely. How fondly her husband must love her, to think her beautiful! She reflected wistfully, yet with joy at their happiness, that this ugly girl knew a triumph that she would never know. For if a man says that you are beautiful, and you are, then he is merely making a statement of fact, and you cannot guess from it whether he is in love with you or not. Even if you know he is, the statement still gives you no pleasure, for there is nothing private or even personal about it, since innumerable people have made it before him and no doubt some have subjected it to the last disenchantment of print. But if a man says that you are beautiful and you are not, then it is a proof that he loves you. The alchemy of loyalty is working on him, he is not separate from you. And since no one else says so it is as intimate as if it were a part of the little language that people who love each other always talk. Decidedly there are other fair seasons than the spring, other conditions than beauty for making people live kindly. A wave of intense emotion passed through her. There was a haze before her mind in which there floated her vast flushed torso, dear Marty, Francis Pitt, this hideous and beloved girl. The upshot was a kind of aching happiness.

'Yes, she's very lovely!'

'Well, I think so.'

'Far lovelier than me . . .'

'Oh no, Miss. I wouldn't say that. But you do see the likeness, don't you? Funnily enough, there's a photo of you in this morning's *Daily Show* that takes you in almost that very pose. I don't know if you've –' He held the folded page beside the photograph. 'Isn't it exact?'

She hadn't seen it. At Clussingford where she had spent the weekend they did not take in the *Daily Show*. At least they may have, for many newspapers and weeklies and reviews lay about on the tables, arranged according to some system of journalistic affinities, so that they lay on the dark wood in curious shapes such as the foundations of an unerected village form on the sward; and indeed they might be taken as the foundations of an unerected intellectual structure, for nobody ever read them, or anything else. The nice fresh-faced people in sports clothes sat about in the library, with the plump, pompous busts, the globe that showed the countries of the world, really so vexed and dangerous, in sweet pale colours like the silks that lay neatly in the work-boxes of long dead women beside it, and the shelves of bindings that made the eye feel as the palate does when it is drinking old port; and it could not be doubted that they knew what it all meant, for these people loved their homes so much that they almost understood them. But they never read. They seemed to feel that their eighteenth-century forebears had done all the reading that was necessary for their class. It was a persuasion that made them restful to visit, but dull to live with compared with these common people, who bent their noses over the cheap prints and tracked down arguments for the reality of their romantic dreams among the trivial, smudgy words . . .

'It's got a lot about you underneath . . .'

He was smiling. Evidently there was something intimate that had confirmed the family in its love of her.

'The latest photograph of Miss Sybil Fassendyll, the famous actress, who is England's favourite representative of the type of blonde beauty. Tall and slim and golden-haired and sunny in face and disposition, she is known to her friends as "Sunflower".'

She drew her forefinger across her lips, compelling them to remain set in a foolish little smile. She felt frightened. There would be terrible trouble over this, for no one but Essington called her Sunflower. He would be furious at seeing his private name for her in print. Though he behaved to her much of the time as if she were his most alienated enemy, he could simultaneously behave to her as if he were an ardent lover in the first and most sensitive days of courtship, so far as the ready harbouring of tender grievances was concerned. On the ground that she did not love him as much as he loved her, that she had missed some fine shade of his devotion, he would hate her malevolently for a week. She knew the line he would take over this. Though it was as likely as not that her secret name had leaked into print through his indiscretion, for he was careless in talking to her on the telephone in front of the servants and secretaries, he was sure to say grimly, 'Sunflower, your little friends talk . . .' He loathed her having friends. She had almost none left. There was really only Maxine Tempest now who came about the house. He would certainly say that it was she who had given this to the press. There would be scenes. She would get so tired, and she had to start rehearsing tomorrow. Again she felt as if she were a rat in a trap. There floated before her once more the images of the vast flushed fallen torso, of Marty, of Francis Pitt, of the hideous and beloved girl, but this time they did not make any meaning of happiness. They had of course no meaning, they could not, for they had no connection with each other. Yet somehow life was not bearable unless they were connected, unless they had a meaning. She tried to steady herself by thinking of the ugly girl, for whom at any rate all was well. Yet was even that certain? For Essington had been very good to her when first they were together. It was not till after two or three years that he had made a scourge of his love. She might come back to this yard in some future spring and find nothing fair but the sunshine and the lilac, sourness on the face of the little man and the only thing that mattered gone out of the place. As it had gone . . .

She did not know what to think. She did not know what to think and be able to go on living. She looked wildly round her and became aware again of the four detestable people who were still standing there lechering with their minds upon her body. There came on her an impulse to throw her arms above her head and shout at them every ugly word she knew, meeting them on their own vile ground and bludgeoning them with her extreme brutality. The world was changing her, spoiling her.

She leaned forward to the little man and said, 'These people keep on staring at me! I can't stand it!'

Again she was obliged to be artificial with this person who had made her so greatly desire to be honest. But she did not mind so much now that she had begun to doubt if he would always think the ugly girl beautiful. So she gave him a consciously exquisite, benignant, and confidential smile, raised her finger to her lips with a gesture that she knew he would enjoy recognising as one she had used in 'As You Like It', and hastened out into the street.

•

When she had thought of the pond with lilies she could not see it, and no idea was any use to her unless she could see it as a picture. She no longer wanted to go there, and even if she had still wanted to she could not have managed the walk, for she felt spent as she did after a scene with Essington. There was something frightening in the way that though nothing had really happened to her during the last twenty minutes, except that four people had stared at her and another had said things that did not particularly matter, she seemed to have been standing up to an enemy, disputing with him, crying out to friends who did not hear, escaping sometimes to safety, but at the last falling under blows. It was as if the situation Essington had created had been given actual separate life by the power of his genius so that it could torment her even in his absence. But here she was, thinking bitterly about him, and that was wrong, for he was a great man, and often so sweet and kind and dependent on her. Nowadays her thoughts were terribly apt to go sour if she let them settle for a moment. Since everything was really all right, and she was of course quite happy, this was ridiculous. She must find something to do in this little town during the hour or so it was going to take to put the car in order, which would not let her think. Across the road there was a picture theatre, which might or might not be open. She went over to investigate, but stopped before she got to the other kerb because she saw that the posters which had looked so attractive advertised one of her own films.

'What's the good of a person going to a film theatre to forget themself if all there is for them to see is themself?' asked Sunflower, almost weeping.

She turned round to go back to the other pavement, but saw that her four tormenters had come out of the garage and were standing about to watch where she was going so that they could follow her. They might as well cross the road as her. She looked up and down the market-place, and decided to go to the more impressive end, where there was a big red-brick building with a clock-tower, because she was always attracted by that kind of architecture, which reminded her of the big buildings around Hammersmith and Chiswick and Turnham Green. Though they were ugly she liked them better than the beautiful places in the West End, which were what they were not because the inhabitants of that detestable part of London really cared for beauty, but they all had nothing to do but talk and criticise each other to bits, so that people who were putting up a building were compelled to make it magnificent out of self-defence. But in Hammersmith and Chiswick and Turnham Green they were busy living, and had no time to chatter about the look of things. Down there it was the little houses that mattered. Not that they were pretty, either, but they sheltered lives that seemed to her, who had to bear the glaring discomfort of publicity, infinitely precious in their privateness. None of the women who lived in the rows of little houses in those ugly parts of London need ever feel as she was being made to feel by the four people who were keeping time with her on the opposite pavement.

22

It was a shame. Because of them there seemed to lie on her a disagreeable obligation to move on, as if she were a criminal shadowed by the police. When a messenger boy, wheeling his bicycle across the pavement in front of her, stared into her eyes and stopped whistling, she ducked her head in a panic; and then made matters worse by looking back at him imploringly to persuade herself that there was nothing in his face but recognition of her beauty, so that it struck him that she was behaving oddly, and he came to a standstill, gaping. She hurried on with her head down until she bumped into a woman who was coming out of a shop. Looking up to apologise she found that the little body's eyes were set derisively on her coat, which was a very lovely fantasy in checks by Molyneux. She was not hurt by that, for often before she had noticed that good clothes, like any other form of fine art, were always greeted with ridicule when they were brought out into the open among ordinary people; and she knew that there is nothing base about this ridicule, since it springs, like the giggling of children who are taken to see a tragedy, not from a lack of sensibility but from its excess. Children are as far as possible from all knowledge of tragedy, ordinary people have few chances of encountering the rarer sorts of decoration, so these contacts are to them news of an unfamiliar variation in life. They are dismayed that it should exist at all, for it intimates that life covers a range far wider than the octave of their daily routine and that the demands which it may make upon them are endless and incalculable. They are dismayed, too, at its quality: for the beauty of tragedy, and the beauty of good clothes, which is one and the same beauty, asks from those who use it a sympathetic nobility and an unembittered but firm discontent with the emotion that is not right, with the colour, the line that is not right. It sends them off on that search for harmony which is as delicious as love for a woman who is perfect and loving, as agonising as love for a woman about whom one knows nothing, not even that she has been born. This is a hard thing to lay on children, on simple people. They will not have it, they pretend that what they have seen is of no significance, and merely a ludicrous accident of folly which calls for nothing from the sane but laughter. Essington had made her see all that when she had told him how the people in Cricklewood Broadway had giggled at her when her car had broken down on the way to the Fairshams' at Harrow, and she had had to step out into the street in a Nicole Groult picture gown and cloak.

23

That had been Essington's thought; it was now hers. Though she rebelled against him, she was a part of him. How could she leave him? How can one leave oneself? And she had nobody to go to. Marty was dead. She could not go back to the people she had come from, the people who were round her now in this street, because of everything that had happened to her in the last twelve years. She did not mean the sexual things, for she knew, as all women know, that these are of the slightest importance. She meant the things that had made her public and exalted. As she walked along she looked up at the big red building as one who saw the towers of a forbidden city, obscure, mediocre, sacred.

It was guarded at all its three doors by policemen. That made her remember something. Mr Justice Sandbury had lunched at Clussingford on Sunday and had taken her a little walk in the afternoon to see the famous white cattle at the home farm. She nearly always liked judges: as a class they were far preferable to retired prime ministers, who were inclined to pinch. This one was specially nice, quite elderly with silver hair and a voice at once rich and thin, like a bell of pure metal worn down by time to paper-thickness; and he had that old-fashioned way of treating a woman as if she were a flower in a vase, which is very pleasant for a little while, though tiresome if it goes on too long, since one is not a flower in a vase. He had told her the old man's story of the stage of the past: of Henry Irving who, with his queer legs that looked like long legs seen through a refracting depth of water, and the ragged plume of stuttered, booming speech that he crazily held between his clenched teeth, somehow made a comprehensive hieroglyphic that expressed all noble variations of romantic passion; of Ellen Terry, who stands for ever in old men's memories in a long white gown holding out paper flowers that have indeed been for remembrance, her face crisped with plaintiveness like a clear pool crisped by the wind; of Adelaide Neilson, who was beautiful, who died young, and in gaiety, dressed in her best, walking on Sunday in a sunny park in Paris with some splendid lover. From conflicting timbres in his voice she could guess that he himself had longed to step on to that stage, but that he was refraining from telling her so lest he should have to explain that he had not done so because in those days it was considered social suicide for a man of his class to become an actor. That made her smile, it was so delicate and so foolish, for of course a gentleman ought not to go on the stage. In the manner of one counting up what is not gain but merely compensation, the nice old man went on to tell her wistfully that of course there was a great deal of drama in his own profession, and to describe some curious cases in which he had taken part as counsel or judge. She had listened very attentively, partly to help him in his task of persuading himself that he had had as interesting a life as he possibly could have had, and partly because she loved to hear anything about real people, so long as it was true and not publicity. So when he said goodbye he had told her, pleased with her listening, that on Monday he would be trying the Assizes at Packbury, and that if she came in to the court for an hour on the way back he would be delighted to see her.

That would be a good thing to do. For one thing she would like to see the old man again. He was so very well-bred; one felt he would place the pleasantest interpretation on everything that was said or done so that life would be nice all round him. One could not imagine him putting a woman in a humiliating position. And it would keep her mind busy watching the trials, though she hoped everybody would be acquitted. She crossed the road and went past the policeman at the main door.

Inside there was a lobby and a stone staircase, with an ugly iron balustrade and a fat policeman with a blue-black moustache looking down from the landing above. She mounted the steps in a sudden glow of tender, familiar amusement, because the prevailing mode of ugliness, and in particular the yellow plaster walls, reminded her of the elementary school she had gone to in Chiswick. The prevailing smell, too, which puzzled the nostrils with a simultaneous suggestion of fustiness and funny astringency, reminded her of school; though indeed it belonged to all places – even the stage sometimes – where charwomen were given plentiful supplies of cleansing agents but kept faith with their deeper natures by applying them with filthy cloths. Funny old things, charwomen! Funny old things, fat policemen with blue-black moustaches! This one was just like the constable that had chased Lily and her all along the Mall after they had picked the syringa from the garden of the empty house in Duke's Avenue, though goodness knows why they shouldn't have taken it, since nobody was getting any good out of it where it was. She felt refreshed, as if instead of being cast in the dreadful, difficult plays that came her way nowadays, like that awful thing by Claudel she had had to play in last Sunday to please Brenda Burton, she had been put back into musical comedy. She supposed it was getting back among ordinary people. This place belonged to them. There was a crowd of them in the big

25

hall at the top of the staircase, standing about in groups. Not one of them was beautiful, their squarish faces were for the most part fair, but negatively, without radiance. Yet they were somehow more moving to look upon than if they had been beautiful. There was a sturdiness about them that seemed the bodily sign of a strong instinct for keeping faith, and on most of the faces was a look of fatigue and patience, like the look on the face of a woman who is going to have a baby very soon. She respected them for what they were doing, which was stupid and obstinate, and yet sensible; for they were evidently talking over the cases that they were concerned in, saying for the hundredth time what they had said from the beginning and saying it too late, since the court was already sitting. Yet it was the right thing to do, it observed the appropriate rhythm. They had talked more and more of whatever their individual scandal and vexation might be as it came nearer the crisis of its trial, and they would talk less and less of it when it had passed that crisis. The tide had risen, it would ebb. Now, when Essington was going to Versailles he had known quite well that he would probably be thrown overboard there and his career broken, but he had not spoken of it. A leader must be proud and impersonal. When it did happen he hardly spoke of it, though night after night he gave way to childlike gusts of angry weeping in her bed. And now he never spoke of it: though he talked perpetually about the ruin that had come in Europe because they would not listen to him at the Peace Conference, he never distorted the logic of his argument to avenge his disappointment. But the thing was in his mind like an abscess that would not mature, so that he danced about in agony, unreasonable, complaining, cruel: perhaps more cruel than could be borne. She wished that he had not been called upon to be a great man, they might have been so happy together. Wistfully she gazed at the crowd, who in their dull clothes looked dark and strong, like trees in winter. Down amongst them, from the tops of the long windows on one side of the hall, there slanted down shafts of pale, dusty sunlight, like blessings from gods that were benign but had begun to doubt their own omnipotence, to vacillate; that could not now match their own creations in sturdiness . . .

Sunflower wanted to move on, to go some place where she would be distracted and would not think. Since she was stupid, there was no good her thinking. Turning on her charm again, she told the policeman why she was there, and he called a man who took her a way round the building that led out of little rooms where ledgers bound in marbled

26

covers lay on dusty tables, and glass doors swung open in front of shelves of crumbling volumes because the key was gone, and there was an air of something just less than disease, as if ageing little men sat there all day in the drowse that comes from security of tenure. It occurred to her that she would have enjoyed spending the afternoon in dusting and tidying up the place; but of course that could not be. So at length she went through a door and found herself behind two chairs, so massive that they formed a kind of screen, on the other side of which Mr Justice Sandbury's voice was sounding clear but very weak, like a fountain whose reservoir is running dry. She turned to the left as she had been told and found herself at the end of a short row of seats that faced the court. As she sat down she smiled over her shoulder at the Bench, and was shocked by the tired old face that smiled back at her, so yellow did it seem between the white wig and the scarlet robe, and as wrinkled as if the tired flesh had fallen back against the bone and was letting the skin fare as it would. She remembered that he had told her that he was going to retire quite soon, because his health had been broken by years of overwork at the Bar. These great men, they hurt themselves so by being great. She wished that some magic power would make him quite little, so that she could go and lift him out of his big chair, his robe flapping round him like a baby's long clothes, and carry him to some comfortable place where he could rest. She looked round the court with hostility, as the place of his martyrdom, and was immediately disarmed. That there was here some honourable work to which a man might think it worth while to give himself, even so that he was spent before his time, was somehow borne in upon her. She forgot her fear that people were looking at her in her intention of taking all this in so that she would not forget it: the court room, which was older than the rest of the building and was planned with the sober grace of the Georgian genius, making its adaptations to its special purpose, its jury-box, its dock, its barriers, with such propriety that they seemed embellishments, declarations of the austere magnificence of discipline, the shining darkness of the oak-panelled walls which looked down on the proceedings with that air of vigilance and criticism that old wood always seems to have in human habitations, as if nature that cannot speak or do were challenging nature that can to match its worth and beauty; the gaping rows of fairish ordinary people at the back of the court, and the huddled others who craned from the galleries with a gracelessness that was a sign of sincerity, since it showed that they did not condition

27

their expression of what they felt by any thought of how they might look; the jury, their gentle, stupid faces perturbed with conscientiousness; the barristers, sitting just below her in two opposing lines, nearly all of them darker than the ordinary people, more alert, one might say more peevish; the young man in the dock. He made her heart turn over. His pallor seemed to be cast upon him from above by a ray that disclosed at once that this was an end of him, and that all his enemies had said was true; and that in some ultimate sense he was in the right, and that the world could not atone for what it had done to him. Just thus tiresome Aunt Emma who drank had looked when she lay dead.

*

Poor, silly dears. The lanky, whitish, celery-like young man who had tried to kill himself by putting his head in a gas-stove, because he had not filled up the proper paper when he moved to a new district, and so had not received his pension and found himself a burden on his family. The funny little puckish man with the curl in the middle of his forehead like a smile done in hair, who had spent his whole life stealing suitcases, so artlessly that he was always detected, but who was not quite mad enough to be put away. The tired old thing with bags under his eyes and the dark iridescence of hair dye on his bowed head, the manager of a boot-store, who had muddled his books and run away so stupidly that they had caught him at once. None of these people would have got into all this trouble if only they had had someone who really loved them helping them to run their lives. She was thinking of them with a wide-eyed and slightly condescending pity, as if they were in an exceptional case which was the antithesis of her own, until she suddenly discovered in her mind, complete and established, the knowledge that her own case was the same. She had nobody who really loved her and would stand by her. Essington pretended to do so but he did not. When anything went wrong he always made it worse. A great many of her rehearsals were dreadful, for though dramatists sought her out on account of her supremacy as a box-office attraction, they were invariably embittered by her rendering of their lines. When she came back from these ordeals and Essington saw her tear-stains he would nag at her for being so stupid and tell her that she must hurry up and learn to act because she was thirty now and would not be able to hold the public by her beauty much longer. If she should fall into any form of this police-court disgrace he would pay the very best lawyers to get her off and then he would take her home and scold and scold and scold her till she would have to go out and kill herself. She was as much alone as any of these people. There opened before her a sense of some danger to which she was liable by reason of her situation. It was so strong that it became a hallucination and it seemed to her as if the floor had been cut away in front of her chair and she looked down at a blue depth where some time she would be shattered. She pushed back her chair and drew her knuckles over her eyes.

She must not think of Essington. Present or absent, he made all things unquiet and unhappy. She looked about her for something on which her mind might come to rest, and found her eyes dwelling, with such pleasure that she instantly smiled, on the face of an old woman. It was such a nice old face; but terribly pale. It struck her with horror that this was the dock-pallor that she had noted in all the prisoners she had seen tried that afternoon. The old woman was actually standing in the dock, with the sallow, cubist wardress at her elbow. But that was wrong. She was a good old woman. One could see that by the way that the dock-pallor made her merely pale, not guilty. The ray of which it was the end had proved the other prisoners right in eternity but wrong in time: it proved this old woman right in eternity and right in time. She was a very good old woman. Sunflower resolved that if there was any need of money for a fine or lawyer's fees she would pay it and not tell Essington. It was so very obvious that she was a very good old woman. But the strange thing was that when one had got over the shock of seeing her standing there as if she were a criminal one ceased to think of what one could do for her but thought enviously of how much she would have done for one if one had had the luck to belong to her. Though she was standing in the dock it seemed ridiculous to think that one could help anybody who was so rich. She was like a barn full of grain.

The judge, who had been bending forward and talking to his clerk, straightened himself, caught sight of her, and exclaimed, 'Oh! Let the prisoner sit, if she wishes.' Sunflower gave him a smile of partisanship. Mr Sandbury was a real gentleman.

She could not make out why this old woman was having this effect on her. She could not even see her face very clearly, for she was so astigmatic that had it not been for the obligations of her beauty she would have worn glasses. Now, Essington could have told her all about this old woman at once. He had a joyless comprehension of all humanity. He could say, 'This man is a liar, but he cares for knowledge, and one can get good work out of him if one gives him enough praise,' and every word of it would be true; only before he had finished saying it he would lose all interest, and turn away irritably. She was so stupid, she could only feel. But there was one way of understanding what was going on inside people. She had discovered it in the course of her struggle with her profession. She had always terribly wanted to find out how one did act; and she had found out that if she imitated the facial expression and bodily motions of a really good actor she began to experience feelings that were evidently what he was feeling since they were not her own and made her understand his conception of the part. Often she had stood in the darkness of a stage-box and mimicked someone great, and found it work; though she had never gone on with it very long, for she found that the feelings that were roused in her were such as she wanted to use not on the stage but in real life, and she stopped in a dark, confused, rebellious dismay. At last this device was really going to come in useful. She looked over at the old woman and noted how she was seated in the chair, and tried to reproduce her pose. The body, which was at once coarse and frail, like earthenware that time had worn to the thinness of delicate china, was held very straight; the bonneted head was held low, so that the onlooker's eye fell first on the puckered brownish silk of her brow and downcast eyelids. As Sunflower assumed the pose a sense of its rightness flowed like water through her body. It meant that about those things concerning which it is right to be proud and hard the old woman was proud and hard, and about those things concerning which it is right to be humble and soft she was utterly humble and soft. But now she was making queer passes with her poor gnarled hands: sometimes making scuffling movements with the fingers of each hand gathered together. What was that? Ah, this one was knitting, the other sewing. That meant that her ordinary life had been so full of goodness that when she was frightened she tried to get in touch with it again by pretending she was doing all the little things she did every day in the household, as a pious person might make the sign of the cross. This was a marvellously good woman.

But they were reading the indictment against her.

'Alice Hester, you are charged with bigamy and the particulars are that on the fourteenth day of March nineteen hundred and twenty-three you went through a ceremony of marriage with Robert Stallibrass, your lawful husband Amos Bullen being then alive.'

But it was not possible.

'Are you guilty or not guilty?'

'Guilty,' she said. Though one could clearly hear the word, it seemed to spin feebly and fall in mid-air, like a quoit thrown by too feeble a hand. Her pale old mouth opened suddenly, and within its vault her tongue could be seen quivering like the tongue of an asp. The wardress gave her a glass of water. She minded to thank the giver before she drank, like a well-taught child. Then she sat with the glass on her lap, shaking her head and murmuring protestingly to herself. She was not rebelling against whatever injustice had brought her into the dock, neither was she feeling fear. Rather was she expressing the embarrassment of one who comes up to town to go to the Horse Show with a friend, and is let in by her for attending a wedding or some ceremony that required other clothes. She had prepared for one event and been precipitated into another. Why, the event she had prepared for was death. This woman would move mildly towards the innermost things.

'Now, what is all this about?' asked Mr Justice Sandbury.

A wigged and gowned figure rose from the bench of his fellows in the well of the court and said in an embarrassed, here-it-is-but-it-is-none-of-my-doing voice, 'The facts of the case are quite straightforward, my lord. Fifty years ago the prisoner married an agricultural labourer who is now in Southend workhouse. Last March she went through a form of marriage with this other man, who has since died.'

'Who has since died?'

'I am informed by the police that he died a few days after the bigamous marriage.'

'Was there any question of fraudulent motive, of inheriting anything from this man that would come to her only if she was his wife, any pension or so on?'

'No, my lord. So far as the police know there was no such motive.'

The judge put his fine white hand to his mouth, and looked deliberately at the prisoner. Sunflower almost hated him, because she knew that he was savouring the quality of this good old woman as he had savoured the quality of Irving or Ellen Terry. It was not right. He might let her go at once.

Kindly he said to her: 'Have you any statement to make? Is there anything you want to tell us, about the reason why you did this thing?'

They heard her remote old voice exclaim to herself, 'O mercy, I must speak now.' She stood up, steadying herself by resting her hands, which were like grey skeleton leaves, on the ledge of the dock; and after curtseying she began to speak. Oh, that one could watch and watch and listen and listen harder and harder, so that one could get everything possible out of the moment. This was a real thing. Everybody in court was feeling it, for there was a hush, and the thin stream of her words might have been trickling through a wood at night.

She said: 'Sir, 'tis true what the policeman says I did. I have been treated fairly, and I make no complaint. But I could not help doing what I did, though I meant no harm. 'Twas this way. My first man was not a good man to me. 'Twas not his fault. He had a mother who came from Foulness Island, and 'tis well known the folks there are outlandish and don't know how to do things right, so he'd had a bad home. Before ever we'd wedded he was used to drinking and that. And 'twas hard on him, too, we had so many little ones. Ten we had before I was thirty, and we had only twelve shillings a week to bring them up on, and our cottage was a poor sort of place. 'Twas not his fault. But when he had been drinking he did knock me and the children about so that it could not be borne, though they was very good children. Then he got tired of it all, and tried to make us go into the workhouse, and I had to stand out against him. None of my folks had ever gone into the workhouse, and I could not let my little ones go there. So we came to having hard words over it, and one night he came home drunk, and he made me get up and dress the little ones, and he turned us all out of the house. We stood in the garden for a while and then he come and drive us into the lane with an old rook rifle my father had given him. 'Twas only because he was in drink. He was a kind man sometimes when he was himself.

'So we walked up and down the lane, for I thought we might go back later when he had fallen asleep. But my little ones cried, and the young fellow who was ploughman at the same farm where my man was, he woke up in his bed where he slept in his cottage across the road, and he came down after us, with a lantern. I had not spoken to him before but to be civil. But he spoke to me kindly as he picked up two of my littlest ones and he took us to the barn, and we slept on the hay, and he stayed by me and begged me not to carry on so. And in the morning he brought us two loaves and some water, and then he took me up to the cottage before he went to work. But my husband had gone. I haven't seen him since. And I did not know what to do; for the cottage belonged to the farmer, and he wanted it for the man he hired to take my husband's place. So it looked as if he had got us into the workhouse, for all I had done against it. But this young fellow said I must not go for to do that, and he wrote to his uncle who lived up over Patchloy in these parts to find a place for him, and said he had married a widow. So we all come over here, and we had another little one of our own, and all was nice and decent for forty years. There was no drinking and not a cross word. He always treated me right, and he was kind to my little ones.

'Then last winter he got a pain in his innards. His food did roar up in him, no matter what I give him. And last February the doctor told him he must go into hospital and be cut. And he came back, and he told me that, and he said, "There is just one thing I would like to do before I go into hospital. I might die, and I would like to be married to you before I die." I knew quite well that it was not right to do it, for my sister who lives in Prittlewell had told me my first was in the workhouse over there and I had sent him some money for baccy and that to be slipped to him private-like without my name. But I knew my man was like to die, and I could see his heart was set on this thing, so I told him I would do it. The pity of it was that my sister's grandson Tom was stopping in the house with us, him not being liked in his own parish. He is kind of queer. He does no good at school and goes about all day playing on a penny whistle and doing what he ought not to do. 'Tis not his fault. His mother was frightened by a ferret when he was on the way. I heard a board creak and I said to myself he had been listening at the door. And I was sure he knew there was something funny about me and my old man, for people had talked in front of him as they should not, and though he is kind of dull he remembers everything. But what could I do, with my man wanting it so bad?

'So we told the registrar we wanted to marry, and then when the day came we went to the office. And all the way going through the streets from the house to the office I heard someone playing a penny whistle just behind me. But I did not turn round, for with my man set on marrying me, what could I do? And while the registrar was writing our names in the big book I heard someone playing a penny whistle out in the street just under the window. But what could I do? And then my man went into the county hospital and the doctors cut him and he died. And as he lay dying he was main pleased he was married to me. So when the policeman came for me I knew it was right he should take me to the station. But what could I do?'

She asked it with her eyes set steadily on the judge, as if she really wanted an answer. It had seemed to her that life had made it impossible for her not to do wrong, and she was grieved by it. She would like to have that disproved, even if the explanation meant that she would have to blame herself. So kind was she, and so honest, that she was willing to clear God's character at the expense of her own.

Sunflower had taken off her gloves and was rubbing her hands, which seemed as if they were charged with electricity. Looking at this old woman made her feel as she sometimes did in church when she looked up at the cross over the altar; only this feeling did not run up and lose itself in the empty sky. Looking at Alice Hester one looked down, towards the ground, and one's feelings seemed to run along the earth, to delve into it, to shoot up into the light, triumphant . . . She found herself living again a moment at her mother's funeral, which at the time had made her jaw drop with amazement. They had lowered her mother's body into the grave. It lay there in its coffin, finished. And round the hole in the earth stood four black figures, Lily, Mabel, Maurice and herself, who but for that body would not have been there. Who had been made by it out of nothing! And now they were putting this marvel-making body in the ground, as if the proper time to sow was after it had germinated and engendered its plant. She had gaped at that extraordinary rite. It had seemed to bring to the surface of life a process that nobody talked about, that could hardly be seen, that she could not have told Essington about at all; that was the most important thing in the world. She didn't know what it was or what it did, but she knew what it was like. It was savagely persistent, it was at once miraculous and the soul of the natural, it went on and on to some aim . . . She could have burst out crying because she was not taking part in the process, and never could do so, since she did not understand what it was, nor how she could force herself into it. She was so stupid! There swept over her a tide of that emotion which Essington most loathed in her, but which she recognised shamefacedly as the most fundamental emotion she ever knew: a desire to be passive which was as acute as thirst. Indignantly she felt that she ought not to be calling on her own will and thought to find a way into this process. Someone ought to have done it for her. She felt cheated because they had not.

Because of that final sagging conviction of betrayal, she had remembered as rarely as she could that queer moment beside the grave: which was a pity, because it was something real, and almost the only thing she had ever found out for herself. But now this old woman

34

made her think of it; and added to her thought the news that if you did this – this thing, without rebelling because it was so hard and feeling love for everybody from the idiot boy who betrayed you up to the God who made you, you got something that was like religion. But better. Religion was like everything that men made. It was all very fine but it didn't work. It was like Essington's ideas which were all wonderful but which didn't get carried into effect and didn't make him happy. It did not work. Religion vanishes out of a building without a spire, as scent vanishes out of a bottle without a stopper. It has to be tethered to people's attention by pretty services with incense and vestments and music; by creeds that men can argue about without coming to any conclusion that has to be acted on; by priests and vicars and district visitors and all. What men do is thin as paper, dry as dust. But this other thing . . . Without being reinforced by being talked about, since it could not be put into words, it had survived for seventy years within this body that had never been beautiful, that had been starved and chilled, vexed with rough clothing, hurt by blows, deformed and torn by baby and baby, laid waste altogether by age. And it had worked. How it had worked!

Mr Justice Sandbury was saying, 'Well, you mustn't do that sort of thing, you know . . .'

If she were punished it could not be borne.

But he went on: 'Still, you've had a very hard life, and you've been through a great deal of trouble just lately, and I see that you may not have known what you were doing at the time. So I am going to bind you over on your own recognisances to come up for judgment when you are called.'

'Thank you, sir,' said Alice Hester. Yet she would rather have had the answer that proved herself and not life at fault. She took trouble to look grateful, for not to do so would have been unkind to the old gentleman, who had done his best for her; but as she turned aside, leaning on the wardress's arm, the interest flowed out of her old face, as if she felt that now she had dealt with this situation she could continue to drift quietly towards death. As she went out of the dock and into the well of the court the wardress and the policeman kept on laying their hands upon her and guiding her, as if she were weightless as a dead leaf and might be whirled by any current of air away from the place to which she ought to go. They brought her to the big book at the table, but there was a hitch in the proceedings. Her bonneted head bobbed up, her tilted face offered some mild objection to the

35

giants above her; their bullet heads bobbed down and offered some reassurance, passing broad explanatory fingers along the page. It seemed that she could not sign her name, but had to make her mark. So she also was stupid.

She straightened herself and curtseyed to the judge. The giants turned her about and patted her, as one pats a ball through water, towards a door in the wall near the witness box, where there waited a bearded man. Embarrassment was on his face like a flickering light. 'It must be horrid to have one's children knowing that one once was loved,' thought Sunflower. But the old woman went straight up to him, laid her hand on his arm, and spoke to him, not, as one might have foretold, brokenly, but chidingly. Peace and docility came into his face. She had done the right thing: she had asserted her authority, and they were back as they ought to be, mother and son. But of course she would always know what was the right thing to do, in any conceivable phase of every possible human relationship. She was inspired. Sunflower thought of all the times in the theatre when she had failed to save situations, when she had let a scene drop or an actor's blunder show across the footlights, because she had not known the right thing to do, because she was not inspired, because she was empty as this woman was full. Hungrily she looked at the door which was now closing on Alice Hester and her son. He looked about forty. Perhaps he was the youngest child. It must have been wonderful, when she had child after child by the husband she did not love, at last to have a child by the man she loved. There could be no child of hers she would not love; but this one must have been covered at its birth with a special sort of love like a caul of light.

The tears were streaming down Sunflower's face. She was amazed by them as by any other sudden and prodigious shower. She dried them with her gloves, for she had lost her handkerchief, as Essington said she always did, and she got up and pushed away the chairs, which seemed interested and resistant, and went out of the gallery into the passage. There she leaned against the yellow plaster wall, whose cold surface was like an admonition to be sensible, and tried to stop this independent weeping. Why should she cry! It was so foolish when Alice Hester had proved that everything was all right if only one had love, which meant that everything was really all right with her and Essington for they loved each other. If she told Essington about Alice Hester it would make him understand that they must stop being unkind to one another. She wished that she could tell him at once, without having to wait to get home. And then her heart sank, for she remembered that he had told her he would stay down at Evescote till Tuesday afternoon, which meant that she would not see him for another twenty-four hours. She could have cried again for disappointment. Things were always happening like this. If she found something in the newspapers that might make him laugh he was never there, and if she clipped it out and kept it then somehow it mattered too much if it turned out not funny enough to make him laugh; and when she woke up and laid her arm across the other pillow and said, 'I have had such a lovely dream,' it was always one of the nights he was not there. And his return to her house was never simple, like the coming home of an ordinary man, but always had to be announced, confirmed, altered, and maybe postponed by that maddening telephone, or to be waited for without any trust that any special hour would bring him. But these were little, little things compared with the adversities against which Alice Hester's love had struggled and survived. She would never think of them again. And at any rate she could go and tell Harrowby. He was not married, she had often wondered why, for he was a very nice man. Perhaps he would get married when he heard this story.

She hurried back through the little rooms, whose drowsiness now seemed a curious affectation in view of the real, rushing nature of life. The hall was still full of groups of ordinary people, standing talking, their good heads lowered. For a little she stood and looked at them, smiling as one might at children who were taking some game very seriously but also wrung with pity because their own seriousness was paining them, and impatient because they had stood there looking down on the ugly linoleum when just behind the courtroom doors a woman had proved to all who cared to listen that no matter what happened life was all right. Regretfully she stroked her useless throat, thinking how bitter it was that with her trained voice she could have made them all hear every word she might have said, but that her stupid brain could not put two words together to convey the brightness that possessed her. But at any rate she could tell Harrowby. She hurried down the stairs and past the policemen, on whom she smiled with dazzling gratitude, since they had upheld the gates of her entrance into everlasting happiness, and she went out into one of these stage-scene hours that sometimes come between a sunlit day and its twilight. The townsfolk were walking in radiance over prodigiously lengthened shadows, like bold and happy souls not awed by any consequences; and in the upper windows of one half of the market-place blazed a piecemeal sunset more glorious than that in the opposing sky. Under the assault of the strong slanting shafts of light no house-fronts seemed much more solid than canvas; the lit shops seemed factitious, sets for the harlequinade; pale householders stepped out of their doors and had ruddiness clapped on their faces as a mask. These appearances seemed to her confirmation of her belief that everything in the world had suddenly been changed by the disclosure of some knowledge, and that now all was well; and she almost ran to the garage to tell her news.

The yard also was wrought on by the hour. The two sides of it, the proprietor's house and the opposite wall, were tepid in shadow, colder than one would have thought anything red could be; but the wall at the end glowed like the wings of a Painted Lady butterfly, and the gate in it seemed to have had its iron convolutions veneered with strips of sunset. The blossom on the lilac bough that bobbed over from the next garden had been dipped in a honey of thick yellow light. Pulled out into the middle of the yard was the Wolseley, its glossy sides suffused with fire in which reflections swam as dilating and contracting islets; and in it sat Harrowby, reading Captain Coe.

He jumped out when he saw her coming. 'Did you find the place all right, Miss?'

'Oh, Harrowby, I didn't go! But I saw something much more wonderful! I went to see the people being tried in that place with a clock, because that nice old gentleman at Clussingford was the judge, and I saw the most wonderful thing I've ever seen in my life. Just think there was an old woman of seventy tried for committing bigamy last March . . .' She had to stop and gasp for breath.

'Dear, dear, Miss!' commented Harrowby mildly, folding up the *Star*. 'An old woman of seventy committing bigamy! That's what I call carrying coals to Newcastle.'

'Oh, but it was wonderful of her! She was the most wonderful person I've ever seen. Alice Hester her name was, and somehow it suited her. I don't think she'd ever been beautiful. You felt she'd never had to bother about all that. But, oh, she looked so nice . . .' She paused again for breath.

'They often do,' said Harrowby, who had evidently not yet found his equilibrium in the story.

'She looked so good, and you felt she'd always been nice to everybody. And she'd had lots of children ever so long ago, and her husband turned them all out of doors, and a ploughman came and took them to a barn, and then they came here and pretended they were married, and they were awfully happy for forty years, though they weren't married –'

'Oh, that,' said Harrowby, with a certain fierceness, 'don't matter any more nowadays. If people are straight, they are, and that's that.'

'Well, then he got ill, and he knew he was going to die, and he wanted to be married to her. And though there was a horrid sort of boy in the house, and she knew that he would tell, she did go and get married, though she knew that she'd get put in prison, and he was awfully happy, and he did die. Wasn't it wonderful of her? Wasn't it wonderful?'

'Yes, indeed it was,' said Harrowby. But it struck her that she had not told the story quite as well as she might have done, though on thinking it over she did not see that she had left out anything. So to clench matters she declared earnestly, 'Really, Harrowby, she was the most wonderful person I've ever, ever seen!' Then she saw she had impressed him, for he stared at her with large eyes and said, 'It does you all the good in the world to take a day off, Miss,' which was so irrelevant that he could only have said it to disguise his emotions. So that was all right.

She drew a deep breath of contentment and looked round her. 'Isn't it a lovely evening?' she murmured. Her gaze ranged lovingly over everything, and came to the sash-windows in the proprietor's house, with their shining panes and neat curtains of Nottingham lace. She smiled happily, for now she had seen Alice Hester she could be unreservedly happy about those people. It was quite likely that the little man would go on loving the ugly girl until he died. She said, 'I'd like to say good-bye to that little man who was there.'

'Well, I shouldn't say there was much chance of seeing him this evening. There's been a lot of coming and going since you went out. A domestic event, I should say. That's the doctor's car over there.'

They gazed up at the little house, which looked stern and knowing there in the shadow.

'She's very young,' said Sunflower.

But Alice Hester must have been as young when she began, and it had turned out glorious for her.

'I wish I knew if it were a boy or a girl,' she speculated with a new shamelessness. 'I'd like to send it something.'

They continued to gaze up at the grave little house.

'We'd best be making a move,' said Harrowby at length. 'You'll be getting tired, Miss. I've got to take you down to rehearsal tomorrow at eleven, I know.'

'It's funny. I am a little tired. But I've had a lovely, lovely day.'
She got into the car, and he settled the rugs round her. She would have her dinner in bed; a boiled egg, and some bread and honey.

II

WHEN Parkyns opened the door she said very quickly: 'My lord is here. He came at six o'clock.'

'Oh I am glad!' exclaimed Sunflower. Now she would be able to tell him about Alice Hester at once. 'Where is he?'

'He is at dinner, Madam, and – '

But Sunflower threw down her gloves and bag on the hall-table, and ran right into the dining-room, which was silted up with late twilight. As she came from behind the draught-screen at the door Essington rose out of the tall chair at the head of the table, which was where she sat as a rule. She could not see his face; on the settee behind him burned the three candles that were as yet the only light in the room. She went to him, holding out her arms and crying, 'Oh, darling! I've seen something so wonderful today! I went to the Assize Court in Packbury, and there was an old woman of seventy who had committed bigamy – '

But he kept silence, lowering his head a little, in the way which always meant that she had done something stupid and that he was not going to help her out of it. There was the sound of another chair being pushed backward. Why, there were two other people in the room. A broad-browed, middle-aged woman with straight black hair and an

41

earthy skin looked up at her over the edge of a wineglass with a curious expression into which Sunflower stared for a moment; it was like the expression that might be exchanged between two servants waiting at table on a troublesome master. And at the foot of the table stood a little man with fox-coloured hair and a very big mouth, and queer eyes the colour of bad weather.

She put out her hand and exclaimed foolishly, 'Oh, it's you!'

He answered in a kind voice, very deep for such a little man, 'Yes, it's me.' His hand was tiny, but very broad and strong.

She forgot her moment's misgiving at Essington's silence in happy wonder that after all these years she should meet this man again, this day of all days. It was odd that she had been thinking of him this very afternoon. It did seem as if life was suddenly revealing its own pattern. She would have liked to say, 'Well, this is a small world, isn't it!' but Essington had impressed on her that, for some reason which she could not fully understand, the use of this and some other equally harmless phrases was far less permissible than the use of really bad language.

But Essington said: 'You don't know this gentleman. This is Mr Francis Pitt.'

Laughingly she protested, 'But I do know Mr Pitt. We – sort of met years ago.'

A tremor ran through Essington. He seemed about to be angry in a different way. 'What's this?' he spoke to Francis Pitt. 'I thought you said you had never met?'

The little man gave a low chuckle. 'Hardly met. We passed each other on the stairs when I was going down and Miss Fassendyll was coming up to the office of a War Charity, of which I was a Grand Panjandrum, a God knows what, and for which she did some real work.' The chuckle ran right through his gruff speech, making it seem the very voice of kindly strength. She thought of the policeman who had found her crying in Hammersmith Broadway when silly old Grandaunt Annie had taken her out and lost her; he had bought her some pear drops and carried her all the way home. 'I remember my eyes nearly fell out of my head, and evidently Miss Fassendyll remembers that too.'

She began to say, 'Oh, no, it wasn't that!' but Essington had gone back to being angry in his first manner. 'Dear Sunflower is as vague about the nature of an introduction as she is about everything else,' he said; and then, suddenly remembering the sallow woman, waved his hand at her, 'Miss Pitt, this is Miss Fassendyll.' The sallow woman smiled and held out a hand so big and broad that it seemed odd that it should be smooth and white, in a manner at once genial and perfunctory, as if she wanted to be nice but was holding herself in readiness to climb a tree if hostilities became more acute. And then Essington went on: 'I've been here since five. I told you I would be back here at tea-time on Monday. It's half past eight now.' His voice cracked. 'I wrote a note from Evescote to say that I'd asked Miss Pitt and her brother to dine tonight. Of course you haven't got it. We're eating a scratch dinner that isn't fit for a pig.'

His words failed him. His hand danced over the comminated table like something stung.

'I'm sorry,' she breathed.

'Well, what does it mean? Where have you been? Who have you been with?'

She wet her lips. 'I've been . . . at Packbury. Harrowby had to do something to the car. I went and listened to some cases. The time passed.'

'It did,' said Essington, 'It did.'

'I'm so sorry. I'm so sorry. But really you didn't say you were coming today. You said you were staying down at Evescote till Tuesday.'

'I did not.'

'But you wrote it.' She tried to laugh. 'Truly you did.' She knew the way of dignity was to be silent; she knew that to defend herself was to crawl in the dust in the way of these strangers. But she was afraid that if she did not speak he would strike her. For she knew, as certainly as she knew that she would eventually die, that he would some day strike her. 'Look, the letter's up there on the mantelshelf, slipped into the mirror.' Recollection of how gay she had been when she put it there, of how she had been moved to do so by her pride in one of his dear minor gifts, made her choke with a sense of trampled happiness. 'I put it up there because your writing was so pretty.'

His eyes found the blue-grey envelope, beautiful as a Chinese print with the exquisite web of his serene and delicate handwriting. His head ducked. It was apparent that he remembered. But in a moment he recovered himself. 'My God! How you love leaving letters about!' he said.

'There's nothing in it but "Evescote" and your initials,' she mumbled. She was shivering, partly because of her humiliation, partly because she was afraid that he had gone mad. There was a magical and ventriloquous quality about his rage. It was as if the voice that seemed to

43

come out of his mouth came really from some lonely, bewitched and baying beast, far out in a desert. There was a silence, so she murmured, 'I'll go and tidy.'

'You will not,' said Essington. 'You will sit down. Then Mr Pitt can sit down. Then I can sit down. Where's Parkyns? She ought to be here. My God, your wayward, woodland charm shows nowhere more strongly than in your domestic arrangements.' He stamped on the electric bell till Parkyns came in; she too was shivering. She had, Sunflower now realised, been shivering when she opened the door. 'Take your mistress's coat and hat. And bring in the soup.'

'I don't want any,' said Sunflower. 'I'll start where you are.'

'Oh, no. Oh, no. You're going to see the kind of dinner we had. We'll wait.'

'Ah, now,' objected Francis Pitt, 'the dinner's been grand,' and his sallow sister broke into a corroborating murmur.

They all sat down. Sunflower felt half-asleep. The misery that filled her mind was not Essington's behaviour, which was so awful that it was raised to a kind of remoteness, like some calamity read of in the newspapers, but the way she looked. She had cried a little in the car, thinking of Alice Hester, and had not troubled to powder; and her hat had been a close one. It was horrid, because Francis Pitt was the sort of man who cared about people being well-groomed. Though his sister was plainly indifferent to those things, since her thick eyebrows were not plucked, she had been drilled into quite a good black dress of the Handley-Seymour sort. And he himself, though his red-brown hair straggled over his ears in bearish disorder, was dressed even more carefully than Essington. He had pretty studs.

She put up her hand to see what she could do with her hair, but Essington said, 'Don't fuss! Don't fuss!' and added, 'Parkyns, turn on all the lights.'

But Parkyns was very nice. She brought Sunflower only a very little soup and hardly any fish. And meanwhile, Francis Pitt leaned forward, chuckling again, and said, 'You'll not be able to guess what I've been doing today.' Sunflower liked the way he laughed on no particular cue, but just on general principles. Essington never laughed except at the exact point of something that was certifiably funny. The little man's way took her back to contacts of her youth: when one went on a visit to Cousin Gladys who was married to the stationmaster at Redhill. She opened the front door, and there was laughter. Then she kissed Mummie and you, and there was laughter. Then one went

44

upstairs. 'This is your room'; more laughter. 'Oh, it's ever so nice'; more laughter. 'Well, I'll be downstairs getting the tea, and you'll come down when you're ready'; more laughter, senseless and kindly. Those were easy days.

'What was that?' asked Essington. She was amazed at his interest. He must really respect the little man.

He chuckled again. 'I went down to my old school in South London and gave the little boys some good advice. I hope to God they don't follow it, or I shall have a grave responsibility on my soul. For I didn't dare tell them the truth about the way I made my money, and maybe what I told them they won't find quite so useful.'

'What school was that?'

'Oh, a rotten private school down at Dulwich. I have no pleasant memories of it, God knows, but the old man who runs it came up to my office. At first I nearly had him thrown out, but he spun a hard luck yarn, and said it would help the school pick up if I came down, and so in the end I said I would.' She thought what a kind man he was; but there flashed across her mind a suspicion that the up-and-down lilt of his voice conveyed so perfectly the ruminations of a stern but good-natured man because it was meant to do so. Deliberately she put the thought away. There was something about his voice, something rich and appetising like the smell of good food cooking, that made her want to like him.

'Lord, those suburban dumps,' said Essington. 'Silly old men and bitter young ones in dusty gowns, an art room with a plaster-cast of the Discobolos, a laboratory with half a dozen test-tubes and miserable little boarders who are mostly the children of licensed victuallers who've sent them away from home because of the pub atmosphere, and more miserable little day-boys who are sent there because their parents are snobs and won't send them to the elementary school though they can't afford a better one.'

'That was me,' said Francis Pitt. 'My father was a Wesleyan minister.'

'Ah, you're like me, an example of what a pious home can do.' They both laughed, that laughter by which men courteously give each other to understand that they are quite sure that they have the more picturesque irregularities in common. 'My father was vicar of Brodip in Norfolk. Eight of us there were.' The note that came into his voice when he spoke of his childhood always broke her heart. It was whining, ungracious, greedy, pathetic: the complaint of a child born with raw nerve-ends into a crowded nursery. Rage ceased to burn in her throat. She would have liked to slip her hand into his under the table, but of course she did not dare. Under her brows she looked at the others to see if they were liking him enough, for she was afraid they must have been prejudiced by his rudeness when she came in. Francis Pitt's eyes slid away from her. Miss Pitt, eating salted almonds, gave her that curious fellow-servant look.

'Six of us there were,' said Francis Pitt. He sat curiously in his chair, his broad shoulders jutting forward, as a lion would sit if he were made to eat at table.

'Lord, how they could! How they could!'

'Well, we got through.'

'We had to pay.'

'Had you to pay much? I thought things had come easily with you.'

'Easily! Oh, my God!' He stirred irritably in his seat. 'I got a Balliol scholarship from my grammar school and couldn't take it because my people hadn't any money. You know how badly one takes things when one is young. I don't feel life's made up to me for that. I had to go to London University, and eke out a scholarship by teaching in one of those private schools. Out at Sydenham it was. A mean little den. Then I got my degree, and I taught at Blagdon. There wasn't anything very good going for me, because I was no good at games. Then I started doing journalism, and read law. I was called to the Middle Temple in '91, and I went into Brandram's chambers. When I was forty I stood for Burdsend. That was a by-election. In 1906. Then in 1910 Brandram died and left me all his money. He was a widower, you know, and his boy had died at Oxford. Strained his heart in that running tomfoolery. The money seemed a good thing at the time. It made it possible for me to give up the Bar and go in for politics as a career. Now I'm sorry the old man wasted his money on me.'

'It's been no waste,' said Francis Pitt. With his deep voice and a gesture of his spatulate hands he made his deference to the older man seem a charming abnegation of his strength's right to dominate.

'It has. It's been utter waste. The old man left me his money partly because he was fond of me, but more because he thought I'd do something for Liberalism. He was a great Liberal. God, if he could see how little I've been able to do for Liberalism; and what the Liberal Party is today.'

'I suppose it would break the old-timer's heart,' said Francis Pitt. 'Now what do you suppose has happened to us? What does it all mean?

46

It seems to me sometimes when I sit in the House and look round at us that we're not only a beaten party, we're a guilty party, and we know it. We feel we've brought it on ourselves. What was it we did? Was it, do you think, that we stuck to Bryce Atkin after the war, when people's minds were clearer and they could see the little villain's quality, and we lost all our moral prestige through having such a leader?'

Sunflower felt unaccountably disappointed at hearing that he too was in politics. But the evening was settling down into the kind of thing that Essington liked. She sat with her head down, doggedly thinking of Alice Hester.

'Oh, no,' answered Essington. 'We all knew Bryce Atkin's quality quite well long before the peace, and even long before the war, for that matter. In point of fact that gave him, and us, our chance in the war. Of course he's obviously a cocotte, God bless him, with his obviously hireable charm and his taste for rich men and those queer perorations of his in which he shows off his Nonconformist quality in a way which isn't decent, like a girl lifting up her skirt to show her ankles. But it's one of the superstitions of the mob that there's no sicknurse like Nell Gwynn if she turns her hand to it. Haven't you read again and again in second-rate novels of the great-hearted cocotte who nurses the penniless stranger through typhoid or what-not? That's why England trusted herself to Bryce Atkin in the war. No, he's never done us as much harm as Oppenshaw.'

'Oh, Oppenshaw!'

'He is our real curse. I often dream of his silly, handsome old face, all curves and whirls of chins and dimples, and soft, soft, soft. It's like a giant nose done in butter for a Grocers' Exhibition. Oh, they both did their bit in dragging us down. But it was the fault of all of us. For we all stood by while those two with their passion for fiddling negotiation made the Party take the first step downhill. That was before the war. Let me see, you weren't in the House then, were you?'

'No. I got in for Braystoke in 1919. I only came to England from California in 1913.'

'Ah. Our paths crossed. You went in as I came out. Well, I wish you better luck than I had.'

They raised their glasses to each other. That was a gesture of friendship; and she knew that Essington's fretful sincerity about even the smallest things in life would not have let him make it had he not meant it. But by throwing the two into the same attitude of bowed

47

head and lifted hand it exhibited them as so different that with a sinking of the heart she feared that they would not remain friends very long; that Francis Pitt might not come to the house very often. Essington sat high in his chair, like some great cat with delicate bones, a puma or a cheetah, with his lean sloping shoulders, and his small poised head, that was broad across the square brow and narrowed suddenly below the wide cheekbones to the little, fine, snapping jaw, over which the silver moustache stuck out like feelers. His eyes were like a cat's, limpid as water, but secretively set; and he had that feline look of having been moulded out of a plastic substance by long, sweeping fingers. He would have been beautiful to look at had he not been disfigured by the expression that the world thought to be sourness, but that she knew to be tortured sweetness. His face was tragic with qualities which life had infected with their opposites: kindliness that because of the million objections which had been raised to his plans for being kind was now chiefly impatience; sensitiveness that because of the wounds inflicted on it had become brutally insensitive in its own defence. She cried out to herself, obstinately, 'I will go on loving him, I will go on loving him.'

But Francis Pitt was a being of a different kind; it seemed, of a different time. With his ape's mouth, his over-large head, and his over-broad shoulders he had an air of having been created before the human structure had added to itself such refinements as beauty and shapeliness. Yet he had as much of a body as a man needs. He looked enormously strong, and as if he could go through anything. Captain Scott. Gold prospectors. Seekers for the source of tropical rivers. She saw them all, on the snow, on the lye-frosted sand, in the green oven of the forest, with his troglodyte body, his unperishable face that also, like his body, rejected certain human novelties. There was there no such tangle of transmuted sweetness and kindliness and sensitiveness as there was in Essington. He seemed to have been created before the human soul had split itself up into these subdivisions. The only modern thing in his face, the only thing which would have been surprising in the death's-head of a mummy found crouching in a grave dug in a place now desert but not so a million years ago, was a certain whimsicality, a certain puckishness, which spoke of an intention to break up life whenever it seemed to be settling down into a form that encouraged these recent psychological inventions. Yet he had surely as much of a nature as a man needs. She tried to put into words what she guessed about it, but since it was his essential quality that he

48

belonged to an age when words were not yet important she could not do it, and simply saw images. He made her think of an iron spade with clods of earth still clinging to it. Suddenly a gust of pleasure at his presence passed over her, and it seemed to her as if she were in a high place, where the air was very clear. Woods ran down to a lake, the green fire of young leaves crackling among the treetops; the milder mirrored woods ran out into the lake, the leaves' fire quenched to a paste of green jewels. She stood among rocks by the water. Something like the fire of the leaves crackled all round her; and within her the mirrored woods were troubled, they were fluted into ribs of thick glass. There was coming a canoe that was driven forward to her, to the fire that crackled round her and in her, by a man with strong arms, with broad shoulders, who cried to her across the water, a round-mouthed cry without words; who was this man.

It was silly to have daydreams when one was grown-up. Under the table she rubbed her hands, which felt as if they were charged with electricity.

'Better luck!' repeated Essington, as he set down his glass.

'And what better luck can you have than to be a great man?' asked Francis Pitt.

She looked at Essington with real interest as to what his answer would be. But he made none, though he acknowledged the implied compliment with a little ironic bow. She turned towards Francis Pitt, hoping he would press his question; but he was thinking of nothing but the turtle savoury he was eating, and it was apparent that he had never expected an answer. She supposed it was typical of her stupidity that she had not seen that it was just one of those questions that men ask for the sake of asking, in political speeches and in newspaper articles: like 'Shall we let Germany?', as it used to be, or as it was now, 'Shall we let France?' But suddenly she rebelled against that customary way of looking at it. It was they who were stupid not to see that the question did need an answer. Most people thought it was good luck to be great. But here was Essington, who was great, and it had been no luck for him. He was miserable. It was of no value to him that the dinner was really very good. It was of no value to him that she had made the room so pretty with its apple-green walls and its black lacquer furniture faintly inscribed with golden beauty. The loveliest thing in it, the dark bush starred with white flowers that stood on the settle behind the windows, he never looked at, though he knew all about it, and when she had brought it home, having bought it because

49

she thought it lovely, he had been able to tell her exactly when it had been made and in what part of China. And it was of no value to him that she was sitting there ready to be nice to him. He knew what she was, how much she loved him, but it did not seem to matter. He looked peevishly past all these offers of satisfaction to a future that was to be reformed half for its own sake and half as an insult to the hated present. That was the fault of his greatness; it was because he had to roll in such fierce grips with his times in his effort to dominate them that he loathed them. It was the fault of his greatness too that he minded it all so much. He could not take anything easily because the knowledge of his power and his responsibility pulled his head stiff and high like an invisible bearing-rein. It had been no luck at all for him. Look at the querulous beauty of his long fingers, for ever restless, now kneading the stem of his wineglass, as if he hoped to change its shape, which could not be done! There must be better luck than his. What was it then that a man ought to try to be? She turned to Francis Pitt, who, she thought, might know. But again his eyes slid away from hers. She looked across the table at Miss Pitt, wondering whether she had come by observation of her male to any understanding of what men were up to; but Miss Pitt's eyes were on her brother's empty plate, and she took advantage of the silence of the two men to ask, with such nervous hurry as might be shown by somebody who had been allowed by the police to cross a street just before a royal procession came along, what the name of this exceedingly nice savoury might be.

'No,' Essington began again, 'the rot began before the war. With our weakness in dealing with the Ulster Rebels. We made it plain that we thought of expediency before principle. That was Oppenshaw, of course. But we should have stood up to him. It meant so much. I myself believe that Germany would never have started the war at the time she did if she hadn't been encouraged to think that we were in a state of anarchy by the Ulster business. And it would have cost us so little to keep order. We need not have shot one of the leaders. We need only have told them we would shoot them.'

'Now, is that true?' asked Francis Pitt, slowly. 'I thought that whatever we might say of them they were at least men of courage. What about Canterton? Wasn't he very resolute on the matter?'

'That drunken lout! If anybody ever knocked the cigar out of his mouth he'd fall to pieces. Nobody has ever tried it, because he fulfils a certain deep human need. Every man wants to believe that it is possible for some human being, even if it isn't himself, to drink eight bottles of champagne a day and suffer no ill effects. Canterton's magnificent physique makes him look as if he could. It isn't till you get to know him that you realise that you see that drink has changed his soul to a stench of vulgarity. Oh, he'd have run all right.'

'But Barstow, now? He surely . . .'

'No. A coward. He hates the Catholic Irish because way back in the eighties he had to go round Ireland prosecuting for the Crown in the Crimes Act Special Courts, and they frightened him sick. He's never forgiven them for that. He's been a brave man because he's gone on in spite of his funk. But one can be a coward and a brave man at the same time, and he was so much of a coward that he couldn't have faced hanging for treason. Dodging assassination is different. It is exciting; you can do it on your nerves. But a cell and the drop – that can't be done on the nerves. He would never have seen it through. Look at the way that long after the whole business was settled he had to have corps of detectives to guard his house down in Sussex. Absurd. Preposterous.'

'Is it true,' asked Francis Pitt, 'that you were the man in the Cabinet who refused all protection of any sort?'

Sunflower, forgetting she was in disgrace, cried out, 'Yes! He never had one detective and Bryce Atkin always had five!'

Francis Pitt laughed outright; and Essington looked at her with his head on one side like a cat that is not sure whether to smack a beloved kitten.

'Well, I've had my question answered,' said Francis Pitt, smiling at her. 'I don't doubt the truth of what I've heard. It came, by the way, from Hurrell.'

'From Hurrell?' Essington jerked back his head as if he were a nervous high-bred animal and someone had held food under his nose which he wanted to see before he swallowed it. The name recalled to her one of those quarrels of his, when secretaries stood outside his door, saying to each other, 'Well, if I were you, I wouldn't post it till the morning. Hold it back somehow. You *can't* send out a thing like that. He'll probably feel better in the morning,you know . . .' He went on, 'I wouldn't have thought you were likely to hear much good of me from that quarter.'

'There you're very much mistaken,' said Francis Pitt, shaking his great head impressively. 'He has a tremendous admiration for you, a tremendous admiration.'

'He hadn't at one time.'

'Ah, but that's a long time ago, and many things have changed

51

since then. I think you'd find yourself seeing pretty well eye-to-eye with him now.'

'Mm . . .'

'No, I mean this. Often and often he has said to me that you were the one man who could have saved the Liberal Party. He ranks you far higher than himself.'

'So he might,' said Essington; and they all laughed.

'You don't think much of Hurrell?' asked Francis Pitt, meditatively. 'Ah, he's a fine man. I met him a week after I landed from America in 1913 in search of my real career, and he's been my best friend ever since. I know him through and through, and I don't think there ever was a much finer man.'

She saw the little man in California, riding a horse on warm white dust, drawing rein, and looking over his shoulder. It was like this large little man that what had caught his eye was nothing less than another continent. She saw him dismount; and later get into a tall American train, as she had seen people doing on the movies. In the blacks and greys of photography she saw him sitting reading a newspaper; she saw the negro porter bending over him; she saw him looking at the women; she saw him eating in the restaurant car; she saw him going down the steep steps and taking a stroll in the clean open air. She saw him doing these things all across the continent; and the effect was like the clenching of a fist. She saw him on shipboard, swathed up to his ugly face on a deck-chair, watching the taut line where sea and sky dip up and down behind the swaying rails; the fist was clenched to hit. She saw him in England, in some open but urban place, its dingy background stained by those dingy and splendid towers of St Stephen's, which are as if London's dreams had wished her fog into shapes of magnificent governances, which have so strange an effect on Englishmen. She saw him walking up to Hurrell, whom she remembered having met, a stooping dull-eyed man on whom intellectuality seemed to be acting like some form of pulmonary weakness; one could imagine his nights much troubled by short dry thoughts. In front of him Francis Pitt came to a halt, as once he had come to a halt in front of her. But he did not hurry away from this man as he had hurried away from her. The fist unclenched, it became a hand held out, held up, like a child's.

It was queer that speaking so baldly he made one think of all these things. It was because his voice was full of character, though his words had none. In this also he was the opposite of Essington, whose voice

52

was without character. Because of his rage at not having been at Balliol he spoke exactly like all men who have been at Balliol; though if he had been at Balliol he would without doubt have disgustedly schooled himself to speak as if he had never seen Oxford. Except for that accent his speech was nearly without attributes. It was silver-bright and unsigned, like a scalpel, a mental instrument as that is a surgical instrument; kept in the locked cabinet of silence when it was not required for real work, never treated as a toy. That was so hard on him, for when he was tired in the garrulous way, and felt the need of just letting his tongue run on and on, as everybody does sometimes, he was ashamed of it, and insisted on thinking, so that his words would be justified by their meaning. His poor head, his poor head. But of course it was obviously more sensible to put one's meaning into as many words as it needed and say them clearly than to let it blow, pungent but vague like a breath of spice, on a booming wind of deep-voiced sentences. This too made her feel that Essington represented a more recent, more edited kind of man than the other. The difference between them seemed to her to be in itself a thrilling drama. She suddenly felt very gay, and began to drink her wine.

Essington said acidly: 'Hurrell wasn't with me at Versailles, you know.'

'No. I know he wasn't. He saw the whole business very differently from the way you did. He thought that to get out when you did was to be a quitter. He had an idea that he could do better if he stayed inside and tried to mould things nearer to what you and he both hoped for. You see, compromise is a very strange thing in Hurrell. Remember he was brought up in a Jesuit school. That leaves a mark on a man. It's left a very deep mark on Hurrell. With him it's always compromise, compromise, compromise. That's made him a good thing in my life. I'm too forthright. I go for what I want, and I must have all I want. Hurrell has taught me to water that down, to take what I can get. But, mind you, he carries the thing too far with himself. I admire him more than any other living man, but I see all his faults, and I know that's the chief of them. But he knows it too. And particularly he knows that he was wrong and you were right about Versailles. He feels very strongly that he should have come out with you. He knows he did no good by staying in with Bryce Atkin. And he owns it publicly now. He was saying so last Sunday when we were all down at Tenby's for the weekend. Tenby was greatly impressed.'

'Mm . . .'

'Ah, you don't believe me. But I tell you Hurrell is with you on this. I should say he'd be willing to be with you on many other points than this.'

'He's never made a sign,' said Essington.

'That's Hurrell's way. He's a terribly proud man. I know him through and through. A lot goes on inside that quiet man you'd never suspect. He's so proud that it's an agony to him to have to climb down. But I think he would do if he met you. I'm sure he would. Indeed I know he would. Now, would you meet him and see if I'm not right? Would you and Miss Fassendyll come over to my house one night this week and dine with Etta and me and Hurrell? Just us five?'

It was as if he had produced a white rabbit from his sleeve. His talk was retrospectively recognisable as conjurer's patter.

'Well . . .' said Essington. He made a little purring sound of embarrassment; and wagged his forefinger at Pitt. 'Vamp!' he said solemnly. 'Vamp!' And he put back his head and laughed silently behind his silver feelers.

Francis Pitt chuckled without real merriment. It was plain that he could not make out whether Essington was really amused or was hiding behind laughter a harsh annoyance that he should have been forced to say whether or not he wanted to meet Hurrell. Essington did not help him. He raised his glass to his lips and drank his port between gusts of silent laughter. Pitt shot a look of hostility at his sister, as if she were somehow to blame for all this; and turned to Sunflower, saying with heavy courtesy, 'Well, what does Miss Fassendyll say? Won't you persuade Lord Essington?'

She was confused by him. The courtesy in his voice was so very heavy. It was as if he stood on the steps of a throne, and she were kneeling to him, and he bent down to do her honour, and cast about her a rich cloak, too rich a cloak, so rich that its weight crushed her. But in the centre of his hard grey gaze there was something that was as if he had not bent down at all, as if he had no intention of doing her honour; as if he were standing level with her, and meant her to take whatever he gave her. She turned aside and looked at Essington, as years before, when she had first sat at meals with Essington, she used to turn aside and look at the thought of Chiswick: the streets; the people; her mother's house; her sisters and brothers; the comparatively simple and unpatterned life she had left behind her. But immediately she forgot Francis Pitt, for she saw what was the matter with Essington. He had put down his glass, and now that he felt himself free from the other man's attention he looked like a child who has heard that if he likes he will be given a certain treat, who longs for that treat more than anything else in the world, but who is prevented by some infantile point of dignity from showing that he longs for it. Of course, he wanted to make it up with Hurrell. It was always like this a year or two after his quarrels, if they were with anybody whom he had known for a long time. If they were with people whom he had met during the last few years, since this curious lack of interest in personality had come upon him, of course he parted with them with no emotion save relief at having eliminated one of those innumerable human annoyances that seemed to his mad nerves to be crowding in and in on his tired middle-age. But about old friends he felt just as if he were an ordinary person. You would not have thought so at the time, for these quarrels were not just a mere matter of having a few words. There was always one of his ideas behind them, and that meant that he went about blue-white like one of the revival preachers that used to come to Chapel now and again, and whipped himself to go on with the thing long after he would naturally have lost interest in it. There wasn't any bright side to them at all, for he got none of the relief that Father used to get by swearing about the place, since he held himself taut all the time lest he should say anything unfair. He seemed to dread being unfair as other people dreaded being sent to prison: for him there wasn't anything worse. But deep down he minded his quarrels in the ordinary way as well. She would see signs of that first some months after it was all over, when a name came up in conversation and Essington pursed his mouth behind his silver feelers and said, with a bruise on his voice, 'Woodruff? Oh, we don't see anything of each other now; not since the Amritsar business'; as, tonight, he had said, 'Hurrell? I wouldn't have thought you were likely to learn much good of me from that quarter.' And then with luck, a year or two later, there would happen a night when she came back from the theatre and found him sitting in his armchair by the fire in the little library, that was so pretty with the birds-of-paradise chintz, drinking his weak whisky-and-water and looking chubby. 'Well, how did it go tonight? That's good. You're getting on, you know. This is a long way the best thing you've ever done. There's quite a quality about your acting now. But what a pretty thing you are! The best part of your prettiness never shows in the theatre. In a little room like this you're astounding. Come here and let me kiss your silly old neck. Well. I've had a good evening too. A dinner at the Jacobsons'. Ooh! Such a rich house. Lots of footmen nine feet tall. And I think there was a pearl in my soup. Very good talk, though. And who do you think was there? Old Woodruff. I haven't seen him since the Amritsar business. He was very friendly. He asked after you. We are the most official pair of sinners that ever were. I'm dining with him on Thursday, just ourselves. Hm. What about going to bed?' He wanted it to be like that with Hurrell, whom she remembered now he had known not very well, but for a long time. He had told her once that they had sat together for the same examination at some very early stage in their careers, and had gone off in company at the lunch-hour and eaten bread and cheese in a public house, united by the link, which was not alluded to then and never had been since, that they were both wearing suits of clothes which they had outgrown to a ridiculous degree. It occurred to her that this must have happened years before she was born. This somehow brought tears to her eyes. It was as if she saw him sitting alone among long shadows.

She must see to it that he met Hurrell; but she must not give away that he wanted to, for he was ashamed of these ordinary emotions, as one would have thought he would have been ashamed of his bad temper and injustice, and as he was not. So she looked at Etta and Francis Pitt, as if she thought them very interesting and charming people, though at that moment she was not thinking about them at all; she seemed as if she were going to say something, but bit it back, and then could not help herself, and said naïvely, as if begging him to let her go to this nice party, 'We could go, couldn't we?' It was queer how she could act better off the stage than on it; she supposed it was because the motive was stronger. She couldn't be expected to want to please an audience of people she didn't know as much as she would want to please Essington.

'There you see,' said Francis Pitt, 'Miss Fassendyll wants you to do it. That settles it. You're coming to meet Hurrell.'

'These women,' protested Essington, 'these women know nothing of the stern moral passion of our sex. I quarrelled with Hurrell on a matter of high moral principle, my dear.' He looked happier already.

'And you'll make it up with him on my Mumm 1901, which is a darn sight better,' said Francis Pitt, with that strange, deep, over-acted chuckle. 'I'm all with the women on this and many other matters. Nix on moral passion for me. Now, when will you come up? Etta, when are we free? Well, we needn't bother about that. It's for you to say.'

'Next week, you said, didn't you? Monday . . . Tuesday . . .' He seemed to reflect deeply, though nowadays he had not so very many engagements; and finally suggested, in a burst, 'Look here, what about this Friday? As a matter of fact it would suit me better than next week, just as it happens.'

'This Friday? That's fine. At half past eight. I count on you for that.'

Etta murmured, 'What about the Dartreys?'

Pitt made a sweeping, advertising gesture. 'Put them off! I know now what I want to do on Friday evening!' He drank deeply, and brought down the glass smartly on the table. 'Ah, this'll help Hurrell to throw off his cold.'

'Has he a cold?' asked Essington. She could see that now he was letting himself be eager for news of Hurrell.

'If you asked him tonight he'd tell you he was dying of one. He's an old woman about himself, God bless him. He's gone off to bed this evening with a face as long as a fiddle because he's got an ordinary cold on his chest.' Again he chuckled, and twirled the stem of his glass between his thick fingers. For a moment he seemed to Sunflower like a tired actor who is getting through the evening on his technique; but that was absurd, for vitality was plainly the thing that he had got. He was the most self-possessed and male person she had ever met.

'Well, I think he really is ill,' said Etta obstinately, re-starting a discussion.

'Fiddlesticks! I'm often as ill as that,' her brother interrupted, rather suddenly. A greyness passed over his face. His features seemed to fall, so that he looked much older, and his eyelids flickered. It seemed to Sunflower that he might have had quite a lot to think about during dinner. But he said, 'Essington, I'm going to ask for some more of your very good port. We must drink to the success of your meeting with Hurrell. May you make it up and – ' he wagged his head portentously, 'may great things come of your meeting.'

Essington filled his own glass too, though ordinarily he drank no more than a sip of port. They raised their glasses solemnly. It was funny the way that men have special ways of being ridiculous that they agree not to consider ridiculous, like the silly clothes they wear at Eton, and going to cricket matches as if they mattered.

'Here, the women are standing out of this!' cried Francis Pitt. 'They must drink this health too!'

'Oh, yes, indeed they must!' echoed Essington, and poured port into Miss Etta's glass with something of the other man's swaggering breadth of gesture, which came so unnaturally to him that for an instant the wine shone above the rim like a bevelled jewel, threw down a tawny veil that draped its calm self, safely contained within the bowl, and clung to the flutings of the stem and became a bright blister on the walnut wood; while the wine left behind shivered, and was again a flawless bevelled jewel above the rim. That pleased Sunflower because it was a pretty thing in itself, and because of the funny little rivalry between the two men that had made it happen. She felt like a mother who, sitting on a beach, watches her son follow some stronger, more conventionally boyish boy over the rocks in some game; she does not mind that hers seems the weaker and comparatively spiritless because she is sure he knows a trick worth two of that; this man was all very well but he was not her Essington, with his honesty, his courage, his wonderful cleverness, and his dear way of looking like a great big lovely cat. She felt very warmly, closely, married to him tonight and plotted how she might move her chair closer to Essington and slip her hand into his under the corner of the table. She smiled at Francis Pitt, as he poured out her port, with the unveiled candour which one can show to a stranger who has no power over one, who will not be able to use it to one's hurt.

'To the meeting with Hurrell,' said Francis Pitt heavily; and they all drank, all of them, even Essington, laughing a little. As they set down their glasses Francis Pitt, assuming the character of a strong man exasperated to distraction and humbly anxious for help from those whom he knew to be cleverer, grumbled, 'And truly I do hope to God you two get talking to some purpose. Something must happen to lift us all out of this mess and if you two can't do it no one can . . .' He was obviously trying to flatter Essington. But it struck her that the obviousness of it was intentional; he knew that though Essington would be pleased to hear someone expressing sincere admiration for him he would be still more pleased that an important man thought it worth while to flatter him. That was clever, but it was male, it was superficial. It was true, of course, but it was beside the point. Essington was going to do as he wished, and meet Hurrell and forgive him, but not for anything that had to do with importance or recognition or getting back into power; simply because he wanted to make it up with an old friend. She looked at him adoringly and wished that she might rub her cheek against his and nuzzle up to him. She would as soon as these people had gone. Sometimes it had seemed to her as if she stayed with him only out of habit, as if the pang she felt whenever she determined to leave him were only such as she might feel if she were obliged to move out of a house after a long tenancy. But now she knew she thought such things only because she was tired. She stayed with him because he was full of sweetness, she did not leave him because that would be to abandon the whole of life that was good. And it would get better and better, there would be more and more evenings like this, as he grew older and less vehement. Then floated before her, and seemed to make a pattern, images of herself, of Essington, this contentment not transitory on his face, of the garage proprietor and his hideous beloved wife; of Alice Hester. She breathed a long, hopeful sigh.

It made Essington turn to her as if he had not really noticed her before. 'Well, Sunflower,' he said kindly, 'What was it that kept you in Packbury, you time-wasting, appointment-shattering young woman? Whatever it was, it's done you good. You look splendid.'

'She does indeed,' affirmed Francis Pitt, settling his grey eyes on her; and Etta made a little enthusiastic murmur. Essington continued to look at her, and shifted the flowers from the centre of the table, so that no spray should veil their picture of her. They were all smiling tenderly, as if she were a child sent into the dining room to show off a new party-frock. She smiled back mistily, uncertain how to take their admiration without seeming either vain or ungrateful; it was a problem she had had to face a million times in her life and there was no solution to it. She never felt right. But this time she did not really mind. She was glad that she was thought beautiful by this man who had set in motion everything that Essington wanted to happen, and his sister who seemed so fond of him. To speed on the still faintly embarrassing moment she said shyly, 'Well, I went down to Clussingford for the weekend.'

'Old Lady Lambert and Sunflower have a curious friendship,' Essington told the others. 'She suspects the poor child of some interesting vice. Someday Sunflower will accidentally reveal the purity of her nature and a car will be ordered to take her to the station.' It wasn't as funny as he could be, but he had only said it because he was enormously proud that famous old Lady Lambert had taken her up, and wanted them to know about it. He really was ridiculously fond of her, and after ten years too.

'And on Sunday afternoon Mr Justice Sandbury took me to look at those white cows – '

'Haven't I heard of somebody else doing that before?'

'I dare say. He's the tenth old man who's shown me those white cows.'

59

'And the plainer women are allowed to stay at home and go to sleep on the terrace. It's a hard world, Sunflower.'

They all laughed teasingly at her, mocking her tenderly for her beauty. It was nice. They knew she was stupid, but did not mind. This was a lovely hour. Everything was going well. She had no troubles, really.

'Well, anyway,' she went on, when she had stopped giggling, 'he asked me to stop at Packbury on my way back on Monday. So when I did get there, and the car chose that very place to break down – '

Essington made a petulant noise. 'Harrowby is no good.'

'Oh, it wasn't his fault.' She put back her head and laughed silently at the dear, silly old thing, for he was scowling and knocking the ash off his cigar and did not see her. It was part of his passion for her, one aspect of his desire to be not only all she loved in the world but all she knew of the world, that he always took a dislike to any of her servants, men or women, as soon as they had been with her long enough to mean anything to her. Actually he would not have let her discharge them except for some misbehaviour, for his sense of justice knew absolutely no exception, save sometimes herself; but he grumbled all the time as if he wanted her to do it. Funny cross old thing that loved her so. When they were alone again she would ruffle up his thick eyebrows and his silver feelers. 'Well, anyway it seemed a way of passing the time, so I went. And it was interesting.'

'Was it? How?'

She grew self-conscious all of a sudden. 'Oh, it just was,' she said weakly, and drooped her head, and bit a salted almond and stared downwards at her empty coffee-cup.

'I loathed going on circuit when I was at the Bar,' said Essington. 'You see then what this earth breeds. But then I don't love humanity. Sunflower does. She would not press the button that meant annihilation for us all, the foolish creature. But tell us, what was it that interested you?'

'Oh, just the people.' She tried to leave it at that, but they worried her for details. Essington wanted her to show off, to let the others see that she was his possession, the most beautiful woman in England but a nice human being as well. And Francis Pitt also wanted her to show off, so that he could flatter Essington by conceding these points. Men were funny! She could not help laughing, and that made them more insistent, which was awkward. And Francis Pitt suddenly made it more awkward by asking, 'Didn't I hear you say something as you came into the room about an old woman who was tried for bigamy?'

She blushed. 'Oh – that was nothing.'

'What was the story?' Essington pursued.

'Oh nothing, nothing . . .'

'Tell me, Sunflower!' He was half-angry. He really wanted to know, because he had seen her blush, and he wanted to know what had made her blush. It hurt him because she was keeping something that had moved her a secret from him. His face was catspawed with growing suspicion and discontent. If she did not tell him he would in a moment or two become capable of something outrageous that would not only express his irritation but would bring the whole occasion to an end, like an angry child twitching a tablecloth by the corner and bringing down the meal it had looked forward to, the favourite food on the favourite plate, crashing to the floor. He might offend them so that the invitation to see Hurrell would fall through. Well, she would have to do as he wished, though she could not tell the story as she had wanted to in front of these two people. But she would say those things after they had gone; she knew that as soon as the door had closed on them he would take her in his arms. And these were such very nice people that she could say nearly all she felt in front of them. In any case she must stop him getting cross, so she began: 'Well, that was rather interesting, I thought. She was an old woman of seventy, called – ,' she looked down and parted hesitatingly with the name for told secrets lose a little of their virtue, 'Alice Hester.'

'That is a very beautiful name,' commented Francis Pitt in his heavy way that was like spoken leaded type.

She had wanted someone to say that. 'Isn't it?' she said, and their eyes met. He was such an understanding person that she wished she might take him aside and tell him the story by himself.

'Well, go on,' said Essington.

'Oh, it isn't anything really. But anyway she was married years and years ago, fifty years ago, I suppose, to a man she didn't like, a farm labourer down in Essex, and she wasn't happy, though she had lots of children. And one night her husband turned her out of doors, and the children too. And then a ploughman came, and took them all to a barn where they slept. And in the morning he brought them two loaves and some water.' Her voice became weak and ashamed, as if she were a child who had been made to repeat a story out of the Gospel to strangers. She turned to Francis Pitt and said, tittering: 'That last bit sounds like something out of the Bible, doesn't it?'

The look on his face struck her dumb. She would have liked to run from the table. It was an odd inquisitive look, as if she had given herself away in some phrase and he was thirsty to follow it up. Ordinarily she would not have minded that at all, for of course she liked people to know all about her. But this was an expression that no one ought to wear when they were thinking of another human being. So might a burglar look, when his fingers had found the right combination and the safe was swinging open, and all that remained to do was to lift out the swag. Defensively she put up her hand to cover her mouth.

'Go on,' said Francis Pitt, 'go on.'

How could she have made such a mistake? In his soft gaze there was nothing but an immense kindliness and protectiveness, and a certain wistfulness. He had simply wanted to hear her story. Of course that would be all, for as a matter of fact she had not dropped any particularly intimate phrases. Probably the beauty of Alice Hester's destiny was so great that it got through even her halting words, just as Shakespeare gets through bad acting. And he was probably in need of help. Though he was so strong he had not that varnished look that happy people have.

'Go on,' said Etta Pitt, too.

'Well, when she went back to her cottage her husband was gone. And she was there, with all her children. And the ploughman fell in love with her, and brought her over to Packbury, because his uncle had found work for them. And then –' it was awkward to have to take her eyes away from Pitt's and probably silly to feel that she ought to, 'they had a real baby. I mean a baby of their own. And they were awfully happy, and he went on always being good to her, and they got quite old. And then he got ill and the doctors said he'd have to go into a hospital and have an operation. And he told her that there was only one thing he wanted to do before he died, and that was to marry her.'

She remembered the look in the old woman's eyes as she had repeated the dead man's words. She stopped her story and said querulously: 'I want something to drink. Give me some water.'

Francis Pitt filled her glass. When she had drunk he said again, 'Go on . . . Go on.'

Plainly he really needed to know. She turned to him as she went on with the story. 'Alice Hester knew she oughtn't to do it, for her sister over in Essex had told her that her first husband was in the workhouse there. But she saw that her man really wanted to marry her, so she made up her mind to do it. But there was a horrid boy living in the house, a kind of idiot, and he overheard them, and she knew it. All the same she didn't stop things, because she knew the old man really wanted to marry her before he died. She just went on with all the plans, and finally the day came for their marriage. And all the way to the registrar's office she heard the boy whistling just behind them. But still the old man wanted it so badly she went through with it. And then the man went to hospital and died. The funny thing was that she did not seem to mind that very much. I don't mean that she didn't feel it but it didn't seem to break her up. I suppose nothing can really hurt one if you've got lots of children and know that everything will go on . . .'

She drooped her head, looked down on the bright wood of the table, and was lost in a dream of an impregnable kingdom of satisfaction; till a movement from Essington recalled her.

'Well, the boy talked, and the police heard about it, and she was arrested. They let her off. Mr Sandbury was ever so nice. But she had to stand in the dock. Though she looked lovely. And you could see nothing mattered to her really, because of the children, and because it had given him pleasure to be married to her before he died. That's all.'

For a moment there was silence. She sat turning the rings on her fingers and looking into the dark corner of the room, until, partly that by speaking she might keep back her tears and partly lest she should in her stupid way have left out the point of the story as she had done with Harrowby, she said hoarsely, 'Wasn't it wonderful that he wanted to marry her after all those years, and that she went to all that trouble to do for him what he wanted?'

There was a stir and murmur from them all. Francis Pitt said deeply: 'Yes, it's a wonderful story. A wonderful story.'

Essington asked in a shrill, complaining voice: 'Did she tell you all this as a coherent story?'

Her lips quivering, she nodded.

'You sometimes get a witness that can tell a coherent story. The general run of them . . . My God . . .'

Francis Pitt asked: 'Did she show any embarrassment at getting up in court, in front of all these people, and owning to having lived with this man?'

She shook her head.

'Ah, women are sensible,' he said, ruminatively. 'They don't believe in these things.'

She understood that he was telling her that he honoured her: that he thought that she had done right in living with Essington without being married. Without looking directly at him, because her eyes were wet, she smiled in his direction. But suddenly there came an acid spurt from Essington.

'Don't they?'

She whirled about in astonishment, and he gave her a second helping of spite. 'Some seem to!' he flicked at her. She was puzzled, not only because she could not understand what his words meant, but because she had thought that he was bound to be in a good mood, since usually he was glad when she said anything that interested people. But it was evident that something had made him terribly angry. Perhaps he was jealous because she had been telling her story to Francis Pitt. Often he was silly like that. She smiled into his eyes but he glared through her. Still, she would get him round.

He said, to the company in general: 'Queer, the range of the scale of humanity. Think what that woman's life must have been. With seven or eight children.'

'Ten, it was,' said Sunflower. 'Eleven, counting the real one. The best one, I mean. The one she had with the man she liked.'

He did not look at her. 'Eleven. My God. This would all be about fifty years ago. She must have had to do it all on twelve or thirteen shillings a week. What a miserable life of hunger and squalor . . .'

'Oh no! She was quite happy,' said Sunflower.

'The vast range in the scale of humanity. Only fifty years from now, only fifty miles from London. Only fifty years and fifty miles from Sunflower . . .' His glance dwelt on her benevolently. She must have been right in her guess at the cause of his rage, for he was not angry with her any more now that she had stopped talking to Francis Pitt. 'Pampered little Sunflower!' he purred. 'Think of the difference between you and that poor wretch . . .'

'Oh, but you don't understand!' objected Sunflower. Since he seemed to be melting she wanted to keep the conversation on these lines till she was quite sure he was placated; for in spite of the sweetness of his tone she felt that there was still something a little wrong. Though of course it would come right in a minute or two. 'Alice Hester wasn't a bit unhappy. She didn't stand up there complaining of all that happened. I've told it you all wrong if I've made you think that. She'd loved it all. She was awfully happy.'

'Sentimental Sunflower.' Caressingly his voice lingered on the

64

syllables, he shook his head at her ever so playfully. 'Of course she couldn't be happy. Unless she was just an animal.'

'She wasn't a bit an animal. She was lovely.'

'Then her life must have been one long misery. Think of having child after child in those conditions. Think of the way it went on, year in, year out. The last child must have been the last straw. What drudgery . . .'

'Oh, no! Oh, no!' She was amazed that Essington, who was generally so right about human motives, should be wrong about anything so self-evident as this. Since she knew that he wanted above all things to know the truth about everything, she felt pleased and proud at being able to tell him something true that he had not known before. Importantly, a little fussily, like a dog racing after its master with something he has dropped safe in its mouth, she put it before him. 'It was that child she specially liked having! She loved having it. You see, she loved the ploughman . . .'

It struck her how oddly, beautifully solvent the love of Alice Hester and that man had been. Town love, the love of the kind of people she knew, the people who were News, had the alarming slippery quality of sudden wealth. Either a man liked a woman because she fitted in with some notion of womanhood he had always held, which made the affair like inheriting money; or he liked her because she surprised him by being something that he had no notion woman-hood could be, which was like taking a chance on the stock exchange. One does not feel confident that either the legatee or the speculator will stay rich, since he will have gained no technique in getting his money that will help him to keep it; and for a like reason these sudden lovers did not keep their love. It was well known that Alan Campbell would go crazy over any girl with real ash-blonde hair and an old-fashioned look that came into his chorus; he was one of those men who like women to do nothing else but that and yet insist on them looking as if they wouldn't on any account do it, which was silly and must make it so confusing for a girl. It was well known, too, that Lord Dunnottar would go crazy over any headliner he met, whether she was an actress or a singer or a dancer; they said he had stood in front of the Nelly sisters, who were identical twins, with his tongue out, not knowing where to begin. Well, she had known of seven girls who had gone with Campbell to what, being an American, he called Cannes-france; and Dunnottar had a standing agreement with the telephone people to change his number every six weeks. She thought of the

65

Embassy Club where she had seen these men with their women; the sallow light reflected from the purple and green walls made all the women pale and alike, as if they were orphans in some funny kind of institution that dressed its charges in fantastic clothes but made them live meanly and monotonously all the same. She shivered, as she sometimes did when it occurred to her that lots of people were starving and that if she had ill luck she might starve too.

But Alice Hester and her man were not like that. What they had had, had lasted their time and more, because of the way they earned it. When peasants make money out of the land, by giving the field what it demands of seeds and strength through all weathers, by reaping all day long though the noon is like a hard thumb of light pressed down on the earth, by driving the wagons to market at sunrise and being craftier than the crafty middlemen until sundown, one does not fear that they will let that money slip through their fingers. Essington had taught her that, telling her why France was reluctant to pay her debts; he would not be unfair even to militarist France. Dear Essington, how he helped her to understand things; even, so miraculously clever was he, to understand Alice Hester, whom he would not trouble to understand. For Alice Hester and her man had earned their love as peasants earn their money; by slow industrious kindness, by the stern will of sweetness not to let itself be soured by hardship, by the patient and wily dodging of circumstances that seem like a rabbit trap for all lovely things. Love earned like that would not let itself be spent too quickly. It must have been slow in its pace, that love, like a runner who knows that he has to run too far to dare to run too fast. Slowly, slowly it had come to them. Sunflower could see, could feel, Alice Hester standing in that Essex lane, with her baby warm on her breast and the others dark, whimpering little things nuzzling and pulling round her skirts. Nothing anywhere was kind. The blackness all about her put out thorny hands; wild things on night errands through the fields made little unchristened cries; the air, so much more tangible than by day, caught on her face like a cold veil; the earth underfoot was cut into cake-hard ruts that might bring her small ones down stumbling. 'Oh, Mammy, I want to go back to my lil bed.' 'Mammy, why was Daddy so vrothered at us?' The poor little things . . . She would be able to take them on in one moment, when she had got her breath again after that run down the garden; and when she had fought down the tears that gushed up from the immense desolation that filled her heart at being alone with her children, at having to be a mother without a father to help her. 'Oh, lovies, quiet all. We mustn't disturb the folks over the road. They'll have to wake early and go to work.' Then came the sound of a window-sash slowly thrown up in the cottage, and she braced herself to move for the woman of that cottage was not kind, and had a good man, and she did not feel strong enough yet to face her and own how bad her man had been. 'Hush, lovies, hush! You've wakened 'em! Come away, we'll go and lie down by the haystack.' So she had gathered them together, and made Jimmie take little Louisa's hand lest she fell in the rut, and bade Mary take care of Tommy, and had picked up Annie to sprawl on her shoulder, though she was all weighed down with her baby, who was so big for his age, and then cried almost petulantly, since she did not want to talk to that woman, 'Hurry, lovies!' for she had heard the cottage door bang. But Annie had been too heavy for her, and she had had to pause to set her down for a minute, and then Jimmie had cried, 'Mammy, there's someone coming after us!' and she had turned, and seen the bobbing lantern.

Slowly, slowly, the lantern had bobbed along the lane. Slowly the kind voice had spoken. 'Why, Mrs Bullen . . .' 'Oh, 'tis Mr Stallibrass . . .'

Slowly he had lifted Annie up in his arms.

Those were the first of kindnesses that were always slow, and therefore certified to have been really meant. When he first told her that he wanted her it must have been with a slow, ashamed drooping of the eyelids, by speech dammed more and more by shyness till there was a heartbeat between every word, and at the end only by deep breaths so delayed that after each one it seemed as though the next would never come. That must have been lovely, for it told her that this was no sudden hunger that would die in sudden satisfaction, but a desire that during its long growth had become part of his nature like his need for air. One would be out of scale with such a lover if one gave him just that silly ridiculous brief thing which town lovers like. One would want to answer him by some slower motion of the body, some motion that would last not minutes, but hours, days, weeks, months, that would end as protractedly in some worthily vast convulsion, lasting not seconds, like the climax of the other, but minutes, hours, perhaps a day, perhaps a day and night. The difference in time would change that culmination perilously, would change it from pleasure into pain. But it would still keep its character of ecstasy.

She cried out, 'But don't you see that if she and the ploughman

67

loved each other so much, they'd have to have a child! They couldn't have borne not to!'

Immediately she saw that more had happened to the moment than she meant. Etta had lost her downcast, servant-like expression and was looking straight at her; and Francis Pitt had let his cigar sprawl in his coffee-saucer. They were both pointing at her with that gun-muzzle attention that an audience gives to a really great actress in her big scene. She could not think why they were staring at her like that. With exasperation she supposed that she was looking more beautiful than usual. It was tiresome, because they had listened to what she had said, so that if they agreed with her they could back her up.

But Essington laughed, so loudly that they all turned to him.

'I must explain to you exactly what has happened,' he said to Etta and Francis Pitt. 'Sunflower has a rival called Maxine Tempest – '

'A rival!' exclaimed Sunflower. 'Why, she's my best friend.'

'Exactly. As actresses have greatest friends,' said Essington.

'But – ' began Sunflower, and was quelled by a patient lift of his eyebrows which conveyed that she was committing the unforgivable offence and spoiling one of his stories, which everybody knows is a dreadful thing for a stupid woman to do to a clever man. She folded her hands, looked down on them, and waited.

'They were in the chorus of "Farandole" together. Sweet children of eighteen. It was then that I met Sunflower.' He laid a slight humorous emphasis on the 'then' which made it more than a mere statement of time. It was as if he had said, you know how attractive girls of eighteen are, to men of our sort; well, that's how I got involved. And then came a little good-natured laugh, as if to add, and really you know, I'm not sorry; she's a good creature, and, you know, I do get extraordinarily fond of people. 'Well, Sunflower is the more comely of the two, but Maxine is decorative enough in her way. And she has perhaps a leetle more understanding of the essentials of her art than dear Sunflower has ever acquired.' He looked at her sideways, with that playfulness. 'Well, ever since "Farandole" there has been a continuous rivalry between the two. Not on the stage, which in their lives, as in the lives of so many young actresses, has never been allowed to assume a disproportionate importance. But in the photographer's studio. In the *Sketch* and the *Tatler*. Once, but not so much recently, on picture postcards. There is a kind of war of pictorial accessories between them that has gone on for years. Maxine has rather the more inventive photographer. He it was who first put Maxine with tulle round her shoulders looking up at a branch of apple blossom. Immediately dear Sunflower put some tulle round her shoulders and looked competitively up at another bigger and better bunch of apple-blossom. And she won, bless her, at a canter. Those were your very best days, my dear. Then Maxine bought a dog. A horrid little dog. A kind of angry powder-puff. This she held up against her face, thus making an agreeable contrast. Then Sunflower went out and bought another little dog, a worse little dog, a more awful little dog. And she held it up beside her lovelier face, thus making an even more agreeable contrast. So Maxine had to find another line, and this time it led her into the kitchen. She was photographed there baking a cake. But Sunflower, though an undomesticated creature, was not to be beaten. Immediately she was photographed making a pie – probably out of the discarded dog – '

The others laughed. She did not, for she knew what this rising tide of geniality usually meant. She sat with her shoulders lifted, as if she expected a lash to fall on them.

'I forget the next stage. Ah, there was gardening. You should have seen Sunflower standing on the edge of a pond with a watering-can, watering – watering – watering – ' his falsetto laughter climbed higher and higher, it seemed as if the tears would roll down his puckered cheeks, 'watering a *water*-lily . . .'

Sunflower protested, 'But we knew that was funny. It was only to use up the last plate. The print was published by mistake.' But no one seemed to hear her.

He went on, his face turned away from her. 'But at last the time came when Maxine got Sunflower beaten. Such a shame! A year or two ago Maxine took to herself a husband. Some sort of actor thing. And the consequence is that now Maxine is photographed with an infant daughter. A preposterous child with a photographic face, the sort of *ad hoc* baby an actress would have. And that, you see, Sunflower can't match. And poor Sunflower's so cross.' At last he looked at her directly, with a smile that would have been easy and rallying if it had not been taut and twitching. 'Poor Sunflower, she's always complaining about it . . .' His voice cracked.

She lifted her chin and smiled vaguely at something above Etta's head. Perhaps now that he had said this in front of people, whatever it was that made things happen would let her off that other moment, which she had dreaded for so long, when he would strike her. Only, if she had been permitted to choose, she would have chosen the other. It would not have been quite so awful.

69

But her smile gave out. It crinkled to something else on her face. She looked round for help, at first to Essington, which was silly, considering it was against him she needed help, but one has those funny instincts, when one has been living with a man for ten years; and then to Francis Pitt. He made no sign of seeing. His heavy, greyish lids were drooped, and if it had not been for the pursing of his great mouth she might have thought he had fallen into a bearish gloom and had not heard Essington's last words. But suddenly and stealthily he laid down his cigar, set his hands on the arms of his chair, and pressed it backwards for a fraction of an inch. Why, of course, she could get up and go. But she always had a queer, obedient feeling that whatever Essington was doing to her she ought to stay until he had quite finished.

She met Etta's eyes, and rose. Essington's hand, trembling, closed the door a little too quickly after them.

The drawing room upstairs really did look rather pretty. She need not be ashamed to take anybody into it. It was always good to come back to the three Ming figures up there on the mantelpiece, the two calm old men with staves who had been on a long journey and brought back peace, the princess whose face looked bland and royal because of her smooth flesh, her little bones. In the grey bowls between the figures the servants had put red roses past their prime; as she had taught them; for she fancied it went well with the agelessness of the old men and the lady, who were seven hundred years old, who were younger than any day past its morning, to hear the wordless lisp of a dropping petal now and then, like the beat of a clock that was truer than an ordinary clock, since it was irregular, and time goes by sometimes fast and sometimes slowly. Between the pale green curtains of the three long windows showed the blossomy branches of the pear tree in the garden below, thrusting through the interstices of the balcony railing, like the muzzles of white furry animals trying to climb out of the London night, where there was only the temporal beauty of the spring, into this quiet Chinese room, where lovely things were continuing for ever. It seemed a shame when one had a nice place like this not to be able to sit down and enjoy it.

'What a lovely room,' said Etta. 'I do like your wallpaper.'

'It is nice, isn't it. It's eighteenth-century Chinese. We found rolls and rolls of it in an Italian villa we once had, never been put up on anything, so we bought the lot.'

'That was a piece of luck. Did you like Italy?'

'I did. Awfully. But he got tired of it in a week or two. He always does get tired of places quite soon.' It was best, she supposed, to talk of him quite naturally.

'So does Francis. Every year he thinks he's going to like Deauville, and he never does after the first two or three days. Then I have to find a new place after we've taken a villa for the whole season.'

'That is tiresome, isn't it.' She would have liked to draw Miss Pitt's attention to the three figures, but she did not feel she could venture on long sentences yet. So she continued to look at the wallpaper through a changing lens of tears. 'I always like that little man coming down the steps of the temple. And look. It's the same little man looking out of the sort of sedan chair. In the procession. And there he is again having his tea in the garden.'

'So he is.'

'I like the grey willows going down all wooshy into the water. It all looks so nice and quiet, doesn't it?'

'Yes, nice and quiet.'

They continued to look at the wallpaper until Sunflower cried out. 'Oh, I feel so cold. Aren't you awfully cold? Would you like a fire?'

Then, seeing the open window, she felt a fool. Of course it was nearly summer. It was only because she was in a state that she was shivering.

But Etta said, as if she had not noticed anything odd, 'Well, yes, I should, if it's only a matter of turning a switch. The evening has turned a little chilly, hasn't it?'

They settled down on each side of the fireplace, stretching out their fingers to the warmth.

'Fancy having a fire in May!' said Sunflower. Her voice would shake about, 'Look, my hands are quite blue. I must have caught cold in the car.'

'Yes, I remember thinking you looked cold when you came in.'

'It was an open car,' Sunflower went on, calculating that one could not see out of the window from the dining room table. 'And there was a wind. Quite a cold wind. I do think the summers are colder than they used to be.'

'Oh, there's no doubt that the climate is worse than it was when we were children.'

'Oh, yes, it must be. Why, Mother never would have a fire lit in the house after the thirty-first of March and before the first of October. Except when some of us children were ill, of course.'

'That was a rule my mother made too.'

'Funny all the rules they had. Changing one's woollies on the first of May.' She sighed. 'Woollies were comfortable, though, weren't they, when it was cold. It's funny to think how one couldn't wear them now. It would seem worse than wrong, somehow, wouldn't it?'

'I don't see why you shouldn't if you want to,' said Etta encouragingly.

'Oh, no. I couldn't. You see, I can't exactly act, I'm just what they call a box-office draw, and it would spoil it. People wouldn't know, of course, but it's what really artistic producers call atmosphere, which means what you can't see. Oh, I'm still so cold. I'm still so cold . . .' She leaned forward to the heater. It seemed as if she would have to press her hands down on the red bar itself before she could get rid of that numbness, that feeling of blueness close to the bone. Perhaps, after all, it would make things better if she did say something about him.

'He's very tired, you know.'

Etta nodded understandingly. 'Oh, I know. Francis has what he calls reactions, sometimes.'

'I suppose it's all the work they do. He works terribly hard, you know.'

'Yes, so does Francis. And they are different from us.'

'Oh, yes, of course they're different.'

They lowered their voices, like nurses talking of their patients at the door of a ward.

'Does Lord Essington sleep badly?'

'N-no . . . I can't say I've much to worry about so far as his sleeping goes. Only after he's eaten duck. I'm always telling him he oughtn't to eat duck. But he always says it's something else.'

'I know. Francis is like that over white port. But he doesn't sleep at the best of times. He really is a very, very bad sleeper.'

'Oh, that is dreadful. It upsets them so, and they can't stand it. They haven't got patience like us . . .' Her jaw dropped. She brought back her hands to her lap. It struck her that from force of habit she was speaking as if she had forgiven him; and this time she had not forgiven him. At last the thing was finished. She wished that she did not have to face him again; not because she was afraid of what he would do or say, but just because she did not want ever to see him or think of him again. It would be difficult to keep her attention on him. She would have to face the other man again, too. She remembered what she must look like.

'Would you like to go upstairs?' she asked. 'If you don't mind, I'd like to tidy. I must look a sight.'

'Yes. I think we'll have time,' murmured Etta.

'We've got to have time,' said Sunflower.

But when they went out on the landing Essington's voice called up plaintively from the bottom of the stairs, 'Sunflower! Sunflower! You know I like sitting in the library after dinner.'

From force of habit Sunflower went down three steps. Then it seemed silly not to go on. Etta did not seem to have expected her to do anything else.

When they went into the library Essington was searching for something among the bookshelves, and Francis Pitt was standing on the hearthrug. He laid a heavy look on her, pushed a chair towards her, and as she settled in it leaned over her and said, 'Are you comfortable?' in a way that would have been suitable only if he had made the chair for her birthday with his own hands. But it was wicked to laugh at him, for spreading it on thick, because he was doing it just to show her he liked her. After he had seen to his sister's comfort, not so portentously, he moved to the other side of the fireplace and came to a standstill, smoking his cigar and watching Essington at his hunt among the books. That was convenient, for now she could take a good look at him. It was funny, how like a lion standing on its hind legs he was. He was lion-colour, with his earthy skin and his tawny hair, and the deep lines running from his nose to his chin were like the folds in an animal's hide. His broad but tiny hands and feet, which she perceived with amazement and delight to be smaller than her own, bore the same proportion to his thick, bulky-shouldered body that a lion's paws do to its carcase. Though he was so short one could imagine him wrestling with wild beasts, rolling about in the dust with them, till the growling stopped . . .

That was what had been in the prow of the canoe he had driven over the waters to her with a round-mouthed, wordless cry: a conquered beast; a slaughtered deer. As the boat came nearer she could see the little head propped up against the birch-bark side, its silken, leaf-shaped ears limp as in docility, its melting eyes set in the saying of that mild, last word that all the dead say, be they beast or human. She would have felt compunction that so lovely a thing should have died before its time had she not felt pride that he had killed it; and had not someone standing by her side, whose voice she loved to hear, sent up a round-mouthed cry that meant that they rejoiced to see food. She wished that she could stay longer in her day-dream, so that the canoe

73

could come to the shore, so that she could learn who the other one was, so that she could understand that feeling of crackling, heatless fire which was in the green forest-boughs, which was around her, which was within her. But she was called back by Essington's fretting voice: 'I never can find anything in this house . . .'

Absentmindedly she asked, 'What are you looking for?'

'Oh, don't fuss me, don't fuss me,' he wailed, and Francis Pitt, with a quickness that showed he had been waiting for a chance to protect her, cut in: 'Have you never thought of going over to the Labour Party, Essington?'

Forgetting her, he wheeled round. 'Go over to the Party that hasn't made up its mind whether it stands for free trade or protection? No . . .!'

*

For a moment after Francis Pitt had gone he dragged their thoughts with him.

'What nice people,' said Sunflower; and Essington purred, 'Yes, the little creature has real charm. But a wicked little creature. They say his financial record in California is shady beyond description. I remember we had qualms of letting him have a seat. And he came here tonight with guile, with guile. He and Hurrell are thinking of trying to pull the Liberal Party together by dropping Bryce Atkin overboard. They want me to come in. But also the little devil has thought of ratting to the Labour Party.' He chuckled. 'An evil little bottle-imp.'

Then their eyes met.

He fixed her with the menacing, justice-invested stare of the outraged schoolmaster; but she lifted her chin as she had never done before when he had been angry with her. For a second he looked astonished and then seemed to doubt whether he really wanted a quarrel, after all. He turned away and began going round the book-shelves, whistling and putting back into place the books he had disarranged; and at length remarked nonchalantly, 'Quite a good little evening. We must ask them again.'

She cleared her throat and said unsteadily: 'No.'

He swung round with an affectation of surprise. 'But I thought you said you liked them?'

'Oh, yes. I liked them all right,' she said. 'But there isn't going to be any more we. It's over. It's finished. I don't want to live with you any more. I don't want ever to see you again.'

He put his long fine hand to his forehead and sighed before speaking patiently. 'Ah, Sunflower. I could wish that you wouldn't always start this sort of thing late at night, when I'm tired out. You have a marvellous instinct for choosing the worst possible moments for making a scene.'

'But I'm not making a scene. I'm just telling you I want you to go away.' She thought of her pretty bed upstairs, with its flat, round, lavender-scented pillow that it was nice to rub your face into, and the embroidered handkerchief linen sheets she had brought back from Switzerland, looking so nice against the apple-green quilt; and tears of vexation came into her eyes. It was absurd to have a lovely Chinese room and not be able to sit in it, to have a comfortable bedroom and not be able to go to bed in it. 'He's like having a pipe-burst in every room,' she thought, and told him wearily: 'I want you to go away. And never come back again. I'm finished.'

For a minute he did not answer but stood raising himself on the balls of his feet and lifting his head, as if to try the air with his silver feelers. 'Very well, Sunflower,' he agreed at length. 'I think the time has come when this is the best thing for us to do.' He rose, he fell, he rose again, on those neat, narrow, long feet. 'For me, I haven't been happy for the last – oh, the last four years.'

She said, 'Right,' and to herself she said, 'It's three years since I nursed him through that breakdown, and had that awful time with him at Madeira. Seems funny that that doesn't mean anything to him. But he's always kind of taken a pride in not saying thank you. I wonder if anywhere inside him he knows what's been done for him. Somehow it would be nice if he did even though we're not going on. But what's the odds. It's finished.'

He breathed, 'Aha! so that's settled!' and crossed the room to the table just behind her, where there were syphons and whisky. There was a fizzing, and his voice passed over her head, purring and benedictory: 'Yes, I think we are very wise to look things in the face and get clear. Without any bitterness. Without any recriminations. In good temper.'

'That's all right,' she assented, through a yawn. 'Is it really going to be as easy as this?'

For a while he drank in silence, and then remarked casually, 'I'll stay here tonight all the same, if you don't mind. Of course I shan't bother you. But I told Brooks I shouldn't want him any more. And . . . mm . . . you know how I hate taxis.'

75

She could have laughed, it was so exactly like him. He would not go away that night, because she had asked him to go then; but he would go away in the morning, and not come back, and persuade himself that this had altered the situation in some way that gave him the advantage over her. After a little it would seem to him that it was he who had ended it, not her. She smiled drowsily, and asked herself, 'Do I really want it to be as easy as this?' and was horrified, as if she had put out a hand to touch some burning substance and found it cold in death, to find that she did want it to be as easy as this.

There was more fizzing. Then his voice soared again. 'We must remain friends, of course, Sunflower. We've had a very pleasant time together in some ways, and there are all sorts of memories that will link us together.'

'Yes, all sorts.'

'You must always look on me as a friend, you know, Sunflower. Always come to me for anything you want.'

He was trying to be nice. 'Thank you, dear,' she said.

Slowly he sauntered to the other armchair and pushed it forward till it faced her; and settled in it with his glass of whisky. 'Yes, little Sunflower,' he went on, between the sips. 'I'll always be glad to help you. For, though I welcome this break in a way – not that there hasn't been a great deal, oh, a very great deal indeed, that's been very delightful between us, but I'm old, I find myself growing more and more incapable of adapting myself to a different type of mind – ' he stopped and gazed thoughtfully into the distance.

'He's thinking of replacing me with one of those political widows with pearl dog-collars who get both volumes of the dull books out of the Times Book Club at once,' reflected Sunflower. 'Well, I don't care. But I wish he'd get on with it. It makes me all shaky to sit and talk like this after I've turned him down, even though he is taking it so well. And I would like to go to my own bed.'

'Still, there's a very real friendship and liking between us, and I'd like to be all the use to you I can. And you know, Sunflower, you may need me, for I'm not sure you'll find life on your own so easy as you think you will . . . Mm . . .' Again he gazed into the distance, until he took another sip, to hearten him after the disquieting vision he had seen. 'I wish I were surer about you in certain ways. There's your work . . .'

'That'll go on for a few years, I dare say,' she said.

He set down his glass, sat back in his chair, again looked into space at some lugubrious foreboding. At length he agreed, 'Yes, I suppose it will,' and, as if to encourage himself, took another drink.

'It's a pity I had to act,' said Sunflower, miserably. 'I've never really fancied it.'

'Yes,' he mused, 'it's a pity, Sunflower. Yet I don't quite know where you would have fitted in better, what your real métier can have been . . .' He dismissed the unprofitable speculation, mournfully drank again, set down his glass, and said, with the air of one putting a good face on a sad situation, 'Well, as you say, that'll probably last for a few years. These new people are pretty good, of course. Perdita Godly and all these youngsters. But you've got your footing. I think Phillips is genuinely grateful to you for the luck you've brought him. He'll probably be loyal to you for quite a long time. Oh yes, you're all right, Sunflower.' He sipped again, his eyes set kindly and pensively on her over the rim of his glass. 'But, mind you, you've got to start being careful. You're a little fatter than you were when we first met, my dear. You eat a good deal, you know.'

'I didn't eat much tonight.'

'No. But it isn't dinner that matters, in point of fact. It's tea that does it. Crumpets, cakes, sweet biscuits, all these little things. That's what gives the slight thickness round the jaw that just takes away the . . . But you're all right, dear, at present.'

'Well, I ought to be,' said Sunflower, shortly, 'for I don't have any tea. And I'm fit to drop.' She raised her finger and ran it round her jaw. Surely it was not so bad. Perhaps, it was a bit heavy. Of course she did weigh a lot compared to all this new lot who were as thin as paper-knives. Still theirs was the type that seemed to be liked nowadays, so maybe being perfect in her type was as bad as being fat. Oh, now that he had started her worrying she probably wouldn't sleep for hours, and she was aching with tiredness. 'Now I'm going to bed.'

He apparently had not heard her, for he went on thoughtfully. 'But anyway that doesn't matter. It isn't in physical type that they've beaten you. It's in intelligence. You're – ' he made a sad grimace into his glass, and gulped the last of his drink, 'slow, Sunflower, slow!' It was extraordinary how she had never quite got the hang of his moods. Of course he had all the time, from the moment she had told him to go away, been frenzied with rage against her. 'My God, the way you kept on coming back and back to it tonight! The way you kept on making a fool of yourself – and me again and again!'

As soon as she had seen that he was angry she had resolved not to answer him back, no matter what he said; but when he reminded her of what had happened at dinner she began to blush again, and the pain of the blunt pricking where the blood swept over her breasts made her cry out, 'Oh! Oh! I never did! It was you made a fool of me!'

He looked at her with eyes narrowed by hate. She cried, 'I don't know what you mean! It was you! I didn't say a thing!'

Softly he said, 'Are you so densely, so cretinously stupid that you didn't see that you were giving away the most intimate details of our private life to Pitt and his sister?'

This was something more than mere blind malignity. He was showing that mixture of hatred of her folly and gloating delight in the fresh evidence he had collected concerning it which usually meant that she had done something really silly. Shivering she said, 'Whatever do you mean? I wish you'd tell me right out.'

'Why, that imbecile story you'd dragged home from the Assize Court – ' his gaze suddenly grew wild and hard with a different, madder accusation. 'Sunflower!'

'Yes!'

'How did you come to be at that court? Had you fixed up the whole thing beforehand? Had you arranged with Sandbury to be down at Clussingford when he was there?'

She gaped. 'Why, I never saw the old man before!'

He clapped his hands over his ears. 'My God, that Cockney whine! I thought I'd cured you of . . . And I wonder, I wonder. Sunflower. I'm not sure about you. You can manage that pure, hurt look wonderfully. But I'm not sure about you. I was looking at your letters before you came in. There are two bills from dressmakers. Big bills. What do you want with all those clothes if it isn't to attract other men?'

'I've told you a hundred times I have to dress because I'm on the stage. You wouldn't think it had anything to do with acting but it has. And you know I'm all right! Tell me what I did tonight. Why shouldn't I have told that story about Alice Hester? You don't mean that either of them had been in trouble for bigamy – or anything – '

'Oh, God above! You fool! You unspeakable fool! Didn't you realise the way you told it gave away that you wanted children, that you were perpetually worrying me to give you a child! You went on and on at it, you wouldn't leave it alone. When one thought the thing was safely thrown out of doors you reappeared at the window with the thing in your mouth.'

She had risen and was standing quite still, with her clenched hands covering her mouth and her round eyes on him.

'Don't you understand even now? You kept on saying, "She wasn't happy though she had lots of children." "I suppose if you've got lots of children nothing can hurt you." "She couldn't have borne not to have a child." If you had told them in a crude sentence exactly what you wanted you couldn't have been more indecent. And the Pitts are nice people. They were out to be nice to you. When I asked Francis Pitt to dine here tonight he suggested himself that he should bring his sister. Said she admired you very much and that they quite understood this wasn't the same as any other irregular ménage. I should think they went away regretting it. I've never had such a ghastly time in my life. And now, to round off the evening you start this nonsense about leaving me. I would have thought you'd done enough, after this appalling exhibition. Oh, my God, can't you say something? Need you stand there looking half-witted?'

She drew a shuddering breath. 'I don't see there's anything I can say. I suppose that must have been it. There certainly was something that made them look at me. I'm sorry.'

'This isn't a thing sorrow can wipe out. It was the last straw, to have the thing dragged up in public, when I'm sick of being pestered about it in private.'

'Oh, Ess,' she said, 'I haven't pestered you. I've hardly ever spoken of it . . . except . . . except when I've liked you very much. And you've spoken of it then as much as me. You know I've never asked you for that . . . by daylight. Oh, I didn't think you'd ever bring that up against me. It doesn't seem the sort of thing that ought to come back to me like this . . .' She bit her knuckles.

He pointed a finger at her and waggled it from side to side. 'That's it,' he said.

She stared. 'What?'

'That thing you're doing to your hands. A silly false movement. No effect. That's how you let down the big scene in "Leonora". No, Sunflower, you shouldn't have been an actress.' He moved towards the table, where the whisky and syphons were, making her feel as he passed her by an exasperated flutter of his fine hands, that it was a piece of intolerable clumsiness for her to be standing where she was. He poured out a glass of soda-water only. Even at this moment he was not forgetful of his austere rule never to drink more than one glass of weak whisky-and-soda after dinner. Having refreshed himself, he went on. 'Yes, I'm inclined to think that if I took you seriously and got out it would be the best thing. I'm sick of this constant suggestion that I've wasted your life, that I'm an old man who's eaten up your youth, that as soon as I got out of politics I should have deserted my poor loyal little Ethel and married you and given you children. I'm bored to death with that story, Sunflower.'

Amazed she asked, 'But whenever did I say all that? You know I never did. Let's not quarrel, let's be friends, like you said we ought to be. I've never said such things. I've never thought them. I've always seen it as I did at the beginning. You're the cleverest man in the world, and I was of no use to you, and I didn't believe it made any difference whether a clergyman said things over you or not, so of course I didn't hold back. I knew it wouldn't be all jam, and it hasn't been, but I haven't ever brought it up against you. Oh, you know I haven't.'

Meeting her eyes he looked away from her, said 'Mm' into his silver feelers, and admitted, 'Well, perhaps you've never said it in so many words. Still the feeling – ' again he waved his long hands, 'is about. Perhaps,' he suggested in a stronger tone, 'you said it without meaning to, as you did tonight.'

The shame of what she had done came over her again. 'Oh, I am stupid,' she said. 'I do say silly things.' She began to cry.

'Oh God, now you're crying!' exclaimed Essington, as if in surprise and despair. 'Haven't you any consideration? Now, Sunflower, dear, try and hold yourself up. I'm always holding you up, and I . . . I can't go on with it. I'm tired. And I'm old. Some people might think it was time I had a little peace. Now do pull yourself together . . .'

But she had already stopped crying. She was looking at him with a deep furrow between her brows. He wailed, 'Oh, for God's sake, don't look so silly,' but she continued to gaze at him thoughtfully. 'I don't understand what you feel about me,' she said. 'You say you love me. But you don't. If you loved me you'd want always to be kind to me and look after me. When I was silly and stupid you'd do something to stop me from going on. You wouldn't do what you did tonight, and stand by while I blundered into it, and then push me further in. And it's all like that. I believe you hate me. If things are bad with me you always make me worse. You know perfectly well I loathe being an actress and that I have to be one and there's no getting out of it now, and all the time you go telling me how bad I am as if I didn't know it. I've never told you of trouble I've had at rehearsals without your looking pained and saying I must have made a fool of myself. I've never had bad notices after a first night without you coming and sitting on my bed and picking out the worst ones in a thoughtful kind of way and saying what a pity it all was. Not that that's what I mind, for most of it is true, though any fool feels nowadays that when he hasn't got anything else to be funny about there's always my acting. What I mind is that you sort of say to me all the time, "Yes, you are a bad actress, and maybe if you keep on like this maybe I'll get rid of you." It is as if when you come here tired out I was to taunt you for having been bested by that nasty little Bryce Atkin at Versailles and say that maybe I wouldn't have you here any more because of it. Which I wouldn't ever do. Now if you loved me you'd say that however I failed on the stage you'd always love me. But you don't because you hate me. It's meat and drink to you to see me miserable. About this marriage business, you've set me thinking. You know I haven't ever talked about it like you said I did, but now I'm wondering. You say you live like this with me because you don't believe in marriage, but you do. You really think it's good of another woman to come and see you because I'm living with you without being married. If you think that then it's wrong of you to live with me. But I'm not at all sure if you don't live with me like this just because it puts me all the time into positions I hate. Staying with me at hotels where people look at me. Like Madeira. While you were in politics you couldn't afford to do that, you just made me cry here, but the minute you were free you rushed at this public thing. And yet it isn't as if I bored you and you wanted to get rid of me. You never leave me alone. I haven't had six weeks on end away from you in twelve years. You just like being with me to hurt me. And yet . . . and yet . . . it's me you like making love to. Oh,' she gasped, shaking her head in horror. 'That – that's what's so awful. It's dreadful. It isn't natural.'

She stared at him earnestly until, beneath his silver feelers, his lips pursed, and she put out a defensive hand. 'Ah,' she interrupted, 'You've thought of something clever that'll make me feel like cat's meat. Well, what's the good of that? I am cat's meat, I suppose. But I'm not going to listen to this one. I know it all.'

As she laid her hand on the door-knob she looked over her shoulder, fearful at her own rebellion. He was wearing the utterly amazed and shocked expression that a bowler in a county match might wear if a batsman suddenly walked off the pitch in the middle of play. 'Ah, it's a game to him,' she thought. 'But, oh, he is looking like a cat. A great, fine handsome cat. It was when he looked like that we used to make up that fairy story about him being King of the Cats and me the Blue Persian Princess. That was a jolly story. Such funny things he thought of . . .' But something in her that was feeling old and desperate cried out, 'You can't give up what's left of your life for a fairy story.' She slammed the door between them.

She ran upstairs, and went into her bedroom, locked the door, sat down in front of her dressing-table, shook her head at the disordered image in the mirror, and said, 'He's mad, he's mad.' Well, it was all over now. The funny thing was that she felt lonely. She would have liked to go and ring someone up and tell them all about it, but there was nobody she knew well enough except Maxine, and most likely she and her husband would be in bed by this time; and she always felt that George was a bit jealous of Maxine being so fond of her. Of course, if Marty Lomax had been alive, she would have gone straight to the telephone and said, 'Mayfair 287169,' and then, 'Is that you, Marty? Well, it's happened like you wanted it to. I'm free,' and he would have answered something slow, something that would have caused her to feel unruffled and full of consequence, and made arrangements to come and see her at some hour on the next day, after which she would never have needed to bother about anything. Marty had been a dear. Alice Hester's ploughman must have been just like him. She put her hand into the back of the drawer under her mirror and took out the little box in which she kept her most private things: the wreath of violets she had worn in 'Farandole', which for some years afterwards she had believed had brought her luck; a photograph of her brother Maurice as a baby; a photograph of herself and Maxine at the first theatrical garden party at which they had been asked to take a stall; and Marty's letter, the only one he had ever written to her.

Hotel Splendide,
Cannes.

Darling Sunflower,

I wish you were here.

Measles has broken out in the hotel. I am awfully sorry for the girl who got them first. I danced with her the day before she got ill.

There is all the usual crowd here. I went up to the Carlton yesterday and saw Fitz playing. He asked after you. He is a good sort.

How old is Irene Temple? I have a bet on it.

I wish you were here. Do remember that any time you cut off I am ready for you. If you wired I would come right back. Or if you think there would be a fuss in London we could meet and get married in Paris. There is a way of doing it that is as simple as it is in London. Metcalfe and Doris did it. I wish you would.

The ponies are all right. I think I shall sell Trefoil to Garside after all. I don't really like her. Never did. So Garside might as well have her.

Roger Westcott is coming tomorrow. His brother is here, and his sister, who married Brixham. I like them all.

I wish you were here.
Much love,
  Yours ever,
    Marty.

Well, Marty was dead. She kissed the letter, put it back in the little box and shut the drawer. There was nobody now who would care whether she left Essington or not. Since he had come out of politics he had made her live such a secluded life that she knew hardly anybody except the people in the theatre. Or it might be that she was getting old and fat, and people were not bothering about her as much as they used to do. After all there were lots of women under thirty.

She looked hard at her reflection in the mirror. Her thoughts rambled on. 'How big I am. I would make two of Perdita Godly. Perhaps it's because I'm so big that I do clumsy things like that tonight. Oh, how silly I am. As if being big in your body could make you clumsy in your mind.' But for all that she felt at the back of her mind a sense that she was unhappy because of something to do with her body; something that, if it was not grossness, had a like contrast with the standards of the world, something that at any rate was in the nature of excess. Puzzled, she continued to gaze at herself. The two lights on each side of the mirror made her bare arms gleam, and she found herself saying aloud, in accents unaccountably tinged with bitterness, 'I could have scrubbed floors pretty well.' Surely she could not really be regretting that life had not sent her an opportunity of scrubbing floors. It was dreadful to be so stupid that you did not know even what you were thinking. The word 'bankruptcy' which came into her head whenever she thought of her relationship with Essington came once again, and she rose and went quickly into her bathroom and turned on her bath. She stripped off her clothes and sat on the

83

edge of the bath, brushing her hair, for she did not want to ring for Luttrell. After all, there were still all sorts of things that people could not spoil by making scenes. She had made this a lovely bathroom; she looked round at its walls that were marbled blue and green like a breaking wave, at the empire dressing-table with the gold legs fine as a high-bred animal, the mirror borne by eagles who seemed to be taking an ecstatic respite from lectern work (but that was Essington's joke); at the array on the broad shelves of bubble-tinted Venetian glass jars and bowls holding the lotions and powders and salts which she hardly ever used, but kept as an assurance to some unformulated power that she was humble, that she knew time was passing. Whatever happened, this was pretty. And through the open door she could look back at her bedroom, at the curtains of rich stuff drawn in solemn folds, and the waiting bed, with the dim lamp beside it. That would always be a good place to sleep. Indeed, she was clever about choosing things. There was perfection everywhere, in the gold hairbrush in her hand, in the Molyneux dress which lay across the chair, in the chemise and knickers beside it, which were of very thick white crêpe-de-chine bound with apple-green, almost as good as any she had got. She looked at them benignly until she was surprised to find herself throwing the brush at them and crying out, 'Well, what's the good of them! I can't eat 'em, can I?' Suddenly the room seemed flimsy as a Chinese lantern. She stood up, waiting for the feeling of solidity to come back to her. The fact was she was so tired she was light-headed. That was it.

She lay in the bath for a little while, thinking of Alice Hester, and sometimes whimpering Essington's name. Then the wedge of vibrant, light-blue summer night that thrust downwards at the top of the two green taffeta window curtains began to torment her. She felt that she ought to go out into the night and do something that would bring her peace. There must be something somewhere that would bring her peace; and she must find it all at once because time was going so fast. This was all nonsense, of course, but she was quite light-headed. Still it made her so restless that she had to get out and dry herself. She was glad she had such nice fleecy bath towels. She did love good linen. If Marty and she had married they would have taken one of those houses that are advertised at the beginning of *Country Life*, and she would have had to buy heaps and heaps of linen for it. She would have liked that. Marty would have left it all to her, he wasn't fussy about that sort of thing. Now, Francis Pitt wouldn't be a bit like that. He'd be most particular, and he'd want everything to be marked with a rather heavy monogram, probably black on white.

She suddenly dropped her towel and stared at the picture of her nakedness held by the eagles. It occurred to her for the first time that now she had quarrelled with Essington she would not be going with him to see Francis Pitt on Friday. With tears in her eyes, with water in her mouth, she remembered the pungent promise of satisfaction there had been about him, which had reminded her before of the smell of food when one was hungry. It was as if a curtain had dropped between her and a conjuror when he was in the very middle of his tricks. She could see him standing there behind the dropped curtain, his vast mouth open on some unfinished turn of his patter, one curious little paw-hand arrested in the middle of a charlatanish gesture, prevented from making for her again that materialisation of spring more actual than the real spring, from concentrating within the trick top-hat he held in his other hand a tiny vision of those lakeside woods crackling with the green fire which crackled too within her body when she thought of it. It could not be borne that this should be the last time she ever saw him. But though he had given her assurances all through the evening that he felt the extremes of kindliness, admiration, and protectiveness for her, he had given her none that he wished to see her again. Though he had spoken of their coming visit to his house with pleasure, it was obvious that it was Essington who was the important guest in his view, though he might be the less liked. He would never think of asking her by herself. Well, she must ring up Etta, and get near him that way. But that would not do, for he would see through it. And as they were sure to have thought her coarse and awful because of the way she had talked at dinner she must be careful not to frighten them. There was nothing to do but let the matter rest. Very probably she would never see him again. She went back to her bedroom and pulled out the little drawer under the mirror again, and sat for a long time looking down with hurt eyes at the box which held Marty's letter, as if this disappointment were a violation of some promise written in that large, round hand.

There was no use worrying about people. That side of life always seemed to go wrong. The thing was to think of one's work. She must try to be more like Brenda Burton, who, when she talked of her life, talked not of her husband and children but of the hundred and fifty Shakespearean parts she had played, investing the achievement with a sort of athletic pride, so that one imagined her being covered with grease by her trainers before she started, and followed by a tug throughout, and fed with Oxo through a tube. It was high time she really began to work hard at acting. Which reminded her, there was a book on the table by her bed she had got out of the London Library specially because it was about acting and it was by that man A. B. Walkley whose notice of her Rosalind had made Essington laugh so much; and she hadn't looked at it yet. She climbed in between the sheets and lay for a minute with closed eyes; and saw the wheeling faces of Alice Hester, of the hideous and beloved girl, of Essington, of Harrowby, of Marty Lomax, of Francis Pitt, whom she would not see again. They would not make a pattern, yet she felt they should. She sat bolt upright, and took up the book. The tip of her tongue began to protrude, as it always did when she read very earnestly.

> This question of temperament is interesting enough to warrant closer examination. Every stage character consists of two parts, one determinate (call it a) indicated by the text, the stage directions, and *nothing else*, the other (x) vague and varying, representing the rest of the character, as it is behind the scenes and was before the curtain went up. The reader of the play forms a mental image of x by deductions from a, and so gets his conception of the whole character of x and a. I may say in passing, that the vice of academic criticism of Shakespeare in this country, as in Germany, is to discuss $a \div x$ as an actual person, forgetting or ignoring that a is the only part of the character for which we have the poet's warranty and that x is merely our own surmise. But that is 'another story'. The point here is that, while we all have to give a value to x, we none of us give the same value, since no two imaginations coincide. That is why the student of Shakespeare is always disconcerted when first he sees a favourite play either illustrated in a picture or performed on the stage. This, he says, is all very well, but it is not my Romeo or my Cordelia. Now the actor's business with a is comparatively simple. He has to speak the words and do the things set down for him. It is with x that his real difficulties begin; for in place of our vague, floating notion of the character as a whole he has to offer us his own real person and temperament. Here the acting side of him is in the long run far less important than what the man naturally *is*. For it is, of course, flagrantly untrue, though often spoken of as true, that an actor can divest himself of his own personality and put on the personality of someone else. Just as an author is always really

86

identical with his work ('for after all', as Walter Bagshot said, 'we know that authors don't keep tame steam engines to write their books') so the actor's histrionic is always part and parcel of his real everyday self. You may so paint wrinkles on your brow, so modulate your voice and order your bearing as to pass, behind the footlights, for a mad old King of Britain, but the fact remains that you are Mr Brunn, a taxpayer of today, with an address in the London postal directory, and a pretty taste in claret and cigars. This fact will for ever prevent you from absolutely realising x. It may even do so in some obvious physical way. ('His weak, white, genteel hands, and the shape of his stomach,' said Tolstoy on his visit to *Siegfried*, 'betrayed the actor.') But even though your disguise be perfect, the fact that the soul within you is not the soul of Lear – or rather the soul of Shakespeare as projected in Lear – but the soul of Mr Brunn must forever mark off a measurable distance between x and your impersonation. The measure of that difference is, inversely, the measure of your success in the part. On the other hand, your reality (the Mr Brunn in you) while it prevents you from fully and satisfactorily representing x – that is to say, coinciding with the spectator's mental image of your part – will give you the great advantage over that pale image of definiteness and substance. What is lost in harmony and perfect propriety of conception is gained in precision and intensity of effect – provided always that your personality is not absolutely at variance with the spectator's conception. You are able to offer him a real man for an imaginary one.

Her hand sought the switch; there was darkness.
She wished she could marry someone really nice.

*

She said, 'I will not open. I will not open.' Then it crossed her mind, 'He may be ill.'

But he was not ill, only dabbled with tears. They stared at each other desolately across the threshold. The lit staircase above them creaked as if a knot of ghosts were leaning over the banisters to watch them.

He turned his face to the doorpost and burst into a fit of noisy weeping.

Well, he could not stay like that all night, she supposed. 'Oh, lovie, don't get into such a state,' she begged him. 'You'll have such a headache in the morning if you go on like this, you know you will. Where's your hankie?'

He felt about in his rumpled pyjamas, in his flapping dressing-gown. 'Lost it,' he said, and choked.

'Come in and I'll find you one,' she told him wearily. The sudden wrench of her awakening had made her feel sick.

He stood beside her, shaken by whimpering breaths, while she sat down in front of her dressing-table and searched for one of the nice big soft hankies she kept for his colds. Suddenly he cast himself down on his knees and buried his head in her lap, sobbing, 'Sunflower, Sunflower, forgive me for being such a brute to you! Why do you let me do such awful things to you, why do you let me say these dreadful things! You don't look after me, Sunflower. A woman ought to look after her man, keep him safe when he goes mad and wicked. Oh, Sunflower, Sunflower . . .'

Turning, she smoothed his disordered crest of grey hairs, and let him have his cry out. Her eyes wandered to the clock. It was half past three; she probably would not get to sleep again for hours, as she would have to quiet him down; and the rehearsal was called at eleven.

Nothing came alive in her at his weeping.

III

IT made her feel hot and cold all over to think of meeting Francis Pitt again after the fool she had made of herself the other evening at dinner, but it did not really matter because there was bubbling up in her causeless joy. She slipped her hand into Essington's and began to hum, beating time with their linked hands, and looking out of the limousine windows at St John's Wood, and liking it all. She liked the neat little stone houses, their whiteness tinted two colours by the evening, bluish with shadow on one side of the road and peachy with reflected sunset on the other and she liked the green pluminess of the spring rising above the garden walls. She liked the young men and girls walking along in light things and carrying tennis rackets, though they made her feel lonely, which was queer, as she was with Essington. It was odd to think that it was only a few hours since she had felt like killing herself because of that tiresome thing that had happened at rehearsal. Well, she didn't care if they did start telling another funny story about her. Let them. She raised Essington's knuckles to her lips, but his hand stiffened, and he drew it away.

'What have you got on, Sunflower?' he asked with querulousness.

'That kind of Greek thing I got from Louise Conlanger. You know, the green one.' She held back her cloak so that he could see it.

'Mm . . .' He looked away, pursed his lips behind his silver feelers, then came back to it. 'Isn't it rather . . . mm . . . dressed up for a quiet little dinner like tonight?'

'Dressed up? Gracious, no. It's what I wore the other night when we went and dined with old Lord Barrogh, and you said how just right it was for that sort of thing. That's why I put it on tonight.'

'Oh, I dare say it's all right. I dare say it's all right.' After a pause he added plaintively, 'Be a quiet little Sunflower tonight, won't she? Not go peacocking about too much and looking too beautiful. Hang up her little 'Reserved' card. I've been hearing things about our little host.'

'What sort of things?'

'Oh, I don't know. He's evidently apt to be tiresome with women. Mechanically and promiscuously attentive. There have been several great affairs. One with a musical comedy actress, I forget her name. Anyway she weighed a lot, and it was all passionate.'

'You mean Dolores Methuen. Well, that must have been a good time ago. For years now she's looked like somebody's rich aunt.'

'Then there was something mysterious with Lady Juliet Lynn. Nobody knows quite what happened but for some years a good deal of money passed.'

'I used to see a lot of her at one time,' said Sunflower. 'Charity matinées and that. She did a lot of war-work posing as the Madonna. She's very lovely. For a titled person.'

'And there have been others,' Essington went on, 'the little creature's evidently an ardent woman-hunter. I thought I'd better tell you so that you could be careful.'

'Who else have there been?'

'I really don't remember. One of the Nelly sisters, I think; and that tiresome young woman with protruding eyes whose husband was one of my supporters over Versailles, Mrs Lovatt, and Veronica Fawcett. Oh, a long list.'

'Well, let's be thankful that he seems to have spared the royal family as yet,' said Sunflower crossly. 'Who told you all this?'

'Young Bramley. He's reliable as a rule.'

'Yes, he is,' she agreed. 'Still, we all know how these things are. You ought to know if anyone does how women crowd round men who've got famous. That Mrs Holtby been ringing you up today again?'

'As a matter of fact she did,' Essington admitted with an elaborate air of nonchalance. 'But it was only about her pet crank.'

90

'Ah, she may say it's the suffering of Transylvanian Magyars under Roumania that's worrying her,' said Sunflower, darkly, 'but if she goes on ringing up you'll find it's the same old thing she's after.'

She sank back in her seat, for the streets now seemed not so attractive as those through which they had passed earlier. But when the car had climbed Church Street and the ground began to fall away from each side of the road, her causeless joy had its way with her, and she pulled at his hand again, crying out, 'Look what a pretty place! Why, you can see right down into the middle of London that side, and it's all a goldy haze. And look at the other side. Why, there's real country quite close. Is this Hampstead Heath? Why haven't we come here before? Oh, did you see that dog running along and everybody getting out of its way? There were lots of people making their dogs swim in that pond we passed a second ago. I wish you liked dogs, I would so love one. But you hated little Li Hung Chang, you did.' She remembered the last time he had spoken of the Pekinese, and there was a second's silence. But the place and her mood carried her on, 'Look, there's a sort of Monkey's Parade, like what we used to have down Hammersmith Broadway and Chiswick High Street, all the boys and girls walking up and down. Oh, I do think it's lovely that almost everybody looks nice when they're young anyway!'

'Silly little Sunflower, who loves her kind.'

'Well, what else is there to love?'

'Me.'

There fell between them one of those moments of embarrassment which happened always, ever since they had had that dreadful quarrel, whenever love was mentioned. It was invariably he who spoke of it now, whereas before it had been more common on her lips; and she could never think how to answer him, but found herself smiling insincerely. To hurry by the moment she said, seeing that the car had stopped outside a public-house, and the chauffeur was asking his way. 'Mr Pitt does seem to live in an out-of-the-way place for a busy man.'

'It's likely to be rather an odd corner. I'm prepared for anything. I have a sort of idea that though our little friend's personality seems so strong to us, it doesn't seem so to him. He probably feels that if he went and lived in an ordinary row of houses he wouldn't be noticed. This out-of-the-way house may be some queer attempt to rivet distinction on himself, to find a style. I don't mean to advertise himself. It's very likely to himself that he's most anxious to make himself clear.'

'I dare say,' murmured Sunflower. But surely Essington was not being as clever as usual, for if there was one thing certain about Francis Pitt it was that he was strong and settled and definite. It was abundance of these qualities that made him able to be so protective.

'Well, I may have been wrong,' said Essington, a few moments later, as the car turned off the deep headlong swoop of the North End Road past wrought iron gates into an avenue of chestnut trees, which confused the seasons as trees of that sort do, being bright with white candles celebrating spring, but casting beneath them a shadow damp with the rich, rotting airs of autumn, in which the downward thrusting spears of sunshine seem to be forged of the strong light of midsummer. 'I may be wrong. This looks as if the little scoundrel had found quite a good Georgian house lying about unwatched. No, by God, I wasn't wrong Sunflower, did you ever see anything so odd? Isn't it queer?' he exclaimed exultantly, 'Isn't it *queer?*'

She exclaimed, 'Oh, I don't know,' and pressed defensively first to one window and then to the other, but there was no denying the queerness of the place. On what seemed, from the tall old trees and the unconfused blossoming of the land, to have been a park, someone had dropped a suburban garden. Wherever there were a few yards on the flat the gardener had put something trim and mean. In a glade of silver birches that at this hour, sunset-flushed, looked like nymphs, there was laid a star-shaped flower-bed planted with geraniums, calceolarias, and lobelias; at the foot of one great cedar there was a clock-golf green, and at the foot of another a clump of pampas-grass; and here and there, at the summit of knolls on whose sides grew flame-coloured azaleas, were plaster urns containing aloes and yuccas. There had evidently been some curious catastrophe here at some time or another; and its traces had not been removed but instead heavily ornamented. After two hundred yards or so the drive passed between two sections of a ruined brick wall, which was so thickly covered with rock-plants, that Sunflower pointed them out to Essington and said, laughing nervously, 'Oh, someone feels over a seedman's catalogue as I do over a shoe-shop – wants to buy the lot! That'll be Miss Pitt! Women do buy like that, don't they!' And beyond it were signs of the same thing, for there was a garden which had probably been enclosed and levelled at the same time that the trees outside had been planted, but which now had a surface broken by all sorts of irregularities. There was a turf-lined, terraced pit which might have been a sunken garden; there were low banks on which had grown hedges at some time; there were grooves that marked the draining of an obliterated path; and over all these was flung an extravagance of star-shaped, circular and rhomboidal flower-beds containing bedded-out plants in acid tints, mauve petunias, magenta begonias, which the powerful oblique shafts of evening sunshine made so bright that they soured the mouth.

'Oh, isn't it awful!' she giggled, and lifted up her arm in front of the window so that the folds of her cloak should prevent Essington from looking through it; but he looked out from his own side, and there was at any rate no keeping the house from him. And that, she found as the car stopped at the base of a wide flight of clipped stone steps with lace-work stucco banisters, and a footman opened the door, was worst of all. It was a villa of the sort that edge Wimbledon Common or Putney Heath, faced with a grey mixture of cement and sand the colour of cold porridge, and surmounted with a useless Italianate tower; but monstrously swollen beyond the size ordinary in its type. She felt curiously reluctant to climb the steps. There was something about the distension of the house and its hideousness that was a condemnation of everybody who had anything to do with it. 'Somebody's been proud,' she thought, looking up at it; and she remembered the pig-face of the grocer her mother dealt with in Chiswick, who had inherited a little fortune and spent most of it building such a corpulent villa as this. One could imagine that it had been built by a man so brutishly stupid that when he was left a legacy that increased his income threefold he could think of nothing better to do than to get himself a house exactly like the one he was living in but three times as big. That accounted for the building of it; but there was no conceivable explanation why anyone who had the money to live there should not live somewhere else. It must, she feared, be another manifestation of that obvious male principle of unreason which made Essington prefer to live with her unpleasantly rather than pleasantly, which made him punish her for revealing intimacies to strangers by going on and on revealing to them things more intimate still . . .

Suddenly it seemed to her as if from all the windows of the three storeys, within their frames of heavy grey moulding, there looked that darkness, radiant yet black, like the eyes of blind men, which shines out of empty houses. She plucked at Essington's coat-sleeve and said, under her breath, 'Oh, Ess, I wish we hadn't come.'

He suggested eagerly, 'Well, if you stagger and faint, my dear, I don't see what I can do but take you home.'

She hesitated. 'But you want to meet Hurrell.'

'I think, Sunflower, that tonight I'd rather take you home than see Hurrell.' He spoke significantly, deferentially, humbly; as if there were a hidden meaning in his words, a meaning dependent on the enormous value which he set on her, and as if he dare not explain it save at her express request, since he was conscious he had done things which would justify her in forbidding him to speak any more of his love for her. His eyes were blinking.

Touched and puzzled, because she could see no reason for such a rush of emotion at this particular moment, she would have said, 'Why, what is it, lovie?' but just then her eye, roving over the house as over some sleeping enemy out of whose presence she was tiptoeing, caught sight of the butler standing by the open door at the top of the stone staircase, and perceived that something here was odd. His face wore a faintly appalled expression, which he was not attempting to conceal under the solemnity of his official bearing, but which he was actually presenting to the arriving visitors as if, for the time being, it were part of his official bearing. She glanced quickly at the footman who was standing beside him and saw on his face a younger version of the same expression: he looked strained and sullen, as if the sky of his youth would have been clear enough if other people had not exercised an unfair privilege and shadowed it with the clouds of their misfortunes. She exclaimed, 'Ess, I believe there's some trouble in this house. Let's go and see if we can do anything!' and started up the steps. Essington, left behind, uttered a faint wheeze of expostulation. She felt his reluctance like a noose cast round her, dragging her back, but she squared her shoulders and went on, for she felt she must have her way in this; and at the door she found him panting level with her.

The butler told them portentously, 'Mr Pitt and Miss Pitt are detained with Sir Robert Cornelliss, but they will not be long,' and stooped forward, as if to expand this statement with some further courtesy, some further ominousness, when his mouth fell open and he looked over his shoulder with an expression Sunflower identified as that which crosses the face of an actor when he sees a cat strolling in the wings during his big silent scene and is not sure whether the audience sees it or not. He seemed to be hearing some sound that they did not. Slowly, looking before them as if they were royalty but not doing it with ease, he led them into the amber shadows of a hall which was so impersonally furnished with large leather armchairs and sofas and the heads and skins of big game, that it might have been part of a club. After a certain point he seemed disconcerted that they were

94

following him, and coming to a halt in front of an armchair in the middle of the room, he made exasperated gestures at the footman, who was standing in the doorway absorbedly watching his progress as one might watch a sportsman performing a difficult technical feat. Suddenly the footman understood what was expected of him, started forward jerkily and took their things, and began to head them off towards a door in the wall opposite to that towards which the butler had been leading them. Essington, who, when people behaved inexplicably always fancied that they were behaving insolently, gave a click of annoyance; and when, just as the footman opened the door, they heard a loud grunt which apparently proceeded from the butler, he spun round and glared at the man, who endured his gaze, but swallowed hard.

Sunflower giggled outright. And that the butler could not bear. He stepped aside and disclosed, lying asleep in the armchair he was shielding, a very tall man. His handsome, oblong face was blotched and scarlet; his large, oblong limbs were flung out in the stark yet loose abandonment of drunkenness. As they looked at him he belched.

Sunflower whispered, 'Ugh! Who can he be?'

Essington could not answer for a minute, so violently was he trembling, 'That is my successor in office, Lord Canterton.'

The four stood in silence for a minute, looking down on the drunkard, feeling drawn together by a community of decent feeling.

Essington murmured passionately, 'When he was lord chancellor I have seen him so on the woolsack . . . The . . . the *shame* of it.'

She slipped her hand into his. 'Never mind, dear, never mind. You're well out of politics if this sort is getting in. You mustn't get so worked up . . . dear . . .' But she realised that she must move him on, for the situation was becoming horrid because the other two men were servants. The butler was looking as if he could have explained to them the presence of the drunkard in a way that would lift the suspicion of disorder from this house whose honour was his own, but could not because they were his master's guests and he knew his place; his Scotch, sentimental face was waterlogged with self-pity and enjoyment of the martyrdom of his solid worth and natural dignity at the hands of social convention. 'He isn't half,' she thought acidly, 'enjoying himself.' And the footman was smiling wetly and meanly, as if it amused him to see his betters shamed by one of their own kind. She wanted to cry out to him, 'You and me are the same class, so I've a right to talk to you! You shouldn't take their money if you feel like that about them!' Rage flared in her at the look of his great healthy body with its broad shoulders and thick thighs, his handsome face, with its sound flesh and lips full of blood. Things had come to a pretty pass when strong men like this were content to put on funny clothes and wait on men they could have knocked down with a single drive of the fist and make it worse by sniggering at them behind their backs. Oddly she found herself thinking of her chauffeur Harrowby and including him in her anger, though he was nice as nice could be and never would laugh at anybody. In the background of her rage she saw the lights of Chiswick High Street and the Saturday night crowds ruddy-faced under the naphtha flares, and there was anguish in her vision of it. Some understanding about life she had found in those early days when she went with her mother and father among these crowds, which consisted of nothing but mothers and fathers and children, had been violated. She was none the better for her journey from those parts. At the end had been deception, abandonment. Irrational fury made her tremble as Essington was trembling. Ah, the poor dear! He would need a lot of quieting down, for Parliament was his church, a public man a priest to him. She said, 'Take me away, that man makes me sick,' and shepherded him through the door.

It was a pity that there were a man and a woman waiting in the library but they did not look as if they would intrude, for they belonged to the smart and jaunty type whom Essington loathed and who usually loathed Essington at sight. The man, who, standing by the vast circular mahogany table in the middle of the room, was pouring himself a drink from a curiously large cocktail shaker, looked at them over his shoulder with brilliant grey eyes that flickered like the tongue of an asp, and then turned away his head. The woman, who was bright with the marmalade tints of the weatherbeaten blonde, was sitting back in a leather armchair by a distant window, her eyes shut, though she held a glass on her knee; her small green felt hat was lying on the floor between her feet. Sunflower wondered who they were; they had the look of being News. She did not like the way they seemed to be at home in Francis Pitt's house. They were in day-clothes, so it did not seem likely that they were stopping to dinner. She was glad of that. It really was a nuisance, these people being there, for there were all sorts of odd things in the room that might have taken Essington's mind off Canterton. The same hand that had overdressed the ruined wall outside with saxifrages had filled the room with an astonishing excess of flowers. There were a dozen bowls of red and white roses on the big central table and on the massive writing-desk, and on the three or four funny little round tables with tops of inlaid coloured marble were vases filled a little too full with crucifixion lilies; and at the four corners of the bookshelves, which wove a hideous pattern round the room out of the solid blocks of harsh colours and grainy textures made by poorly bound complete sets, stood brass jars from which grew flaming azaleas. 'It's as if a railway waiting-room had gone gay,' she thought, feeling cold, because she had to admit that there was something deeply wrong about the room. Like the house itself, it cast discredit on everybody who had anything to do with it, but more heavily on the man who lived there now than on the man who built it. This man lived in a better age, he had the money to live anywhere, he liked flowers. How could he bear this room? That perversity, that preference for the unpleasant rather than the pleasant . . .

She must say something to Essington, who was still trembling. 'Isn't it awful?' she murmured. 'Furnished in the year one, I should say. And the pictures – !' She rested her hands on the hideous brawn-like marble of the mantelpiece, which was almost entirely covered from end to end with vases of the scarlet-spotted lilies, and looked up at the picture hanging above it. It was a Victorian historical tableau, representing one young woman in Saxon costume handing a crucifix to another similarly clad. Hopefully she asked, for he liked making jokes about that sort of thing, 'What's that supposed to be?'

'Oh, that's St Walburga giving the rood to St Editha.'

'What's she doing that for?'

He gazed at her severely. 'That's a rude question,' he said with an air of rebuke.

She tittered delightedly. 'Oh, you are . . .' He would be better in no time.

The footman came to them with cocktails. As they turned to refuse they found that the man who had been drinking at the table had come up behind them, and was standing there holding out his hand. He was a hard and glittering creature, with his steely eyes bright among wrinkles that were there not because he was old but because his expression was contracted on too tight a spring, his nutcracker chin, hard and smooth as a metal-casting, his hair that was turning aluminium at the temple, his sporting suit that was the colour of an armoured car. At the sight of his smile they knew only the modified reassurance of those who come on a dangerous animal in one of its rare genial moods. Essington made no move towards taking his hand, so he raised

97

the glass he was holding in his other with a hail-alligator-well-met expression, and said, 'Ah, you don't know me, Lord Essington, but I feel I know you. I'm Sir John Murphy. Jack Murphy to my friends, I hope, to you.'

He bowed extravagantly from the hips. 'He talks Irish like we used to on the stage before the Irish players came,' thought Sunflower. 'I often think it was a pity they came. It was easier and what did it matter.'

He continued with pomp. 'I feel warm things towards you, Lord Essington, for honour came to me at your hands. I received my baronetcy from the government of which you were a member.'

'No, you didn't.' Essington's voice had gone thin and high and polite, as it always did when he was going to be really rude.

'Ah, but I did.' He slapped his chest. 'I'm Sir John Murphy, Jack Murphy to my friends. And your government gave me my baronetcy.'

Essington said, 'No.'

'Ah, but yes. You great men grow forgetful, you have so many – '

'Didn't you say you were Sir John Murphy?'

'That's who I – '

'Of the firm of Murphy & Brace in the City?'

'Yes, that's – '

Essington gently shook his head. His voice had become a mild squeak. 'Then you certainly didn't get a baronetcy from any government of which I was a member.' He wheeled about and faced the mantelpiece.

'Ah, sure, you may be right!' cried Sir John Murphy to his back, with undiminished cordiality. 'Indeed, I know you're right! You went out in the spring, and I got my baronetcy in the autumn! What a memory you've got!' He threw back his head unnecessarily far, drained his glass, and exclaimed apparently without irony, 'Now, I'll always be flattered that although the men you've known who've got titles in the last few years must run into thousands, I might say millions, considering your great position, you remembered when I got my baronetcy.' He pressed between Essington and Sunflower and tried to find a place for his empty glass between the vases on the mantelpiece, muttering contemptuously, 'Flowers, flowers, Pitt is mad on flowers.' It occurred to Sunflower that he spoke as if he did not like Francis Pitt. They could not be close friends, then. She was glad.

Having found a place for his glass he started work on her. He flashed his eyes at her and raised the corners of his mouth in an expression of lustfulness, that was evidently, from a certain mechanical quality about it, part of the etiquette he always observed when meeting a lady. 'And for different reasons I feel as if I knew this charming friend of yours here!' He did not seem abashed when the introduction he waited for did not come. She gazed at him in amazement and perceived suddenly that he was drunk. The curious, flickering, restless impression he gave was due to a constant succession of fine muscular adjustments he was making to compensate for the waves of unsteadiness that passed over him; all the time he was shifting his weight from one foot to another, or laying a finger ever so lightly on the mantelpiece, or resting his knee against an armchair. With his slim, jockeyish body he was riding his intoxication as if it were a horse. She thought that perhaps his condition was the cause of his indifference to rebuff; but also it seemed to her that there was an adamantine core to him, which would never get drunk no matter how sodden the rest of him might be, which was inaccessible to ordinary notions of honour and dignity as it was to drunkenness, which might not improbably decide after experiment that the most disarming way to take an insult was buffoonery. She felt a flash of pride in Essington. She wished she could get away from this horrid man, but he was standing right in front of her, thrusting out his nutcracker chin under one of his too tightly sprung smiles, and speaking unctuously into her face. 'I've no hesitation in telling you to your face that I'm right pleased to meet the woman who's known as the most beautiful woman in the world, for I don't expect that a true woman, and I can see that you are a true woman, will be ashamed of being known that way. 'Tis not human to be ashamed of your distinction. I'll not conceal from you that I'm proud of mine. It's the fashion to laugh at titles nowadays, but I'm proud of mine. Yes, I'm proud of my baronetcy. And, dear lady, will you tell me that I have no right to be? I'm one of the only two baronets in whose patent of nobility it is written that the honour was conferred because of "exceptional services" – "exceptional services", mark you, "rendered to England in time of war." What man's going to be ashamed of that, I ask you, dear lady? Proud I was to serve my country, though I'm Irish. Old Irish, we are, though for a generation or two the family has been settled in Liverpool. Twelve of us there were,' he said, beaming at her with a face suddenly grown soft in contemplation of the domestic virtues, 'and all double-jointed.'

He lifted up his hands, which had more character than most hands, since they were exquisitely shaped, dark brown with sunburn, grained and horny like shagreen, and adorned, even over-dressed, with gleaming rose-pink nails; and, awed by his inconsequence as one is bound to be by any quality when carried to an infinite degree, they watched him while he bent back each finger with a loud crack. Fortunately he lost interest at the middle finger of his second hand, and basked again in the sun of sentiment. 'Yes, twelve of us there were, and I've given all of them that grew up, for I lost a dear little sister, sweet little Bridget, when she was twelve years old, God rest the little angel, I was saying I'd given all the others enough to rub along on, yes, enough to rub along on. I've not been forgetful. Only the week before last I gave my dear old mother one of the largest hotels in Paris. Nobody can say I haven't been a good son to my old mother, ever since I struck it lucky in California.' He turned about and faced Essington, putting on the unnatural ecstasy of a man in an advertisement. 'There's where I met our good friend Francis. Ah, he's a fine fellow, our Francis! I can tell you that. We had our rough times together when we were finding our feet out there, and I saw the worst and the best of him, and let me tell you the worst of him is better than the most of us, and the best is something that brings tears to my eyes. And, by God, he is loyal to his friends.' Shaking his head tenderly, he lifted his glass from the mantelpiece, found that a drop had collected in the bottom of it, gulped it, and remarked absently, 'Yes, I've always been a good son to my old mother.' His eyes roved towards Sunflower, his face, which seemed beginning to fall to pieces, pulled itself up into that polite and mechanical look of lustfulness, and he said to Essington in a flattering manner, 'Ah, I'm like you. I like a woman who looks like a woman . . .'

Essington's long hands motioned her to go at once. She turned and went towards the window. Sir John called after her. 'Yes, go and say a word to my little daughter Billie. Get her to show you the diamond ring her father's given her for her birthday. I have five beautiful daughters – Billie, Rhoda, Fay, Myrtle, and – ah, I was forgetting – and my little Fay. And I grudge them nothing . . .'

As her father spoke her name the girl in the chair opened her speedwell blue eyes and lifted her tousled golden hair, so Sunflower had to go to her. She sat down beside her in a higher chair and murmured a greeting. She was all of a tremble. She hadn't liked Sir John Murphy at all. He might think he was paying compliments, but it was like having your face licked.

The girl did not return her greeting, but looked at her for a minute in a hard, rather hostile way before she spoke. 'I've seen you at the Embassy sometimes with Maxine Tempest at lunch.'

'Why, yes, we do go sometimes,' said Sunflower. 'She's my best friend. She's a sweet girl.'

'Hm,' said the girl, disagreeably and portentously. Sunflower saw that she too was drunk. Her golden head was nodding, her blue eyes were vacillating, like buttercups and speedwells swung by the stream in a flooded water-meadow.

Sunflower exclaimed, 'Oh!' She wished she could have got the girl some coffee. It was difficult in someone else's house.

The girl said, as if making conversation with a bore: 'We've been out seeing Ted Dawkins training at his quarters at St Albans.' As Sunflower looked enquiringly she explained irritably, 'Oh, the heavy-weight! He's fighting Larodier at Olympia on the third of June. I thought everybody knew that!' She flung herself back into the chair, and shut her eyes again. 'I've got such a head,' she grumbled. 'Dawkins' manager gave us a new long drink of his. The Tired Tart's Refresher, it's called. Filthy stuff.'

'I've got an aspirin in my bag,' said Sunflower.

It didn't seem right that the poor thing should wash it down with another cocktail from the vast shaker, which her own father must have left at her elbow. Sunflower looked for help towards the two men, but Sir John was describing with gestures how he had once saved someone's life with a lasso, and Essington was looking at him with the expression of a cat which sees a bird too wet and muddy for its fastidious claws to kill. She looked back at the girl and found her staring shakily at Essington with a tipsy, exaggerated smile of contempt. For a minute she closed her eyes, but opened them again and said, as if she must find a vent for her scorn, 'I've seen you with him too.' She jerked her head at Essington. 'At the Berkeley and places. I suppose you think he's wonderful.' She laughed bitterly. 'Well, you should have heard Canterton this afternoon while we were at St Albans. Showing him up. Saying what rot all this business about the League of Nations was. Nature red in tooth and claw. Oh, he was *brilliant* . . .'

She drained her glass, drew her hand across her mouth, which had become loose, leaned forward, and tapped Sunflower on the knee. 'Now, there is a really great man, Canterton!'

'I'm sure,' said Sunflower.

'Marvellous memory. Read everything. The other night he sat in the Embassy reciting Keats till three in the morning. Made me cry. Far the best speaker they've ever had in Parliament. Making a most marvellous success of his ministry.' She glared at Sunflower, trying to make her little flower-like face as much like a bulldog's muzzle as possible. 'Essington's a failure.'

'Well, he is and he isn't,' said Sunflower, 'it all depends on the way you look at it.'

But the girl had dropped back into her chair again and closed her eyes. 'My head does hurt,' she grumbled.

'I've another aspirin, if you'd like it.'

'It's no use,' refused the girl crossly. 'I wish I could be sick, but I never can.'

On the other side of the room Sir John cried, 'Ah, my dear Francis!'

*

So she had been right when she had guessed outside that something awful had happened in this house. He had been shocked, shocked right out of that thorough clumsy neatness, which she suddenly perceived, now that she was faced with its absence, to be piteous and lovable, since it was a defence he had built between his odd appearance and the world. His fox-coloured hair was wild about his ears; his shirt-front was bulging so that his queer lion body looked more top-heavy than ever; even his features seemed not so tidy as they had been, for his mouth was gaping in amazement. It was as if a violent emotion had been thrown over him like a jugful of water. There must be something terrible, something terrible. When he tried to give all these people he found in his room a general greeting he could not lift his face into a smile, for the strong anguish in him had moulded it into a heavy mask, a massive symbol. He was uglier than ever, the poor dear, for he was thrusting out his lower lip and stiffening his upper, like a child trying not to cry, and this made the creases between his nose and his mouth prodigiously heavy, like folds in a rhinoceros's hide. That look he had had of vigilant, missionary mockery, watching life lest it crystallised into seriousness and had to be set moving again with laughter, had gone as completely as his neatness. His defences had failed, he wore instead the astonished look of a captive who right up to the moment of capture had believed in his luck. It had been his intention to have his life lit only by such flames as the azaleas that were set in the four corners of the room, and there had come on him this fire that had burned him till his flesh was ashen. Puck might have looked like this if he had stayed out in open country too long after dawn, been snared by mortals, christened though he kicked, and forcibly acquainted

102

with human grief. At his sorrow something came alive in her. She got up to go across the room and comfort him.

She stopped because he had seen her. He had seen her and he had been enormously interested. His interest ran through him like an electric shock, jerking his chin up from his shirt-front, lifting his loose eyelids. He looked straight at her, and it was as if he had shoved in front of her for her signature a printed statement that she had risen to come and comfort, because he wanted to keep forever a record of her kindness to him. Helplessly she looked back at him, and it was as if she had signed that statement, and would never be able to go back on it now. Well, she was not ashamed. If a person was in trouble you wanted to do what you could for them. Nevertheless she began to blush. It was the second time that she had blushed in his company, one of her awful blushes which could be seen a mile off, which ended by travelling right down over her shoulders. She drooped her head and felt a fool, lifted it again and smiled as foolishly at the top of the walls, at the bowls of roses on the bookshelves. But of course he did something kind about it and stopped looking at her immediately, and busied himself with greeting Essington and Sir John. Of course she had been wrong in her moment of resentful feeling that though it was subtlety he had been displaying he had forced her to take notice of the display with a compulsive gesture that was the very opposite of subtle, that was bullying and detective. Really he was the soul of protectiveness. He gave her quite a lot of time to get right before he ranged the men one on each side of him with an authoritative gesture of his paw-like hands and crossed the room towards the women.

To her he said heavily, 'I *am* very glad you have not disappointed me,' and then looked down on the girl who was stirring stupidly in the deep armchair, wanting to get up but having so much trouble shifting her glass from her right hand to her left that she could not give her mind to it. His eyebrows drew together and his lips tightened. He was evidently surprised and grieved to see that she was drunk. But he said kindly, as if to a child, 'And how are you, Billie?' Probably he did not know these horrid people at all well, but was just nice to them when they pushed in on him. She knew what it was. Often enough people she hardly knew pretended to be great friends of hers and rushed at her when they met, and really it was very hard to know what to do.

'Me dear Francis!' answered Sir John. 'How goes it?'

'Badly, Jack,' answered Francis, shaking his head, 'badly.'

'Now isn't that truly tragic, truly tragic!' continued Sir John, happily and expansively. 'I just had to come up and see how you were. I said to Billie, "I shan't be able to eat my dinner till I know how Frank is," and she believed me, for she knows her dad. It's you I'm feeling for, my lad, more than him. Ah you've a great gift for friendship, Francis Pitt! And I always say so too. For I myself can stick up for my friends.'

'That I know well!' said Francis Pitt.

The girl blurted out, "S'pose it's hopeless?'

There was sweat on his forehead. He moistened his lips before he answered patiently, 'Why, yes, Billie, that's what they say. It's hopeless.' He was evidently schooling himself to speak without expression, lest he should seem to be rebuking this poor tipsy child for the tactlessness that was caused by her condition.

'Well, me dear boy,' rattled on Sir John, his iron will keeping him to the matter of condolence, though his drunkenness was dissolving him into a confusion of glittering, unaimed smiles and springy, happy, wavering movements. 'I'm sure nobody in God's own world could be doing more for him than you are. Well I do know it. I was telling Thurston and Laidlaw so at lunch at the Savoy today, I was saying to them, "If there's a way of saving him depend on it my old friend Francis Pitt will find it." Yes, that's what I said to them. I said, "I have known Francis Pitt since the old days in San Francisco, and let me tell you . . ."'

There seemed no reason why conversation based on this formula should ever come to an end. Not knowing what had happened to him was making her feel faint. She would have turned aside from the group had she not been anxious to prove to him that though she had been so silly and impulsive the first time they met she was really as calm and collected as anybody who wasn't on the stage, who wasn't living with somebody they weren't married to. So she stood smiling politely, though every moment made it less easy. It struck her that now Francis Pitt was speaking to Murphy his American accent became much more marked than it had been when he talked with her and Essington, and that made her realise sharply how little she knew of his past, and that lots of people, some of them quite horrid people like Murphy, had shared in it and would know more than she ever would even if she got to know him quite well and he told her everything. She was annoyed to notice that Murphy also was speaking with a stronger American accent than he had used before Francis Pitt had come. These two wrought upon each other, they gave each other responses, there

104

was a real comradeship. That was dreadful, because Murphy was a really bad man. It was loathsome the way that as he was talking to Francis Pitt he kept on patting and pawing him with insincere gestures of affection which distressed the eye with their falsity as a note sung out of tune distresses the ear. They were exactly the kind of gestures that she had made when she first went on the stage, that Essington was always saying she still made, that she would perhaps make as often as he had pretended had she not remembered what old Frederick Turner had taught her. He had always said that no gesture was valid unless when it was exaggerated it led straight to the climax of the emotion it was meant to illustrate. If a gesture of hate were really appropriate it should, performed with violence, become the motion of a blow or a dagger-thrust or a strangle-hold, and a gesture of love should bring friends side by side or man and woman breast to breast. But if these movements of false goodfellowship had been exaggerated absolutely nothing would happen. The two men would simply have toppled to and fro like those Russian skittle-shaped dolls that are weighted with lead in their feet, if Sir John had put all his force into clapping his left hand on Francis Pitt's shoulder and Francis Pitt had put all his into clapping his right hand on Sir John's upper arm . . .

For Francis Pitt was doing it too. He was returning these false gestures in their own kind with adeptness, without repugnance. She shivered. It was as if behind her she had heard a whistling, a crazy whistling, that warned her that the enterprise on which she had come out was not safe.

A feeling of resistant doggedness came on her. She compressed her lips and to shift her thoughts she turned her head away from the two men. Her eyes fell on the girl in the armchair, who was pressing a little handkerchief against her lips and looking as if, though she was so sulky that she did not want to call anything by its right name, she would soon have to admit that she was feeling sick. Sunflower sent an imploring glance at Francis Pitt and found his eyes just shifting from her face. With deliberate, canny, good humour he said, 'But true friend as you've been to me, Jack, I refuse to take on the burden of all your friendships. I see no reason at all why I should have your friend Canterton parked in my hall!'

The pleasantness was suddenly sponged off Murphy's face. 'And what's wrong with Canterton?'

'God knows, God knows!' chuckled Francis Pitt. 'Something that cost about twenty-seven shillings a bottle, I expect. Lanson '11, I should think, if he's been in your company for some hours. Anyway, Jack, it's time you took him out of my hall.'

Drunkenness was at last dissolving the iron will's determination to be currying. 'I'd like to know since when Canterton stopped being good enough for you! Let me tell you he's my friend, and I am loyal to my friends . . .'

Francis Pitt swung round so that his back was turned to Essington and Sunflower, but they could see from the thrust of his head and shoulders that he was ramming a steady stare into the other's flushed, brawling face as he might have rammed a revolver muzzle. After a second he chuckled again, shifted his weight to one foot and said easily, 'Yes, yes, I know well that Canterton's a grand fellow, but just at the moment he seems to me not so good as I've seen him. So take him home, take him home.'

'Sure, I'll do that,' responded Sir John, suddenly genial. 'And I'm sorry it's happened like this. 'Tis his sense of the responsibilities that weigh too heavy on him at times and then he just helps himself over the stile, that's what it is, he just helps himself over the stile. Let's not forget that with all his weakness he's a great man, a great man.'

'Hurry along, Jack,' said Francis Pitt, firmly. 'The morals of my butler and my footman are going down by inches every time your friend snores.'

Sir John shook hands exhaustively with Essington, who emitted a faint, distasteful, mewing sound. 'It's been one of the best days of my life, and mind you I mean what I say and am no flatterer, that I first met the man whom by and large I admire as much as any man who's alive today.' With an air of having been brought up to behave politely to ladies when he was young and never having forgotten it, he was careful to reassume an expression of urgent concupiscence when saying goodbye to Sunflower. Then he called, 'Come on, Billie!' in a tone that dreadfully expressed the minimum to which the relationship between father and child could be cut down. There was a sort of loyalty in it, as if the grizzled wolf would fight for his cub against the rest of the pack, a sort of kindness, as if he would let her bury her fangs in one flank of the carcase of his kill; and there was nothing more. With such late human inventions as her honour he would not concern himself.

The girl stood up. The stubborn little golden moon of her face was preternaturally blank and stolid, and her body swayed to and fro

106

like an inverted pendulum above her pony-like stance. She said contentiously to nobody, 'I'm all right.' They all, except her father, who was walking with a jockey's springy tread to the door, watched her in agony. It seemed as if at any moment she would fall foward on the floor. Sunflower heard the breath hiss through Francis Pitt's teeth as he moved forward to the rescue. He must be feeling awful. If you had these people carrying on like this in your house you would want to send everything away to the cleaners, they were so sort of dirty. And it was so dreadful for him that it had happened when he had got visitors, and one of them was Essington, whom he respected and would want to have everything nice for. She remembered how poor little Mummie had cried after she had the insurance manager's wife who lived at the big house at the corner in to tea and Aunt Emma had come in in the middle smelling of whisky and asking riddles. It was lovely of Francis Pitt to be so patient with the girl, to take her arm so gently and say so kindly as he led her out of the room, 'You must come some day soon and tell me what you think of the new hard court.' And he looked over his shoulder with a most apologetic air when he passed Sir John, who had paused at the open door to shout, 'And I shall expect you and Miss Fassendyll at me party next Wednesday. Number one hundred Carlton House Terrace! 'Tis slightly larger than the other houses in the Terrace. I'm giving this party for the Rajah of Kuda Tala, who's a very old friend of mine, and we're going to have a grand time – I'm having the Embassy band to dance to and Tetrazzini and Pachmann and Chaliapin and Nora Bayes for a spot of music, and me secretary – Pearl La Salle – ah, she's a fine woman – ' he waved a hand at Sunflower as if to explain what he meant, 'she's thought out a colossal scheme of floral decoration! There's going to be nothing on our tables but the best champagne and nothing on the walls but the finest orchids! And in my house, let me tell you, we allow a magnum of champagne for each person! So goodbye to you till then! From now on, Lord Essington and Miss Fassendyll, I count you as among my friends!'

'Oh, too good of you!' wailed Essington; and at last Francis's short bearish arm came round the door, plucked Sir John by the coat sleeve and turned the handle.

In the sudden peace Sunflower and Essington drew close together and slipped their hands into each other's. They were both breathing deeply, as if they had been involved in a brawl.

'Say what you like, it's worse for a woman to get drunk than a man.' She shuddered. Supposing it had been she whom Francis Pitt had seen

107

flushed and staggering . . . She went on gravely, 'I really oughtn't to touch anything at all. You know, Ess, I had an aunt who used to take a drop too much, I did tell you that before we began.'

'My dear, sweet, clean little Sunflower, I don't think you need to be frightened,' he said; and stopped to give her a tender kiss. 'You don't belong to the same breed of animal as Miss Billie, and the things that happen to her won't happen to you. And don't worry your dear muddled head about Aunt Emma. All this talk about heredity in these matters is bunkum. If Aunt Emma hadn't lived in a dreary little warren like Chiswick – '

'Oh, it wasn't so bad,' she murmured. 'It wasn't hardly ever so bad as this . . .'

' – she probably wouldn't have had to get the colour and romance she wanted out of the whisky bottle. But these people! These people! Sunflower, that man's a thief. He's robbed decent people all over the world. There are men and women living on crusts in garrets because of his knaveries. And he spends his loot on this guzzling and swilling, this belching and reeling – '

'Wasn't it dreadful for poor Mr Pitt!'

'But why does he have such people in his house? If he's got friends like these it isn't any sort of place for us. I wish we hadn't come. You didn't specially want to come, did you?' He looked at her plaintively and searchingly. 'You didn't specially want to come, did you, Sunflower?'

She hesitated. 'I did . . . rather. I . . . liked the look of Miss Pitt.'

'Yes, yes!' he assented heartily. 'You two did seem to get on very well together, I remember noticing that. I dare say you'll be able to pull off quite a jolly friendship with – '

'Also,' she added, 'you wanted to see Mr Hurrell.'

'Yes, of course, of course, that was really why we came. I wish to God he'd turn up.' He looked at his watch and gave it an irritable shake, as he always did; for whatever hour it might be, he always wished it different. 'Well, I don't know that I particularly want to see him after all. I learned at Versailles that he isn't as scrupulous as I am, but he's even less scrupulous than I thought if he can bear to come here and be smacked and elbowed by the Hiccuping Wing of the Tory Party.'

Now that he was not standing right beside her she began to think of Francis Pitt's face as it had looked when he first came into the room. After a moment she cried out to Essington, though he was still walking about speaking angrily of politics. 'Who can it be that's ill? It must be someone that he's very fond of, he looked so awful. Who can it be?'

He said acrimoniously, 'And in any case Hurrell was one of the cabinet who gave this rogue his baronetcy. Sunflower, it can't be borne! Of course honours have always been bought – both parties have sold them by the score, by the hundreds! – but never till now to men who could not turn up at the accolade without special permission from the Governor of Portland Jail! That verminous little shyster got his baronetcy from Bryce Atkin's coalition just after I left, and they gave it to him knowing what he was – '

'You could see Mr Pitt didn't think much of him, if you watched him closely,' said Sunflower, nodding wisely.

'They knew his whole record. Birtley came to me about it and I went to Bryce Atkin myself. He *knew* – '

'It must be awful to have friends that you can't very well turn from the door, can you, and yet know they'll carry on like this. But I do wonder who's ill. They said it was a he . . .'

'I told Bryce Atkin the whole story with my own lips. And he used a lot of his filthy tobacconist's girl-charm on me, and swore he'd do something about it. And the next week it was in the Birthday – '

There was a soft thud against the door, and it was opened with a sound of scuffling. No one came in and the handle rattled as if someone were making a counter-attempt to shut it again. A pretentious voice, foppishly powdered with a lisp, declaimed: 'Let me get at Ethington. I want to talk to him. Abthurd that a man of hith talent shouldn't be with uth . . . Thethe mad ideath, nothing in them. Nature red in tooth and claw. I could ecthplain it all to him in five minuteth . . .' Pitt's voice cut in, rough and humiliated, 'For God's sake, Canterton!' and the door banged.

'Oh, it's a shame, it really is!' said Sunflower. 'When he's got visitors, and there's trouble in the house! If he were a woman he'd burst out crying. Why, of course he's been crying. That's why his face looks all funny . . . Oh . . .'

Essington sat down as if he had suddenly grown very tired. 'Sunflower, I wish that drunkard Canterton hadn't got my job.' He spoke with a kind of noble peevishness that was at once complaining and selfless. 'There are good people in that ministry, steady little people who've given their lives to building it up. People who always made me feel rather ashamed when I got any credit, as they'd done twice the work I ever did, and never got their names in the papers since they weren't – ' he smiled up at her as if this were a joke that would perhaps strike her as funnier than he quite liked, 'great like me. And now they're under this fuddled oaf, and one day there will be such a mess. There'll be some act of tipsy impudence – of quarrelsome instructions to one of the tipsy cads he has as secretaries – and there'll be a row that'll bring the sky down with the trade unions or whatever it is he's lurched up against. Think of that lout butting into a delicate nego-tiation with the Triple Alliance, the pet plan of some spectacled little man who was ordinated to the job by Sidney and Beatrice Webb and has done nothing else all his good little life destroyed with a hiccup . . .' He closed his eyes, took her young hand and held it to his forehead; and for a moment was silent. 'Only . . . it's his kind of man England seems to want nowadays . . . not mine . . .'

'Oh, lovie, don't fret, don't fret,' she said; and found something to say that might have comforted him, if she had not at once forgotten it, turning her head to listen if there were not the sounds of an automobile engine starting outside the drive.

He did not raise his wrinkled old lids. 'And when his lot go out the country still won't want us. They'll call in the Labour Party . . . which isn't a Party but a bazaar of ideas got up by a vegetarian mothers' meeting . . . Bolshevism . . . anti-vaccination . . . lunacy reform . . . mm . . . the sad case of Comrade A. at Peckham . . . trivial special cases . . .'

'They've gone,' she said exultantly. A car had rolled down the drive. 'He'll be back in a moment.' She drew away her hand.

He sat up, rubbing his tired eyes. 'Anyway it all works out in dinner being preposterously late.' He groped for the hand she had taken away, but started and exclaimed, 'Sunflower, how beautiful you look! Such a lovely, tender, grave Sunflower it is tonight! And yet she's wearing her little girl face too! Really, you don't look a day older than you did when I first met you twelve years ago, only far, far lovelier. And you've such a glowing colour! You haven't been putting things on your face, have you? No, it's natural!'

She smiled at him, happily, shyly, turning the rings on her fingers.

'Oh, such a beautiful Madonna Sunflower it is!' he went on proudly. 'What queer beasts women are! They put on different degrees of beauty as they might put on different dresses. Lately you've been just a handsome woman. I haven't thought the kind of dresses women have to wear nowadays suited you particularly. But tonight you're astonishing, you are a queen of beauty. And there's no reason for it . . .'

She turned away from him, because Francis Pitt came back into the room.

All the commotion he had had to go through to get rid of these horrid people had left him more dishevelled than ever, with his tie slipping round to one side and his hair straggling right down over his ears, so that he looked like a flop-eared spaniel pup which had been rolling about in the dust with the other puppies. It was queer how he kept on making one think of some sort of an animal. It would be lovely to touch him, his body would be warm like an animal's. If you found him lying asleep and woke him he would make funny whimpering little noises just as a puppy would. But there was more than that to him, he was far more than just dear and fubsy. As he crossed the room to them, his massive head down on his chest, his half-shut eyes just glinting grey under his heavy brows, force seemed to pour out of him. He was great, like Essington. And there was something pleasanter than greatness pouring out of him . . . She had heard the phrase, 'A wind from the Spice Islands' . . . It was like that, a rumour of things hot and sweet in the mouth, or gentle pungencies . . . He was a fragrance, and he was a time: the hour when people say, 'The tide has turned, now we can start', or, 'It will not hurt any more', the hour after which all things are fortunate and easy. She would be happier for days because of the little time she was going to have with him this evening, she would not mind Essington so much. It was so wonderful of him to do all this for a person when he was utterly miserable; he must be very miserable, for his face was all crumpled with crying, and though men did cry a lot, much more than you were warned beforehand, he wasn't the sort that would cry easily. She wished she could put out her hands as he came near and take his grief from him. She saw it as a warm bundle, of a size that would be easy for her to carry in her arms.

With an encircling movement of his little paws he seemed to draw them together into a ring of intimacy that excluded everybody else in the world. He conveyed to them with a spent smile, that, though miserable, he was now enjoying the relative relief of being with people that he really liked; and he said very simply, 'You folks must be dying for your dinner. I should have chased those rogues out long before you came but for – what's happened here.'

Soothingly she asked what she felt he wanted to tell them. 'Why, whatever's happened?'

He looked down. His face worked.

111

'Why . . . Hurrell's dying.'

Essington exclaimed testily, 'Hurrell! Hurrell dying! He can't be dying! Why, he's no older than I am!'

Francis Pitt said dexterously, 'That's the devil of it. He's no age at all!' and then turning to Sunflower and looking on the ground at her feet, he repeated, slowly and pitifully, 'Yes, Hurrell's dying!'

It seemed to hurt her hand that she could not lift it to stroke his ravaged face. She murmured, 'Oh, I am so sorry! Then you won't want us about. Hadn't we better go away?' It would be dreadful if he said yes. She did not want to go away from him.

His eyes shot up to hers, and he exclaimed: 'For God's sake, no! I have been looking forward to this all day!' He gave her a deliberate, pressing glance that was a reminder of the other glance he had given her when she first came into the room, and held out one hand towards her, as if he would have liked to go on talking to her and wanted her to stay there so that he could get back to her at the first possible moment, while he turned to deal with Essington, who was complaining irritably, 'But he can't be *dying*! He wasn't dying when you dined with us on Monday night!' She watched him fiercely, wishing she could get the grief out of him by some simple, violent physical act, as one sucks poison out of a wound, while he answered grimly and patiently, 'He is dying now, and he was dying then. Of a thing called galloping consumption which I daresay you thought, as I did, a handy device of the novelists. Which is rare enough in real life, which is nearly unknown in a man of his age. "Acute miliary tuberculosis", the doctors call it. It got its teeth into him six weeks ago, when he got a chill speaking in a draughty marquee down at some damned women's Liberal federation in Sussex. It will finish him, they say, in six weeks' time. Of course he doesn't know. We've kept it from him . . .'

She loved the way he loved his friend. She had to keep her lids lowered in case she cried too. 'I don't know what I shall do without him. I've known him ever since I came to London. I've lived by him ever since I came to London. I don't know what I shall do . . .' She wished that she could have pressed his dear hideous grief-ruddled face against the warm flesh at the base of her throat, not that she wanted to be familiar, but because that used to quiet Essington when he had his crying-fits after Versailles. Looking hard at him, partly in case she might read in his expression some way she might help him, and partly in order that she might remember him as completely as possible after they parted that night, she noticed that the brownish tints of his hair and skin were the colour of fireside shadows. Something at the back of her mind which had not been impressed by any of this scene, which was refusing to attach any serious importance to an emotion felt by a man about another man, seized on this note of warmth exultantly and prophesied that there would come a time when all this nonsense would be given up and the real business of living would begin, satisfyingly, nutritiously. Shocked, she forced herself back to her loyal duty of pity and distress. Pitching his voice deeper and deeper lest it should squeak up into tears, he was saying: 'It was easy to move him out of his stuffy little hole of a flat in the Temple and get him out here. You see, he's practically had a bedroom here for years. I used to keep him talking so late at nights, I hope to God it wasn't bad for him . . .' Now, Essington had hardly any close friends, and none that he loved like this. He was kept from it by the dreadful justice of his mind. It was really justice and not mere censoriousness, even now it was making him say very clearly and distinctly, so that the meaning disadvantageous to himself should not be missed, 'It's plucky of you to have him here. I . . . should have been afraid of the infection.' But it kept him from friendship just as much as the meaner quality might have done, because it never let him pass through the first phase when you are silly about people, when you believe that they are perfect and want to be with them all the time, and get so fond of them that it doesn't matter much when you find they've got their faults like anybody else. There had been a time when she'd been an idiot about Maxine, and would have told anybody that she was unselfish, though really old Maxi was dog-lazy and never did a stroke if she could put it on somebody else; but by the time she had found out that she had found also that you could tell old Maxi anything and she would understand and not say that you hadn't any self-respect because you stayed with Essington though he was cruel to one; and anyway she had by then got so used to seeing Maxi's face about that it had a special value like places that one has known all one's life. She expected Francis Pitt had been silly about Hurrell like that when he first met him, and that it had worked out all right. He had pretended that the old man had got everything, and in the course of the pretence he had found out what he had got. But Essington could not go through such a process, for by merely looking at people he knew the truth about them. His eyes would close up from below like a cat's, and he would purr a phrase which would record the bad in them without malice and the good in them without affection, and that was that. So he had no

113

friends as she had Maxine, as Francis Pitt had Hurrell. Yet he was not unloving. If you got to know him, you could see that often he had an aching feeling in his heart like anybody else. He had wanted dreadfully to make up his misunderstanding with Hurrell, he was minding it that Hurrell was going to die. Querulously, he was now trying to alter that fact by talk. 'But can't anything be done for him? Is Cornelliss the best man, do you think? . . . Doctors are always such fools . . . Mind you, I was told thirty years ago that I had just six months to live . . .' He was always like this when he heard that anybody was dying. Indeed he was always like this when he was faced with any evil which could not be brought to an end by being clever about it, or for that matter with any good which couldn't be completely accounted for and controlled by reason. That was why he was so horrid to her, although he loved her. Their love wasn't reasonable. It wasn't logical that he should have grown really to care for a woman who was quite stupid, who couldn't be of any real use to him except to make love to, so he was constantly examining this state of affairs with distrust and suspecting that he must be allowing himself to be governed by appetite and base emotion like the bad leaders who were responsible for most of the woes of the world. Also the situation arising out of their being in love vexed him because he had worked it all out cut and dried and everything in the garden should have been lovely. They lived together without being married because they did not believe in the institution of matrimony; they lived together openly enough for it to be generally known because it was wrong to be hypocritical; they did not live together quite publicly because that would have been to violate other people's susceptibilities unnecessarily; they did not have children because it would have been difficult with servants and governesses. They ought to have been perfectly happy. It was unreasonable that she should mind what quite negligible people said about her; it was unreasonable she should mind doing without things that if she had had them would have caused endless trouble. It was his sense of her unreason that made him go bickering about her house – or was there another twist to it? Did he mind her unreasonably minding those things or did he mind the still more unreasonable way he minded her minding them? Did it not turn a sword in his heart when he saw her grieving, and was not his bickering half a squeal at his own pain and half a quarrel with the fate that had hurt his beloved woman and not at all the sheer callousness it pretended to be? She looked at his fine, fretful face and knew that she was right. Here, as always, his soreness was

114

sweetness tortured into the likeness of the opposite. But she did not feel, as she always used to when she had found out some excuse for him, any flush of tenderness. It did not take away from her that feeling that she was caught in a trap, that she would die starving . . .

It was like food to be with Francis Pitt. He did not deny the death of his friend, though to admit it was anguish to him. The truth was wringing out of him in sullen phrases . . . 'There is no hope. None at all. The only thing is to get him through it as easily as possible. There are little things one can do . . .' He narrowed his eyes and lowered his head as if he talked of some way of cheating in a game, and that the other player might overhear. 'Keeping him quiet at the time when the haemorrhages are most likely to come . . .' She could see him standing by a campfire in defence of something that lay long and white and still, drawing himself to his full little height as death came down on them from the dark sky, his long arms crooked and his little paw hands stretched out flat in front of him ready to do things more cunning than direct blows, his eyes a little open so that he could watch his enemy but nearly closed so that his enemy should not see what he planned, his feet set dancing-light so that he could dodge and feint. The first men in the world must have looked like him. They too would have no need to be tall. For hunting and snaring it would be better if they were little . . .

The footman had said twice that dinner was ready, but they had not heard. She wished that they had. She wanted to see him doing something sensible like eating, building himself up instead of spending himself on this emotion about another man. And if he was sitting down at table people would not be bursting in on him, people that she did not know anything about, people who knew things about him she did not. After a minute she touched him on the sleeve and said timidly, 'They're saying dinner's ready.' He let her see by a slight tired movement of his head that he had heard her, that he longed to go to dinner but was too exhausted to deal with the technical problem of how to interrupt with politeness Essington's description of how obstinate and incompetent and without ideas the government had found the medical profession when they were drafting the Insurance Act; and that he resigned it all to her. So she set them off by moving slowly to the door. It was nice, as dancing with him would have been, to feel him walking beside her, keeping time with her. She bowed her head and stooped so that he would notice as little as possible how much taller she was. From now on it was all going to be lovely. He would be settled in

115

his chair at the table, a thick wide mahogany door would be shut on them, they would become involved in the undisturbable ritual of dinner. He would eat, he would feel better, they would be able to enjoy him, his queer earthy face, his queer rough voice, the force that flowed out of him.

But nothing nice ever happens easily. Out in the hall was Etta, looking very harassed and wearing one of those dark dresses that were quite good but made one feel depressed because they so obviously had been bought without any particular person in mind, and she was standing by a table where a greyhound sort of man with glittering pince-nez sat writing something with an attaché case open beside him. At the sight of him Francis Pitt drew a little away from her and moved closer to Essington and came to a halt, saying, 'Ah, Cornelliss, I thought you had gone. You are good to us, giving us so much time. Miss Fassendyll, Lord Essington, this is Sir Robert Cornelliss, my doctor and my friend . . .'

Sunflower smiled vaguely at the doctor, and looked away from him at the clumsy Victorian furnishings, the gross carvings of the staircase banisters, the soup-like colourings of the woodwork and wallpaper. This was a mighty little gnome that had taken this mediocre house that was built to be the home of a butter-merchant with six plain daughters, and filled it with great people, a great drunkard, a great thief, a great man dying, a great man grieving for him, a great doctor . . .

Wistfully Francis Pitt enquired, 'When ought you to hear from this Viennese chap who says he's got this serum?'

Cornelliss answered, kindly but oddly without deference, 'Tomorrow, sometime. But remember I don't believe in it myself.'

A sudden scratching on the paper told of a pretentious signature. He gave what he had been writing to Miss Pitt and began to shut up his attaché case. Francis Pitt watched him with the attention that children give to the most purely mechanical proceedings of greatly respected adults. She wished she could have pulled him on by the hand.

Cornelliss stood up, but did not go. Sunflower looked at him to see why not, and found his eyes set on her face. She assumed an expression of blandness. Not even now could she bear to throw away that tedious triumph, though she felt sick with the frustration of her desire to see Francis Pitt seated at the table, fixed, eating, resting, sealed to her society.

Cornelliss said, 'It is interesting to meet Miss Fassendyll after I have admired her so often on the stage.'

She shuddered. She had forgotten that she had to act. His eyes shifting to Essington, he continued, 'I think you know my wife. She has spoken several times of having met you at bazaars and charity matinées and so on.'

'Oh yes!' She felt pleased. It was nice to think that dull people like this met other dull people and were happy together. 'Lady Cornelliss. Why, of course! She's wonderful. She gets on so well with all the princesses you have to have for those sort of things. But then when you come to think of it,' she meditated, 'she looks just like a princess. Why, she might be one of the royal family herself, to look at her . . .'

Francis Pitt made an involuntary grunt of amusement, and Cornelliss sharply turned his back on them while the footman put on his coat. She supposed she had said one of the stupid things that made Essington so angry. Well, she did not care, so long as it had cheered up Francis Pitt.

Cornelliss swung round again, and remained before them for an instant exhibiting the expression of one who sees a joke perfectly but must not see it because it would be bad form to do so. She did wonder what she had said. Then he picked up her eyes again for a second, let them go, and said to the company, 'Goodbye. I shall be out in the morning about eleven.' He made a sweeping bow; and when he was in the doorway, black against the blue dusk, he turned round and bowed again.

Harshly, violently, with the air of a man who throws something away from him for the sake of hearing it smash, Francis Pitt exclaimed, 'That was for you, Miss Fassendyll! He cut that caper to show you that he's a damn good figure for a man of fifty-three. My God, Etta, got on with it. These people will be thinking I asked them for breakfast tomorrow.'

The two women went on together, padding softly, talking in undertones, like temple servants.

'This must mean an awful lot of work for you,' said Sunflower sympathetically.

'Oh, it's beyond anything. If only he'd eat, I shall have him on my hands next. They *encourage* themselves to get upset, don't they? And he won't eat a thing.'

'Well, you know, I found in the war that they're apt to eat better if you cut out the little things. Soup and that. Just get straight to a

117

nice piece of sole, or if they're very tired, right on to the chicken. Then they start with what they like.'

'I'll try that . . .'

At last he was sitting at the head of his table. Surely nothing in the world could prevent them all being together for the next hour or so. Satisfied, she leaned back in her chair, smiling at the Victorian pattern of heavy gilt frames, thick bell-ropes, fringed damask curtains, and coarsely gleaming red woods that made the shadows of the dimly lit room seem like a sort of dust in the air, so close was the link in one's mind between such furniture and dust. Now she understood why he lived in this queer house. That spurt of feeling in the hall gave away the secret. Francis Pitt had been shocked when Cornelliss had showed off in front of her, as a schoolboy would be if he caught out his father taking undignified trouble to catch the eye of a mere schoolgirl. He was thinking of Cornelliss as a child thinks of a grown-up. In fact he was one of those people who cannot realise that they are adult, who feel themselves as children playing truant from the nursery and fear they may be clapped back there at any time with punishments for all the damage they have done while trespassing in the grown-up world. Houses and furniture were things that grown-ups always control, so he had felt frightened about meddling with them; he had doubtless painful memories of a day when he had painted the grandfather clock with robin's egg enamel. So rather than initiate a house he had taken this preposterous place, which had the sanction of having been arranged by a grown-up. Probably this childishness accounted too for the excess of flowers which here clotted to a sweet-scented extreme, covering the whole table save where the places were laid with a trough of many-coloured carnations. It must be the realisation of some childish promise that when he was grown-up he would never get mean as grown-ups are and unable to use their power to order as much as they want of the really good things in life; so might a little boy, left by accident in charge of his home, order twice as much ice-cream as his mother usually did. Wishing she could tease him about it all, she turned towards him with a smile; and was appalled by the sallow, tear-riddled gargoyle of his face. Again she had that fantasy of his grief as poison in a wound. She saw the wound as a dark fleck on his shoulder: she imagined dropping her lips to it and sucking, sucking, till he was whole. A tremor passed through her. He could not have seen her, for his eyes were nearly closed, but at that moment a tremor ran through him also. He hid his face with his hands as if to shut out something

118

and grumbled behind that screen: 'Thank God you people are here tonight . . .'

Essington raised his glass as soon as it was filled. 'To poor dear Hurrell,' he said. From the wistful cantankerousness of his voice she knew his eyes were wet. Mechanically she pointed out to herself that people didn't know the feelings that he had.

Francis Pitt echoed deeply, 'To our poor dear Hurrell.'

She dutifully participated in this queer male ceremony, and stared down on the tablecloth, trying to think of Hurrell, who oddly enough was now a vaguer personality in her mind than he had been this morning, although everybody had been talking about him for the last hour. She could not feel interested in him. As soon as was decent she lifted her eyes to Francis Pitt again, and was amazed to find that as he set down his glass his face wore the expression of one who embarks on a journey which he has often made before, which he has always liked, which he expects to find more delightful this time than ever. Immediately it faded, and his face became a mask of misery again. It was extraordinary that just for one second, in the midst of his grief, he should have felt such glee. It occurred to her that no doubt this was due to a result of early poverty that she had often noticed in herself. No doubt his parents, like hers, had been so poor that they could hardly ever ask people in for meals, and no doubt he, like she, felt therefore a perpetual delight in being able to have people in whenever he liked and have things nice for them. That was it, of course. But though Etta, poor Etta, was like that too in an ordinary way, she was evidently too tired to feel it tonight, for she was looking at Sunflower with an expression of pity. She must be thinking of what had happened with Essington the last time they met. Sunflower smiled at her to show that it was all right. Never in her life had she felt happier.

*

'Well,' said Francis Pitt, his face still puckered by laughter at Essington's story about the Nationalist members and the Egyptian patriots. 'If anybody had told me two hours ago that I should ever be as happy as I am now I should not have believed them.'

Leaning forward, he dipped his paw-hands into the trough of carnations and clumsily patted the flowers aside till he found a large white one. He shook the water from its stem with the prudent look of an animal and held it out to Sunflower. They all looked at her

119

benevolently, pleased with her beauty. She remembered that it was just at this stage of the meal, when they were sitting over the coffee and brandy and cigars, that they had begun to make a fuss of her the other night. As a matter of fact that was nearly always the time when people took notice of her at a dinner.

'She'd look nice with a pink one,' suggested Etta.

'Yes,' purred Essington, quizzical and proud, 'Sunflower can raise pink to her own dignity.'

Francis Pitt said levelly and casually but obstinately, 'I've given her the flower I think she ought to have.' As he spoke the door began to shake under bouts of delicate scratching, and he swung round in his chair shouting, 'Hey, my beauties! Hey, my beauties! Frederick, let those dogs in!'

'They're his borzois,' Etta explained to Essington and Sunflower; and added, as if complimenting them, 'He hasn't let them near him for the last three days.'

The door was thrown open and four great moonlight-coloured dogs came springing down the long dark room. Nooses of pale flowers cast by athletes might have parted the air swiftly like this, have landed on the ground as softly. They did not seem dogs of this world, for their barking sounded so hollow and echoing that they might have been coursing through the caverns of some magical landscape superimposed on the ordinary scene; and when they came near the brightness of the table their eyes changed from the points of blue radiance that had gleamed from their snake-flat heads in the dark to common affairs of lash and liquid iris, as if they had had to make some compromise of substance before they could enter the society of human beings. With the motion of wind-driven flames they leaped up and down round Francis Pitt, who cried out at them lovingly and cursingly, but did not look at them because he was pouring port into his empty champagne glass. 'Ah, will you be quiet, you devils! Get down! Get down!' One of them wrangled at his cuff with its teeth, and the brown stream of port swirled round the glass's edge, made a blister of brightness on the mahogany table, and foundered on the peach-parings on his plate. 'My God, my God, making a mess of your good home! Are you trying to make out to the visitors that you've never been taught manners?' he grumbled, and slipped his elbow into the open jaws, jerked it up, and threw the long beast back on its haunches. It flung up its tape-thin muzzle, uttering coughs of lament, and he argued with it, cramming his hands down into the glass of port. 'Try and have some sense, you

120

fool dogs. How can I get drinks for you if you're all over me like a pack of old women after a handsome curate? Give me time . . . Now then!' He flung himself back in his chair, stretching out his wet hands level with his shoulders, and the tall dogs leapt up and licked his fingers. 'Ah, my beauties, my beauties, my delights!' He watched them with an expression of gratified cunning, as if he had won some advantage over them by pandering to their appetites, which was absurdly, lovably inappropriate to the innocent occasion. It was that he was the harmless kind of man who likes to be taken for worse than he is. 'Ah, you know good port when you get it. When I die I'm going to leave these dogs all my port and they are going to drink every night to the glory of my soul.' He snatched back his hands, wet them afresh while the dogs leapt and whimpered, and thrust out dripping fingers again. 'Aren't they wonderful? Aren't they the finest dogs in the world? Two gentlemen and two ladies. Tamerlane and Jenghiz Khan the gentlemen's names are, and the ladies are called Peggy Joyce and Jean Nash. No you'll not get a drop more. You've had enough, you devils. I know that. I gave you more once upon a time and you blundered round my house in the most disgusting condition, each of you trying to rub off the second tail and the fifth leg you thought you'd got against my poor furniture. Oh, such ongoings, such ongoings.' He gathered them all close to him, stacking their forepaws on his knees, rubbing his face against their frosted shoulders and the frail hoops of their ribs while they passed long pink flannel tongues over his hands and ears and neck and every bit of his bare flesh they could find, he and they all swaying to a rhythm of turbulent animal tenderness, keeping in time to it with grunting little noises.

It was a pity that Essington did not let himself go like this sometimes, doing things that certainly hadn't any sense in them, but kept one human.

'Yes, we're fond of animals in this house,' said Etta, though the dogs took no notice of her and she made no movement towards them.

'Narrow, passionate faces,' mused Essington. 'A pity they can't participate in human institutions. They would have a talent for patriotism . . .'

'They are darlings,' said Sunflower. 'Do they have puppies?'

'They do, they do, at God's appointed times,' Francis Pitt assured her, 'and you shall have a puppy from the next litter. If you care about keeping dogs, that is.'

Sunflower and Essington met each other's eyes and looked away.

121

Essington said acidly, 'Yes, do give Sunflower a puppy. She likes dogs. She calls them doggies when she thinks I'm not listening.'

Nothing but laughter on his face, Francis Pitt was down bickering with his dogs again. 'Jean, will you keep still while I turn your ears the right side out? Do you think the lady I named you for would come down to dinner at Deauville with both her ears outside in? Let me tell you that a good woman looks on her home as a perpetual Deauville. You keep that in mind or you'll be losing your Jenghiz Khan and your Tamerlane to Peggy who's the trimmer wench of you two, and keeps her ears as a girl should.' Then, beating all four off, and holding his head back to dodge their muzzles, he called to Essington. 'The reason I offered Miss Fassendyll a puppy is that she's one of the very few women who continue to look beautiful when my dogs are in the room. Isn't that true, Etta?' His face was flushed with his scrimmage with the borzois and he spoke loudly to drown their barking; he was like a man reaching the top of a mountain and shouting with delight at the view. He did not pause to give Sunflower that hard gaze referring to the future with which most men follow up their compliments but passed straight into a fit of chuckling. 'It's a test I don't pass myself. I've had that brought home to me. Etta, shall I show them that drawing of Goleath's?'

'Oh, that horrible thing . . .'

'I think I'll put myself in your hands, Essington, and let you see it. Etta, where is the thing? I thought it was hanging up somewhere in this room.'

'No, indeed, it's in the top drawer of the right-hand book-case. I took it down the other day when some people were coming to lunch. I couldn't bear it any longer.'

'God bless our loyal women,' chuckled Francis Pitt, and heaved himself out of his chair. With the dogs ambling beside him he padded out of the bright zone round the table over to the mahogany dinosaurs of the furniture creations that towered in the shadow beyond, and stayed stooping in front of it for much longer than Essington, with his feline faculty for swift movement, would have needed to do. There was a curious quality about his movements whenever he did anything with his hands; it was not exactly clumsiness, rather was it as if he was not used to finding his paws split up into fingers and that the use of these finicking new instruments made it necessary for him to readjust the whole of his body which had been used to simpler motions. It somehow made one feel fierce with tenderness, like the stumbling of a

122

child learning to walk. When he had found what he wanted he stayed for a moment with his back to them, looking down at it, then gave a guffaw. 'My God! Am I as bad as that.' He was laughing; but there was something in his tone which told that the little creature really minded being ugly quite a lot. But he was in high spirits again in a second, crossing the room with the picture held by a corner so that its frame nearly swung against the floor, and saying happily, greedily, as if he were tasting some gross, rich flavour of life, some trace of garlic in the universe: 'Goleath is an ungrateful devil. God knows how much government money I got him for his war pictures, and how much of my own I've lent him, and how often I've saved him from jail and expulsion from France and suchlike calamities. Nevertheless he did this drawing to amuse my enemies more than me. Mercifully he showed it to me one day when he was drunk and I bought it off him then and there. Look at the damned thing!' He put it down in front of Essington with a flourish. 'Isn't it awful?'

Sunflower went and stood at Essington's shoulder.

'That's real wit in his line,' said Essington; and laughed.

Sunflower went back to her seat. 'Horrid,' she said to Etta, who pulled up a chair and went and sat beside her.

'Wit and beauty,' gloated Francis Pitt. 'And look at the lovely little writing round the edge. "The brute creation contrasted with man (made in His image)". It's as exquisite as the drawing. But don't I look a loathsome brute? Don't I look a monster?'

'Of course,' said Sunflower to Etta, 'I don't ever see the sense of caricature, really. What's the good of drawing people as they aren't?'

'In any case he's very difficult to do,' said Etta. 'Even photographs. I've got lots, but he never takes well.'

'Neither does he,' said Sunflower.

'They always leave out his character.'

'So they do his, too.'

Patiently they watched the two men.

'Yes, this is genius,' muttered Essington. 'Wit and beauty and ingenuity. Look at the way he's given a gothic touch to the dog's ears, setting up a suggestion of spirituality in the eye of the beholder. Ten to one he did that unconsciously, probably he doesn't know to this day that he did it. That's why in my hearts of hearts I loathe art. It's done so blindly, so uncontrollably. It's the best thing we've got, but we can't yoke it to the world's service.'

'You certainly can't yoke Goleath to the world's service,' chuckled

123

Francis Pitt. He was very happy. He had liked Essington admiring what was evidently one of his cherished possessions; and now he was going to talk about Goleath, who was evidently one of his pet subjects. 'Did you ever meet the fellow?'

'Yes. He drew me during my brief visit to Versailles. We were all drawn then. Roughly speaking, anything that happened to a musical comedy star happened to us great statesmen then. I constantly had an impression a face cream was being named after me, but I may have been wrong . . .'

'Didn't he strike you as a horrible fellow?'

'Odd, odd. I remember he told me some story of a widow in some French town who had refused to yield to his embraces till they had visited her late husband's grave and prayed. The results of their embraces showed her to be a woman of a strong but rather unpleasant sense of humour. Not the sort of thing I should have told a stranger . . . No . . .'

'That was Goleath all over. He has no shame in him.' He set back his huge head and roared with laughter. 'God, what a man! I'll never forget what he did to me in Paris. Never. It led to a lot of trouble, some of which is going on still. I had a job in Paris, you know, and part of my duties was being polite to British subjects who were doing war-work there. Soothing duchesses who were running hospitals and thought they weren't being appreciated, and assuring little men with glasses and independent means who were running billiard rooms that the British Empire was sensible of the sacrifices they were making in staying up two hours later than they used to at home in Bournemouth. And when we were winding up the thing I had to give a dinner party to the whole damned lot of them. By that time I was sick of my job. I wished that every one of them were at the bottom of the sea. And that very afternoon I was sitting in my office, feeling I'd go mad before I had done with it, and who should come in but Goleath. He wanted me, not for the first time, nor the last, to lend him some money. He'd met a negress whom he assured me was far more beautiful than the Venus de Milo and I didn't feel competent to dispute the point with him and apparently she'd been exorbitant in her demands. So I gave him some money and, God forgive me, I asked him to my party.' Choked with silent laughter, he strutted a few steps on the hearthrug with his feet wide apart and a proud expression of conscious wickedness gleaming in his eyes; he looked ragged and muddy and young: he seemed to be changing into the naughtiest boy in the district strutting at the street corner while the rest of the gang gape respectfully from against the paling. 'And God and all His saints forgive me, I put him next to a duchess. I'd never fancied the woman, and she'd given me a lot of trouble, treating me as one of those low little men who make money. She's the sort of duchess who gets her clothes where Queen Mary does, and she was a great big woman with masses of hair piled up under a tiara that was obviously made by the same man who built Euston station.'

'It wasn't the Duchess of Grantham, was it?' asked Essington.

'That's the woman. Well, it all went quite all right till we got to the ice and then there was a yell. My God, there was a yell. And there was Goleath tearing down the duchess's hair.'

'Pitt, you are an excellent fellow,' said Essington, 'I have detested that woman for years. She was one of the Ulster lot. Gracious Englishwomen. Who came up to one all the time one was in office and bullied one as if one was an insolent footman because one wasn't shooting some large class of God's creatures without trial – trade unionists, the Irish Nationalists, Hindus . . .'

'Well, this night she wanted to shoot Goleath without trial. You should have seen that woman with her tiara over one eye and Goleath going at her hair, not vindictively, you understand, but as if he was giving the negress a rough-house before they got friendly again. And there was such a shouting and such a hullaballoo as you never heard outside a low-class pub. Then suddenly Goleath stood up, looking like a king, and quieted them all with one wave of his hand, and said, very gravely and impressively, "I see that I have done wrong. I must apologise. My only excuse is that at present I am living with a woman who adores brutality." And with that the devil went out and left me to settle up with the duchess. You can guess how easy it was for a man of my size, and my unfortunate air of not minding very much if things do go wrong so long as they're funny, to placate that rearing carthorse of outraged virtue. But I smoothed her down all right, and lied like blazes, and said it was a secretary of mine who'd asked Goleath, and that I'd known nothing about it, and that my heart was broken, and finally I got her pretty quiet. So we finished our dinner, and then we all went into the ballroom and listened to music, the real right stuff that experts had got in for me. And all my Mutts and Jeffs were sitting like lambs drinking in some Italian woman when – *yowp!*' – his eyes were like eddies in the wicked grey Thames that flows under London bridges – 'Goleath had come back, and he'd come up behind some damned woman who'd taken two million colonial troops to hear organ recitals in the Invalides, or provided them with some such entertainment that would naturally appeal to colonial troops on leave, and he'd smacked her hard where one doesn't smack ladies, though it's convenient enough. He said he'd gone out into the streets and that suddenly he'd felt that we were all going to have a dull time, so he'd come back to make the party go. And, by God, it did. It went within the next half hour. We couldn't get him out. He's over six feet, you know, and as strong as a bull. So the rest of them went instead. There wasn't a soul in the place by eleven o'clock barring me and the waiters. I didn't mind. In a way it was the best party I ever gave. But I got hauled over the coals for it finely before I was done. Hurrell was furious – '

He stopped.

The glee went out of his face, it became again a mask of sullen misery. His eyes, old under his reddened lids, above the baggy pouches, passed from one to other of his listeners as if in resentment that they had seduced him into forgetting even for a little. He turned his back on them and walked draggingly into the shadows of the room, looking down as people do at funerals. There was a bell-rope hanging near the door. He felt for it as if he were blind, tugged it, and leaned back against the wall. Through the darkness they could see his face as a still patch of sallowness, not so high on the wall as one would expect. Essington began to say something in a high, nonchalant voice, but the words caught in his throat.

When the butler came in Francis Pitt said, 'Frederick, will you ask Nurse Vyner if we can see Mr Hurrell now?'

'She's just been down to say that she'd be obliged if you'd come up as soon as possible, sir, so that Mr Hurrell won't be kept awake too late.'

He came back to them, pouting out his lips as if he were trying to make a thick, solid mouth to stabilise his face, which was in danger of becoming muddled with tears. 'Will you come, Essington?' he asked humbly.

'I should be very sorry if you did not let me,' said Essington gently.

'And you, Miss Fassendyll? He was saying today he'd never seen you, and that he'd like to.'

'I'd love to see him.'

'You're sure you're not afraid of infection?'

'He's used to horrid women!' she thought savagely; and clenched her fists as there passed before her mind's eye certain faceless women's figures; and said aloud, 'Thank you. I don't ever catch anything.'

126

'That'll be good of you. You're being very good to me, you two . . .' Mumbling, he led them to the door and held it open for them. It was dreadful to pass so close to him and not be able to touch him, to see quite close by one's shoulder his earthy, pudgy little face downcast to hide the working of his mouth, so that it looked all bulging forehead and angry eyes, and not be able to tell him that it didn't matter if he did cry, everybody cried sometimes. 'I'd better go first . . .' It was as if his grief was a fluid interpenetrating his body and making it immensely heavy. Shuffling up the staircase in front of them, his hands in his trouser pockets, his head well down in his collar, he moved as if his limbs were leaden, he almost waddled. And in this part of the house he looked smaller than ever, for here things were even more monstrously swollen. All the way up the stairs hung subject pictures vaster than his others, with Saxon princesses and Dutch fisher-girls eight feet high, and gold frames thick as a ship's cable; and on the landing the banisters became a kind of reredos, and at each side of the three stained glass windows were curtains which, had they fallen on a child, would have stifled it before it could beat its way out. The door at which he knocked with such a meek, tense bridling of his strength, towered up and up above his little crouching back.

He put his fingers to his lips. 'Remember he doesn't know . . . He hasn't the least idea . . .'

As the nurse went out her cap was reflected half a dozen times in shining cliffs of mahogany. It wasn't a homely room; and that broad bed must be dreadful for the servants to make; and it was heart-rendingly too broad for the man who lay in it. He made so little of a mound under the bedclothes that he must be nearly as spare as the rain-polished bones one sees lying on the turf on the Downs. Blue shadows lay like pennies on his closed eyelids, and on his high cheekbones was a flush like firelight seen through the hands. There was on his long Scotch face a look as if he were nourishing something within himself at the cost of a continual physical sacrifice. It was the same look that is on the face of a woman who is going to have a baby. Only there were these colours painted on his skin, like a plague sign daubed on a door, as warning that what he was cherishing within him was not life but a disease, that its birth would be a death.

He raised his blue lids and stared up with huge, brilliant eyes. Avariciously Francis Pitt bent over him to receive his gaze. After some seconds of stillness the man in bed gave a weak, sweet smile.

127

'Well, Gordon, how are you?' asked Francis Pitt. 'Are you feeling any better?'

'I'm feeling fine, thank you, Francis,' answered the man in bed, with a slight Scotch accent. There was a little weariness mixed with his sweetness. It was apparent that Francis Pitt had asked him this question several times before during that day, and during the preceding day also.

'I've brought some people to see you, Gordon.' He spoke with exaggerated distinctness. Evidently his sense that his friend was every moment being borne further and further made him want to shout at him, as one would at someone who was moving physically away from one; and as that plainly could not be done in a sickroom he tried to get the same effect by speaking very clearly. It could be seen, from a little irritable twitch of the head on the pillow, that this puzzled and annoyed Hurrell, who however made no reference to it, but said with the same sweetness: 'If it's who I think it is, I'm glad.'

'Yes, it's the folks I spoke of, right enough. Here's the famous Miss Fassendyll . . .'

He gave her one of those beautiful looks which men who have had nothing unworthy to do with women all their lives can give women when they are old; looks that are half holy memories. He was smiling at Sunflower, he was smiling at some girl who had looked lovely when the wind blew her full skirts round her at a street corner in a Lowland village fifty years before. He said, 'It's very good of a young lady like you, who must have such a quantity of gay engagements, to come and see an invalid.'

Remembering that he was out of office, and that Francis Pitt had said that he hated exile, she told him, 'Oh, I wanted to! You see, you're one of the few great men I'd never met.'

Gently he laughed and took away his hot, damp hand, and said, 'Well, I'm afraid you must have found us a poor lot.'

'But I wish you hadn't been like this,' she went on. 'I'm sorry you've been bad.'

With that piercing sweetness he said, 'It's nothing. Nothing but a feverish chill of sorts. A kind of ague you might call it. I make the most of it, I'm afraid, because I've always enjoyed unusually good health, and now when a little real pain and discomfort comes my way I make a terrible fuss. And Francis here spoils me and encourages me to get good treatment by malingering. It's no wonder that it's got about that I've got galloping consumption.' He gave a mild laugh. 'That was

128

how they put it in – Francis, what was the paper? I showed it to you the day before you made me come out here.'

'The *Chicago Standard* was the fool thing's name,' said Francis Pitt heartily.

'The silly things they put in papers!' marvelled Sunflower, and stepped back.

'And there's someone else,' said Francis Pitt.

'My dear Hurrell . . .' mewed Essington. She was proud of him. He was at his best in emergencies like that. Nobody could have told from his demeanour that there was any shadow on the occasion. He moved towards the bed with the slow grace of a cat, put his head on one side like a cat wondering if it is safe to jump on a stranger's lap, and laid his hand on the quilt very lightly and tentatively, as a cat puts a paw through a railing towards a bird. 'Tell me . . . am I your dear Essington?' His tone suggested, 'If not I shall run away and play by myself, it's of no real consequence. But I should like . . .'

Hurrell's fingers closed over the offered hand. Huskily he said, 'You are my dear Essington . . . indeed. There's a saying we have in Scotland . . . It sounds foolish in English . . . A sight for sore eyes . . .'

'It certainly does sound wrong,' said Essington querulously, dropping into an armchair by the bed. 'Sore eyes . . . It reminds me of the days we were in opposition together and used to join forces to bully that ass Prester when he was at the Home Office. We used to allege that he exposed Russian immigrants to stricter eye tests than the other immigrants because they were free-spirited rebels against the Tsardom. I wonder now if that was true . . .'

'Let not two politicians in the autumn of their days sit down and distress themselves by discussing how much of what they used to say was true,' objected Hurrell, 'particularly what they used to say when they were in opposition.' He got back to what was evidently a little prepared speech. 'But I couldn't tell you you were a sicht for sair een, for I would never dare use Scottish dialect to you after an evening we spent at a play by a compatriot of mine called Sir James Barrie. Your comments were most unsympathetic. Do you not remember? We were taken in a party by Lucille Oppenshaw.'

'How I detest that woman,' said Essington. 'We Liberals brought our own ruin on ourselves. We ought to have seen that no man was fit to lead a Party who had been fool enough to marry that woman. There were no sensuous inducements. That toasting-fork figure makes celibacy seem a life of riotous self-indulgence.'

129

Hurrell said 'Tchk! Tchk!' in a shocked, delighted way, and laughed into his pillow. Sunflower moved to a sofa that was set against the wall, facing the end of the bed. Francis Pitt was standing looking at the two men with a gratified yet wistful expression, as if he had arranged this meeting and was very glad that it was going off well, but that he had not wished it to go so well that they would both forget all about him. Presently he strolled over to his sister, who was sitting by a table near the sofa, and lounged over the back of a chair. Suddenly he caught sight of a bottle on the table and started up right, exclaiming in a vehement undertone: 'But he's still taking that French stuff! You know Cornelliss said he was to have the German brand! Oh, Etta, Etta!'

'It's only because the German brand hadn't come when it was time for him to have his last dose. But very likely the German has come by now, and he can have it next time. I'll see if you like.'

'Go now, go now . . .'

To the closing door he said, but too late for her to hear, 'Thank you, my dear,' and went and sat down in an armchair on the other side of the bed.

Hurrell said: 'I've often thought of that evening. The things you said. I missed you a lot after you left. I don't know how often I've said to myself, when something ridiculous happened, "I wish Essington had been here. He'd have laughed at that, and maybe said one of his things!" Nobody else ever said things like you. I've always told people who've come in since you've left, "There was never such good company as Essington."'

Francis Pitt jumped forward on his chair as if he expected to have to give corroboration of this; but this was not asked, and he sat back.

'Yes, we were always good friends,' said Essington, with an air of grudging the admission, of cantankerousness reluctantly giving way to amity.

Hurrell meditated: 'It's funny what a lot jokes count for in life. And just seeing the humour of things. Even if you hadn't said those things the mere fact that we laughed at the same things meant . . .' his voice faded away; and came back crisp and Scotch, 'almost more than anything.' It was apparent that though his mind did not know that he was dying his spirit had learned it, and was not afraid, but was calmly casting its accounts of what it had gained and lost in its sojourn on earth. He closed his eyes and was still for a minute. Then he said

130

feebly, 'There was something I saved for you . . . Something that I thought would make you laugh . . . Francis . . . What was it?'

Instantly Francis was on his feet, bending over the bed.

'I know . . . The letter in that packet we were going over yesterday . . . The letter from St Audrie . . . I asked you to put it by for Essington . . .'

Francis Pitt went smartly to a writing table in the corner of the room, opened a drawer, took out a paper, and brought it back with the fussiness of a retriever bringing back its bird.

'Read it out, Francis.'

With comic pomposity he read: 'My dear Hurrell, I hear that Lord Longchester has called on you and has suggested that he should be given the power to raise the fourth Draconian Loan. This news has caused me to feel the greatest perturbation, as I can hardly imagine a less suitable person. He has gone from bad to worse ever since he left Eton. Some time ago he left the lady who is his wife and ran away with a woman. Recently he had to sell his place. I do not think that any Englishman of his class who sells his place after he has been left sufficient wealth whereby to maintain it is the kind of person who ought to be associated in any way with the operations, whether financial or otherwise, of the Empire. May I say that though the duty which has fallen to me of writing this letter is painful – and may I say that that duty has been made more painful than it need have been by my consciousness that I write in response to no enquiry on your part, but have to intrude unasked to avert a calamity that may be I know not how near final accomplishment – I consider that this occurrence should not be forgotten but should be kept in mind as a proof of how undesirable it is that Downing Street should permit itself to parley with approaches that should have been made to the Foreign Office. Yours sincerely, St Audrie.'

'Oh, glorious, glorious! . . . What a man . . .'

'And I had but told one of my secretaries to give this Longchester rogue a cup of tea and a bun.'

'But do you remember the personal letter he wrote to the Postmaster General in our time? "The Marchioness of St Audrie was twice disturbed last night, once at 11.30 p.m. and once at 11.45 p.m., by persons ringing up her telephone number and enquiring, 'Are you the Coliseum?'"'

'Oh, the man's a wonder!'

While the two men laughed, Francis Pitt neatly folded the letter,

131

took it over to the desk, and went back to his seat on the other side of the bed.

'Oh, often and often I've wanted to hear what you would say about things like that. There was Mussolini.'

'Yes, he came after my time. Of course you had to meet him over that League of Nations advertising business. What sort of wonder is he?'

Hurrell closed his eyes again, said in a very soft, very Scotch voice, 'The man's a lunatic,' breathed deeply and nuzzled into his pillow as if he were going to sleep. Francis Pitt moved forward anxiously, and a fretfulness came over the sick man's face. With a broken word and a flutter of his hand, as if he were trying to find some reason for the change and were too tired to achieve it, he summoned up some last resource of energy and rolled over so that he lay with his face to Essington and his back to Francis Pitt. There was a silence of some moments. Essington bent forward and covered his eyes with his hands. Francis Pitt sat cupping his podgy chin in his hands and staring at the back of Hurrell's head, which was all he could see of him. A clock ticked, a flame drove, behind the maroon curtain and the navy-blue blind an owl smudged the night with its blurred cry.

Hurrell stirred in his bed. Both men sat up to attention. He was lying on his back staring at the ceiling.

Suddenly he said, 'Man, your suit was smaller on you than mine was on me.' His Scotch accent was quite broad. He said, 'Your shirt!'

Essington's laughter was almost weeping. 'Hurrell, you flatter yourself!'

They looked at each other steadily. It occurred to Sunflower that they might have been brothers. But perhaps that was just because they were both the same age, because they were both old.

Francis Pitt wriggled on his seat and looked round the room. His eyes fell on Sunflower. He looked back at Hurrell who had put his hand on the quilt. He watched Essington, who, making the gesture as light as could be, torturing his eyebrows into a quizzical shape, laid his hand on it. He pulled himself out of his deep chair and went over to Sunflower.

'Will you come and see my garden?' he asked softly.

*

As they were going down the stone steps to the gravel he paused and

132

laid a protective hand on her arm, 'Are you cold? Would you like your cloak?'

Amazed by the idea that she could feel heat or cold when she was wholly absorbed in him, she exclaimed, 'Oh, no!'

She saw that she had spoken with too much emphasis. He had lowered his eyelids and was compressing his lips, plainly he was filing the fact of her excitement for reference, and meant to examine it at leisure. Deep down in her she realised that her delight in him was shot with fear. Embarrassed, she ran down the last few steps and stood on the gravel, looking up at the stars.

He padded down after her, standing a little behind her, took a cigar out of his pocket and slowly, clumsily lit it.

'That's a clever thing to do, to ask a lady to see my garden, when it's pitch dark and she can't see a thing,' he said, amiably but stiffly.

It was all falling so flat. She had wanted to be alone with him so that she could get to know him and be nice to him. But they had nothing to say to each other. He was in the grip of a queer mood. He seemed so penetrated with heavy grief that a sense of weight, of suffering under weight, hung round him, yet she had a suspicion that he was bathed in a sense of satisfaction at being there with her, a satisfaction so strong that if she had made a movement to go back into the house he would have stopped her with a vigorous gesture, a satisfaction so utterly unconcerned with her well-being that the gesture would have been definitely threatening. She hated this satisfaction men got out of people, which did not make them gay and caused them to feel cruel instead of grateful to those who gave it. Essington's unsmiling, complaining glee in making a fool of her and scolding her for it afterwards was like that. Sharply she turned her head and looked at Francis Pitt. But at the sight of him she could believe nothing bad. He was a simple, loving, unhappy little man. She had been imagining these things. Living with Essington had spoiled her nerves. There was nothing wrong with the moment except that it was falling flat, she supposed because he wasn't interested in her.

Weakly she murmured, 'The moonlight looks nice on the flat top of that yew hedge. It might be frost.'

'Ah,' he said, brightening up because she had given him a line to follow, which showed how bored he must have been. 'Come and see what lies behind it. That's my paved garden. It's very old, it belonged to the Tudor house that was on the site of this one till it got burned down about sixty years ago. The other gardens were burned with the house, and the old ass of a city merchant who built this house just planted his idea of a nice suburban garden all over the ruins of them. I dare say you noticed how queer it looked as you came down the drive. And I dare say you think the house is queer enough too.' He gave one of those deep chuckles which were comic and endearing and piteous, since they were so obviously nervous prostration of the sort of maleness which has no nerves, so obviously timid attempts to avert criticism by pretending that this was the rugged strength which laughs when it is criticised. 'Well, I like it. I like queer things. When we first came to England Etta buzzed round looking for somewhere to live and I got sick of it, and I could see the woman would spend the next two years finding a house, and then two years after that picking up bits of furniture, and that I'd have to go on living in hotels till she'd finished. So when we stumbled on this, with its crazy gardens and its Noah's ark furniture, I said, "For God's sake, let's buy the thing, it's somewhere to live and it's too damn good a joke to let out of the family." So here we are.' Having reached the end of his defence, again he chuckled.

She walked beside him across the moonlit square of gravel, smiling to herself. It was funny the way he took his childish feeling of diffidence at doing such a grown-up thing as furnishing a house and represented it as the curt gesture of a strong silent man. To her face she held the flower which he had given her at dinner.

The passage through the yew hedge was cut aslant so that no vista of the garden within should be seen from without. There was a second when they could see nothing before or behind but walks of twiggy darkness. He gave a mutter of pleasure as if he liked being hidden, he dawdled as if he did not want to leave this cache.

She went on ahead of him into the garden. It was like a sampler worked by some grave little girl who liked quiet colours. There were the four tall hedges like a frame, and flagstones like the canvas that had to be sewn on, and yew beasts and plants whose flowers had now the hueless lustre of faded silk, set in four beds within box borders, all as neat as stitching. At the other end of the garden, in a vaulted alcove cut in the middle of the yew hedge, was a stone bench, dignified and melancholy, that was like the moral emblem worked at the foot of the sampler.

Francis Pitt, coming up behind her, said: 'In here you're shut right away from all the rest of the world. I come in here and sit on that seat when I'm feeling too miserable. I have sat there a lot . . . during the last few days . . .'

She made a little tender noise, but could find no words to say. She looked hard at the stone bench. She could see him sitting there, his bulging shirt-front gleaming in the moonlight, his martyred face tragi-comic with strong shadows, his feet not quite reaching the ground. She could imagine herself running across the flagstones to him in the dress of some other age, in the full skirts of the eighteenth century, throwing herself down at his feet, drawing his head to her breast with bare arms, petting him and saying things that didn't mean anything, that you couldn't argue about, but that would make him feel better. It would be impossible to do it in ordinary clothes. If she did it in the dress she had on now it would look as if she were making love to him. She wished that when a person was in trouble one could get up a sort of masque about it, when all his friends would put on fancy dress to show that what they were doing was something separate from everyday life and did not have to be followed up in any way, and would make beautiful, stylised gestures to show what they really felt about him, and said lovely, vague things in poetry. But people never put on fancy dress in gardens except to do pastoral plays for charities (she wondered suddenly who 'Our Dumb Friends' were) and then it was usually 'As You Like It', which was a horrid dull play when you came to act it. You couldn't believe that the people you saw going down to Kew on Sunday didn't say warmer and kinder and more unexpected things to each other than Orlando and Rosalind did. It was queer how nothing connected with the stage, like fancy dress, ever could be made handy for anything that would be really useful, as running over the flagstones to him would be.

As it was, everything was falling flat, so flat.

She said timidly, 'Are you sure you wouldn't like to go back to the house and be with them?'

Like a sulky child he answered, 'Well, they seemed to be getting on quite well without me, didn't they?'

She looked at him in surprise, and exclaimed, 'Oh, but go on, you understand all that, don't you?'

'Understand what?'

'Well, what I mean to say is, you do see, don't you, what's happening when Mr Hurrell seems to think you a bit fussy, when he's glad to see other people? You know, it's like this, you're looking after him with special care because you know he won't get well, but he doesn't know he isn't going to get well, so naturally he thinks you're fussy, and it gets on his nerves. But you can't do anything about it.

The only thing you could do would be to stop giving him special care, and goodness knows you can't do that. It's just a price you have to pay for feeling like that about people. You see, I know, because Mother was like that. Just an hour before she died, she said to me and my sister, quite cross, "I could get to sleep if you girls would leave me alone and not sit gawking at me like that." And we just had to go. But, mind you, it didn't mean anything, not really. She thought the world of us girls. They don't *mean* anything by it, really they don't . . .'

He looked at her searchingly, 'Do you think it's that?'

'Oh, I'm sure it is.'

He dropped his head and stared down on the stones. 'I believe you're right,' he said, in a voice as childish as that in which he had made his original complaint. Then he repeated in a harder, more adult voice, more strongly tinged with an American accent, 'I believe you're right.' It was as if faith that what she had said was true had given him the strength to test it by reason, and that he felt more at ease using the tool of reason. 'Why, yes. I believe that's what it is.'

'Well, don't worry about it any more,' she murmured.

'Oh, I won't,' he said, 'I know your explanation's true. It's got the turn to it that means it's true. I've made my money by backing tips that had the same turn to them. Well, well, that's how it is. I must just put up with it. It's part of what I have to do for my old man.' He took some puffs at his cigar. 'Thank God you've told me this. You see, I'd been thinking that maybe I'd been boring him all these years and that he'd been too good-natured to let me see it . . .'

'Oh, it wouldn't be that!' she exclaimed in wonder. Didn't he know that everybody would be bound to like him?

'It might have been, it might have been,' he said, with an air of scrupulous fairness. 'Yes, I'm glad you talked to me about this, because you see I know nothing about death. All my life I've been an extraordinarily lucky man, in every way. And I've never lost anyone I've been fond of. My father and mother are still alive down at Bath, and all my brothers and sisters are kicking about somewhere. So I don't know a thing about people who are dying. And one hasn't got a lead. Death is one of those special occasions in your life when people are apt to have the same special needs, however different they may be in ordinary life, and though it keeps on happening again and again, yet nothing about it ever gets out, no one knows what those special needs are. Now, one realises when one's having a love-affair with a woman that she's apt to have this and that emotion because of the situation.'

She was shaken by a tremor of disgust. He spoke in a level, matter-of-fact tone, and there was certainly nothing coarse in his words, yet for a second she felt outraged as if he had said something indecent. But she realised that was mad and silly of her.

'She may be jealous then, though at any other time she'd be fair-minded enough. But one knows all that the first time one needs the knowledge, because all the time love's being talked about, love's being written about. But no one talks about death, no one writes about it. We're all afraid of it.' His voice was desolate, his voice was shuddering. 'So when the damned thing comes on us we blunder about anyhow . . . unless a friendly soul comes along and will take the trouble to look closely at a stranger's troubles and read the right meaning of them.' He spoke gravely, and evidently under the influence of deep feeling. For a little while he puffed at his cigar in silence; and then said, suddenly, 'God bless you, Miss Fassendyll.'

She had always been sure that people did in real life behave just as they did in plays that were considered quite bad.

He muttered, 'I believe I shall sleep tonight.' It was a measure of his need for rest, she supposed, that when he spoke of it his voice was charged with gruff voluptuousness, as if he meditated indulgence in some rich food, some heady wine.

It was queer and lovely that anything she had said should have been useful to him; and it had really been useful, he was not merely being polite. The new placidity of his movements, the unctions of his speech, showed that he had been reconciled to life in the last few moments. It had been left to her stupidity to serve his need because what he said was true, nothing was written about death, nobody talked about it. That was because men did most of the writing, and nearly all the talk that was listened to, and they always avoided as subjects things that could not be altered by argument. It hadn't been a man who had given her the idea why dying people get cross with those who cared for them most. She and Lily and Mabel had been sitting, very sad about it, in the kitchen, when someone had come in, someone wearing an apron, someone whose name she had forgotten or never knew, just a neighbour who had popped in to see what she could do, and she had explained it to them. Her own mother had been like that too. There had been lots of women who had come in to see them, during those last few days, women wearing aprons, with unimportant names, and had told them all sorts of things that had helped through that time.

It occurred to Sunflower, with a sense of having been sold into a desolate country, that since she had left Chiswick and moved into the centre of London nobody had told her anything that would have been of use to Francis Pitt in his trouble. She felt a sense of guilt about this, as if she had broken a tradition, had done something like moving out of her place during a church service. She couldn't have helped being an actress, so far as she could see. It had just happened to her. But all the same it didn't seem right she should be one; not really right. And she felt that possibly he might have done something wrong of the same indefinable sort in becoming a very rich man and a politician. That might account for the faint sense she got now and then that he was not perfectly good. They should neither of them have been standing in this formal and enclosed garden, the air of which was melancholy. They should have been somewhere else, cosy and less tidy.

Because of his grief she felt a bodily pain, a bruise over the heart. Through the darkness and behind him, so that certainly he could not see her, she moved her hand as if to stroke his stooping shoulders. She could not even say anything, lest she should seem to be making capital out of his sorrow, to be using it as an avenue to intimacy with him. In any case she was nearly paralysed by stage-fright. She felt as if everything she did or said when she was with this man had to be weighed on very delicate scales, and if it were too light he would turn away, and if it were too heavy he would stand by and be courteous and gloomily decide not to see her any more. It was lovely to be with him, but it was torturing, exhausting.

He was looking at her as he smoked. Evidently he thought that as there was only moonlight she would not be able to see that he was doing it. She could not bear that for long, so she put up her hand in front of her face on the pretence of smoothing her hair. At that he took the cigar from his mouth, and said, not at all casually, but as if a long train of thought were coming to the surface, 'What was that play you acted in where you went to a man's rooms at night, wrapped in a great silver cloak?' He spoke gloatingly; his little hands greedily described the way the silver folds had fallen. 'You made a most beautiful picture. I have never forgotten it. Can you remember what I mean?'

'Why,' she answered in a little, weak voice. 'I don't know which that would be, I'm sure I've acted in such a lot of plays. It must have been some years ago if I went to a man's rooms at night. Nowadays all that happens before the curtain goes up, and it isn't considered

138

specially interesting . . .' She found it difficult to speak to him, but not because she was feeling the boredom and embarrassment that usually came on her when people praised her beauty. Instead she was feeling as if this was the first time that anyone had ever praised her beauty. It was as if an utterly new thing were happening to her, and had taken away her breath. She murmured, 'Oh, I think I know . . . That would be "The Nightingale". It was by Mr John Richard Smith, and he's ever so old, so those sort of things go on happening in his plays . . .'

'Well, whether he's old or not, he wrote a play that had one wonderfully lovely scene,' pronounced Francis Pitt solemnly, shaking his head for emphasis, 'a wonderfully lovely scene . . .' He went on smoking with an air of rumination, till with an abrupt, twitching movement, as if his high spirits had suddenly flared up, he threw his cigar high in the air over the flowerbeds and exclaimed in a voice full of good humour, 'My God, why did I bring you into this gloomy old garden where I come and have the dumps! I've lots of other things here I needn't be ashamed of! Come and see my chestnut walk.'

He was indeed very happy, far happier than she could ever have thought he would be while this trouble was hanging over him. They had to walk quite a little way, through the passage in the yew hedge, across the gravel in front of the house, which was the colour of india-rubber in the moonlight and had coarse blunt edges to all its copings and angles like the edges of hot water bottles, and up a winding path through a shrubbery of all those plants whose leaves set out to be shiny and are dull, laurel and rhododendra, but his mood held. He moved lightly and springily on his little feet and made broken, grunting, satisfied noises, and sometimes whistled tunelessly and exultantly through his teeth.

At the last turn of the path he stopped and said proudly, 'Now!'

They were at the end of an avenue of chestnut trees, that drove along a flat terrace on the hillside to something too distant for anything to be known of it in this light save that it was high, and white, and stamped with the mould of human fancy: a statue, a fountain. Wide bays of brightness scalloped the pathway, for there were but half the number of trees on the valley side that there were on the side of the rising ground, so that at her elbow were wide windows of landscape, a landscape of vague radiant woods that seemed to be adhering to hills sticky with moonlight in the manner of treacle-caught moths, and of sky, the dark sky that is always a little strange to human

139

eyes, since though it is more lawless than the land with its unmarshalled, moving clouds, it is by night more formal, pricked out with the patterns of the hard stars. There were floating here and there silver vapours that might have been passing over the world on some alchemic task of making beauty of what was not, a changing the character of what was beautiful to something rarer. The hideous house below them now served the eye, for its slate roofs looked like shining waters; and the candles on the unpartnered chestnut trees, lit by the full light of the moon, which the fine matt surface of the petals did not reflect, seemed to have the short, crumbling texture of snow.

'Oh, it is lovely!' breathed Sunflower.

He was innocently pleased, he was childishly proud of his possessions. 'Ah, you must come and see it by day! It's a fine view over to Harrow, and the candles on my chestnuts are at their best. Pink and white they are, the flowers we're walking on.' He ploughed them up with his feet, whistling as if it gave him a sense of luxury to be treading on fallen flowers.

'I love them when they're mixed,' said Sunflower. 'There was an avenue of them in a park where I lived when I was little. Strawberries and cream, we used to call the flowers on the ground.'

With gleeful, generous inconsequence he asked, 'Do you like strawberries and cream? We might have had some tonight. My gardener forces them in some corner hereabouts, though God knows I have to go on my knees to get some of what I pay him to grow on my land with my money. But it's a pity we didn't have some for you tonight.'

'It's awfully kind of you, but they're no good to me, ever. I like them, but they don't like me – '

She bit her lip. This was one of the phrases that drove Essington into a frenzy. But Francis Pitt seemed not to be offended by it, for he went on happily, as if to talk of trivial things were a holiday. 'Mm. Now I loathe asparagus, and we're in the thick of the season now. How I hate those weeks every year when I have to sit in front of a plate that's stocked with that anaemic, water-logged timber . . .' No, he hadn't minded her being common. It was a rest to be with a man who wasn't porcupinish with different subtle sorts of fastidiousness. One could tell him anything. She remembered suddenly something that had been a lump in her throat ever since the morning because she couldn't get it out of her system by telling somebody. In the automobile coming there she had felt quite sick because she didn't dare say anything about it to Essington. She wondered if she could possibly tell Francis Pitt.

140

She paused, and stood looking over the moonlit landscape. He checked his walk and came to a halt beside her and asked, 'Not cold, are you?' with so obvious a desire to do everything he could for her, that she felt a rush of confidence, and began penitently, 'I did make such a silly of myself today.'

'How was that?'

'Well, you see, I'm rehearsing a new play of Mr Trentham's just now, and I'm playing a person who isn't very well educated, not quite what you'd call a lady, really. Well, in the first act I have to say, "My husband's uncle's got mines in the Andes, not that I know where that is, I never was good at geography." Well, that's how I've always said it till today. But this morning Mr Childs, who's our producer, stopped me while I was saying the line and said, "Miss Fassendyll, if I were you I should say Jography." Well, naturally, when he said that, I thought I'd been saying it wrong and that it ought to *be* Jography. Well, I'm not the sort of person who pretends to know more than I do and never have, so I said, "Thank you very much, Mr Childs, and I'm sure I'm very sorry but I always thought it was Geography." Well, you could have heard a pin drop, and then they all laughed, and what's worse, they all stopped themselves. Well, wasn't it awful of me?'

'Awful of you? No, by God, it was not. It was awful of them. The fools, the silly little fools. Such a little thing to snigger about.'

'Oh, but it was a dreadfully stupid mistake.'

'But such a tiny mistake. It just shows what small minds people have. It's a mistake anybody might have made. My God, the words in the dictionary I can't pronounce . . .'

'Really?' she asked, very pleased. 'Do you have trouble that way? Oh, but you aren't stupid. You see, it isn't just that I'm ignorant, I do such silly things. I suppose you heard about the interview I gave the *Evening Mail* when I first signed up to play in "As You Like It"?'

'Not a word,' he told her stoutly.

'That was awful. I told the young man I was looking forward to it because it was the first time I'd acted in a Barrie play. Wasn't it dreadful of me? And he went and put it in the papers, though he had stayed on and had his tea. I never heard the last of it. But really it wasn't such an out of the way mistake to make, because Barrie did write a play called "Rosalind". All the same, people laughed.'

'The fools, the damned fools,' he said with mounting indignation. 'As if all that stuff mattered. But I hate to think of you exposed to all

141

this spite and jealousy and meanness. I wish to God you weren't on the stage.'

She began to move on along the avenue. 'I don't like it much,' she murmured.

'A woman like you,' he said gravely, 'ought to be at home, ought to be . . .'

He did not finish his sentence. They walked in silence, ploughing up the flowers, looking down at them. She felt ever so much better. How this little man understood things. He saw how horrid it was for her to be laughed at; he would realise how she felt when people talked about her and Essington. She felt a sense of gratitude and affection not only for him but for this place where so many lovely things were happening: where a great man was waiting sweetly for death, and this little man was loving him so warmly, and Etta was serving them both with such devotion, and where, when she had come in for an hour or two, they had cured her of a worry that would have choked her for days, just by being simple and kind. She stopped and leaned against a tree-trunk, and looked at the pale hills and the roof that was shining like water, so that she would never forget them, and this night.

'It's nice here,' she said huskily.

He stood beside her, his feet wide apart and his shoulders hunched, a kind little Napoleon. 'Yes, it's nice.'

They stood in silence for a little while. Her eyes brimmed with tears, but not because she felt unhappy. It was part of the relaxation brought about by the place. Of late she had always had a few tears just under the surface and now that she was all loosened these flowed, but none took their place behind her eyes. She was utterly happy, utterly at peace.

Suddenly she felt very shy, and wondered if he were not thinking her odd, and boring, and silly. She began to move away.

'Wait a moment,' he said very softly. 'That's a London tree-trunk you've been leaning against. Most likely it's left a mark on your frock. Turn round and let me see.' She watched him over her shoulder while he peered at the silk. He was very careful not to touch her. There was a beautiful decorum, a respect for physical reserves, about all his movements, though they were so friendly and cherishing. 'No, not a thing. I am glad. It's a very lovely frock.' He was speaking very, very softly and she answered him as they moved on in a whisper. A cloud was passing before the moon, and it seemed right that all other things should be muted like the light.

But suddenly she uttered a loud cry.

'My flower! I've lost my flower!'

'What flower?'

'The flower you gave me at dinner! I've let it fall.'

'But there are lots more in the house. I'll give you another – '

'That wouldn't be the same! I want this one! Oh, I had it this very minute!'

She hurried back to the place where they had been standing and knelt down on the ground and scrabbled among the fallen flowers, the other flowers that were not valuable. He stooped over her but did not help her in her search. Almost at once she looked up into his face and called out happily, 'Look, I've found it! I knew I had it when we were here!' She rose to her feet and he straightened himself to his little lesser height. She stood smiling at him and twirling the flower in her fingers, wondering why he did not say he was glad that she had found it. It was lovely that he was so small, it gave him the charm of a child as well as a man. Yet in a queer way it had been nice when she had been kneeling and he had been standing. She would have liked not to have got up but to kneel in front of him and take his hands and kiss them. Then perhaps he might have bent down and kissed her on the lips. It came to her like a thunderclap that there was nothing that a man can do to a woman in the way of love which she did not wish him to do to her. She was in love with Francis Pitt. Pleasure swept over her, pricking the palms of her hands; and she seemed to have been promised the kind of peace she had always longed for, an end to the fretfulness of using the will, passivity. She felt as if she had become as stable, as immovable as one of the chestnut trees. But this passivity would be more passionate than any activity, for like a tree she had a root, force was driving down through her body into the earth. It would work there in the darkness, it would tear violently up through the soil again and victoriously come into the light. She thought of that moment at her mother's funeral when the four dark figures stood beside the hole in the ground where there lay a black box holding the body which had caused them all. The ground, the ground, she had at last become part of the process that gets life out of the ground. She felt so grateful to him for somehow doing this for her that she could have licked his hands as the dogs had done.

It seemed to her inevitable that he should say something in his deep voice that would tell her what to do, that would bring her the beginning of her passivity. But he said nothing, standing turned

143

sideways to her, his head down, his hand covering his mouth, till he was caught away from her by another of those rushes of good spirits. All of a sudden he was striding along in front of her with his hands in his pockets and a lift in his tread, crying out in a ringing, hearty tone, not so deep as his ordinary voice but more ordinary and jolly, 'Well, we must go back to the house now! That nurse woman will have turned Essington out long ago! Poor Essington! Poor Essington!' He flung his head back and laughed loudly. Sunflower wondered what sort of a woman the nurse might be that he found the thought of an encounter between her and Essington so exquisitely amusing.

Following him was a pleasure, but she looked over her shoulder regretfully. 'What's that . . . that white thing we were walking towards?'

'A statue of love!' he called gaily and perfunctorily. 'I'll take you there some other time! You'll be coming here often, you know!' He was hurrying, he might have been an excited boy who had found something wonderful in the garden and wanted to show it to the people at home. When they came to the steps down through the shrubbery and she had to go slowly, because she did not know the way, he showed what would have been impatience had it not been so utterly unclouded by anything like ill temper.

'You do seem happy all of a sudden,' she said as they crossed the gravel square. She had to say something. She felt as if a great bird were beating its wings within her breast.

'I am happy. I am happy!' he answered gravely. 'How should I not be happy, when you have lifted a load off my mind? You have done that for me by what you said about Hurrell.' Whistling softly, he ran up the steps to the front door. He liked her, at least he liked her.

On the threshold he came to a halt and laughed aloud.

Over his shoulder she saw Essington sitting in the hall alone, stretched out very low in an armchair, his face nearly hidden.

Francis Pitt strolled across the room, rubbing his hands, and stood looking down on him with an indulgent air. 'So you've been turned out by that nurse woman.'

'Yes. Yes. With a great show of efficiency and womanly spirit. Odd that the profession of attending the sick is so often taken up by the female equivalent of the more powerful and relentless type of prize-fighter . . .' He did not show them his face, but he sounded very tired and querulous. 'Sunflower we must go home. I'm tired. And I have to do something tomorrow. I don't remember what it is. Don't you remember, Sunflower? I'm sure I told you.'

144

'Well, you can go home,' Francis Pitt told him good-humouredly. 'Your car's outside and your chauffeur's standing by it, admiring the stars.'

'Was he out there?' asked Sunflower. She had noticed nothing.

'We nearly fell over him,' said Francis Pitt. 'Have a drink before you go, Essington? Whisky? Or some brandy? The brandy's the best thing I've got.'

'No. No. Yes. I'd like some brandy. I feel cold.'

Francis Pitt went over to a tray on the table and poured out some brandy with steady easy movements. He was amazingly better than he had been when they had arrived; better even than he had been that first night at dinner at her house. He offered the glass to Sunflower.

'No, I don't touch it, ever,' she said. Because he gave her a straight, deep look, she became uncertain that she was so very beautiful after all.

'Yes, our Sunflower is very respectable. Sunflower has all the puritan prejudices of the lower middle classes,' grumbled Essington, putting out his hand for the glass. She thought he needn't have said it like that, particularly when they had had that talk about Billie Murphy before dinner. But when he was tired things seemed to slip his mind. 'And when one gets the dear thing to drink she likes her wine sweet.'

'God bless her, that's one of the ways one knows a good woman,' said Francis Pitt, pouring out soda-water for her and some brandy for himself. She settled down in an armchair, facing Essington across the hearth. Francis Pitt went and sat on the high padded kerb of the fender, his little legs drawn up under him, his feet hooked across the metal bars. Over the rim of his glass his narrowed gaze swung like a pendulum between the two. When he had finished drinking the corners of his mouth were turned up as if he had liked his brandy very much.

She wished that a magician would change her into a cat, so that she could come and live in this house without the question of love being raised; for of course nothing like that could ever happen, not the way they met. Though there wasn't any use worrying over that, for if they hadn't met this way they wouldn't have met at all. If she were a cat he would lift her off chairs, saying funny, rough, loving things to her as he did to the borzois, and would give her bits of food in his fingers. Thinking of magic made her remember the name of a clairvoyant in South Molton Street that one of the girls at the theatre had been talking about. She would like to see if she was any good. But that would be sly, for she would not be able to tell Essington. There wasn't anything he hated quite as much as clairvoyants and spiritualist mediums.

Abruptly Essington asked, 'When will he die?'

He was miserable, miserable. She must pull herself together and take notice of him.

'Six weeks,' answered Francis Pitt.

Oh, God, he was so miserable, she had done nothing for him, she could not do anything for him, she could not even touch him.

'Very good brandy,' said Essington cantankerously.

'Some more.'

'No. No. I haven't the capacity of your friend Canterton.'

'Canterton is not my friend,' said Francis Pitt. He spoke with a touch of stiffness. 'He was brought along tonight by Jack Murphy, to whom I am bound by various ties of my misspent youth. But he's no friend of mine, and I am sorry that you saw him here in that condition.'

'Oh, don't apologise for his condition. Indeed, I don't think, and I've watched our friend Canterton ever since he came to the House, that I've ever seen him to such advantage before. I've seen him unable to walk, prostrate on the woolsack; I've seen him leaning on a table to support himself through one of those speeches that consist of sham eighteenth-century epigrams delivered in a bar-parlour voice. But I have never seen him absolutely speechless before. No, I don't think I've ever before seen him to such an advantage.'

Francis Pitt was lifting his glass to his lips, but he lowered it. 'My God, Essington,' he said, 'I would not like to have you for an enemy.' He looked at the other man steadily for a minute, and then repeated, 'No, I would not like to have you as my enemy.' He lifted his glass and emptied it, then turned round and set it on the mantelpiece and stood looking down, as if he were considering something from a fresh point of view. She wondered what was troubling him now. It could plainly have nothing to do with the words he had repeated. As tired people do, he was simply taking a chance phrase he happened to find in his mouth and saying it over and over again, making it relevant by fitting it to the rhythm of his distress.

'Sunflower,' said Essington wearily, pulling himself out of the chair, 'I want to go home.'

Francis Pitt wheeled round, walked slowly across the room, pressed the bell, and stood dusting his fingertips against each other, as if he had finished a delicate job.

*

'Sunflower, little Sunflower, why are you crying?'

She would not say, she pressed her face against his shoulder so that it should not be found by the lances of light the street-lamps drove through the car window.

'Oh, little Sunflower, is it because you think I'm old like Hurrell and may die too? Oh, you silly little Sunflower, come close and be comforted!'

For a moment she stared into the darkness of his coat. But there was no way of being honest. She went on crying.

147

IV

IT was plain that he did not love her, for he never wanted to see her alone. She walked for a time in the desert of that thought; and then perceived that Harrowby was still standing at the door of the car, waiting for orders.

She began, 'Up to – ' and then checked herself. 'Harrowby, you don't look well.'

'I'm quite all right, Madam.'

'But you can't be all right. Not when you're looking like this. I've noticed for some time back you haven't been too bright. But I haven't seen you look like this, ever – '

'I suppose, Madam, it's up to Mr Pitt's as usual.'

'Yes, Harrowby. But if you would rather not drive today, I'll take a taxi and you can go home.'

He slammed the door. But it was not rudeness, just jumpy nerves, for he opened it and shut it all over again, very softly this time, and his eyes travelled towards her face, though they got no further than her throat, and his mouth worked as if he were trying to smile. Poor thing, he did look so white. He looked almost as bad as he had after that motor accident they had last year on the road from Cannes to Grasse, when she had opened her eyes and found herself lying on a bank by the roadside with him kneeling beside her . . .

148

Her mind turned its back on his misery and forgot it. Keeping her eyes on the dove-coloured carpet of the car so that nothing should break the thread of the fairy-tale, she thought of what it would be like to stay at Cannes with Francis Pitt. It had never been quite right with Essington, for he did so hate places where people enjoyed themselves; he himself went just because of the climate. It would be nicer to go with Francis Pitt. It would be nice to have tea at the casino about four o'clock, sort of listening, but not too hard, because it did not matter and the air was a little too warm, to somebody quite good singing; and after an hour or so go out and stand for a while looking across the wide bay as the sun set behind the mountains of Cap Estérel. The little harbour by the town was always so pretty then, with the old fortresses lying up on the hill, looking as if life really was like a bad play, the kind of play Lewis Waller used to act in, which, say what you like, would be nice; and the avenue of plane trees by the sea looked lovely, for their dark trunks and branches were dissolved by the dusk and the last few leaves which had survived from the autumn into the winter seemed to hang unsupported, a suspended shower of golden rain. Along the road behind them flashed the automobiles, the great luxurious Riviera automobiles, with their air of being, as one would have thought it impossible for machines, no better than they ought to be; their air of wearing jewelled garters on their axles; stopping outside the little but inordinate Riviera shops, cubby-holes of yellow light, where people who were laying up money for their children sold pretty things who had not that idea in air warmed to stew away what might remain of thrifty resistance, and wrote in ledgers with an expression of petty victory after the bell on the closing door had given that glutted, muted note, which was so different from the ping with which it let in the customers. Funny, silly, trivial, amusing place. But on all that they would turn their backs and they would walk, her hand on his coat-sleeve, along the quay where the millionaires' yachts are moored, their rigging like nerves against the red and gold, the fine intricate nerves of some fleet, capricious, veering beast. They would walk right to the end of the quay, she and Francis Pitt, and would stand looking at the lovely sunset, which now would be covering the sky with all the colours one could not wear because one was fair; which was a pity, still if one ever had a daughter who was dark one could dress her in them. With the flames behind them the Estérel mountains would be like shapes cut wildly out of black paper. It was funny how you could not do even a simple thing like looking at the sunset if you were with Essington. He would slew one round till one looked to the south-east, towards the dull, flat islands instead of the mountains, over grey waters untouched by the sun. Beauty seemed to irritate his mind as an unshaded lamp irritates the eye, it was too much for his poor nerves, he put up his cantankerousness as a shield against it as he would have put up his hand against the light. When she said how she liked the romantic fortresses he looked up at them, made one of his disparaging, mewing noises, and rather spitefully, like a man alluding to the advancing age of a woman, pointed out how trifling a piece of modern artillery would be needed to blow them to pieces. And the shops and the automobiles and the cake-like casino made him gird at the injustice of the social system; though she knew it was really their pettiness he disliked, for he always kept quite calm when they were motoring out of London through the nasty little brown brick houses and the stores where poor people are sold rubbish, and those were surely far horrider results of the social system than Cannes. But with Francis Pitt one would not get the beginning of any such wranglings with life, because one would do nothing, absolutely nothing, not even anything mental, not because one was lazy, but because if one was with him one would be doing something that absolved one from the duty of doing anything else . . . something interior and secret that would give one the right to be purely passive. It was true that he did not give her that feeling now when they saw each other, but she felt that at any moment their relationship might take a different turn of some sort and she would get it. It was as if she were holding a berry in her mouth and waiting for a signal to crush it between her tongue and teeth and flood her palate with the flavour that she wanted. Well, to go on to Cannes, maybe she would dance a little with him after dinner, for he loved to dance, though he was terribly bad at it. Foxtrotting with him was like being adrift on a choppy sea not in but with a small boat. But his clumsiness was not annoying, it made one smile and think of the squarish stumbling limbs of a child just learning to walk. That would be the only time she would be active in the whole day. Probably the best hours of all would be those spent furthest away from activity, in utter lethargy, in the warm nearest that waking can come to sleeping. Her teeth denting her lower lip, she imagined herself lying quietly on her bed in a darkened room, her arms close to her breast, her hands folded against her cheek, so that they felt companionable, as if they might have been someone's face, a child's

150

face, her lids just raised so that she could look at the bright oblong between the half-closed shutters and see Francis Pitt standing on the balcony outside. He would have his back to her, he would be leaning over the rail looking down into the well of warm afternoon beneath, up which were coming the broken voices of people who were walking about, playing tennis, doing all the things she was not doing any longer. She did not want him to turn round and speak to her, for by that time everything would have been said, they could take each other for granted. Simply she would lie and notice how, standing black against the sunshine, he looked taller and broader than he really was; and would try to accept the illusion, to see that picture with uncorrected vision, because he did so hate being small. It occurred to her that perhaps that was why men shut up women in harems in all hot countries, so that the women should sit in the shadow and see the men silhouetted against the glaring light, bigger and stronger than they really are. She laughed, but not at him; at them all. He was not nearly so bad as lots of them.

The car stopped with a lurch and a grinding of the brakes. Harrowby had nearly driven past the signals of a policeman on duty and was now having an argument with a red face under a helmet and a couple of swinging white gloves. The face got redder, evidently Harrowby was being very rude. This was the second time that week there had been this sort of trouble, for just a day or two before when she was on the way up to lunch with Francis Pitt there had been the same sort of unpleasantness at one of the crossings on Finchley Road. He never used to do these things. Something very disagreeable must be happening to him. At this reminder that the characteristic quality of life was always to be a little upsetting she realised that she would never go to Cannes with Francis Pitt, because he did not love her. He could not love her, since he never wanted to see her alone.

Again she looked down so that nothing should break the threads of the story, and thought of what she had got out of life in spite of its determination not to go quite smoothly. She had seen more of him than she had ever hoped. It had been wonderful. While the play was rehearsing Essington and she, and sometimes she alone, had gone up there nearly every other night for dinner; but she could not do that now, and would not be able to till goodness knows when, for the play, bother it all, was a great success. Essington seemed to like going to the Pitts', which had surprised her. He did not even complain of the length of the drive across London, though ordinarily he hated going further for his dinner than a ten minutes' journey. The truth was that he was really very deeply moved by what was happening to Hurrell. Every time he made the visit Hurrell's room was more exactly what his terror of the disagreeable most resented: his old friend's body under the sheets had less of human roundness and more the rectilinear shape of a narrow box, and the face on the pillow, which had been familiar to him all his life, which it was urgent that he should continue to recognise, for if it became different anything and everything might become different and he would not know where he was, had in fact become terrifyingly different, because it was patterned as definitely as a moth-wing with the shadows of monstrous pits of emaciation in the cheeks, at the temples, around the eyes; and there were horrible times when the sick man made a strangled noise and they had to leave him quickly because of some breakdown in physical dignity; and there were worse times still when he suddenly fell asleep, falling like a man who has been clinging to a ledge over a precipice and whose fingers have let go, and they could not leave him till they had gathered round the bed to make sure that he had not fallen further than sleep. One would have sworn that all this could not have been tolerated by Essington, who took it as a breach of loyalty, a betrayal of the citadel to the forces of unpleasantness, if anybody belonging to him was so ill that they had to call in a doctor. But miraculously he was kind, he was bravely, wittily kind, he made constant visits to the dying man that were increasingly beautifully unconcerned, brilliantly trivial. It was amazing to see him padding the room with his cat-like grace, spinning round on the balls of his feet, while with delicate buffoonery he made a monstrous fuss about a cold he alleged he had caught, though there was no visible sign of it, or purred awful things about Oppenshaw and Bryce Atkin and, in short, behaved so exactly as one would not behave in a death chamber that Hurrell ceased to say as he did every few minutes if she and Francis Pitt were left alone with him, 'Of course I know well I am not really ill. I shall be about in no time.'

All this had made her very proud of Essington. It seemed to her that the shock of finding his old friend about to die had burst the dam he had built against the springs of tenderness in his own heart, and that at last he was going to admit that he was really quite nice about all sorts of things. And she had taken it as confirmation of this, though on thinking it over she supposed there was indeed no logical reason why she should have done so, when he came home one evening with a diamond and emerald bracelet from Cartier's as a present for her. It was the first time he had given her any jewellery; indeed, it was one of the very few times he had ever given her anything. And it was a beautiful one, that crackled with light on one's arm, and had a pattern of emerald scattered like leaves among the frosty brightness of the diamonds, so that it was as if spring was diving headfirst through a winter sky; and he must have gone to the shop specially, and spent some time choosing things, and paid out quite a lot of money all at once. It was all right really, he did love her, he was very generous at heart. She cried a little and kissed him, and he seemed glad in a curiously anxious, humble way, that she liked his gift. Then she suddenly exclaimed, because she had caught sight of the clock and perceived that if they stood about looking at the bracelet any longer they would be late for dinner with Francis Pitt, and hurried him out to the car. Once they had started she realised that she had put out the glow there had been between them. But that could not be helped, they would be five minutes late as it was, and as Francis Pitt ate hardly any lunch he ought to get his dinner punctually. Anyway it had been established that her Essington was kind and dear, and that he was going to admit it more than he had ever done before, so she began talking of what she planned to do for Parkyns who that morning had been told by the doctor that she had phthisis. It was not that she was giving him gloomy details, or that she wanted him to help her, for she could easily do it all out of her money. What she did want were suggestions as to how she could do for Parkyns what he was doing for Hurrell, make the heavy thing light.

But almost at once he began to click his tongue impatiently, to twitch his long fine hands; and she had to stop, in case he should say the thing, so clever that it must be true, which would worry her when she woke up at night and make what she was doing for Parkyns seem silly. It was evident that he was not going to be any kinder than he had been before. In spite of Hurrell there was no real change in him. She saw what he had done. It was his cleverness again. Life had forced him into a position when he had to feel pity, but he had got round it by putting a peculiar male twist on the situation, by deciding to specialise on Hurrell as the dying man, the only dying man, his dying man, on whom he should lavish so much tenderness that he would earn absolution from being kind to anybody else, as one who has served on a jury in a lengthy case gets exempted from such service for seven years. It was the same sort of prudent investment he had made in his wife, Mabel, whom he had selected as the woman he was good

153

to. He had given her everything material she could want, that fine quiet house in the country which he visited politely and did not rush into to upset, and a great deal of money for her famous simple clothes and her collection of snuff-boxes and miniatures; he wrote to her every other day when he was away, not scratching letters saying that he had been thinking over her last performance (for one thing, the lucky woman did not have to give any) and it was so stupid that he would have to leave her, but friendly letters suggesting ways by which she might get her gentle pleasures out of life; then, since he could not enjoy being the lover of a woman to whom he was kind, he turned to his mistress and could enjoy illimitably his relationship with her because he could make her life a misery, and always argue that that must be her fault, since he was a kind man to women, and could prove it by his relations with his wife. He was utterly inhuman. He was a monster. Her face flamed. But he did not mean it, he had been betrayed by his false religion of thought. It was his faith that nothing could be evil save the passionate instinctive gesture: thought was the means by which mankind was saved from its vile propensity to instinct. Because the means he took to batten his egotism on life was cool and intellectual he felt they must be saved and should be pushed to the extremest lengths. It was as if a masseur became infatuated with the mere idea of kneading flesh so that he pounded and pounded the body of his patient into lifeless pulp. Finding herself forced again to a point at which she felt horror for him she looked down at her bracelet. He had given her that, he loved her, he was generous. She took it off her arm and clasped it tightly between her fingers, as one clasps an amulet, as one clasps an amulet in which one does not quite believe, in which it is absolutely necessary that one should believe.

It had been good to get out of the car and go into Francis Pitt's house. That evening he was sitting in the hall waiting for them. Darkness was thick among the curious ugly furniture which had the look of defiant artists' squalor that tombstones and pews have, as if the clumsy craftsmen who made them knew that the human occasions they catered for befell so inevitably and so innumerably that they need never fear unemployment and could let their blunt fingers make mean-ness with impunity. She did not have to see them unless she tried, she did not have to ask herself the question of why he chose to live among such ugliness. If she kept her eyes wide, in the way that makes them look most beautiful when one goes into a room, all she need see were the flowers, the excess of flowers that was the trademark of this house, clots of delphinium and peonies, seeming suspended in the darkness, since the vases which supported them and the tables which supported the vases were drowned in the rising night, and his face, his earthy, bedabbled face of grief, all of him that was visible above the black blur of his clothes. It was as if this was a place where one could have the things that mattered, beauty and that other thing, the thing that was behind great plays and acting (real acting, the sort she could not do) without having to pay all one's attention to the creaking mechanism of intellect that did not even make them, that merely hoisted them up to a position where they could be viewed by the human mind. When she thought that she had a feeling as if she had plucked a cloth from a globe and found it gleaming crystal. She saw the way life should go, and turned sullen eyes on Essington because it was not his way, but slipped from whatever it was she had been thinking, and she was not quite sure what that was, into joy based on the fact that Francis Pitt was not dressed for dinner. That meant that she and Essington would be the only guests. It was true that there was a sleek-headed young man sitting beside him, but he would not be staying, he was taking something down in a little book, he was a secretary from the office in the City which Francis Pitt kept just to collect the current earnings of the fortune he had so miraculously made before he was thirty, which he had so obstinately and with such distinction refrained from increasing since he had returned to England and fallen in love with politics. She was very glad, for it was never so nice when there were other people. For one thing, Francis Pitt, oddly enough, considering that above all things he wanted to be liked, was a very bad host. When there were more than half-a-dozen people meaning seemed to fade out of him; his brows came down so that one could not see his eyes, his mouth pouted round a big cigar so that it became merely thick lips, he sat on at table long after everybody else wanted to get up and there was no conceivable reason why he should linger. It appeared to her part of his unique perfection that he should be a bad host. Obviously it proceeded from his childlikeness. Just as he could not put the ugly furniture out of his house and get in new because he felt that that was a thing for grown-ups to do and he was never quite sure that he had really grown up, so he could not entertain guests because he felt that his father and his mother ought to be doing it instead. It made her want to touch him, to stroke him.

Those were still the days when he used to look at her at the first moments of their meeting, with a hard, grinding look as if he were

155

rubbing some thought they both knew of against her consciousness. Then, as on every other night, as soon as his hand unclasped she would sit down in the chair which he seemed to want her to sit in, and the two men would exchange the duetting remarks about the day's news which are not intended to be penetrative, which are merely the equivalent of the sniffing and snapping that goes on between dogs at a street corner, a ritual performed to soften strangeness. Francis Pitt would sit with his knees crossed, one foot swinging rhythmically and his heavy-lidded glance sliding nearer and nearer to her face, till they looked into each other's eyes and his hand would flash up and cover his face. She too would have to cover her face, for always during this time of waiting two things would come into her mind which made her features not know what to do. There had been one night, a week or two after they first got to know each other, when he had brought her home from dinner because Essington had been telephoned for to go to his country place at once, as there was a Liberal Association market day breakfast he had forgotten all about, and goodness knows there were so few Liberals one ought not to discourage them, and it must be so awful for them in the early morning, so he had gone off in her car, and Francis Pitt had taken her back in his a little later. It was the first time they had been alone since that night when he took her to the paved garden and the chestnut alley, and she had felt shy, largely because he seemed to be worried about something. The light from the street-lamps showed his right hand clenched on his crossed knees. But he began to talk about adventures he had had in California when he first went out there as a boy, and that seemed to interest him. When the car stopped and they went up the steps to her house he was right in the middle of a story which he evidently liked telling about how he had gone to a succession of people and said, 'Now we'll talk turkey!' a form of address which was apparently very compelling and ultimately remunerative, so she did not ask him to turn on the switch by the door but stood with her latchkey in her hand. She did not listen to what he was saying, for he was not telling the story at all well, he was being too consciously shrewd and whimsical, he was like a bad actor who has read with his mind's eye a notice, 'Mr X gave a performance full of quaint and kindly humour', and quirks his head and makes crinkles round his eyes and mouth. But after all there was no reason why Francis Pitt should be absolutely perfect. She swayed in a drowse of happiness, noticing wonderful lovely things about the moment. The steps on which they stood were painted with that lovely pattern which

London's pavements wear by night. The purplish vignettes, which surely could have nothing to do with London leaves, must be the shadows of grapes growing in some magic world co-existent with the ordinary framework of earth, the same world whose invisible caverns echoed the barking of his borzois when they ran round his table. She put out her foot and trod the shadowed ghostly grapes into the stone, smiling to think of the unseeable wine that would be pressed from them, smiling to imagine a world full of magic, in which one would probably always be having abrupt alterations to something lovelier. She stared at her front door, which by day was sealing-wax red but was now a neutral tint that looked as if twilight were trying to remember colour, and pretended that the house behind it had suddenly been changed. The staircase would be on the right instead of on the left, and the carpet would be beige instead of black, and the dining room would be at the back instead of at the front, and she would not mind if all the furniture were eighteenth-century instead of Chinese; she had always disliked that style because it was fussy and feminine, but why shouldn't one be that sometimes? And nothing that had really happened to her in that house would have happened, and it would have been Francis Pitt who lived there, and he would have lived there all the time, and not just rushed backwards and forwards. She thought what it would be like to come in and know that he was in the little library and not go in because he had been there millions of times before and would be millions of times again, so one would not bother, though probably one would. Now he had come to the end of the story about talking turkey and was chuckling reminiscently, so she laughed and said, 'Oh, how delicious!' and saw the light shining on his funny fingernails that were so wranglingly bitten and so glassily manicured. He was holding out his hand for her key. She wanted to touch his hand. What she had been doing was silly, she was dreaming about things which could not happen, she wanted to touch his hand at once. So she pretended that she thought he just wanted to say goodbye, and she slipped her fingers into his palm as if she were going to shake hands. At the contact she felt a thrust of emotion so strong that it seemed to have mass and colour and to be outside her, a white arch binding horizons. It was something real, it was something invisible, it was a part of that same magic world of the grapes and the caverns: it was there all the time whether one happened to be feeling it or not, it could only be apprehended directly through the touch of his flesh, just as one knew of the grapes only by their shadows on the stone and of

157

the caverns only by the harmony between their rounded vaults and the rounded voices of the hounds. She saw a vision of intersecting planes of life: but was immediately distracted from it by her sense, which she knew to be not less important, of the amazing warmth of his hand. Though the night of a cool summer was about them his flesh was glowing as if they stood in sunshine. It seemed as if he were drawing heat from some external and invisible source, a great fire burning perpetually in a clearing deep in a forest, somewhere in that same magic world of the grapes and the caverns and the white arch, a fire higher than the height of a man, higher than the height of the men who danced around it. She saw again the picture which she always used to see when she first knew him, of the lake among the woods where he drove a canoe with food in it across the waters and she waited with the children on the shore. A wave of loyalty and tenderness swept over her, but while she was still in its depths she realised that she had not quite brought off her gesture. His fingers had been contracted to grasp the key, so that if she had honestly thought he wanted to shake hands she would have known she was mistaken as soon as she touched him, and she had to exert a little pressure to get the movement through, a very little, but just enough to make it unnatural. These things had not escaped him. He lifted his shoulders but otherwise stood quite still, as if he had been flicked with a whip he was reluctant to obey; and he gave a deep, nervous chuckle, saying, with an evasive, an almost cunning quality in his voice, 'Oh . . . I'm not saying goodbye yet, it was your key I wanted.' She was ashamed. She did not turn on the switch by the door, but let him fumble for the key-hole in the darkness. It was awful, too, that he did not ask her to turn it on, for she remembered that he himself had found it for Essington a few nights before. And it was awful, too, having to go through the formality of asking him in to have a drink and standing there while he said he had to go back to Hurrell. But it was all nonsense, there was no reason why her face should sting with shame, even though he had seen through it all; a woman does not do a man any harm by being in love with him. She was not going to lay any obligation on him, for obviously nothing could come of it, she was with Essington.

Surely he loved her too. Why did he want her to be with him, to be there in his house, every possible moment she could spare, if he did not love her? Why did he look at her like that, his eyes saying sullenly that at least he could look at her, there was no harm in looking, if he did not love her? What could it be that he longed to say to her and could not, so that whenever they were together silence fell on them that hummed and buzzed and sang in the ears because of the strength of his unspoken words, save that he loved her? There are only four ways a man can feel about a woman, aren't there? There is hate, and he did not hate her. There is indifference, and he was not indifferent. She had seen the hair on the back of his hands stand up because the sense of her coming across the room was like a wind blowing. That is not liking either. There was nothing left but love that he could be feeling for her. And surely that was the meaning of what happened that other night a little later, when she had gone up without Essington to dine with Francis and Etta, and had found that the fourth, for of course there was a fourth, was that queer Georgy Allardyce, the playwright. They had great fun, for Miss Allardyce was good company. She was not pretty, not at all, for she was one of those red-haired women whose appearance seems to have taken a Puritan offence at the flagrant beauty on her head. Her greyish-white face, with its pale, narrow eyes and thin, bitten lips, might have cried out for protection against the wild force that had her by the hair, as Daphne did when Apollo seized her and was changed into laurel, and been granted it in an ungracious form, for her body seemed to have been turned into wood. It was angular without being slim and had the coarseness of bad carpentry about the joints. It must be dreadful to be like that. But she had a very good shingle, and was beautifully and carefully dressed in a traily Vionnet dress, which surprised Sunflower because she had always heard that Miss Allardyce was dowdy and untidy. She had expressed this surprise afterwards to Francis Pitt, who had given one of his chuckles and said, 'Yes, Georgy's taken to dressing very well lately.' She supposed he was amused to see that even professionally strong-minded women take to pretty clothes as soon as they make a little money. Anyway, it did not matter what Miss Allardyce looked like, she talked so wonderfully. She had a funny husky voice with a crack in it, which made you feel that you were alternately eating crushed honeycomb and drinking something with ice in it, and she said the most unexpected things all the time which doubled you up, they were so amusing. Her talk was rather like Essington's, only it was more just about people. She nearly made them die telling about a weekend she had spent in a Scottish castle sitting over the fire between two septuagenarian beauties who croaked the most awful scandal about each other because they were both stone-deaf and knew

159

the other couldn't hear. She would have been quite a good actress, only of course it could not have been done with her looks. It was the greatest pity the evening had to break up quite early because she and Sunflower had to go, as a matter of business, to the party that the actor-manager, Sir Aubrey Balmcourt, was giving on the stage of the Olympic to celebrate the three hundredth night of his play; but, as Miss Allardyce said, it was so good of Sir Aubrey to have spared so many nights from his social duties that he ought to be encouraged. When they came to go something happened that made her like Miss Allardyce a lot. Miss Pitt had asked a question about this party which had been faintly tinged with wistfulness, and Miss Allardyce had pounced on it. 'Haven't you ever been to a stage party? And you want to? Then come along with us! We'd love to take you! Go up and put on your cloak!' She forgot to say anything clever, she forgot to give her lips that slight twist which seemed to process the phrase that was coming between them, to change it from statement into wit. There came into her voice an exultant generosity, as if she were sitting in the sunshine with her lap full of lovely things and tossing them to everyone within reach. It was plain that something good had happened to her, probably she had just placed a new play very well and she wanted everybody to feel as jolly as she did, and she loved being able to do it so easily as just by taking Etta Pitt to a party. That was a nice human emotion for anybody so clever to feel. They all settled down in the automobile, feeling very cosy and happy with each other, Etta quite flushed over her new social adventure, when the queer thing happened. Francis Pitt was standing on the steps looking very impish and vagabondish, not as if he possessed the great house behind him but as if he had only temporarily got into it by a series of comical rogueries. Even his dinner clothes had an air as if he had but recently removed them from a wardrobe while the real owner lay snoring a few yards away. He stood smiling his broad gnomish smile on them, and suddenly, as the starter began to jiggle, he ran down the last three steps and called out, 'Goodbye . . . dear . . .' and broke into nervous laughter. Ostensibly he had said it to Etta. But it was not for Etta he had meant it . . . you could tell.

Those were the two things that used to come into her mind to vex her, to soothe her, to leave her in such a state of suspense that she felt faint, as she sat with the two men. They always had to wait a little because poor overworked Etta was late, and the conversation would run dry. She would stir and look down at the floor, feeling that Francis

Pitt was in the same state that she was, that he would like to shy and bolt like a frightened horse; and presently he would invent some curiosity that could only be satisfied by leaving the room, he would want to know whether it was going to rain and would go out to look at the barometer in the hall, he would become doubtful whether the butler understood about the port he wanted opened and would stray off in search of him. And Essington would say, 'The poor little man looks bad tonight. He takes this Hurrell business too seriously.' Yes, that was what was the matter with Francis Pitt. His best friend was dying, of course he was upset. Things were better when they went into dinner. The tired men began to eat and drink and say more individual things and enjoy them. But there was a little time before the women would be quite sure that what they could say would be well received, so she and Etta would sit silent while the man-talk went on over their heads, hard, metallically glittering, fire-spun, incomprehensible, like the sort of things, the tangle of wire and girders one sees, if one lifts one's eyes as one passes a great office building when it is being put up. Essington moved among the affairs of the world in his characteristic way, like an artist moving among the easels of his pupils at an art school, rubbing out faulty strokes in their drawings and sketching in the perfect line with a fretful gesture that would be intolerable if it were not that he really was a great artist, that the drawings really were botched, that better than anybody he knew how to correct them; and Francis Pitt trotted after him, using his little paw-fists without fretfulness but with mischief to smear any drawing that was being too beautiful, too highfalutin', that was not subjecting itself to the censorship of commonsense. Always, every evening, however much below their own form they might be, she recognised in them the quality that great actors have. Only sometimes it occurred to her queer that the end to which they were bending their greatness was the rebuilding of the Liberal Party. Thinking of the running backward and forward of weak people that had been the political spectacle just before the war, as she remembered very vividly because she was just starting with Essington then and was trying hard to understand what he was doing in case he got tired of her because she was stupid, she saw no hope that if they did get the thing going again it would give them any opportunity to be nearly as wonderful as they could be. Instead they ought to . . .

They ought to what? There was nothing else for them to do. It was worthwhile following an art or a science, but one could only do that if one was definitely the sort of person that gets ordered about, a subordinate, a private soldier, and these two were officers. They could not be led by something vague outside themselves, as artists and scientists have to be, they had to lead; and as nobody knew where humanity ought to be helped there was bound to be a lot of futility about the business of leading them. Human beings were like the lovely old wineglasses on the table, that were of crystal, that had the form and substance of falling water held for ever to its momentary beauty within them, that were painted with gold patterns as beautiful as the markings of flower petals, that would not change with time, but that would hold nothing but wine, which is not so nice after all. Babies are born, they grow up into these wonderful things with these bodies that may be ugly but affect one as if they were beautiful and these great brains, and they can cancel out death by giving one children so that the race goes on; but, gorgeous and deathless as they are, life fills them up with an activity that is not good enough, with politics, with wars that end in neither victory nor defeat, with things that, say what you like, don't really please anybody. What men make is not so good as the making of men. Having a baby and bringing it up has more of the quality that belongs to a good gesture, to the fine performance of a part, than all this niggling. She felt a flush of pride because she was doing what Essington always said all women in general and she in particular never did: thinking about principles; and then with dismay she realised, as she nearly always had to do when she felt proud for that reason, that it wasn't any use her having done what Essington wanted her to do, since it had led her to conclusions that he would not approve.

From thoughts such as these she was always called by her need, which was as insistent as a drugtaker's desire for his dose, to look at Francis Pitt; and every time she looked at him his eyes had just slid away from her face. Surely he was always thinking of her just as she was always thinking of him. Every now and then he would say something that showed he had been furtively watching her all that evening and all the other evenings. 'Miss Fassendyll doesn't like endive salad. Take it away. Remember she likes lettuce.' Sometimes it made her quite sure that he loved her. Sometimes she thought she was under the spell or a delusion, for it seemed to her that Essington also was furtively watching her; and even Etta too. But that was understandable, for when Etta looked at her she also looked sorry for her. Sunflower knew that she was thinking of how dreadfully Essington had behaved at that first dinner, and she was probably imagining that he was like that all the time whereas he had been so much, much better lately. She used to smile at Etta reassuringly. But fortunately at that stage in the dinner there would come suddenly a burst of that good fellowship which was drawing them together night after night to the exclusion of all other friends. As if a whip had been cracked as a signal the two men became extravagantly genial, they brought the women into the conversation, they teased them, they made a fuss of them. Francis Pitt told stories that illustrated Etta's Marthadom, Essington demonstrated, but was nice about Sunflower's stupidity. 'It isn't that the dear creature's stupid, she's guileless. She can't believe that anybody can say anything that they don't mean. It's astonishing how that incapacity eats through modern life . . .'

But it had all been different, it had not been so breathless, so torturing, since the night which was the last they had spent together. After dinner Etta had gone to telephone the nurse's ten o'clock report to the doctor, and the rest of them had gone up as they always did to try to help Hurrell through the period before midnight, which was the worst time in the twenty-four hours for him, because he woke from the doze of exhaustion which followed the effort of eating his supper and lay tossing and sweating in a state that was as different as sleep from ordinary wakefulness, that was as if bright lights had been turned on inside his brain. Essington was sitting by his bed, twirling his moustache in his fussy way, and purring scandalous insinuations against all the more respectable members of the Liberal Party when the smile died on Hurrell's face, which was now so terribly thin that it was just a cage for his spirit, and there was a queer rattling noise as if his spirit had run in terror to the bars of its cage and was shaking them. Francis Pitt, who had been sitting hunched on the other side of the bed, sprang up with an air of coming into his own, saying, 'Go out, go out.' Sunflower ran out on to the landing and called over the banisters, 'Nurse! Nurse!' and Essington came and stood beside her, breathing quickly. The nurse ran upstairs with a flouncing of starched petticoats and asked an unnecessary question without waiting for an answer. Essington muttered squeamishly, 'The human machine, the human machine,' and covered his mouth with his hand. She murmured, 'Go downstairs and get some brandy for yourself, dear,' keeping her eyes on the door. Presently it opened and Francis Pitt came out. He remembered to shut it very gently, and then leaned heavily against the latch. She went to him and put out her arms for him to take, and said, 'Come away with me.' Without speaking he lifted his head so that she could

163

see what had happened. His shirt-front was soaked with the sick man's blood. His great mouth was working with disgust, but his loyalty to his friend was making him choke back all sound. She felt angry with Hurrell. She said, 'Which is your bedroom?' She hated not knowing. He wagged his head towards one of the mahogany doors, and she led him to it. There was blood on his hands too, so she had to open the door. It was a very ugly room with nothing personal about it; poor dear, he had not been able to furnish even his own room. Without turning on the light in case he wanted to cry she took him to the bed and said, 'Lie down, lie down.' Afterwards she was quite sure she had not called him dear. He obeyed and lay down across the bed. He was so little that he did not reach all the way across it. She went to the dressing-table and found a pair of scissors, calling comforting things to him softly over her shoulder. He whimpered just so that she could hear it, as if to ask her to go on, as if to tell her there was need of it. Then she went back and cut the starched front of his shirt away from the soft linen body. All the while he was shuddering with disgust and making these little whimpering sounds. It struck her as queer that he should love his friend and yet get into such a state over contact with his blood, particularly as it wasn't really very bad, for the blood had not soaked through the starched shirt-front, it had not stained his vest, much less touched his skin. It did seem odd that unless men were trained to it as doctors, they cannot do what almost any woman can, and perform a kind of alchemy in their minds which takes the horror away from any substance provided that it belongs to somebody one is looking after, so that when one is minding a baby or a sick person one never thinks of that sort of thing. He loved Hurrell, but he simply could not do that for him. As her hands worked over him, slipping down between his flesh and his collar so that she could pull out the stud and free the shirt-front, she realised that there were many things which, like this, he simply could not do. Even should it happen that he loved her, if they went on a journey together and met with hardship he would not be able to go on being sweet to her; if she made herself ridiculous in front of other people he would not be able to be loyal; if he had to choose between hurting her or himself he would not be able to choose to hurt himself. But all that was not really of the slightest importance. She had strength enough for both of them. Seeing that he was straining to lift his head and brace himself, she murmured, 'Don't try, faint if you want to, it won't do you any harm,

164

it's trying not to that makes you feel so bad, just shut your eyes and let go. Pretend you're asleep . . .' His body loosened, he lay quite still. She had to slip her hand under his neck to take out his back collar-stud, and his big head wobbled. It was funny having him this way. It was like undressing a drowsy baby; one felt that the next thing to be done was to pick him up and carry him with his little tummy against one's shoulder and his big mouth uttering woeful sleepy cries into a steaming bathroom full of warm fleecy towels. She had cut away all the bloodstained linen by now, but she continued to stand and look down on him, for she knew she would never have him this way again. It was safe for her to do that, since his eyes were shut. She bent quite low over him, trying to note all the dear oddness of his appearance through the darkness that the wedge of light from the open door just raised to twilight. Then she saw that his eyes were not shut. He was lying there looking up at her. For a long time they stayed so. Then Essington's voice spoke meekly from the door. 'Can't I do anything?' She turned and saw him standing on the threshold, the light striking on his bowed head, and his long, fine, wrinkled hand, which he was resting on the door-post, very high, above his head, as if that helped him to pull up his bowed shoulders. She answered, 'I know, I know, I shall be out in a minute.' Francis Pitt rolled over on his side and lay with his cheek on his folded hands. Now his eyes were shut. She lifted his dressing-gown from the chair where it had been left ready for the night and laid it over him, whispering, 'We'll go. You needn't come downstairs again. I hope everything'll be all right.' He did not seem to hear. A long deep breath shook him. She took the bloodstained linen in her hand, in case the sight of it should upset him when he rose and turned on the light, and went out on to the landing to Essington. He was leaning on the banisters. Looking down into the hall, he said, 'Stay with him if there's anything you can do.' She answered, 'No, I want to go home.' He turned and ran very quickly down the stairs, saying, 'I hope Harrowby is ready, I hope the car is there . . .'

She did not know what had happened then; only that something had happened. When one is falling from a great height one knows nothing except that one is falling. But after that she had never worried so much about how things were between them. Why should he have lain like that, little and not moving, unless he felt happy at being looked after by her? And what could one want more than that? Anyway it was lovely to remember, particularly that little time when he had just lain still and looked up at her, and perhaps it was as well that she had never been back to the house by night, because now she never thought of it with darkness among its heavy hangings and in its raw-toned rooms without feeling again that atmosphere which had throbbed with grief, and tenderness, and gratitude. But of course when her play had first started she had not felt that way, she had missed going up to dine with him quite dreadfully. That first night she had sat in her dressing-gown in front of her mirror, pinning her orchid to her shoulder-strap, because that was the sort of thing nobody could do for you, not properly, and thinking, 'If I did not have to act, I would be driving up to his house now, the car would be going through that funny garden, I should be going to see him in a few minutes, if I did not have to act.' And as she stared into the glass she suddenly perceived that there was looking back at her a face haggard with hunger. Two great lines were stamped upright between her eyebrows, her lips were thin and drawn backwards. In fear she exclaimed to herself, 'What, do I care as much as all that?' It could not be wise to care as much as all that. There stirred in her mind a recollection of how one day when she was so small that she still played on the floor a woman carrying in her arms a new loaf which smelt nice had come and stood for ever so long with Mother at the front door, while they talked in low voices of someone who was in a bad way, a very bad way, because a soldier had left her. She trembled with fear, she opened her powder box and shut it again, and pulled the lid off a jar of cold cream without looking what she was doing, as if her flesh, more foolish than her eyes, hoped there was something really useful kept in these little china things, something magic that one could eat and be happy. She was even glad when the call-boy came and she had to go on the stage and play that silly part.

It was queer that people liked her better in this than in anything else she had ever done, because she had never hated acting so violently before nor gone through a performance so blindly. She could not keep her mind on what she was saying, she walked about the stage in a fluid, desperate state, never holding a pose because she had no clear sense of what pose she was taking nor confidence that any of them were relevant, speaking and moving with a special intensity because of her need to work off the restlessness that nowadays was always tormenting her like prickly heat felt inside instead of outside the skin. But it was true that though you would have thought that going on like this you wouldn't get anywhere, she found herself establishing a relationship with her audience which had more life in it than anything she'd ever got before. When she cried out those lines in the third act, her mind blank of all sense of what they meant and dizzy with the effort to keep from abandoning itself to thoughts of Francis Pitt, she felt an extraordinary effect of strong impact with the audience. It was as if she had become hysterical and done something violent and satisfying with her hand and then heard the smash of breaking china. What she was doing could not be quite right, for though this was just the same passionate effect that great actors got they knew what they were doing as they did it, and achieved a serenity contemporaneous and co-equal with their passion. But at any rate she had broken out of her old stupidity. She was not being bad any more in the way that Essington had always laughed at. She was not imagining this, other people felt it just as well. The papers said quite a lot about reversing their opinion. There had been several marvellous notices, some of them so good in this new allusive way that you had to go and look things up in the encyclopaedia. One young man who, she learned on enquiry, had been considered very clever at Oxford, wrote in one of the evening papers: 'In her difficult moments we hail the great, glowing, grape-golden compeer of El Greco and Scriabin, with this and that of the simple magic of Michelangelo and Bach, when she has but to sweep loveliness from the ambient air with common motions of her fingertips and the flatter remarks of the not ever nearly worthy (as who could be, save maybe Euripides and WWerfel) dramatist.' Essington himself had said after the first night, petulantly and yet with a kind of awe in his voice, 'You've changed, Sunflower. I don't know that you'll do any good by confusing your public . . .' And Francis Pitt had seen it too. He had not been at the first night, for she had begged him to stay away in case she made a silly of herself, but he had sat in a box all by himself on the second night and came round afterwards to take her out to supper at the Embassy. He had stood in her dressing-room, rather silent and awkward, which she quite understood for it was the first time they had met since that queer time when she had cut out his shirt-front. She had been immensely amused to see how his queer shy eyes which appraised everything within sight, not avariciously but in the spirit of a child waiting with its mother in a greengrocer's shop who pinches the fruit just to see what it feels like, lingered on the tubes of greasepaint in front of her mirror, the stage costumes hanging on the pegs, the gold silk wrapper lying in a semi-circle on the floor where she had stepped out of it, the flowers, the telegrams pinned on the wall, the dresser in her tight black gown eyeing the visitor with a flattering air of discretion. She fancied she saw him holding himself with a self-conscious swagger, pouting out his lips into a bad man's expression. Naïvely, childishly, it seemed to her, he was saying, 'I am in an actress's dressing-room.' Then she remembered the stories about him and Dolores Methuen and the Nelly Sisters and she perceived that what was thrilling him about the scene was not its novelty but its familiarity, its association with past private delights. For a minute she looked away from him and continued to powder her neck and arms, trying to bring back to mind various sermons against jealousy that Essington had read her from time to time, particularly in the middle period of their life together, when she had cared more for him than he did for her. But it wasn't any good, she couldn't bear it, she found herself doing what one so queerly does towards men, and appealed to him for help against the hurt he himself was inflicting on her. She twisted round in her chair and cried out to him vehemently, through something ordinary he was saying about the play, 'But what did you really think of me? What did you *really* think of me?' He seemed embarrassed by her importunity. He thrust out his chin, lowered his eyelids, and said stiffly, like a man who has been begged by a woman to speak of intimate matters that he himself would have been too delicate to raise, 'You're acting quite differently from the way you've acted in any other play I've seen you in. You've . . . altered completely.' Oh, he hadn't liked her! There was something disagreeable, something resistant, almost a sneer in his tone. She dropped her powder-puff and clasped her hands and cried out, 'Then you didn't like it!' His face changed. For a minute he looked at her with an expression that was startled and honest and kindly. Then his eyes flickered, and the blood rose under his skin, and he said in that thick voice he often used to her, which sounded as if he were tasting good wine, eating delicious food, 'I never liked anything better in my life.' She had a curious feeling that in saying that he had abandoned himself to a temptation which he had meant to resist.

It was after that he suggested they should go to the Embassy and telephoned for a table. She was glad, for they had a lovely time. She had never liked the Embassy before at night, but he saw to it that she enjoyed it. He did look after one well. When he told her in the car that Maurice and Leonora Hughes were dancing there just now, and she said she'd never seen them before as Essington didn't care for that sort of thing, he was so pleased that he was going to show her something lovely for the first time, and he took ever such pains to make sure that she should see them properly. He wouldn't take the table that had been reserved for them because she wouldn't have had a good view, and they had to wait in the doorway till another was put in for them right in the corner of the dancing floor, which was embarrassing, for it meant that they had to stand under the white spotlight which was trained there ready for the dancers' entrance. He felt shy too. She could feel him shaken by silent nervous laughter. Then when they sat down he was quite fussy about ordering something that she'd fancy, not a bit like Essington, who never picked up a menu without reminding her that she oughtn't to eat anything or she'd get fat. He let her have sweet wine, too. And Leonora Hughes was the loveliest thing she'd ever seen. She was like the smell of one's hands after one has been picking lemon verbena, and she looked so really nice, as if her life was like her feathery, floating dress, as if when she was disappointed about anything she wouldn't work it off by being nasty to anybody else, but would just go away and cry and then suddenly stop crying and be very happy because of nothing in particular, as if her emotions were shapely and slim like her legs. During her funny dance, when she and Maurice pretended to be a stenographer and a travelling salesman at a New York palais de danse, and everybody was shrieking with laughter, it broke on Sunflower that at last she was having as good a time as the people at the next table. She was enjoying herself in the way she ought to have enjoyed herself during her twenties and hadn't. Because of Francis Pitt she was not, after all, going to miss anything, though she was thirty. Enjoying her own laughter as much as any part of the treat, she turned her laughing face towards him, so that he might see what he had done for her; and was appalled by his appearance. He was sitting hunched up in his chair, his great head pressing down his short neck to nothingness between his shoulders, looking troglodytish, queer in shape and queer in substance, for his blank and joyless face had turned the grey-brown colour that a chip in coarse china shows. His narrowed eyes stared across the lit space where Leonora twirled like the crescent moon trying to be buffoonish, over the smiling faces of the people who sat up to their necks in indistinctness at the tables, to the middle of the purple and green wall, which was now supported at regular intervals as by caryatids by the men and women who were standing up on the plush benches so that they could see better, almost dissolved by darkness to mere stripes of decoration, alternately magpie and gaily coloured, save when laughter made them sway forward and bring their shadow-patterned faces near the light. There the door was an oblong of darkness. He wanted to be outside it. She saw his spirit wandering down some unlit street that led to no home. She gave a little moan of distress and sympathy and put out her hand as if to stroke her wrist. He turned and looked very gravely at her, seemed to make some resolution, and made a slow reluctant gesture towards the orchestra, as if when the music stopped he would tell her something important and not pleasant. Again she had that sense of being strong enough for both. It did not matter what he had to tell her, she could bear up under it, she could make something of it.

But when the music stopped he told her nothing. It happened that one of the men who were sitting at the table behind them stood up and in the wildness of his applause pressed quite close against Sunflower, so that his coat touched her bare shoulders. Both she and Francis Pitt looked up at him sharply, and they saw it was the Duke of Victoria, a big fair man, whose downy face now as always bore an aggrieved expression, as if he were slightly hurt that he had not been born a bull. Francis put his arm round her with a protective movement so intimate that it surprised her, so vehement that it jogged the Duke's attention away from Leonora. He stared hard at Sunflower whom he had been trying to get to know for years, quite unsuccessfully, for he wasn't the sort of person it did one any good to be seen with, since he'd kept everybody that you can keep and married several of the rest. Then he looked at Francis and said in an astonished, congratulatory tone, 'Oh, it's you, Pitt!' It was funny what a child Francis was in some ways. He couldn't have given himself away more if he had tried than he did by his sleepy, happy, preoccupied smile, his vague, friendly, remote, definitely dismissive greeting, which begged that he might be left in peace with his delight. But of course it didn't matter. She turned to him as soon as all the clapping was over, and asked, 'What is it?' He faced her with an expression that was so satisfied with the moment that in anybody else it would have been gross. 'What is what?' She stammered, 'When you looked at the door I thought . . .' He said patiently, as if she had been tactless to remind him of his lapse into depression but would be forgiven because he liked her so much, 'I was thinking of Hurrell. Let's dance now. It's "Horsey, keep your tail up".' For a little she was uncomfortable because she had been so stupid, but then she looked furtively at his face to see if she had really upset him, and found it heavy with a secret joy, the eyes veiled, the lips slightly parted, and again suspected that he loved her. Certainly he must love

170

her. Why, when they got up to go during a lull in the music and went across the dancing-floor towards the door he walked beside her with so contented an air of possessiveness that they might already have been lovers.

That was the last time she had ever seen him at night. He had asked her to go out to supper again, but Essington had made a fuss and said she would lose her looks if she kept late hours. She had hopes that perhaps they might dine together on Sundays, but Essington had just about then developed a queer passion for going away with her every weekend. It was true that she still saw him in the daytime but that did not make up for the lack of seeing him at night. There was a funny way his shirt-front bulged, like the cheeks of a cherub, that she wanted to see as if she were starving and the sight of it food she could eat. But of course she ought to be thankful because now she lunched with him nearly every day except when she had a matinée. And that was lovely, for one met so many interesting people. Always, always, there was somebody else there. To begin with, there was Etta, who was a dear but got on her nerves because she would look at her as if she were sorry for her. Once Sunflower and Francis had been in the library together, bending over the central table and turning over the pages of a huge old Bible, the illustrations of which amused him for some reason that she couldn't understand though of course she laughed, when she got a feeling that she was being watched. She raised her head sharply and looked out of one of the windows and saw Etta standing on the terrace outside in a petrified attitude. Her eyes were fixed on Sunflower and her brother, her right hand held a pair of scissors open above a rose on one of the standards, her left hand was crushing a sheaf of bright flowers against her flat and heavy bosom so tightly that it was apparent that she was so absorbed in what she was seeing that she did not know what she was doing; and her swarthy face was darkened a second time by a cloud of heavy, foreboding compassion. Sunflower flashed a smile at her to show her that it was all right, and Etta gave such a start at having been seen, and so forced an answering smile that it was apparent she obstinately believed it to be all wrong. After lunch, when Francis went up to see Hurrell, she had done her best to make it plain to Etta (as she had already tried to do more than once but the woman didn't seem capable of taking it in) that Essington had been ever so much better lately and that anyway she was gorgeously, marvellously, indestructibly happy just now. This Etta had handsomely but uneasily pretended to accept, saying, 'Yes, they do have their ups and downs, don't they? And the ups are just as up as the downs are down,' but she had worn such an expression of infinite pity that Sunflower could have smacked her face.

But after all Etta did not matter, for she had a right to be there. If Francis Pitt had not wanted her there, he still could hardly have helped having her there. It was her home. But all those other people had no right in the house, they could be there only because Francis Pitt wanted them to be there. Now as the car swung down the chestnut avenue she stared ahead of her at the open gates that were hinged on a blank of green brightness at the end of the shadows and bared her teeth at the thought of the enemies that were behind them. There were so many of them. While Harrowby drove the car up the drive, which he was doing with such ill temper that several times they lurched on to the grass kerb, she looked from right to left as she might have for an ambush. Of course she could see well enough why he liked some of them to be there. It was indeed a proof of his unique virtue, of the shaggy beauty of his character, that he should have them there. He had Bryce Atkin and Mr Macbride the banker there rather more than their connection with his political party made necessary, but that was because of his great sense of humour. It was so funny to see the pair of them facing the politician's problem in such different ways: Mr Bryce Atkin conscious, with a roll and momentary dulling of his bright little robin's eye, that he was going to too many places for his soul's sake, and then brisking up and shaking out his feathers and deciding to work off any moral blame that might have attached itself to him by giving as good a show as he knew how at every place he went to so that nobody could say he was accepting hospitality for nothing; Mr Macbride conscious, with an increasing concavity of his Scotch jaws, of the same disquieting fact and, after assuming a silent lankness just too clenched to be called limpness, making a sustained effort to repudiate the whole situation by giving no sort of show at all. Their presence there was really quite lovely, because it was proof not only of Francis Pitt's sense of humour but also of his beautiful modesty. He invited them just as he invited the colonial administrators and foreign potentates who some-times gave his dining-room a Pathé Gazette look, because it was a constant amazement to him that such important people should bother to visit the ugly, undersized son of a Wesleyan minister. He thought nothing of himself, the poor little thing. It was that which accounted too for his passion for having nice-looking, wild people about him. He used to hang round his own tennis-court when Teddy Drayton and

172

Lord Orisser were playing a singles as if he thought that it was good of them to let him look on, and watch them with the most pathetically worshipping, unjealous envy. It was the same desire to know at secondhand what it was to be physically active as he was not that made him fill the place with young people like Peggy Bryce Atkin, and the three Cornelliss children, Lionel, Michael, and Susan, who looked so nice playing tennis in their white things with their long legs and their lovely straight backs and their sleek brushed heads, and who sounded such ducks when they called to each other in the high voice that girls and boys who have been well brought up have, a thin, pure voice which wouldn't be any use on the stage and is lovely in private life. It was nice of Francis Pitt to have them about; it wasn't every man who liked children. And it was nice of him to have their father, Sir Robert Cornelliss, because it must be just out of gratitude for the way he was looking after Mr Hurrell, for he was the most awful old bore. He was one of those people who embarrass you terribly because they sit around not saying very much but making you feel that they are telling themselves some silly kind of a story about you. He would come and stand behind her while she was watching the tennis, very tall and greyhoundish, resting his fine, long hands on the back of the bench miles away from her shoulders, so that it couldn't be that which made her feel so uncomfortable; turning his distinguished, high-bridged profile swiftly and suavely from player to player; occasionally making a remark about the score in his pleasant voice and keeping an easy, unfidgetting silence in between the games. He did not do or say a thing that was objectionable, yet when he said a courteous farewell and strolled away she had a horrid sense that he had pinched something from her, that he had put her at a disadvantage. But there wasn't any denying that he did everything he could think of for Mr Hurrell, and didn't mind coming over any time he was sent for, day or night. Of course Francis Pitt had to give him the run of the house.

But there could be no reason at all why he should have to ask those beastly people, Billie Murphy and Lord Canterton! It made one sick to watch Billie Murphy running about the tennis-court with the movements of a stocky little pony, wearing an expression of bluffness and healthy commonsense, calling out shrewd technicalities about the new court to Francis in a quiet, jolly, schoolboy voice, being no end of a good fellow till something happened, her foot slipped or the sun overpassed the great cedar and dazzled her. Then there would show, printed greyly on the stubborn golden moon of her face, a second face,

173

the peaked, vacillating, lonely face of the drunkard, who does not think lovingly of anything in the world but the next drink, who does not feel anything for the surrounding scene but headachy peevishness. It made one sick to watch Lord Canterton go out on the court, carrying his racket in one large oblong red hand and tossing up three balls in the air with the other, in a manner that would have been just excusable if he had been the only man since the beginning of time who had been able to perform that feat; wearing the pompous and meaningless expression that is affected by the statelier and less efficient sort of manicurist when she carries her dish of soap and water across the room, the eyebrows raised, the chin dropped but the mouth closed, the whole advertising a state of bored superiority over somebody who was not here in an issue which was purely imaginary; carrying himself with such slow swaggering vulgarity of movement that his white flannel trousers looked as loud as loud checks and his sleek black hair seemed a facetious and ungentlemanly way of treating the head like a billycock worn on one side. One could not blame poor little Billie, for she was so young that someone must have worked hard to make her what she was. But certainly both of them, whoever was to blame for it, were coarse and greedy and futile people. There was not an ugly thing in the world they would not do. There was not one fine end that they served. They could not fulfil any real need in Francis Pitt. There could not even, considering that Francis Pitt was a Liberal and that both Canterton and Sir John Murphy belonged to what Essington called the hiccuping wing of the Conservative Party, be any worldly reason why he should ask them to his house. He must have them there simply because he preferred having them there to being alone with her. Once she had forced herself to admit that, she tore up the argument she had been weaving for days and, staring at its loose threads, admitted further that it was utterly amazing that any at all of his guests should be in his house just now. It was against nature. Bryce Atkin and Mr Macbride and the princes and ministers might satisfy his ambition and his sense of fun and his humility, Teddy Drayton and Lord Orisser and the schoolboys and schoolgirls his touching wish that he had been born better-looking than he was, Cornelliss his desire to be loyal to his friends and kind to those who were good to his friends, but those were not real needs compared to their desperate common needs to be alone together. Nothing could happen, of course, because she was still with Essington, but they ought to be alone together just once.

174

She was pale now, not only because she was going to meet Francis Pitt in a few seconds, but also because of the way of their meeting. Yet, though that was agonising, she felt not depressed but exalted by it. There was a quality of importance about Francis which was not of her imagining. She had verified its existence by watching Bryce Atkin and Mr Macbride when they were watching him, and noting how there came quite often into the amused brightness of Bryce Atkin's eye a hard, computing, and ultimately respectful sparkle, and into the unamused dullness of Mr Macbride's eye a grudging gleam. Both of them were almost contemptuously entertained by Francis Pitt's charlatan ways, but they both felt it not impossible that some day he might produce from his coat-sleeve neither a rabbit nor a guinea pig but a sceptre, which he would nurse for a while in his short, folded arms and chuckle over with narrowed eyes and then suddenly lift in a gesture of rulership which the world would not disobey. This quality of importance gave the strange circumstances of their close and remote companion-ship, their intimate separateness, the dignity of a historical mystery. She felt as if she were some girl with a high white coif on her head riding on a led palfrey through the forest into a clearing wholly ringed by armed men leaning on their spears, where she would find him between two tall guards, his hands tied behind him, his hair wilder and worn longer, his face more kingly and more wolfish, while the one who had for the time being gained the upper hand of him sat on a stool amongst his counsellors and watched their meeting. Well, if that were the only way that one could go to him, it was the best thing in the world. And it was glorious to know that if the armed men and the enemies were not there and there was only the short grass, and the wild rose briars, and the dark sweet-smelling arcades of the forest, he would fall so gladly at her feet and bury his face against her body, kissing the stuff of her gown with his great mouth. But what could not be borne was that the armed men were there because he wished them there, that he himself had tied his hands behind him, that he himself was the enemy who mocked their love by making them meet publicly. What could it mean? Why was he torturing both of them like this? Was it just that he knew she wanted to stay with Essington – which she did, of course she did – and he was helping her? Or was it that there was another woman? There did not seem to be. Surely he had not time. She knew fairly well what he did with his days and he seemed to be always in the open, either up here in the house and gardens, or at political parties and dinners. Yet she could not be quite sure. She knew from something Etta had said that he had been out on Thursday night, but she did not know where. Of course there were lots of interstices in his time, hours here and there when he might have been with someone he loved. But he was in love with her, why should he go to any other woman? That was a silly question. He might have tied himself up to somebody in a way that could not be broken. Perhaps he had made love to a married woman who had wanted to be good and had gone against her conscience because she loved him so, and now of course he could not leave her. At that some force much fiercer than herself leaped up inside her body and ran like mercury through her flesh, arguing that though this was the sort of scruple she had respected all her life it must go down before the work that she and it had in hand. Instantly she deserted to its side; and had once more that feeling which she had had so often since she knew Francis Pitt of being called to some tremendous battle and having an inexhaustible store of power with which to fight it. She straightened herself, feeling in her shoulders, her back, her loins, the strength of a great tower.

But a thought weakened her. Maybe the case was simpler than this. Maybe he did not love her and she had only thought he did because she wished he did. It was something one could not disregard, that he never wanted to see her alone. Maybe he loved some girl for her beauty. The force that was running through her flesh ran with less spirit now. There were some lovely girls about nowadays, and far more of them than there used to be. And they wanted so little. They did not care if the man loved them. She would be dark, probably, this girl; men did not seem to care for fair women the way they used to. And without any figure. And young. As young, most likely, as she herself had been when she first went with Essington. If Francis Pitt would tell her she would not mind so much. She might be able to help the girl, tell her the best places to get clothes. Girls often made mistakes when they began to dress.

Feeling a little sick because of this thought, she got out of the car and found Francis Pitt and one of the sleek-headed young secretaries from the City office standing at the foot of the steps. Rehearsing serenity, she smiled first at the young man; but found his face scarlet, his eyes bright and blind with anger.

She turned to Francis Pitt, and saw that he was hideous with rage.

In a voice that climbed shakily down from shrillness to his usual register he greeted her, 'Ah, Sunflower, that's a lovely frock you've got on. Beautiful, beautiful!' and gripped her hand. Still holding it, in a curiously familiar, fondling gesture, he wheeled round on the secretary and said in a tone of dismissal, 'Well, goodbye, Harrop, and don't ask every girl you meet to marry you.'

The young man mumbled something. From his trembling, jerking hands slipped a notebook. A fan of loose leaves scattered on the gravel. Francis Pitt stooped and recovered them with one swift movement that was an insulting comment on the other's clumsiness. He held them out to him without looking at him, smiled into her eyes, and said slowly and deeply and happily, 'We are going to be alone together today, Sunflower.'

·

She said timidly as they went into the hall, 'Whatever has upset you so?'

Gravely he shook his head. She need not have been afraid. The lines on his face were those of grieved fatherhood. Of course he was not doing what Essington did, and making himself feel better by making other people feel worse. 'That young fool has made the mistake of his life. I'll tell you later. Just now I feel too badly about it.' He checked himself on the threshold of the library with a curious hunching movement of his shoulders, like a butting beast that sees barbed wire in front of it, and growled over his shoulder to the footman, 'There are not enough flowers today!' She hated that footman. A great strong young fellow like that ought to get something better to do than carry round two cocktails on a tray. Every time she saw him she felt as she had done that first time she came to the house and found him sniggering over Canterton, which hardened into an angry recognition that he and she were of the same class and that in some way he had failed her. Now she could have smacked his face, as he moved his full lips in silent acknowledgement of his master's complaint and looked past him into the library with a gaze which was certainly insolent, since it dwelt gogglingly on the froth of flowers that dripped from the vases set nearly rim to rim along the bookshelves and on the tables, but which meanly protected itself from rebuke by its blankness. Well, if he felt like that he shouldn't be his servant. There was plenty of other work in the world for a big hulk of a man.

When he left the room she drew off her gloves, looking round her. Certainly they seemed to be alone. There was no other guest. She turned to Francis Pitt and found that he had taken up one of the

177

cocktail glasses and was holding it out to her. His eyes were running over her with less disguise of their interest in her beauty than usual; and there was a certain grossness in that interest, which he was making no effort to hide, but was rather parading, that was not what one liked. But if it was part of his troubled state, one took it from him, of course.

'Drink, Sunflower!' he said.

She told him gently, 'I don't, you know,' but took the glass because his trembling fingers had so nearly dropped it. He gave a heavy, disgusted look at his hand and did not turn back to the tray. She perceived that he wanted a drink very badly, but would not take the other cocktail in case he could not manage to hold it. So she lifted her glass towards his mouth. But he drew back his head as an animal does, when it is offered food by a stranger. He was ashamed that a woman had observed his weakness and was helping him. To get round that she smiled in a silly sort of way, as if she were doing it out of flirtatious-ness. Then his brows looked lighter, he flung back his head and laughed into her eyes, lowered his lips to the glass, looking wisely and lewdly over the brim at her. She smiled back, saying serenely to herself, 'This is not where I want to be with him, but I can withdraw from this minute when I have given him his drink, I have the strength to climb out of it.' It struck her that this was the sort of thing that people who were lovers did quite a lot, particularly at the beginning of their time together. She regarded it with a sense of achievement, yet coldly, almost contemptuously, as an ambitious boy who meant to be a millionaire might think of the first weekly wage he earned as an office boy. She felt a pang of compunction at her own inexorable intentions towards him.

He raised his head and looked at her with his huge lips pursed with the act of drinking, with the thought of an enjoyment. 'Ah, that's the way to take a drink,' he said jocularly, and with a steadier hand took the glass back from her.

There was a pause while he set it down. The fact that they were alone, that for the first time they were alone, seemed to make a loud humming noise in the silence. He did not do anything to help her, even when he turned round. He did not say anything, and she could not make out what he was feeling, for his face and body were twitching with movements that were nothing except records of excitement.

Of course it might be an accident that they were alone. He might

178

not have wished for it at all. She bit her knuckles at that thought and asked, 'Did – did Etta have to go out?'

He must have happened to think of something funny at that moment, for he had to suppress a gust of laughter before he answered gravely, 'I sent poor Etta out. I thought it would do her no harm to have a day's shopping and lunch with a friend. It is hard on her having to go through this Hurrell business with me. And anyway I wanted . . .' his voice died away with an air of embarrassment. He took the other cocktail, looking down as he drank. Again there fell a silence.

Just for the sake of doing something to break the strain, she pointed through the window at the sunlit gardens and murmured, in a voice that shook like her pulse, 'It's summer now, the spring's gone, another spring's gone . . .'

He was just in the middle of turning up his glass for the last drop with a gesture that in its mechanical avidity made her think uneasily of how she had seen Sir John Murphy do the same thing in too nearly the same way, but he brought it down abruptly and stood staring at her, his mouth a little open. She realised that she had uttered those words which were of no importance, which she had chosen at random, with an absurd tragical emphasis. But she could not dispel the impression with laughter, for whatever he thought her words had meant had reminded him of something sad and something important to him, and he was saying with a shame-faced earnestness which she could not possibly interrupt, 'Sunflower . . . Sunflower . . .'

It was a pity that the footman should have come back to announce lunch just at that moment; and that Francis Pitt should have started up so violently at his entrance, and burst into nervous laughter, and moved away from her. It looked as if they had been kissing or doing something silly, and she could see from the footman's face, from an infinitesimal thickening of those coarse lips, from a shifting of his eye under the drooped lids, that that was exactly what he thought. She couldn't but admit that this was Francis Pitt's fault. He hadn't been thinking of touching her when the door was opened, he'd been feeling far too upset about whatever it was that her words suggested to him, and he wouldn't have anyway, since she was with Essington; but his mind had had some comic postcard stuff about kissing in it, and that had showed. If one stayed ever so quiet in a scene where one ought to be listening intently, but instead got thinking of whether Essington would still be cross when one went home, they felt it out in front at

179

once. It occurred to her, and the suspicion strengthened as she crossed the hall and felt him snort with a silent chuckle and brush against her as they got into the dark part outside the dining-room, that quite possibly he might be cheap and common when he made love. She had always known that he was not a gentleman as Essington was, that he had not been so nicely brought up. It did not matter at most times because he was nice inside and never had anything to express but kindliness and protectiveness and strength; but she could imagine that when he was feeling jolly and wanted to have a good time with somebody he liked he might get vulgar and enjoy meaningless noises and scufflings like those she used to hear when she was little and there were family festivities and cousins went to help each other wash up in the scullery. Even then she had not liked such things, they seemed an injury to beauty like footmarks on a sheet of snow; and in the life she had lived since they would have been counted as certain evils had they ever been thought of, for they were akin to bad acting and would have been more disgusting than any sin to Essington, who so greatly hated all sounds and movements that were not fine-pointed with purpose. She knew that in this matter she and Essington and her world were right, and that Francis Pitt was wrong. But if it were the way that Francis Pitt felt, then she would put up with it. Again she had that feeling of being a great draught-horse that could drag any load.

As they entered the dining-room the footman, plainly embarrassed by having to ask a question he ought to have asked in the other room, said, 'You'll not be waiting for Mr Harrop, then, sir?'

There was a third place laid at the table. Sunflower and Francis Pitt both stared at the diagram of knives and forks on the white cloth in silence. Francis Pitt pulled himself together. 'No, no. Mr Harrop's not lunching with us! I never meant him to! Take those things away!'

It was all right. He had wanted to be alone with her.

But she did hate that footman. He made such a clatter taking away the silver, and looked so rudely at Francis Pitt while he did it, as if he wanted to answer back. But it was lovely when he had left the room. She had been thinking of something disagreeable just before he came in, but now she could not have imagined what it could have been, although she was so shaken by the beating of her heart that she felt dizzy. Life suddenly seemed to have changed its gear and to have become calmer than she had ever known it. The heavy curtains were looped back from the window and she could look straight up into a dark blue sky, which because it was crossed by bright white clouds like galleons in full sail seemed not like a dome of warm summer air but like an inverted salt and invigorating sea. The spinach and eggs she was eating, and the iced lemonade she was drinking, had a clean taste, and the flowers in the room were all of cottage garden kinds, with dark sprigs of sweet-smelling herbs among them. And Francis Pitt did not look silly any more, but sat at the head of his table as one would like to see a man sit at the head of one's table, dignified and leisurely and sensible. There was not a thing she would have wished different.

'Well,' he asked after a while, 'how's the play going?'

Absurdly she found that she was shy. Her voice came in the funniest little husky growl. 'All right.'

A minute later he tried again.

'Has the man who's been rehearsing Cosmo Davis's part played it yet?'

'Yes.'

'Did he give a good show?'

'Mm. Rather.'

It was dreadful. She must sound quite rude. She wanted to cry.

He ate a few more mouthfuls, set down his fork, put his elbows on the table, and cupped his face in his hands. Looking into her eyes, he said deliberately, 'Dear Sunflower, who hasn't a word to say for herself for ever so long after she comes into a room. Just sits mum. But who all the time is the best company in the world.'

She set down her fork too. He continued to sit quite still and look at her. She could feel that the intimacy of his words and their undisguised affection were as much of a delight to him as they were to her, as much of an indulgence after long famine. Her hands fluttered up to cover her mouth. Through her laced fingers she smiled at him plaintively, begging for mercy. He must not make her too happy.

He went on, 'Do you know that, Sunflower? There isn't a soup ever made that has heard a single word from your lips. It all goes down to its grave behind the waistcoat buttons without ever getting a whisper of that lovely voice of yours. There isn't a fish that ever heard it either. The roast beef or chicken may get a little bit of it. May get a "Mm" or the beginning of a sentence that gets chopped in two on a pink lower lip by two remarkably handsome white teeth. But nothing but the ice-pudding has any real luck. I could sing when I see that stuff coming in, though I haven't touched it for years. I say to myself, "Now we'll hear what Sunflower has to say". And then she does let us know what sort of pretty things she's been thinking and feeling about this old world of ours, and it makes us all very happy. And that's how it goes every time.'

She smiled and moved her lips, but no sound would come.

'Tell me, Sunflower, why are you so shy with us? Are you bored with us?'

'Oh, no. Oh, no,' she murmured.

'Are you sure? Are you quite sure that you don't find the talk tedious between us old men who care for dry things like politics? Are we asking too much of a kindness when we ask you to come here?'

'Oh, no!' she cried, finding her voice, 'I'd rather be here than anywhere else in the whole world. I don't know what I'd do if you stopped asking me!'

He blinked. She saw that he was enormously pleased; but he continued to speak very gravely. 'I am glad of that. I am very glad of that. Sometimes I've been worried by your silence. But I suppose it only means that you and I, Sunflower, are the kind of friends who do not have to talk to be of use to each other.'

He took up his fork and went on with his eggs. She could not. She did not seem to want any food. To make things quite clear between them, so that he should never be troubled again by any suspicion that she did not like being with him, she explained timidly, 'Really, I don't talk because I haven't anything to say.'

'Nonsense. You have a great deal to say.'

'Really I haven't. I'm ever so stupid.'

'You are not.'

'Yes, I am. You don't know how stupid I am. A head like a sieve. I can't remember a thing.'

'Yes, you can. You remember your parts. And you remember them well. That's a very long part you're playing now. And never once in all the times I've seen you in it have I heard the prompter helping you.'

'What? What? Have you seen it more than once?'

He was embarrassed. 'Yes . . . two or three times . . .'

To shield his embarrassment and her glowing pleasure she stumbled on quickly, 'That's different. I can't remember other things. History. Dates. I don't know when kings were. I tell you I'm stupid.'

'I tell you you are not. You show intelligence in lots of ways. You run your house well. You are shrewd about practical things. You never spent foolishly in your life. You have good taste in art. You notice fine points about people. You are not a stupid woman.'

Perturbed, because this was such a reversal of what she had heard from Essington, she murmured, 'But I am stupid, really I am . . .'

'I tell you you are not. If you have not mastered the world of intellectual things that Essington and I live in it is because you haven't taken the trouble. You are reserving your energies for something else. That is how you always strike me. As being full of strength you will not spend on anything that you are doing now, because you are saving it for other things.'

She looked at him with interest. She had felt that about herself quite often. Sometimes her body tingled from head to foot with undischarged force. Then she would want to get up and run round and round the room, and at the same time would want to go and lie down on her bed and cry and cry because there must be some more sensible thing to do when one was like that but she did not know what it was.

'What are you saving your strength for, Sunflower?'

She stared at him with knitted brow.

'For your acting?'

The idea made her laugh. 'No.'

'Well, what do you really want to do?'

When he put it that way she understood the whole thing. She gazed down at her plate and pouted her lips, trying to look as if she did not understand it.

'Supposing you could change your whole life and spend the rest of it doing what you like, what would you choose to do?'

It was awful. He was keeping his eyes on her so insistently. Surely he ought to have sense enough to know what almost every woman really wanted to do. A blush was pouring over her face, her neck, her breasts; and the blood seemed to be dragging a harrow of pleasure through her flesh, so that tears of delight and agony stood in her eyes. It was awful. There was nothing more unthinkable than that one should tell a man that one wanted to have babies unless one was going to have his babies and it was almost all fixed up. And she was with Essington, she was with Essington. Yet she felt as if, were he to go on any longer, she would cry it aloud in simple words that they would never either of them be able to forget. Her gaze shifted from her plate across the table, seeking for something to talk about, to break the domination of his easy, innocent inquisitiveness. She remembered the place that had been laid just opposite her, and muttered, 'What was it about Mr Harrop that made you so angry?'

There was a silence. She heard his heel come down smartly on the

183

electric floor bell. 'He has made a fool of himself. Ruined his career at the beginning.'

She knew from his gruffness that he did not like the subject but she could think of nothing else to keep him from the other. 'How?'

'He's got himself engaged.'

'Who to?'

'A girl who works along with him in my office.'

'A typist?' The footman was back in the room. She had to keep this talk going. It would be too awful if Francis Pitt started off again in front of him.

'No. Higher than that. She's an American girl who handles a good part of my American business.'

'Oh, not that Miss Wycherley whom I met here one day?'

'Yes. Miss Greta Wycherley.' He said the name ironically as if it were a romantic statement of an ugly fact.

'But I thought you liked her! I thought you said she was clever! And she's ever so pretty.'

'She's all that.' He spoke sharply and indicated with a nod at the footman that he would give her an explanation when they were alone once more.

'She's quite lovely,' said Sunflower lamely.

'Quite lovely,' agreed Francis Pitt, with nearly a snarl. He sat back in his chair, suddenly looking grey and tired. He nodded his head silently and impressively, with the movements of an old man, as if he were repeating to himself some judgment he had recently delivered which had been so closely based on Bibilical morality that it had made him feel like a patriarch. It occurred to her that perhaps underneath everything he had old-fashioned ideas. It might be that Miss Wycherley had been silly when she was young, that she'd made a mistake as people do before they know; and that Francis Pitt thought that men oughtn't to marry a woman who had been with anybody else. Men were so queer, you could not tell in what direction they would fail you next. She must find out about that at once . . .

As soon as the footman had given them the cold chicken and salad and gone out she began timidly and obstinately, 'This Miss Wycherley – '

He shot out a forefinger towards her wrist. 'I've never seen you wear that before in the daytime.'

'What?'

'That bracelet.'

184

'Oh . . . I put it on because I wasn't sure that I'd go home before the theatre.' She had prayed that he would ask her to tea as he sometimes did. In a panic lest he should guess she had prayed for that she added, 'I've got some things to do.' Oh, now he probably wouldn't ask her, since she had expressly said she had other things to do. Life was so difficult.

'It's a gorgeous thing. One of the finest I've ever seen. You used not to wear it when you first came here.'

'I didn't have it then. Essington hadn't given it to me.'

'When did he give it to you?'

'Just a week or two ago.'

He was so long in speaking that she thought he had tired of the subject, and was going to try and turn him back to Miss Wycherley, when he said genially, 'Well, you're an exceptionally happy couple, you and Essington, Sunflower. I don't know many women who get presents like that after ten years.'

'I know. I was ever so pleased. It's the first thing of the sort he's ever given me.'

'What do you mean? The first bracelet?'

'No, the first jewellery. He hasn't seemed to care for jewellery.'

'Then what has he given you?'

She tried to remember. 'There was a Spanish shawl, about three years ago.'

He held out his hand for the bracelet. She made haste not to keep him waiting.

'This is a very magnificent thing, Sunflower.'

'I know it is. It must have cost quite a lot of money.' She spoke with a puzzled air.

'When did you say he gave you this?'

'About a fortnight ago.'

He turned it round and round in his little paw-hands. Something in the design seemed to be amusing him.

'Why are you laughing?' she asked at last.

He looked up in surprise. 'I am not laughing.' She saw that she had been mistaken, his face was quite grave. 'Here, put it on again, Sunflower. Well, I suppose there's no need for me to tell you that Essington's very fond of you.'

'I know he is.' It occurred to her that this was a good opportunity to correct a view which she was sure Etta had, and which she thought it possible he shared, that Essington was always as horrid to her as he had

185

been that night when they had all first dined together. 'And you don't know how specially lovely he's been to me these last few weeks. He's been getting nicer and nicer to me. Why, he never used to make me go away with him every weekend like he does now.'

'And how do you spend those weekends, Sunflower? I've often sat here cooped up with poor Hurrell and thought of you two off in the country, and wondered what you were doing, and envied you.'

'Oh, you needn't, they're nothing much,' she said. They were, indeed, rather more than one wanted to undertake after a week's hard work. Late on Saturday night they motored down to some country inn, and early on Sunday morning, before she had had her sleep out, she would be wakened by his discontents. He missed his bathroom, with its boiling water and its army of bottles with which he could nurse all the suspicions he was constantly conceiving about his health, about coming colds and poisoned scratches. He missed his valet. He missed the breakfast he always had at home, on the simplicity of which he would expatiate, of freshly roasted and ground coffee, with milk and an egg just sent down from the farm, and the best peach from the greenhouse. When they went out for a walk he missed the seat on the terrace where one read all the Sunday papers, and hated the mob of staring people who infested this open country as they never did his park. She had to soothe him perpetually but never dared to say the only words that were really apposite. 'Essington, you are too old for this sort of thing. You don't want to be romantic at your time of life, and I never did. We both want to be comfortable. Let's get married so that we can have a nice place together and stay quiet.' After lunch, which infuriated him by the contrast with the kind of meal he would have got in his own home, he would go upstairs and lie down on his bed. She would have to go too. It worried him if she went out for a walk by herself; and also he needed her to open and shut the window, to lower and raise the blind. She would sit in an armchair, drowsing, listening to all the sounds of the automobiles and charabancs and motor-cycles as they carried the free people along the road outside, seeing Francis Pitt against the darkness of her lowered lids. Then there would come a querulous voice from the bed, 'Sunflower, what are you thinking of?' And she would start, and throw the thought of Francis Pitt away from her, and stutter, 'I was thinking . . . of that scene with the wineglass in the second act. I don't feel I've got it right yet', or, 'I was thinking . . . of that article in *The Times* yesterday by the explorer about the tombs he found in that cave in South America. He

186

found one girl in her coffin dressed like a bride. I wonder what had happened to her, whether she had just been married, or whether she was just going to be . . .' He would give a little grunt. She would hear the creak of the bed as he turned over on his other side. There would be some time of silence, and then again a querulous voice, 'Come and put your arms round me, Sunflower . . .'

Perhaps she ought not to have said, 'They're nothing much.' It was a giveaway of Essington. But Francis Pitt had said he envied them, and it might be that his imprisonment in that bleak bedroom with the dying man had seemed worse when he had imagined Essington and her having a lovely time in the country, and she couldn't bear by even so little to darken any further the life that, because of his sensitiveness and his inordinate, unfashionable capacity for love, must be dark enough just now. To put matters right for Essington she went on, 'No, they're nothing much. It's my fault. I'm tired before I start, you see. But Essington's lovely to me.' An incident which had greatly moved her when it happened came into her mind, and she turned to him with shining eyes, immensely relieved to find that she could back her defence of Essington with a true story. 'Why, the other day he did the most wonderful thing – !' She checked herself and said primly, 'But it's very private.'

'Count me as big brother who never tells,' said Francis Pitt easily; and when she hesitated, and inclined towards thinking that it would not be right to repeat that story, he added gravely, 'and who is very glad to listen. My own life has not gone too well in these matters. I will tell you the whole long tale of it some day. But it does me good to hear from your life of an affection that seems to go on being warm and passionate and romantic after so many years.' She still kept a doubtful silence; and he went on, 'Or so it seems to me. I hear on every side that Essington is an irritable, unloving man. But I think you could tell me differently.'

'Oh, I can, I can!' she exclaimed indignantly. 'The nerve they have to say such things! Listen to this! I thought it was too private to tell you – but if you know it you'll be able to stick up for him. The other weekend we went to Virginia Water. Do you know Virginia Water?'

'No, Sunflower.'

'Well, it seems a funny place to go for a weekend. It's quite near London. Lots of motor-buses go there. But it's lovely. It's one of the loveliest spots in the world. I always hope dying'll be like what it is. You see, there's a pub on the highroad, and you stop there. And it's all dusty and noisy, with the motor-buses starting and people getting out of charabancs and kids crying. And you go inside the pub and that's noisy with people having drinks and all. And then you go out into the garden, and there's lots of parties having tea and waiters running about between the tables. And you go into a shrubbery, just a common sort of shrubbery, and through a wicket gate, and up among some trees that aren't specially nice, and then all of a sudden you come out on a lake. A great big lake. Oh, miles round. With trees on the edge, reflected in the water like a face in a glass. And it's calm, ever so calm, like those Chinese paintings in the British Museum. That's why I say I hope it's like dying. You feel you've got home at last after all the dust and bother. You see there's something unlike other lakes about it. It lies differently, somehow. That's because it isn't natural. The Prince Regent made it. Dug up a lot of earth and ran water in from miles away. And pinched a lot of columns and things out of the courtyard of the British Museum and stuck them by the side of the lake, just how he thought they'd look pretty. And they don't look quite natural either, for the way they're put together they couldn't really have ever been. So that too makes it look like some other world. Oh, haven't you ever been? We must go, we must go!'

He said softly, 'Yes, we must go.'

A vision of another loveliness diverted her for an instant. She stared at it, her mouth a little open, smiling, and looking very young. 'And there's another place. In France. A place I went to. I want to take you there, too.'

He said again, as softly, 'Yes, we must go.'

'Well, I was forgetting. We went down there the Sunday before last. And in the evening, before dinner, we were taking a walk by the lake. Lovely it was. Just like a mirror, and a swan drawing lines over it. Well, there was a poor old man in among some trees right away from the water, gathering sticks. You know the sort of old man I mean, goes about the country catching moles and things, nothing regular. Well, usually Essington doesn't take any notice of that kind of person. He isn't interested in just people, you know. He's tired of them. But this time he left where we were walking and went straight over to this poor old man. At first I didn't notice what he was doing because I . . . was thinking of something else. But all of a sudden I found ourselves standing by this poor old man and Essington takes out a pound note and gives it to the old man. You could have knocked me down with a feather. You see, Essington doesn't ever give to beggars and that in the

188

street, not ever. It isn't that he's mean, for he's most generous, but he doesn't hold with it. So I said to him when we got away, 'Whatever did you do that for, all of a sudden?' And he said, 'It was a thank-offering, Sunflower. A thank-offering because you're down here with me today after ten years. And a bribe to heaven to let me always have you with me, for I should die if I lost you.' She hesitated, wondering if she should tell him that there had been tears in Essington's eyes as he spoke. But that was too private. So she ended, 'Now wasn't that a lovely thing to do?'

Francis Pitt dropped a lump of ice in his glass with his pudgy fingers and took a long drink before he answered. 'That is a very beautiful story, Sunflower. Thank you for telling me that. It has made me feel . . . much better.'

She had known he would appreciate it. 'Wasn't it lovely?' she asked delightedly. 'And he's always doing things like that just now. I'm glad I told you, because you do understand, just as I knew you would. And in a way, you know, you're responsible for it all.'

'How's that?'

'Well, it's only since he's been coming up here that he's been like this.'

He started bolt upright in his chair and turned on her a face blank with astonishment, though not with incredulity. It was not as if she was telling him something that he did not know, but rather as if she were disclosing to him her knowledge of something with which he had long been familiar but which he had thought to be hidden from her. He laughed deprecatingly, and tilted his face down, smiling up at her puckishly. But when she smiled back amiably and uncomprehendingly he again started and seemed confused. 'Well, how do you account for that?'

She wagged her head to give impressiveness to her words. 'Believe me or not, I think it's Mr Hurrell!'

'Mr Hurrell?'

'Yes. I think meeting Mr Hurrell after all those years, and in those circumstances, turned him all inside out, and made him feel more like when he was young, before he got fussed-up and upset about things.'

'Oh, I see what you mean!' exclaimed Francis Pitt. 'Yes, yes, yes. I agree with you entirely. It must be Hurrell. And indeed I should think he would be bound to have just that effect on someone who was being reconciled to him after many years. He would bring him back to all the best that had ever been in him. His own goodness is such a real and powerful thing that it would be bound to be infectious.'

He spoke quickly, almost mechanically, and she heard his heel go down on the floor-bell. Of course he loved the dying man too well to want to speak of him. She should have had more sense.

But when the footman had left the room she realised that he was in tremendously high spirits. He rubbed his hands and said, 'Ah, Sunflower, look what we've got to eat.'

'Raspberry tart,' she said. There didn't seem anything extraordinary about it.

'Yes, raspberries, and not strawberry.'

'Mm.' You couldn't help laughing when he looked at you like that, his grin stretching right across his face, mischief quivering across his face like sunshine on the face of a gargoyle.

'Raspberry, not strawberries.'

'I don't know what you mean.' He was leaning right over the corner of the table, his face was close to hers, their laughing mouths were near each other. She wanted to throw her head back and giggle as if he were tickling her.

'You don't remember?'

'No! No! No!'

'Raspberry, not strawberry?'

'No. I tell you I don't know what you mean!'

'Don't you remember telling me that first night you came here and we walked in my chestnut alley?'

She leaned back sharply in her chair. There came over her like sickness a hideous feeling that he would have liked to jump out of his chair and thrust her backwards and put his face against her neck and munch the flesh with wallowing, insulting kisses. But why did she think such awful things about him every now and then? Was it that she had been so greatly disappointed in Essington that a part of her which was tired out with pain kept begging her not to invite such pain again by hoping too much of Francis Pitt? It must be that. For the whole thing was a delusion, there was nothing in his face when one looked into it except the most innocent gaiety, such a will to be happy that he was laughing heartily at something that was not really funny, that was just nice.

'Fancy you remembering that.'

'Dear Sunflower, I remember everything you say. Everything. You have style, dear little Sunflower. You have always had it as a woman.

190

Now you are beginning to have it as an actress. And when one has style everything one does has a meaning, everything one does fits into a picture. Sometimes when I cannot sleep or when I have to sit beside Hurrell, I think of all sorts of little things I've heard you say and little things I've watched you do, and they all fit into a picture. And it is a picture that does me good to think of. So I have said over to myself more than once, dear Sunflower, all the pretty things you said to me when we were walking in my chestnut alley.' She smiled at the naïve, childish vanity of possession that made him always say 'my' instead of 'the' when he spoke of anything he owned, and make a slight pompous movement of the hands. Yet he would give away anything. He was funny, he was lovely.

Smiling, because of what he said, because of what he was, she murmured, 'Yes, it was nice up there.'

'We must go up there again one night. Would you like that, Sunflower?'

Shyness changed her voice to a croaking whisper. 'I would. Sometime.' She cleared her throat. 'You said there was a statue at the end there. You haven't ever showed it to me.'

'Why, so I will one night. It is a statue of love, Sunflower. Yes, we must do that. The trouble is that we are both of us busy people. Both of us have other engagements. But we must squeeze this in somehow. That has got to be.' He spoke grimly, portentously; but hardly altered his tone when he went on to say, 'My God, this is extraordinarily good raspberry tart. We're each going to have a second helping.' His heel clicked on the bell. She stared at him in wonder. Was it all a joke or was none of it a joke? And if there was a joke, what was it? He carried on, still rather ponderously, 'Frederick will think I have gone mad. I haven't had a second helping of anything since heaven knows when.' As the footman came in his face suddenly lit up with a grin but instantly grew dark again. More heavily than ever, he said, 'Though God knows I shouldn't eat this stuff. My doctor says it's very dangerous for me to eat these things.'

She gazed at him anxiously and exclaimed, 'What do you eat them for then?'

He shook his great head and said mournfully, 'I am past caring for what the doctor says.' He had helped himself and the footman turned aside, thinking he had taken enough; but Pitt called him back. 'Here, I haven't finished. I want more than that.'

It was really an enormous helping. She couldn't eat her own

though it was really lovely. She was all upset and said, 'No, thank you,' to the cream, though of course she hadn't meant to. The minute the footman went out she put down her spoon and pressed him, 'Did the doctor really say it was dangerous to eat these kind of things?'

'Mm.' He nodded and filled his mouth with raspberries.

'Did he say it was actually dangerous?'

'Mm. My God, these are good. These are very good.'

'Then you mustn't eat them. I suppose he's afraid of the seeds irritating the – you mustn't eat them.'

'Mm.'

'You mustn't. You mustn't. Oh, I don't know how you can be so silly!' She jumped up from her seat and ran round to him, and tried to make him put down the spoon he was raising to his mouth. He shouted with laughter, crammed it into his mouth and kept it there, looking up at her impudently. 'Oh, you're silly, just silly!' she exclaimed indignantly. He took the spoon out of his mouth, and made faces at her and lowered it to fill it again. She moved her hands down to grip his wrists, but the sight of the thick hair curling from under his cuff, rather redder than the hair on his head, made her feel shy, so that she spread out her fingers for a minute stiffly and then drew them back and instead shook his coat-sleeve. That was, of course, not much good and when he put down his spoon it was only because he had laughed so much that he had spilt some raspberry juice on his dinner-mat and he was as tidy as a cat. He fell right back in his chair, puffing and choking, and she stood over him, crying, 'Oh, you are silly to do what the doctor said you didn't ought! Weren't you ever taught – ' Suddenly, as if a match had been struck in her brain, she was alight with real anger at his folly, at his recklessness, at his lack of care in tending the pearl that was himself. She put her hands on his shoulders and shook, and shook, and shook him.

'Oh! Oh! Oh!' He gasped through his laughter, in time to her shaking. 'If you let me go – I'll tell you – what it was the doctor said.'

She bent over him in fierce and tender concern.

'He said . . . well, he said . . .'

'Go on! Go on!'

'Oh, Sunflower, Sunflower . . .'

She slapped him on the hand, quite hard, trying to hurt him.

He was giggling so much that he had to force it out. 'He said that if I ate sweet things – I would get fat – and God knows it's my beauty that got me where I am.'

'Oh!' she cried. 'Oh! You are awful! Oh, indeed you are! Making fun of me!' And she slapped him again, harder still, and then as he went on laughing she had to laugh too. Well, she oughtn't to mind if he had teased her, he was so pleased with his little joke, and surely he wouldn't dare to make such a donkey of himself in front of anybody he didn't like and trust quite a lot. Dutifully she stood over him, laughing and looking down on him to see when she might safely stop. He had pushed his chair back and was sprawling in a beam of sunlight that lay without mercy on his ugliness, over which his own merriment was travelling like the distorting pencil of a caricaturist. She marvelled once again at the wrongness of every bit of him: at the glazed, earth-coloured skin, stretched so tightly over the queer broad forehead which, because of something bulging in the contours that made one think of bad engineering, one suspected of being no thicker than an eggshell; at his straggling hair; at the sly setting of his eyes and his great pale and shapeless lips; at his nose, which might have been pinched in wet clay by a savage; at his head which was so badly set on his neck, at his neck which was so badly set on his shoulders that round the collar he had the look of a badly packed parcel. She had never seen him look more hideous, more unborn. Yet she had never known him to give out so powerfully his peculiar emanation of warmth and impish sweetness. Suddenly and keenly she wanted him to be immediately her lover. For the first time she knew desire not as a golden cloud but as a darting line of light. But of course it could not happen, not anyhow, since she was with Essington. Looking down on him hungrily she perceived that he had slipped one of his arms up behind him and was resting his head on the crook of his elbow, gorging himself in the comfort of this moment, lying in it as if it were his mother's lap. Without any doubt he was happy to be with her. She flung back her head and laughed, not as she had been laughing, to oblige him. This laughter shook out of her without the knowledge of her will, like a pulse made audible. It seemed to rise up into the room, to stand upright in the air above her like the climbing song of a lark. He became silent, his face was soft with pleasure as if he were a little drunk, his eyes watched a bumble-bee that was swinging slowly in the scent above the flowers on the table. Jealously she wondered, 'Why does he watch that bumble-bee? Ah, I see! He likes the slow sound of its drumming, he would like life to move at that pace while he is with me.' She felt cruel and triumphant like an angler that drags a great silver fish out of the water, pulls a scarlet hook out of its beating gills,

193

and throws it down to flap and wriggle on the wet boards of the boat, caught, caught. His eyes were nearly closed, but his fingers were twitching. He lifted his hand a little way in the air, clenched it, and dropped it back on his knee. From his tight, tortured smile she knew that he had resolved to deny some longing that still was making him see pictures behind his drooped lids, and she was certain that for a minute he had had the intention of gripping her by the wrists and swinging her down to him so that he could kiss her lips. If he had done so she would have cried out with terror, if he did so now she would have to cry out, for it would be like letting him drive a spear into her body. But the thing in her that was implacable towards Francis Pitt was implacable towards her also. It held her there, though she put one hand behind her so that he should not touch it, though with the other she covered her mouth.

But a shadow of annoyance passed over his face. He turned sharply and looked over his shoulder at the door as if he had heard something. 'Frederick,' he said.

She went back to her place. They sat and waited. She felt giddy, as if she had had a glass of champagne.

'H'm, I must have been mistaken,' he said at last, in a queer, dispirited voice. 'But God damn it, he will be coming back in a minute. There's cheese, Sunflower, and there's fruit.'

'Goodness gracious, I don't want any.'

'No, Sunflower, of course we don't want any. But because we have risen in the world, you and I, we have to sit here while a damned fool brings us fruit and cheese we can't eat, and takes an hour to do it too.' He spoke with a real, a despairing petulance.

'Well, we don't have to. After all, we're just as good as the servants, really.'

He broke into a sudden, an inordinately violent yell of laughter. 'Sunflower! Sunflower! You darling! Who says out loud what the rest of us timorously think! Oh, Sunflower! Sunflower! That's what I've been saying to myself in the dead of night with my bedroom door locked, and here you say it out in the open!'

'Well,' she said, her giddiness making her feel restless, 'I don't care how funny you think me, there isn't any reason why we shouldn't go out into the garden.'

'My God, I'm on. Down with the cheese and the fruit. Down with Frederick.' He jumped up, swung her out of her chair, and went arm-in-arm with her to the door. He was her jolly brother now, her schoolboy comrade. She liked it, of course, in a sort of a way.

194

For fear of Frederick they hurried through the hall, lifting their fingers to their lips, peering over their shoulders, making comic grimaces to each other. Her giddiness made her stop and pout into his face, 'I hate this house.' To which he guffawed, 'What a woman! What a woman!' But it was a horrid house. She didn't care if she had said it. The front door was a square of radiance in the darkness of the hall, which seemed like its adhesion to a grim philosophy, that dared to be so thick and umber because it knew that the time would come when that square would not show its contradictory brightness, when the outdoor world would come over to its way of thinking. He ought not to live here. He must move. A house in town. If he had to have one that was queer, there were those big ones by the river, in Chelsea. A house right out in the country. Some healthy place . . .

He ran down the steps, whistling, and waited for her. They strolled beside each other for a minute or two, silent, embarrassed. She had lost her tipsy feeling in the fresh air, he had lost his schoolboy spirits. There was no mood between them. Except the perpetual ache of her passion for him she felt nothing. It was like one of those nightmares in which one finds oneself on the stage before a huge audience and with no part, with no play, with only this vast and terrible obligation to entertain. He said as pompously as he might have said it to any stranger, 'Come and look at my flowers.' They turned aside from the drive and walked along the grass terrace outside the library windows, looking down on the preposterous scene, on the flower-beds that tossed like moored boats on a choppy sea over the broken levels of the old garden, on the flowers that grew so thickly in the beds, in the borders, on the ruined walls, that one thought of the glass shelves under the counter in an artificial flower department. He clicked his tongue and grunted good-humouredly, 'Funny place, funny place,' as if he were tolerating some other man's folly in living there. 'Let me give you one of my roses, let me give you one of my roses . . .' Standing beside him while he got it for her she shivered. Now she knew that everything they said about the way he had made his money was true. He did not pick the rose, his paw-hands stole it from the tree. He was a thief. Well, that was nothing, nothing. She lifted her head and frowned into the sun, then dropped her face to the rose.

He lumbered on clumsily among his rose-trees, with his queer look of being a lion walking on his hind legs, growling a tune to himself with incredible tunelessness. He broke off to say, 'I am happy, I am

195

very happy today, Sunflower,' and went back to his humming; and broke off again because from behind the trees that masked the turn of the drive there came the hoot of an automobile. The sound seemed to cut at his balance for he put out his short arms in front of him, just as a rearing lion would try to steady itself; and he swore violently. 'Oh, God damn . . . Oh, God damn . . .' She was reminded of the rage that had convulsed him when she first arrived. 'This is that fool Cornelliss.'

'Oh, bother him!' she exclaimed. 'It just would be Cornelliss.'

He turned on her sharply. 'Don't you like Cornelliss?'

'Of course not. He's a silly old thing, always standing about as if he were saying, "Well, at any rate, I'm not one to intrude", and then somehow intruding without saying a thing more than anyone could talking nineteen to the dozen.'

He seemed pleased. 'Poor Cornelliss. He has tried so hard to make you like him. Do you really not like him?'

'No, I think he's an awful old bore.'

His eyes were glinting. 'Shall I hide you from him then? Come on, I'll hide you.' His hand closed round her wrist, he hurried her round the corner of the house. They both laughed gleefully, they were conspirators together as they had been when they ran away from Frederick. 'In here, in here . . .' As he held the French window open for her he shot a furtive, grinning look at her, as if there were an amusing and rather improper implication in what they were doing and he wondered if she perceived it. She found herself in a very small room that she had never been in before with hardly anything in it but bookshelves and a desk stacked with papers and two big armchairs. It was evidently what Essington would not have let her call Francis Pitt's 'den'. He pushed forward a chair for her and went out of the door, but put his head back to give her a last look. 'Well, make yourself comfortable till I come back,' he whispered, with that ingenuously knowing grin. He had that air of naïvely enjoying a situation that looked improper though it was not because that was as near impropriety as his innocence ever reached, which he had worn that night in her dressing-room. 'I am in an actress's dressing-room', he had boasted to himself then. 'I am hiding this very beautiful woman because someone is coming and they will think we are lovers', he was boasting to himself now; and he was enjoying himself because he had never hidden a beautiful woman because someone was coming and they were lovers. She had altered her reading of what he was thinking in her

196

dressing-room because it had occurred to her that he must often have visited Dolores Methuen and the Nelly sisters at the theatre. But this time she knew she was reading his thoughts right. She reminded herself, 'Juliet Lynn, Mrs Lovatt, Veronica Fawcett', but it meant nothing that she could believe. She was sure of his innocence. If he were spending his glee on a reality he could not have so much left over for an appearance.

He whispered, 'Well, goodbye, till I've slaughtered Cornelliss.' She sat down in the armchair, took her hat off, leaned back and smiled up at him.

He made a slight exclamation, as if he had run a splinter into his finger and stepped back into the room.

'What is it? What is it?'

'Nothing, only that you're looking so lovely.' He bit his lip, gave an awkward laugh, jerked his head over his shoulder at sounds of arrival in the hall, and went out.

She sank back in the chair, laid her cheek against the leather cushion, closed her eyes and murmured, 'Dear Sunflower, who hasn't a word to say for herself for ever so long after she comes into a room. Just sits mum. But who all the time is the best company in the world . . . Sometimes when I cannot sleep a wink or when I have to sit beside Hurrell for hours I think of all sorts of little things I have heard you say and little things I've watched you do, and they all fit into a picture . . . I am happy, I am very happy today, Sunflower . . . Nothing, only that you're looking so lovely.' He said that, he said that . . . She started up and looked at the desk to see if there were any photographs. There were none there or anywhere else in the room. She did not think there had been any upstairs in his bedroom either. She ranged round the room trying to find out more about him. She knew all the books he had in the library, she wanted to see what he had there. She could not bear to think there was anything about him she did not know. They were much the same kind of books that were in the library but shabbier, possibly the worst he had found in the house when he bought it, possibly some he had bought before he was really rich. This was evidently the place he came when he was in the mood that makes a woman want to go out in her oldest clothes; there was something obstinate and perversely unlike his ordinary habit of neatness in the way the papers were stacked on the desk, and it was perverse of him to be using the horrid little slit of a room at all, for it was in the north-west half of the house, and the green bank of the

197

hillside rose only a few yards from the French windows. He was queer. Trying to lay hold of his queerness, she pried among his books, her hands shaking. She pulled out one red leather volume of Longfellow and found it was a prize that he had got for arithmetic at that school in Dulwich he had told them about that first time at dinner. There was a Scott bound in the same way just beside. And a Shelley. And a Wordsworth. They all had the same white label edged with gold pasted on the marbled flyleaf which said over the flourishing signature which failures use that it was a prize which had been awarded to Francis Pitt for arithmetic. She burst into nervous and delighted laughter, it was so just like Francis Pitt to have kept these prizes all these years. It was so utterly unlike Essington, who if he received any honour of any sort waved it away with a gesture of sick distaste, who if he were awarded a prize by any of those international committees of something dictated letters so shrilly squealing with annoyance that the secretaries went to unheard of lengths to delay posting them for a couple of days, who if he had found one of his school prizes would have rung the bell for it to be taken out as if it was something old that smelt. The idea of giving any prize seemed absurd to him in itself in view of the inadequacy of all human effort to cope with the human task. It was as if instead of building an ark Noah had met the warning of the flood by holding a swimming gala . . . But Francis Pitt was not like that. He was little and humble, he was not arrogant enough to criticise an established custom like prize-giving, he was so doubtful of himself that at the back of his mind he was glad to be able to say, 'Well, anyway in 1895 I was first in arithmetic in the fourth form at Everett College, Dulwich.' Of course it wasn't as clever a way of going on as Essington's but it was more useful. Since there wasn't any society but human society for a human being to take part in what could a human being do if it lost patience with human society? You might as well put a rope round your neck. Poring over his comical and serviceable kind of nature she sought among the shelves for further traces of it. There was a shelf of those books, Casanova and Rabelais, that men have agreed are amusingly virile just as they have agreed that cricket matches are not dull; which is so much what you wouldn't naturally think about them that you feel they made the agreement formally at a meeting in one of the older clubs, the kind where the senior members nearly died in the war because they had to have waitresses, and all signed their names to a long paper after lots of people who had been at the same school had proposed and seconded things. She had taken a look at the silly things. Casanova told the same sort of stories, only not so decent, that the favourite brother of the lady next door told the night when he turned up for the first time for fifteen years, and then the next morning they found that he hadn't any money but expected to stay with them till he heard from a friend in New Zealand about a treasure hunt. And Rabelais. She had talked that over with Etta only the other day. 'They're always talking about Rabelais and how jolly he is, but you don't ever come on them actually reading Rabelais, do you?' 'No, nor anything else either,' Etta had replied tartly. 'They don't read half as much as they think they do.' 'No, they don't, do they?' She flung her arms the length of the shelf, rested her face on them and laughed at those books, and at some other things: the way he always looked badly dressed though he went to the best tailors and, if you thought, you could see it was because he would not let them make the shoulders broad enough nor cut the coat short enough to fit his queer little body, as he liked to pretend that he had a body like other men's, not seeing that his was somehow better. A languor came on her so that she sank down on the floor, keeping her fingertips on the shelf, pressing her smiling mouth and drooped lids against the bare flesh of her arms. For some reason she felt as if her thirst for passivity were about to be quenched. The will inside her was like a spinning top, running down, running down; soon it would give a jerk and fall, twitch and lie still. She pulled herself up, and without troubling to open her eyes more than lash-deep swayed over to the armchair and threw herself down there, burying her face again in the leather. Inconsequently she thought of Alice Hester, the old woman whom she had seen tried for bigamy at the assizes, who when she was young (but not so very young after all) had been sought out by the man she loved where she waited in the darkness, not able to see the faces of her many children though she could hear them crying to her. He had turned the long ray of his lantern on the darkness and had shown her her children one by one . . .

Sunflower nearly slept; and passed into that fantasy which had come upon her often when she first met Francis Pitt, when it was as if she stood in a high place among the hills, by a lake, where there were woods bright with the young fire of spring, and there were children round her, crying out because he brought food for them across the water. With interest but without distress she noted that though she was lying still and half-asleep her heart was beating fast, as if she had run a race. She laid her hand on it and smiled to feel the hard hoops of her ribs. They reminded her of a half-finished boat she had seen on the stocks in a shipyard at some fishing-port she had once visited. It was a ship the man who showed her round had been proud of making, a ship that they said would stand all storms, it had sturdy hoops of ribs like hers. 'I am strong,' she murmured, 'I am strong!' Now everything pleased her, even the little room. Its darkness seemed like the snug darkness of one's bed, and good to lie in. That the blue and white day could be seen only high above the green bank which pressed its dampness close to the French windows struck her as an amusing architectural feature, as a fantastic chimney-piece might be. She passed into a state of pleasure no more inscribed by thought than the petals of an unfolding flower are inscribed with words. Once she said aloud to herself, placidly, comfortably, 'It is a pity that nothing can happen, that I am with Essington . . .'

He was back sooner than she expected, in something less than half an hour. He looked very pale and drawn, which did not surprise her, since for some time she had seen that he was finding his care of Hurrell purely tedious. The inspiration of his grief had failed him. Evidently he had found that he did not care for Hurrell as much as he had thought he did. Well, she was sorry it had happened, but perhaps it was as well that he should have found out how little use a man can ever be to a man really.

Stretching herself she murmured, 'I nearly went to sleep.'

Taking no notice of that he said, 'Will Harrowby be here or shall I send a car with you to town?'

In alarm she asked, 'Is Mr Hurrell bad?'

'No. He is quite all right. Cornelliss has gone.'

She rose slowly, saying icily, 'Oh, Harrowby will be there.' She put on her hat and found her gloves and bag, taking care to move without haste.

He made it much worse by showing that he knew what he had done, muttering awkwardly, 'You said you had some things to do in town this afternoon.'

Calmly she answered, 'Yes. The Times Book Club. My hairdresser. A fitting at the dressmaker's. The things one has to do.'

'Mm, busy life we all lead, busy life,' he mumbled, and went towards the door to open it for her; but it was opened in his face by Frederick, who held out a tray with a letter on it, saying, 'Come by hand.' Francis Pitt picked it up disagreeably as if it were something Frederick had invented to annoy him, looked at the handwriting, started, and turned to Sunflower, exclaiming piteously, 'Excuse me, excuse me!'

She waited stiffly.

There was the sound of tearing paper. He said to Frederick, 'No answer,' and crossed to the fireplace and scattered the pieces in the empty grate behind the screen, exclaiming petulantly, 'I wish there were a fire, I would like to burn this damned thing.' Then, keeping his back to her, he told her with hurt nonchalance, like a little boy reporting that they hadn't picked him for the second eleven after all, 'It appears that young Mr Harrop and Miss Wycherley have already left my employment. At least so they tell me.'

It was nice of him to be so much concerned about these young people. 'Oh, they'll marry and be happy in some little house,' she told him, ready to be nice.

He was shaken by a convulsion of rage, he brought his clenched fist down on the mantelpiece, he began to snarl and choked it, he sunk his chin on his chest and became a huddled heap of sullenness. Well, if he chose to be so queer and would not let her know about him as somehow she had a right to know, he could do it alone. She wanted to go home and cry. She moved to the door.

At the sound of the turning handle he wheeled round and in quite a high voice cried out as if astonished that she could be so unkind, 'Oh, but you're not going! You mustn't go!'

'I must,' she said coldly.

'Oh, but you mustn't! You needn't! Sunflower, please stay and talk to me!'

In a strangled, throbbing voice she asked, 'Do you really want me to?'

'Oh merciful God, I do, I do.'

Tears were forming behind her eyes. 'But . . . I thought you didn't . . .'

There were tears in his eyes, too. 'Of course I did, of course I wanted you to stay.'

'Then, why – '

'I thought you had to go, you said you had to go, oh, for the love of Christ, stay and talk to me. Sit down! Sit down!'

She sat down. 'Just for a minute,' she sniffed into her handkerchief.

He muttered as indistinctly, 'That's good of you . . .'

They were both near crying. He turned aside and busied himself in taking a cigar from a box on the desk. For a minute he sat there

201

smoking and muttering to himself, till a twitch shook him, uncrossing his legs and bringing his feet down on the ground heels first, while his clenched hands struck his knees and his head jerked backwards. He wheeled round in his chair and called out to her, loudly as if he could not see her because of some mist, 'Well, you're there, Sunflower.' Lightly but with a core of obstinacy, she answered, 'Yes, I am here.' He got up and strolled about the room, holding his cigar in a shaking hand but strutting more with every puff. 'Ha!' he breathed presently. 'I feel better. I am a fool to take these young people so seriously.' He put his hands on the back of the other armchair and pushed it along till it faced hers, looking very comical as he waddled behind it. Genially he grumbled, 'But I am a fool about these things. I make friends of my subordinates.' He plumped himself down on it. The chairs were so close that his knees were close to hers. 'And I am loyal to my friends.'

'I'm sure you are,' she said fervently. His nostrils dilated as if her assent were something good to smell. 'So when my friends are not loyal to me I feel it.' He sighed. 'Yes, I feel it.'

'Of course you do.'

'But perhaps I ought not to blame those poor young people. They are up against sex.' He spoke the words with a demure gluttony, looking obliquely downwards. For a short time he sat puffing at his cigar, then took it out of his mouth, and said very clearly, keeping his eyes on hers, 'Sex causes a great deal of trouble in this world, Sunflower.'

She flinched. She did so hate that word sex.

He seemed to become lost in thought, frowning at the book-case behind her head. She tried to work her chair away a little, so that she need not be quite so near him.

His eyes flashed back to hers again. Kindly and concerned, he leaned forward. 'Are you not comfortable, Sunflower?'

'Oh, quite, quite . . .'

He seemed satisfied. His gaze swung away from her again. 'It has caused a lot of trouble in my life, Sunflower. That is why I very often feel envious of you and Essington, of the steady, continuous union of you two. Though I suppose it is my own fault that I have nothing of the sort to make other people envy me . . . the fault of my unfortunate temperament . . .' He shook his head and chuckled reminiscently. She wished she was not so very near him. 'I have not been all that I should have been in the past, Sunflower . . .'

But why need he tell her all these things? It could not be of any

202

use to him to tell that horrid story of how he had met a woman who he had thought very beautiful (though probably she was not, probably he was as apt as Essington to mistake good clothes for good looks) at a luncheon-party during the war and had . . . been taken with her (he need not have put it into that hatefully coarse way) so that he had risen as soon as the meal was over and made the excuse that he must go back to his ministry and had muttered over her hand as he said goodbye, 'I will call on you at three o'clock,' and had gone to her house at that hour and found her waiting (what sort of a woman could she be to do a thing like that?) and had then and there . . . Why did it hurt her so to hear that? She had known well enough that he was like that. She had been told all those women's names, and though from time to time she had fooled herself that those stories were a pack of lies she had known that the chances were that they were true. There was something round his mouth that showed that he had often done that kind of thing just as when he was a little boy a smear round it must often have shown that he had been eating jam out of the jar. But one was made so funnily . . . A thousand times she had talked this over with herself and been tortured by pictures of him making love to other people which she had deliberately held in front of her mind's eye so that familiarity should make them hurt less. Yet when she heard about it from his own lips she felt as great a shock as if she had suddenly been thrown into icy waters. Her surprised lungs had to battle to force her breath back into her body. But at least he did not notice what he was doing to her, for if he had he would not have gone on to tell that other story about the American girl that a friend had brought over to London after an unfortunate attempt to start in business in New York . . . 'It was so like him to come back with no money and a girl . . . Helen . . . now what was her name? Helen . . . Helen . . . By God, I have forgotten her name . . . that's too bad, that's too bad!' He was humorously scandalised at his forgetfulness of one whom, it appeared, he had such abundant reason to remember gratefully. That story and all the others made her want to cry out, partly because he was making himself so ugly. He looked old-womanish while he told them; it was as if his grossness were the turned-up collar of a dirty old dressing-gown he had huddled round him because he felt a cold coming on, and the stuffy warmth of his stories might have been steam rising from a basin of mustard and water in which he was soaking his feet. And the stories themselves made her see ridiculous pictures of him, running after women taller than himself through immense rooms

203

furnished like hotels so that his little legs looked comically short. She shut her eyes tight and shook her head when in those pictures she saw him catching up the woman he pursued, she was so sure that his love making would be slobbering and silly. Amazed she asked herself, 'Why do I bother about this man? There are many others. I am beautiful, I am not so old. This man is horrid. He is common.' For a moment she felt as if she had only to pull down a latch and walk out into such peace and freedom as she had not dreamt of for weeks. But the force that rode her after him, as a huntsman rides a horse to hounds after the fox, dug its spurs into her and said, 'You fool, he has something that you need.' That was true. His strength, his power, she must have that. The lake among the hills swam before her eyes, not as a place where it would be delightful to be but as a place that she must go to if she had to crawl there on bleeding knees. Besides, this was not all of him, he was a million other things as well, he was kind, he was warm, he had charm like the smell of spice, he was a king among men and made them serve him; and the part of him that was these things was utterly hers. Indeed, though it might not look like it, though nothing had been said about it, there was a way in which he was utterly hers. She could not think in words about it, but images formed before her mind that told her the truth as well as words could. In that magic world which once or twice since she had known Francis Pitt she had perceived to be superimposed on the real world, where there were the caverns that echoed the barking of the borzois, the grapes on whose shadows they had trodden at her door, the white arch of the love that proceeded from her when she touched his hand, and this lake to which she had to go, she enjoyed among many other forms the likeness of a sphinx, crouching in a vast desert and thick darkness, unappalled because her head reared high into the night and was changed to something more suited to her fierce intentions than her present loveliness, because her breasts were not flesh that would die but rock that would endure and were great enough to suckle the earth, and because her hands were now huge claws between which he lay in the likeness of a swaddled child with a sceptre beside him. Yet also she felt degraded and ashamed and contaminated. It was shameful, it was disgusting, but she would rather have been any of the women Francis Pitt had done that thing with than be herself. From his stories she knew that they had been so easy that their love-making can have been no better beauty than the iridescence grease makes on water and that they had seen him silly and vulgar, but for all that they had kept that tryst with his body that she had to keep or go down alive into her grave. The only thing was that at least he wasn't saying that he had really loved any of them.

But that was just what he was saying now.

'Still, Sunflower, all this sin and wickedness is perhaps not so much my fault as it seems. I like to think I might have been like you and Essington if things had not gone badly with my one real love affair. This is a story I do not tell to everybody, Sunflower. It hit me hard, it hit me hard for a long time. It still . . . upsets me to think of her, though I have not seen her now for many years, except for a glimpse at Juliet's wedding . . .'

She asked fretfully, trying to divert the story from its channel, 'Who's Juliet?'

He threw her a sharp and furtive look, as if he were surprised to see that she had evidently not heard of some story relevant to her question, and that it concerned him in such a way that he could not possibly tell her about it. With patent, over-acted quietness and discretion he answered, 'Lady Juliet Lynn.'

Remembering, she started and almost moaned, 'Oh, yes!'

He smoked until she thought she would not be able to bear it. He looked very well and chubby, as if it nourished him to tell this story.

'It was this way, Sunflower. Two days after I landed in England on my return from California, I met a woman. A very beautiful woman. And I knew from the moment I set eyes on her that I loved her. I sat next to her at lunch, and before she had opened her mouth I said to myself, "That is the girl I am going to marry". And then I looked down and saw her hand. Her left hand. She was wearing a wedding ring. It was the last thing in the world I had expected. I had not heard her name when we were introduced and she was very young. I tell you, my heart dropped dead in me for a minute. Well, she was married right enough. She bore a very famous name. She had a great position. She had children. There was nothing to be done. Openly. There was something to be done secretly. And by God we did it. I may have to pay pretty heavily for that in the hereafter, for it was all my fault. She had the scruples that good women have and I had hard work to overcome them. But I did, and whatever I have to pay, it was worth it. Seven years of the wildest happiness. Seven years . . . I am very faithful, Sunflower.'

Seven years was a long time. He must be saturated in her. No other woman would be able to wipe out the memories he must have of her. If only he were not sitting so very close to her . . .

'That was a wonderful time. I have much to be grateful for, Sunflower. I have some intoxicating memories. I had a little flat in Cork Street. She used to come to me there. And sometimes with careful plotting and scheming we used to meet abroad and have a few days together at some place. Once we had three days at Fontainebleau. And we had nearly a week at that place outside Rome. What is it? Tivoli. But we were nearly caught that time. My God, she was a marvellous woman, a marvellous woman. In our room at night we could hear the sound of the waterfall, and there was a nightingale used to sing. Sunflower, are you quite comfortable in that chair?'

'Quite comfortable, thank you . . .'

'You were moving as if you wanted to get up. Well, we had seven years of it. Seven years. Then the crash came. We were caught. She was speaking to me on the telephone and her husband happened to pick up an extension and heard what we were saying. Then, by God, the fat was in the fire. Her husband was a very decent fellow, but he would not have it. Small blame to him, he wouldn't have been a man if he had. I wanted her to face the music with me. To be divorced and marry me. But there I lost her by the very thing that held me. She was a good woman, and she would not give up her children. She had three lovely children. So we had to part. That was an awful business. Her husband let us meet for the last time in the park of their country seat. I had to wait for her in a clearing at the end of a long grass avenue. I had to give my word not to go up that avenue, to stay right there in that clearing. I saw my poor darling coming down that avenue, dressed all in white, because she knew I loved to see her so, running to meet me, running desperately like a hurt thing that wants to get home and show its hurt and be comforted. And I could not go to meet her. I had to sit there and wait. When she got to me she was all dabbled in tears. I cleaned them up with my handkerchief. We had just an hour together. I had given my word to keep her no more than an hour. Then I had to sit and watch the white figure stumbling all the way back up the avenue. Back to her home. Away from romance and passion and all the delights we'd had for seven years. Once she fell on her knees. I couldn't bear it. I swung round and hid my face against the trunk of a tree, but when I turned back again she was still there, a white heap on the grass. And I could not go to her. I was howling like a kid when at last she picked herself up and staggered to the end of the avenue. God help all of us who live outside the law . . .'

Unctuously he rambled on, 'Then after that I went to pieces. Nature is very brutal. A man's heart may be broken, but his body doesn't cease making certain demands. And women have always been kind to me, too kind to me . . .'

Why would he go on talking about things that do not matter? She cried out from the bottom of a deep pit, 'Those three children, were any of them yours?'

He did not answer.

She cried out a little louder, 'Were any of them yours?'

A long while afterwards he answered, 'No.'

Because his voice sounded muffled and did not come from the direction she had expected, she took her hands down from her eyes. Now why, when a minute before he had been sitting up in his chair as pleased as punch and smacking his lips over this story of this woman who had made her think him so wonderful, paunchy and sleek with self-satisfaction, should he have slipped down sideways in his chair and be lying in a huddled heap, his face buried in one arm, the other one hanging limp between his knees as if he had had a stroke? She rose and stood looking down on him in terror.

He spoke again. 'None of her children were mine.'

And then again he grumbled out of his collapse, 'I have never had any children.'

She snapped her teeth together so that it could be heard, and drew her hand across her flat hard stomach and the strong hoops of her ribs. But she was alarmed at him. She took a step towards him.

'Sunflower,' he querulously muttered.

Prowling, cautious, like a dog that is afraid it is being manoeuvred into a position where it can be whipped, she crossed the room and stood over him. She was not quite sure that he would not look up at her and jeer. But from his heavy breathing she knew that his distress was real. She sank on her knees beside him, not touching him, because he would not say anything that gave her the right to do that, but coming very close to him. 'What's the matter? What's the matter?' she asked tenderly, crooningly, fiercely.

Without lifting the arm which shielded his face he muttered, 'What can I do to be saved?'

'What do you mean?'

'What can I do to be saved?' Mockingly he said it, as if he were quoting from some sermon that would strike every sophisticated person as preposterous. 'That's how my old father would have put it in the pulpit. What can I do to be saved? How am I to live so that God will not send me to Hell?' Then awe and terror flooded his tone and he asked in deadly earnest and despair, 'How am I to live so that people will think me a great man? How am I to live so that it will last, so that there is some sense to it all?' He lifted his head from his arm and looked at her with something like hatred. 'It is easy for you! You are a woman. You know what you want.'

'Why,' she said, in wonder, 'what do I want?'

He closed his eyes, which made his face look very ghastly and smiled. In a whisper, he said, 'You are so terrible as an army with banners, Sunflower,' and turned his head away from her.

She did not know what to do. If only she had the right to touch him, she might be able to comfort him, but she could not find any words, she did not understand what was the matter with him, why he could not go ahead and be happy. All she could do was to bring her face closer to his and murmur kind, inaudible things, while he muttered brokenly, 'What am I to do? What am I to do? What's the way to live? Essington and Hurrell, I thought they had it, I thought they'd got the trick. Hard thinking and public service . . . Hard thinking and public service . . .' He repeated it owlishly, making a faint charlatanish movement of his brows and hands. 'But Essington and Hurrell . . . Look at them. Look at them. Hurrell is dying. And it all means nothing. He's missed something and he knows it. Every minute of the day I can see he knows it. And Essington . . .' He gave a hard, dry snigger that in the midst of her pity for him struck her as unusually disagreeable. 'Essington is a great man. But he is old. He is losing the things one loses when one is old. And it all means nothing. He has missed something too. Hurrell mourns over it, Essington bickers over it. And they are fine men. If there had been anything there they would have got it. By God, it is better to be like Canterton and Jack Murphy. At least they have their drink and their fun.'

'No, no! You don't want to be like them, the nasty beasts! Why do you have them about? It isn't wise, when you're feeling low like this, you might get into their ways. It doesn't do you any good to have that man Murphy round.'

He sat up in his chair and grasped her wrist. 'Murphy?'

'Yes, he's a horrid man, and it isn't as if he were fond of you, he isn't fond of anybody, the old crocodile. Look what he's done with his own daughter and Canterton. There isn't hardly anybody would do a thing like that . . .'

He pointed a shaking finger over her shoulder. 'Is that door shut?'

'Yes, dear, you shut it.'

In quite a tiny whisper he said, 'Sunflower, I want to tell you why I have Jack Murphy in my house. It's something I've never told anyone else in the whole world.'

'Oh, don't tell me if you don't want to.' She was whispering too.

'I want to tell you. I must tell somebody. Not even Etta knows. I can't tell her.'

'Oh, you poor dear, you poor dear, tell me whatever it is.'

'I know. I know. I could tell you whatever it is. You would forgive me. Sunflower, it is good to have you here. Well, I was out there in California when I first went out as a boy, and everything was going wrong. Nothing fails like failure in the States, and I was a failure all right. They laughed at me, because I was so short and such a funny-looking little devil. I had a job as a clerk in a store for eight dollars a week, and I was damn lucky to have that. And I wanted money, and I wanted drink, and I wanted women. I wanted all the things that other men seemed to get for the asking.'

Oh, if she had the right to touch him. She writhed where she knelt and pressed her knotted hands against her face. 'Oh, you poor little thing . . .'

'I was nineteen,' he almost whispered, and his great head rolled on one side, while he wallowed in her pity. She gave a little cry, and he stiffened up in his chair and exclaimed with consternation, 'No, I am lying, I was twenty-one, I was twenty-one. Do you hear, Sunflower?'

Fiercely defending him from himself, she said, 'That was young. Terribly young to be there all alone, far away from his people.'

'But listen to what I did. Sunflower, a man from Vancouver left me his fur coat to look after, while he went down to do a job in Panama. Sunflower, I sold that coat. I sold it, and I got a good bit of money for it, for it was a good coat. I spent that money giving a grand dinner at the Poodle Dog and having two of the best women in the best whorehouse in the town. I was a fine fellow for that night. The men clapped me on the back and called me a good guy. And the women said that I was a wonder and that they liked little men. God, those trollops. But I thought I'd never have any woman but a bought one, I thought I'd never be able to buy any but these. Then in a month or so the man came back and wanted his coat. And when he found what I'd done he got mad. He'd been kind to me, because he was a big chap and had felt sorry for me. Do you hear, Sunflower? I'd stolen from a friend.'

209

She moved miserably. 'You were so young, you were all alone, oh, don't fret about it.' She was sitting on the floor, resting her weight on her two hands, rocking herself from side to side, her head hanging down.

'He had me arrested for it. I was taken through the streets to a police station. I was locked up in a cell. I was tried in a courtroom. Oh, Christ, I was so frightened of the jail. I cannot bear the feeling of being shut up. Do you know that to this day I cannot bear the law courts. However much interested I am in a case, I can't go up and see it tried. Last autumn my firm was sued for a quarter of a million. We won of course. I had taken care to be well on the right side from start to finish. But I could not bear to go near the court. It would have brought me right back to the day I had to stand up before a judge while they told the kind of cur I was. I had to stand there and listen to it with a sore head, because I'd been sick with fright out in the passage and a policeman had hit me on the head with his club for being such a dirty little beast.'

'Oh, my dear, my poor dear . . .'

'And that's how Jack Murphy gets into my house. At the last moment he came forward and defended me. I'd helped him to figure out something in a saloon one night and he'd seen I was worth backing. He was an attorney then and in with the police. I walked out of that court a free man – or a slave to Jack Murphy, put it whatever way you like. I hate and loathe him, the dirty devil with his gab about friendship. And he's always there, making me toe the line. If I were to go back on him for one moment, he'd be at my throat, he'd be spilling the story all round London and I should be done.'

'How dare he! The nasty beast!' she cried savagely. 'But don't you know anything against him so that you can fight back?' As she spoke these words she realised how far she had travelled out of Essington's country. Defiantly she gave herself up to the proud, growling, outlawed loyalty of the poacher's dog.

'I do. By God, I'll say I do! But that's no good to me. He doesn't need to care about his reputation. It's all out about him in the City. Nobody who is worth anything there will give him a bean. He makes his money out-swindling other rogues or getting hold of fools that will disregard the family lawyer and the broker because of this good kind man, God damn him, with his shark smile. But I'm different! If I'm to get on in politics I must be respected.' His voice squealed high and querulous. 'I've got to make people like Essington think I'm all right!'

'He likes you awfully,' she murmured.

'Does he?' He seemed pleased, yet muttered derisively under his breath, 'Essington!' Panic came down on him again. 'But my God, supposing I pull that off what is the good? Essington and Hurrell! What ought I to do? Sunflower, what am I to do? How am I to live?'

'But what do you mean?' she cried in desperation. 'One just lives.'

'Yes, but how? But how?'

'One lives, one lives, one just lives the ordinary life! Things go on!'

They were facing each other with bared teeth, as if they were enraged with each other.

'But how? I'm asking you how?'

'I tell you, one just lives! Oh, why do you fret, why do you worry?' She began to cry and stretched out her arms to him. He did not take them so she drew them back and beat her clenched fists on the ground sobbing, 'Why won't you be happy? Don't you want to be happy?'

He screamed out furiously in a very high-pitched voice, as if she were asking a question idiotically disregardful of some torture he was undergoing, 'Yes, why can't I be happy? Why can't I? Why can't I?'

She crawled right up to his feet, put her hands on his knees and shook him. 'What is the matter?' she shrieked. 'Why don't you tell me what the matter is? How can I help you if you don't? And you are torturing me, you are killing me!'

His face grew sullen and obstinate and hostile, it grew vacant as a skull. His mouth was a round hole, his eyes were round grey holes. He sat in a heap in his chair, looking straight in front of him, letting his head and body wobble as she shook him. 'Have mercy on me!' she sobbed. 'Have mercy on me!'

Suddenly his face lit up. He gripped her wrist. 'Frederick.'

Though he had pulled her up from the floor before the footman came in he forgot to take his hand away from her wrist.

'Miss Allardyce is in the library, sir.'

He burst out laughing. Then checked himself, and said in his usual, gruff, genial voice, 'Tell her I'll be with her in a minute.' When the footman left the room he got up and walked with a deliberate conscious strut to the window, and remained staring out for a little while. Then he turned round and went to the mantelpiece, and picked up her bag and held it out to her, saying, 'Pretty bag. Dear Sunflower, who has everything pretty about her.' He looked her clearly in the eyes. It was not possible that there had ever been the scene between them which had just happened.

211

She drew on her gloves.

'This is a pity,' he said lightly. 'I had forgotten that I had told poor Georgy to come here and tell me her troubles.'

'Has she troubles?' she said, as lightly. 'One thinks of her as such a lucky person.'

'Ah, clever women get into the same jams as stupid ones,' he said with cool amusement. He strolled about the room with his hands in his pockets, his spirits quite restored. Suddenly his head slewed round, he looked over his shoulder at the chair where he had lately been sitting. Her eyes followed his. That scene had happened. It was true that he had sat crying out for help against some terror, that she had lain at his feet, weeping and beating the floor with her fists, because he would not let her help him. There seemed to be an invisible yet material record of it remaining in the room. It was as if the air had not been able to rush into the space that had been filled by their bodies during that scene, because it was stuffed out with the violent emotions they had generated. Abashed, Sunflower and Francis Pitt turned away from each other.

Thickly he said, 'Sunflower, who sometimes blurts out the truth so that it makes one tell the truth oneself.'

She murmured, 'I wouldn't ever tell.'

'Well, would it be easy to describe?' he asked sardonically, in mockery of himself and all he had done, spreading his hands across his chest. Then he seemed to see that she meant something less profound than he at first had thought, and said hastily, 'Oh . . . about Jack Murphy. I know you will not give me away.' He repeated this, the second time making it seem as if he were paying himself and not her a compliment. 'I know you will not give me away.' Strutting, he took another turn about the room. She heard him mutter between his teeth, 'Georgy . . .'

He swung round on her. 'The play! Tell me about the play!'

'The play?'

'Yes. How long is it going to run, do you think?'

'Oh, a year, it might. Mr Trentham is so sure about it that he wants to put Joyce Marbury into my part and send me to America with it in the autumn. You see, he's never had a success there, and he thinks I might make it go there.'

'Would you go to America, Sunflower?'

'No!' Then to explain away her fervour, to make sure that he would

212

not guess she was staying in England because she wanted to be with him, she added, 'Somehow I've never wanted to go to America.'

'Now, how would a change of cast like that be managed? I mean, what would make an English manager fall in with Trentham's desire to have an American success?'

'Well, it's like this.' She explained the business arrangements involved, and he followed that up with other questions, which she found it delightful to answer. He would see that she was not really so stupid, that there were some things she understood. And it was wonderful to see that he was not embarrassed by what had happened, he would ask her back again, and next time she would be more quiet and cunning, and would find out what was worrying him, and then everything would go right. She stopped in the middle of a sentence and compressed her lips obstinately. Then, trying to grope for the rest of the sentence and reckoning where the argument had brought them, she realised that they must have been talking for about ten minutes and exclaimed, 'I must go, you're keeping Miss Allardyce waiting!'

'Oh Georgy will wait, Georgy will wait,' he said, smiling. 'But tell me, is this arrangement common?'

It was lovely to think that he should be making excuses to keep her there. She answered that and some other questions, and moved to the door.

'Oh, don't go!' he begged.

Primly she murmured, 'I've got to do all those things I told you about.'

'Oh, yes,' he said, 'The Times Book Club,' and laughed.

With an entrancing slowness, he paced beside her across the hall. Quite certainly he loved being with her.

'Georgy,' he said with a chuckle, and jerked his head towards the open door of the library. They could see her standing at the other end of the room, looking out of the window with her back to them. The contrast between her fine head, so well held, and her stocky body and thick legs was so great that she reminded one of a bust on a tall cylindrical pedestal.

'I like her,' said Sunflower, 'and that's a lovely dress. It's one of Vionnet's best this year. Did you say she has only just started dressing up?'

'Yes, just recently.'

'Ah, that's why she's standing up. I used to do that when I first had good clothes.'

'What do you mean? Why is she standing up?'

'To keep the pleats in.'

He guffawed. 'To keep the pleats in! Women are funny things.'
They moved on towards the front door. On the top step he checked
her by laying his hand on her arm. 'Well, God bless you, Sunflower,
for bearing with me this afternoon. I suppose you think I'm a crazy
fellow.'

'No, I don't,' she said stoutly.

'Then come back and bear with me some more. I do not know what
I would do without you.'

'It's lovely of you to say that.' Harrowby had driven the car up to the
steps and was now looking up at them. She exclaimed, 'Oh, doesn't
Harrowby look ill?'

'He certainly does. I've never seen a man's face so white. What's
the matter with him?'

'I don't know. I can't find out. He's been like this for the last two
weeks. It's terrible.'

'Ah, he's in love with you and jealous of me.'

She smiled at his joke and said, 'Now you must go back to Miss
Allardyce.'

He kept hold of her arm as they walked down the steps, almost
fondling it. After he had put her in the car, he called through the
window, 'I will telephone you tonight . . . When you get in from the
theatre, just to say goodnight.'

That was wonderful. He had never done that before. 'Very well.'

'And now,' he said, 'I must get back to Georgy, poor Georgy.
Goodbye dear.'

She had done him a world of good. He ran up the steps like a
schoolboy.

*

She felt ever so embarrassed when the dresser said, 'Why, here's
Miss Tempest! She's quite a stranger here nowadays!' She had quite
forgotten that dear old Maxi had written to say that she hadn't seen
the show yet because she'd had to take the baby down to Herne Bay to
convalesce after whooping cough and had come back for a couple of
days and was going to be in front with George that very evening. It
was lovely to see her again, fatter than she used to be but still well,
and hear her burst out not listening to one word of what you were

asking about baby, though usually you weren't allowed to talk about anything else, 'Well, Sunflower, who's the clever little actress now? Oh, I'm so pleased, I can't tell you how pleased I am!' and break into those funny laughs that used to make the other girls say, 'Hello, old Maxi's laid another egg!' Only it was funny how men did get in the way of a girl's friends. Sunflower couldn't help remembering how Essington had previously described the greeting of any two actresses as a violent outburst of affection unaccompanied by cerebration, not unanalogous to a sneeze, and she felt miserable about remembering it, because though Maxi was noisy she really meant everything she said, and you ought to quarrel with a person who says things like that about your friends, but you can't do that if the person is somebody that you have to be loyaller to than your friends. Also she had to dodge when Maxi hugged her and not hug back for fear of spoiling her make-up and her hair over which she had worked so carefully that several times she'd made a complete mess of it all and had to start from the beginning all over again. For if Francis Pitt had been to see her several times without telling her, he might be there that night. But she did love old Maxi, she was so warm and understanding.

'Sunflower, I can't tell you how wonderful you are! Of course you look too gorgeous. You're the one woman in the world who looks well with long hair. But it's your acting, darling, it's your acting!'

'Oh, Maxi, do you really think I pull it off? There's one thing I wish you'd tell me about. I'm never sure I got that scene with the wineglass quite right. Doesn't it look all wrong from the front?'

'My dear, you're marvellous, there and everywhere else, marvellous. Well, you know what George is. Born in the theatre, my dear, and you can't get a rise out of him in the ordinary way. I give you my word, he's been sitting all the evening saying, "Well, where's Brenda Burton now?" Though speaking for myself, I always knew where that Shakespearean Art gets off. My dear, you're right there, up at the top.'

'Oh, Maxi, you can't think how funny it is to have your acting spoken freely about in front of your face instead of having it glossed over. The times I've nearly burst out crying because people kept on saying, "Charming, charming", in that kind way. But of course it's rather difficult now. I never know what to say. You can't contradict people when they say you're acting well, and yet you can't agree with them, it seems so conceited.'

'Well, my dear, that's a very good line you had just now.'

'Which?'

215

'The one you just said to me. "I'm never sure if I get that scene with the wineglass quite right." You keep on saying that.'

'But I might get the scene right any time. I feel it's something quite small that's wrong. You could probably tell me what it was.'

'Yes, dear, but in any case go on saying that, it sounds well. People'll say you're modest, and that you're beginning to work so hard. Don't you dare not say it. You couldn't have a better line.'

'Well, I don't want to be a fraud.'

'That isn't being a fraud. You asked me that question when you came into the room, didn't you? Well, you weren't being a fraud, then, were you? Then there isn't any harm in asking it again, is there? You silly girl. You always did waste things . . . And you're a silly girl too about that scene with the wineglass. It does go wrong, but it isn't your fault.'

'But it is my fault. It must be, because it's wrong when I play it with Cosmo Davis and it's wrong now this other boy's playing it. It isn't likely that they'd both go wrong in the same place, is it?'

'But that's just what happens. The scene does break, you're quite right, but it isn't your fault. Don't you see what happens? You work the scene up and up till you pass him the wineglass in that lovely soft, floppy sort of way, as if you were just ready to keel over, and he ought to grab it in a he-man sort of way, as if he were a bull at a gate. Well, he can't do that, being a nancy-boy, as anyone can see, and neither could Cosmo, who's a lamb, but we all know what he is.'

'Well, it isn't Cosmo's fault, poor dear. They all seem to be that way nowadays.'

'My dear, don't I know it. For years before I left the stage I never played a love-scene that wasn't just a romp with the girls. Well, you can't make bricks without straw so the scene drops. But you're all right. Oh, my dear, you're going to be a fine actress. And the funny thing is I don't mind. I'm just glad. I've minded all sorts of things about you before. I used to mind dreadfully because when we went out out together, everybody looked at you first. Of course you never guessed that, because if it had been the other way round you wouldn't have minded. You're much nicer than I am, Sunflower.'

'Oh, don't be so silly. There isn't anybody who isn't nicer than me, and especially you, Maxi. And just to show it, I did mind dreadfully the way that however much people looked at me, they were always readier to laugh and joke with you. When a man danced with me, he used to just stand about and stare at me afterwards, as if I were something in a museum, and the men were always jolly and friendly with you. Why, don't you remember how nobody but the principals ever spoke to me in "Farandole" and you had the loveliest time larking about with everybody.'

'Well, you were so beautiful that they felt as if you were set apart and only the most important people had the right to speak to you.'

'It's not much fun being set apart.'

'Anyway I envied you that, and the way you could slip into anything and look lovely. With my bust I had always to be so careful. It's haunted me for years that I once told you a dress didn't suit you when it did. It was a lime-green silk with three flounces like how we used to wear them in a little shop in Brompton Road. It was before you had money, so that a cheap dress was something you ought to have laid hold of. I told you it didn't suit you, because I just couldn't bear the way it did. I've often worried about that.'

'You silly.'

'But the funny thing is that now you've come out as a great actress.'

'Oh, go on, not a great actress, just a good actress.'

'Well, my dear, there was a time when the one thing seemed just as unlikely as the other. And now you've got there, I'm just glad, I don't feel any envy.'

'Well, who would?' Sunflower asked languidly. 'Acting doesn't really matter very much, does it, when you come to think of it!'

'Well, no. I see what you mean. No, of course it doesn't matter, not really, it doesn't make you happy. But still, there's a sort of working agreement that it does, and after all, we all draw our money from it, don't we? Even George!'

'How is old George?'

'He's fine and he sends his love and he's been saying all that I've been saying. I left him down in front because I wanted to have a talk with you. How are you, old thing? Apart from all this, I mean? How's old Essington?'

'Very well.'

'Still the gentleman who hangs his hat up in your hall?'

'Yes. And always will be.'

'Oh, go on. You'll wake up some day and turn that silly old pope out of doors.'

'Maxi, dear, I wish you wouldn't. You don't understand him.'

'You bet I do. Better than you do, a lot. I hate the way he thinks he's a good man and isn't. Prides himself on not drinking and made

217

just as much a pig of himself swilling down your youth as other men do when they swill down champagne. He's never hidden what he thinks of me, so I don't see why I should hide what I think of him. George saw you at the Embassy the other night.'

'Did he? I'm sorry I didn't see him.'

'George said he didn't think you saw anybody. Said your eyes were like stars and you just floated. With Francis Pitt, weren't you?'

'Yes.'

'Seen much of him lately?'

'A bit. You see he's in trouble. His best friend's dying. And he wants company. I go up to lunch with him nearly every day.'

'Is he nice?'

'Yes.'

'Straight?'

'Yes.'

'Do you really like him?'

'Yes. But we're just friends. Nothing but friends. I lunched with him today. We're just friends.'

'That's just what I've always objected to about lunch. One's apt to be just friends. I always say lunch isn't worth the trouble of dressing for it. You can do as much with two dinners or one supper as you can with five lunches.'

'But Maxi, it isn't like that. I wouldn't try to make anything happen. It wouldn't seem right. And anyway, I don't care if nothing ever happens. This is different. So long as I can see him . . .' She turned way and fumbled on the table for her powder puff.

'Oh!' breathed Maxine in consternation. 'You would take it like that, wouldn't you?'

There was a pause. Sunflower said, 'People aren't talking, are they?'

'A bit.'

Insincerely she muttered, 'Horrid of them.' For the first time in her life she glowed at the thought that she was being gossiped about. It was better that she should be embraced by Francis Pitt in the imagination of others than nowhere at all.

'Hasn't he said anything at all?'

Sunflower shook her head.

'Do you think he cares for you?'

'Yes. I'm almost sure.'

'I wonder why he doesn't come across? Do you think there's a Reason?'

'I've thought sometimes there might be a Reason.'

'If it's a Reason you'll get him all right. You're so lovely. You needn't worry. But I wish there wasn't so much of this lunch business. It's so much easier to make things happen at night.'

'But I tell you I don't want to make things happen. It would spoil it: I want to stand back and let it happen.'

'My dear, I know just how you feel. Isn't it awful when it makes you come over all religious like that! I do hope it'll be all right, I do hope it'll be all right, I do hope – you're sure he really is nice?'

'I'm quite sure.'

'I do want you to have a bit of luck after all you've been through with that old beast. Do . . . do you think he'd marry?'

'I don't know.'

'Sunflower, you ought to try for that. Don't be too good-natured. You're far too soft. Not that I mean you've ever done it with anybody but Essington. But you're soft about everything. It's made me sick sometimes, the way you've let girls copy your best dresses that wouldn't have given you a loan of their lipsticks. Don't be a silly girl over this. You don't know how good it is afterwards. After you've got through all this stage you're in now. There's something after that. Sunflower, I'm happy. I really am happy, and I didn't think I ever would be again.'

'You did go through an awful time with Jerry.'

They stared at each other palely, shaking their heads.

'Without so much as a by-your-leave,' said Maxine.

'I often wonder if they never think.'

'I don't suppose they ever do.'

Sunflower turned back to her dressing-table and fiddled with the jars and bottles.

'Maxi, dear.'

'Yes, old Sunflower.'

'There's something I'd like to ask you, only . . .'

'My dear, we've slept in the same bed in the old days and used the same hairbrush when mine wore out. There isn't anything you can't ask me.'

'Well . . . does George mind about the others?'

'Oh, that. Well, I don't suppose he actually cheers when he thinks about them, but I don't think he does think about them much. Men don't nowadays. They're much more sensible. They realise that unless we were born twins with our husbands, which would be incest, which is horrid, there's bound to be a few mistakes while you're waiting round. Anyway it doesn't seem to worry him. Except Jerry. He wouldn't like me to see Jerry.'

'Do you ever run across Jerry now?'

'Once in a blue moon. At Ciro's. And the Fifty-Fifty. Always with a girl. Different girls. He doesn't ever seem to keep a girl long. Not longer than three months.'

'Well, you were with him much longer than that.'

'A year and ten days. October the third, October the thirteenth. Friday the thirteenth it was that day I came round to you.'

'You don't care for him any more, do you?'

'Oh no. I can think of him now without crying. And look right across the room at him as cool as a cucumber and bow. I'm always so glad George is good-looking when I see Jerry. He's better looking than Jerry, you know, really. You think George is good-looking, don't you?'

'Oh yes, he's very handsome.'

'You wouldn't say he looked Jewish, would you?'

'Oh, no, not really. A Spanish type, I'd call George.'

'Mind you, I'm glad George is a Jew. It's a good thing to marry a Jew. They don't look on their wives and children as being something they let themselves in for when they were silly, like how a lot of Christians do. But I don't see any sense in anybody looking like a Jew, just because they are a Jew, do you? I mean, it isn't necessary, is it? But then George doesn't look Jewish. You're quite right, he's a Spanish type. But anyway he doesn't mind about the others, not so that it matters. You see he's fond of me. And if they're fond of you they never think of it.'

'You really think so?'

'I know it . . . And you see . . . by the time baby grows up it'll be forgotten. It's funny how people forget one. I'll be forgotten in no time. Why, the doorkeeper downstairs didn't know me tonight, though I played here for six months for you in "Ashes of Roses". You see, I'm not like you. You're News. You always were from the start.'

'Oh, but I'm not so much News as I used to be. People aren't taking half the notice of me they did.'

'Never took more, my dear. And small wonder after this performance.'

'But I'm dropping out! I'm dropping out more and more every year. Haven't you noticed?'

'Noticed nothing! Everybody's crazy about you. Why, the paragraphs you get all the time.'

'Oh, but I'm bound to drop out at my age!'

'Nonsense! Oh . . . I see. Well, dear, I see what you mean. I think you're right. Maybe your paragraphs are more about your work and less about you. I think you're right. In ten or fifteen years nobody won't ever remember a thing about you and Essington. Not a thing.'

'I don't think they will,' said Sunflower; and fell to fooling again with the jars and bottles on her tables.

'Maxi . . .'

'What is it?'

'Is it really so bad having a baby? I mean, does it really hurt such a lot?'

'Well, yes and no. You can't call it a picnic. But then what I say is you get something for it. Think of the people that are operated on for appendicitis and this and that and have all that pain and all that expense and three weeks spent in bed and nothing to show for it. That makes having a baby seem more sensible, doesn't it? And anyway it's awfully interesting. Sunflower, you can't think how interesting it is. I mean it makes you think. It's all so queer. I mean, one day the baby's you, it's just a part of you. And then there it is, on the other side of the room, with its own ideas about things and making a noise. Well, you know, that's wonderful. I dare say I don't make it sound anything, because I'm not one of your talky birds, but really it is quite wonderful.'

'Oh, it must be.'

'And you know there is something queer about the whole business. Really there is. Don't you think it's extraordinary that a baby shouldn't look like its father, even though its father is its father, which George certainly was? Will you tell me how science can explain that? I tell you it's all very mysterious. But, oh Christ, it does tear you to pieces. Sunflower, you haven't any idea of the things that happen to babies, the things that are let happen to them. You couldn't believe it. Just take this business of whooping cough that baby's just had. Do you know that poor child used to get black in the face? And it's really dangerous. Baby might have died. I tell you that he might have died. And the whole thing's so badly managed. Did you know that a boy baby can rupture himself as easy as anything just crying? And then they let them have things like whooping cough that make them cry. Is that sensible? And it's like that all the time. People talk as if having babies were dull and settling down. It isn't a bit like that. You have to stand between them and the bloody silly universe all the time.'

'It must be lovely. I mean, you must feel you are doing something.'

221

'Oh, yes. And the pain isn't really so frightful. And if they're nice they're awfully good to you while it's coming. George was a dear all the time. Home every night as early as could be. And when I was silly and thought I might die he didn't scold me and say I wouldn't, but just held me tight and then I felt that anyway I'd been so happy with him these eighteen months that if I did die it would all have been worthwhile. Oh, Sunflower, George is a white man. He really is a white man.'

'I know he is. I didn't worry a bit about you after I saw him at the Registry Office. I said to myself, "Well, Maxi's all right for the rest of her life". Use my powder, dear.'

'Thank you, darling. I am a silly to go on this way. But you know what it is. I didn't think I'd ever be happy again. This is a lovely powder. It's a mixture isn't it?'

'Yes. Bayard's Naturelle and Favot's Blanche. They go well together because the one's too sticky and the other's too light. But it's too white for you. You're so lovely and creamy.'

'Oh, my dear, who wouldn't rather be you!'

'Get on with you. And kiss me, Maxi, dear.'

'Mm. You sweet thing. And there's the call for beginners. We have had a show. Give me another kiss. Oh, my God, how you're shaking! Why, your heart's killing you!'

'I'm like that all the time.'

'You . . . you're quite sure he's nice?'

'Quite sure.'

'You do hear of him picking people up and dropping them.'

'Well, I haven't noticed anything of the sort. I shouldn't think it was true. He's awfully kind. Fatherly. But I can understand how it might get about he is like that. You see, there aren't many people who'd understand him. They'd fail him. He does take a lot of understanding. And then he'd get through most people very soon, because he's so clever. Not many people could keep up with him. I quite see how the story might get about.'

'Well, you ought to know. You're used to clever people. I never got on with them. Well, goodbye, dear. I hope to God you're going to be happy. Send me a telegram if anything happens. And thank you so much for all you sent baby. He loved them.'

'I'll be along to see him some time this week, I expect.'

'You don't want to go tying yourself up with engagements just now, my dear. Leave yourself free. We'll expect you when we see you. Well,

222

here's goodbye again. It's funny . . . Somehow I wish you didn't care for him quite so much. But it'll be all right. You're so lovely, you'd get any man you wanted. And you wouldn't lose him, either, which is more. Oh, it'll be all right. Or the man's mad . . .'

*

When she got home the house seemed to be dreaming a dream about itself, to be giving an invisible party, as London houses often do by night. The black cat, Sambo, lay curled up like a soft dark ammonite on the bottom step of the staircase, instead of being in his basket down in the kitchen, which never should have happened to such a god-fearing tom had there not been strange comings and goings to disturb his habits. The chest and table in the hall had more than usually that air which all old furniture usually has, of being taciturn as a good servant is, never speaking in the presence of its masters, never saying as much as it knows at any time; the dull highlights on the lacquer seemed like respectful and vigilant eyes. She sank down on the step by Sambo, and lifted him into her lap. He snapped open one eye and with the flip of an ear thanked her for nothing; for though she might be the talk of the town she was not Cook, who is the arbiter of cream. She murmured to herself, smiling because she was pervaded by a pleasure, aloud because she was light-hearted with fatigue, 'My cat, my funny cat, my house, my funny house.' Though for years she had poured nearly all her private energies into the business of making this a beautiful place, she suddenly felt, quite without pain, almost flippantly, a sense of detachment from it. She looked at the letters which lay waiting for her on the table and didn't want to open any of them, since it seemed impossible that anything in this house could really be relevant to her, though there was one packet, which looked like a cheap weekly paper, which she would have liked to take away and tear up, because it was such an ugly acid violet-pink. But that could wait, that would wait. Sitting and stroking Sambo, she fell half-asleep, she had silly thoughts. It seemed to her that if she went upstairs and opened any of the doors, she would find people sitting in the room, not speaking, not moving, not able to do anything when she came in save arch long waxen necks and turn rose-and-lily waxen faces with a condoning expression, because they were but waxen people such as dwell in shop windows and could not become flesh and blood till she had given up this fantastic practice, which condemned

223

the whole world to unreality, of living in this house which was a stranger to her. But she must not doze like this, she must keep awake, she must keep awake at any cost. She set down Sambo and wandered upstairs, partly because she feared she would sleep if she were still, partly because she had that impulse to range round the house that one has when all the furniture is packed up and the vans are coming in an hour.

But she felt ashamed of her callousness about the house when she went into her Chinese room. It was hers, it was perfect. There were the Ming figures on the mantelpiece, the two old men with staves who had been on a journey, there was the princess who had not needed to go on a journey because she was royal and had been born with peace in her heart, as she had been born with fine bones in her body. There was the vase that was grey, nothing but grey; but surely the thought of far-off hills, which are blue, had crossed the mind of the potter who made it. There was the wallpaper where the little old mandarin drank his tea for his private pleasure in the house among the willows, and only a few inches away looked out of his sedan chair in the procession which he had joined for the public good, and a few inches further on than that walked up the temple steps to worship the gods whose will it is that in private and public things alike there should be decorum; being, as a sage must be, everywhere in the whole range of life in the same moment of time. This room was a miracle. The wallpaper had been made four hundred years later than the figures, and the vase had come into being somewhere in between them. She had bid for the Ming figures at Christie's, she had found the vase in the must of a shop in Pimlico, she had unrolled the wallpaper and seen its pattern through tears when she had strayed into the lumber room in the villa at Settignano as a refuge from the sandstorm of Essington's irritation, for that was one of the many places which he had disliked at sight, but lingered on at interminably, because of his mysterious preference for disliking things. Yet because of an inclination towards harmony which had been built in them by their makers, these things, made far apart in time and gathered together on no principle but that they had struck her as pretty, made a room which was a whole as a gem is a whole, as a flawless emerald is a whole. It had an enduring beauty, it had gone on being a calm and beautiful place; no matter how cross Essington was, no matter how badly she acted, it would go on being beautiful for her so that she could enjoy it when she was quite old. She should not so bitterly miscall her life up to the present. There had been this room in it, there had been moments of a beauty like the beauty of this room, moments when Essington was kind, or was not there. The time had not all been wasted.

Reconciled to her house, she went downstairs, gathered up her letters from the hall table and went into the little library, where they left her supper for her on a tray. It didn't look very good tonight. This was the third time they had given her cold chicken that week, and she didn't think she ever really liked it. It was too much like an ingénue part. Suddenly she felt jealous of her servants, moving about in her kitchen as if they owned it, and giving her what they chose of her own food, and she made up her mind to go downstairs and find something she did like to eat. In the hall she paused and called Sambo, who put his three-cornered head between the two lowest banisters, and narrowed his green eyes at her and plainly said to himself, 'Well, I think but little of her, but all the same I suppose that if you're about the other ones will go, and I can get back to my bed.' He accepted a lift in her arms down the stairs to the basement, but was careful to jump down at the first possible moment, so that she should not use this condescension as a pretext for familiarities. 'Very well, you silly old thing,' she said, and went to the ice-box and found a hard-boiled egg and some cold potatoes and some celery, and put them on a plate and took it to the kitchen table. It was nice, eating them in her fingers, and anyway she loved being in her kitchen. It was the only part of her house which made her feel that she was any richer than she had been when she left her home in Chiswick. She would never have been surprised to find out that she enjoyed all the possessions in her other rooms temporarily and conditionally, like the dresses she wore during the run of a play. But when she looked at the plates on the dresser, and the sewing machine on the side table, and above all at the rows of red canisters on the mantelpiece with 'Flour' and 'Tea' and 'Rice' written in gold on them, she felt that these were real things that one really owned, that one could keep always because one had paid real money for them, that would always be useful. Finishing her meal, she put her elbows on the table and rested her head on her hands, looking drowsily round her, pleased with the kitchen that was hers, that was full of nice things, that was clean as a new pin. The scrubbed wood of the table was clear as a slice of cheese . . . She became full of a sense of joyful departure, she was in a ship that was swinging on the tide and with the turn of the tide they would set sail on the fortunate journey . . . What was swinging? Her sleepy head, held on her hands. Why was she joyful?

Because Francis Pitt was going to ring her up that night. There was not any harm in being rung up. Oh, but if she went to sleep down here, she would never hear the telephone bell, for the servants would have disconnected the one downstairs and it would be ringing by her bedside. She must go upstairs, she would read her letters to keep her awake, she must not run the risk of losing that . . .

On the threshold of the library she drew back, and screamed, because there was a strange man sitting there.

He stood up. It was not possible that she should not have known him, for it was Essington.

He said, 'You seem startled. Who were you expecting to find instead of me?'

She answered, 'I wasn't expecting anybody. Only somehow I didn't recognise you. I suppose it's because I'm tired.'

He repeated, 'Who were you expecting to find instead of me?'

Plainly he was in tune for one of his long, slow, persistent, cross-examining scenes. There was no way of quieting him down in one of these except by standing still and letting him do it until one cried, when he melted and was benevolent and appeased. But suddenly she knew she could not do that any more and that some change had taken place in her which would have made it impossible for her to do that even if she had wanted, and she exclaimed in exasperation, 'Do you mean that I'm expecting some man here to make love to me? Don't be stupid! You still have your latchkey to this house, haven't you? That's how you got in, isn't it? Then how could I have any man here?'

'Sunflower. You are getting very clever. Very hard and clever. And I think I know what's making you so hard and clever. There is a certain instinct so strong that it puts bones into those who are naturally spineless as jelly-fish, intelligence into those who might otherwise be classified with the amoebas. Sunflower, I saw you play tonight.'

'Well, that was nice for you. We gave a good performance.'

'Sunflower, I saw you play your love scenes with that new young man. That Jew-boy with the wave in his black greasy hair and the little hands and feet. By God. I have never seen such doings on the stage.'

She stared at him in horror. 'But you are going mad,' she said gravely, 'You are going mad.'

'Sunflower, I saw you. I saw you in his arms. I saw you kiss him. Real kisses. I saw you – linked with him . . .' His words seemed to bring the sharp point of his tongue out with them through his teeth.

226

He had to stand quivering while he bit it back. 'You've never acted like that before. You've always acted like a decent woman. Not like . . .' His intellectual conscience, which was important to control his malice but would never be quite gagged by it, refused to let him say the words because they were not true; but the other passionate part of him had what relief it could by making his mouth shape them silently.

The corresponding point in her seemed to hear what they were, and she made a sweeping gesture which she immediately checked, feeling that sick terror she always felt when an argument between them slipped towards a primitive plane. It had something to do with her fear, which was beyond all reason, which was greater than her fear of death, that he would some day strike her. Their eyes met nervously, and they consented to disregard this moment of dumb show and its significance. She said, as if she believed that an intellectually convincing explanation convinced people, 'You know you're talking nonsense. I play that scene like I've always played love scenes, the way old Sir Charles Mordant taught me when he was pushing me through my first lead and I couldn't act at all. "If you want to play a love-scene that gets across the footlights," he said to me, "get your feet mixed up." And that's what I've always done. That's all I do in this play. You've seen me do it a hundred times before. What are you being silly about all of a sudden? And as for this man, of all men. Why, you know he's a nancy-boy.'

He shuddered. 'Your hideous slang. About things you might have found too hideous to know.'

He had shifted his ground. She had him beaten. But she liked him none the better for that, for it showed that he had made this accusation against her without having a case, without really believing he had one. 'Well, as to that,' she said coldly, 'they're all round us. They act with us, they write our plays, they make our dresses, they decorate our houses. Sometimes there seem more of them than of the other kind. We can't help knowing of them.' There passed through her mind a picture of Cosmo's birthday party at the Ladrone restaurant a few weeks before. She had not been playing then, so she had gone early, and had sat at the host's table opposite the door and watched all the guests coming in; the lovely little girls in their teens and early twenties, who had rid themselves of all the traditional signs of womanhood, who had cut off their hair, who were so slim that their frocks rose over their breasts only as they might have over two flower-petals worn that way for a charm, yet who remained utterly women,

227

with soft young faces that glowed in expectation of adventures the cause of which would be submission; and with them these dapper boys, their heads sleek as men's are, their bodies straight and lithe and dressed in black and white as men's are, yet who had become utterly not men, whose faces were sparkling with enjoyment of adventures in which women had no part. She had felt very sorry for the girls then. Now, perhaps because she was goose-fleshed with that sense of danger which always came on her when her relationship with Essington took this turn towards unreason, she felt ashamed about herself. At the moment she seemed to hold plenty of cards: but if they were struck out of her hand it would not be so easy to get others. She said aloud, 'Yes, I don't know what the world's coming to!' She felt perturbed, flimsy, hollow, ephemeral, something that would disappear if people stopped thinking about her. The sight of her letters, which she had left lying on a table, encouraged her. They would be all about her work, they would prove to her that she had a career, that she solidly existed, she would feel much better if she read them.

Essington called out loudly, as if instead of sitting close in the room she had gone out of the door and he had to bring her back at any cost, 'I am hungry! I want something to eat! Go and make me some coffee!'

This was a habit of his when he had risen to a certain pitch of rage against her. He would wait till there were no servants about and would order her loudly to cook something for him. It was not such a bad thing as it seemed, for it was not a mere explosion of tyranny, it was more like a little mechanical adjustment which made it possible for their relationship to run smoothly for a little while. For after she had obeyed, and gone down to the kitchen and made him coffee and scrambled eggs or a welsh rarebit, and brought it up to him, he would explain that he really had needed the food, that for some reason he had had no dinner, that he was very grateful to her for giving him this; and after that he would be very kind and good for some time. She had often wondered what was in his mind when he did this. It was perhaps the attempt of somebody who was clever in general but not at handling human beings to make a relationship run right by forcing it into the groove along which such relationships traditionally ran; just as a clever person without a mechanical turn of mind who found himself faced with the problem of making a broken-down machine work again would try to make it look as much as possible as it did when it was first delivered by the manufacturer. If they had been mates in a primitive society she would have tended all his bodily needs and he

228

would have been grateful to her for it; that was the way she had been delivered by the manufacturer. The imitation of it was so nearly right, was at any rate so allusive to rightness that it always felt sweet. But it was play-acting, it was pretence, and tonight she couldn't go through the performance. For it was the extremest fatigue and tedium, like doing exercises when one is dropping with sleep, for her to take any notice of him at all. And it was all preposterous anyway; if he wanted to be kind to her why couldn't he just be kind to her instead of staging over and over again these pointless dramas of the unjust accusations and repentance?

She said, 'There's plenty of cold chicken on the tray over there.'

He grumbled, 'I wanted something hot.'

'I am too tired. There's whisky there too.'

She did not look at him in case he got her again by some familiar piteousness. When she heard him sit down by the tray and take up his knife and fork she picked up her letters. First of all the folded newspaper she had noticed on the hall table because of its acid violet-pink. The sooner she got the ugly thing into the waste-paper basket . . .

Essington flung down his knife and fork and cried squeakily, 'You needn't have let him . . . lip you as he did in that third act.'

Rage flooded her. She threw the paper down into her lap. 'It's in the part! I can't play the part as it's written unless I let him do that! And how dare you suspect me of this! Me who you've known all this time! With a silly little thing like that who's seven or eight years younger than me! How dare you! It's hateful of you, it's mean of you, to use something that I have to do as part of my work to goad and hurt me!'

'Yes, part of your work,' said Essington; munched for a minute; and then came back to it purringly. 'Your work. That's been one of the chief difficulties of our relationship. Your work. The limited farming out of the practice of the least dignified of the arts by one not particularly competent to deal with the difficulties of such a situation.'

If he began to talk about her work he would go on forever. 'Don't talk about my work,' she said. 'I had to have it. For one thing, I had to have the money. We couldn't have had as comfortable a house if I hadn't worked. You couldn't have spared enough money for all this. And I needed it for itself. You're away so much that I'd go mad with loneliness if I hadn't had the theatre. And you had a lot of fun when you've been feeling as you are now making fun of my acting. No, there isn't any use talking about my work.' She took up the newspaper and tore off the wrapper.

'Sunflower,' he said, so imperatively, so weightily, so much as if he were going to lay by her some new and important fact bearing on their relationship that she put down the paper again and waited. But all he had to say when he had got her to look at him was, 'The misfortunes of us men. Particularly in connection with the necessities of sex. Think, think, if because of our need to eat, to consume from time to time a mutton chop, one had actually to take a sheep about with one. To make constant concessions to its sheeply nature. To train oneself to think – so as not to be rude and give offence – as much like a sheep as possible.'

She bit her lip, took up the newspaper again, and unfolded it. She had never heard of 'The West End Topical Titbits' before. Essington's knife and fork rattled fussily.

When she had read the paragraph on the front page marked with a cross she covered her face with her hands and cried out, 'Oh, God! Oh, God!'

Essington squeaked in irritation, 'What is it? What is it?'

'This paper! There's a paragraph in it about you and me! An awful paragraph!'

'What paper? Oh – that pink gossip-rag!'

'Oh, Essington, it's dreadful, dreadful!'

'My dear Sunflower,' he wailed, 'don't be absurd. You ought to be used to that sort of thing by this time.'

Surely that was a frightful thing, an incredibly callous thing for him to say to her? She knew in her heart that he was going to fail her for the thousandth time, but because of this new agony this paragraph had brought her, which surpassed any she had ever known before, she had not the courage to accept that. She got up and staggered across the room to where he sat at the tray, holding out the paper and turning her face away from it, and crying out, 'There's never been anything as bad as this before! How can people write such things and go on living! You'd think they'd be ashamed! Oh, read it, read it!'

He struck the paper from her hand. 'Stop making such a fuss!'

'But Essington, you must read it! It's so dreadful!' If only he would read it he must feel sorry for her, he would have to pity and comfort her and she would die if someone did not cover her eyes with kisses and persuade her that everything was well so that she could be relieved for one moment from the anguish of the thought that Francis Pitt might read that paragraph about her, might see her nakedness made a mock of . . .

Essington nearly screamed. 'But I've read it.'

'You've read it?'

'Yes! Of course they sent it to me too. I threw the thing in the waste-paper basket. But I knew you'd make a fuss about it. I knew you'd make this hideous fuss!' He waved his hands as if by her impetuous folly she had ruined a situation delicious in its serenity.

She took a step nearer to him, and bent down across the tray, putting her face close to his. 'Essington, you've read it?'

He blinked. 'Aren't I telling you so?'

Appalled by his wickedness, she drew a deep breath.

'Now what's the matter?' he asked tearfully. 'What did you want me to do about it? What good does it do to get excited as you're doing?'

Gravely she said, 'You are mean, you are stingy. I see it all now. When you read that paragraph you saw how awful it was. You're clever, you couldn't help doing that. Why, ever since you came in, you've been trying to prevent me from reading. Every time I've picked it up, you've said something that's put me off. You knew it was awful, you knew I couldn't help being hurt. But you can't bear giving any sympathy, because you hate giving anything to anybody. You couldn't even bear to admit that anything horrid had happened to me on account of you, because that would make me your debtor. So you invented all these things to be angry with me. That silly stuff about the Jew-boy. That endless business about my work, so that it seemed as if it was you whom I ought to be sorry for, and I who was in your debt in every way. Oh, you are mean, you are grudging.'

She stopped suddenly, her finger to her lip, considering a memory as if she were listening to a distant sound. It had crossed her mind that he had been very kind to her one summer night about four years before. They had gone down for a weekend to Southend, because it was the kind of place where nobody would recognise them, and on Saturday evening a tooth that had been giving just the tiniest twinges during the week suddenly began to dig twitching lobster claws of fire down into her jawbone. He couldn't have been nicer to her. He hadn't once said that she ought to have had it seen to when she was in town, and had held her in his arms all night, and when she cried a little because the pain was so bad he had made up a funny silly tale to amuse her, a tale like one of the Just So stories, about an Elephant that had an Ache in its Tusk. Her face wrinkled up, she nearly weakened and let him be a little cruel to her, so that they could start all over again. But she remembered what had happened the next day, how on the Sunday morning they had gone

231

out to find a dentist, and when the second one had proved to be out he had suddenly grown tired of being kind. He had waited sulkily in the waiting-room of the third, while she had had the tooth pulled out, having begged her to get through with the business as soon as might be, since it was a pity that anyone who was working so hard as he was should have to spend one of the few decent days of that summer indoors; and at lunch, though she was still feeling sick from the cocaine injection and the wrench, had spoken with humorous pity of her acting, as he had done often before, as he had done often since, as he would do an infinite number of times again, if she did not break up this thing. It was no good. One could not face life with this man who had frayed his nerves by perpetual rage with all that exists, any more than one could cut the pages of a book with a knife that was saw-edged because an ill-tempered user had hacked it down on every sort of substance. She had to put an end to this.

She took her finger from her lip, sighed, shook her head and said, 'You must go away.'

'I haven't finished this chicken.'

'You mustn't finish it. I want you to get up and go.'

He paused, his knife and fork in the air.

'If you don't go,' she said, her voice going flat and unmusical with fatigue, 'I'll take that tray and throw it on the floor. You've got to go.'

'Sunflower, let's talk this thing over first.'

'No. I know everything you have to say. You're clever, I'm stupid. My acting's rotten. I've minded petty things about my position more than I ought to have. It's all true. But what matters is that this is my home and if I don't want you here you've got to go.'

He rose and came out from behind the table and stood close to her. He suddenly became immobile. His eyes became fixed, like the painted eyes of a china figure, looking slightly above her left shoulder. Something awful must be happening within him to change his substance from its normal sensitiveness, which responded to each tremor of his nerves as water does to wind. He was probably planning to do something frightful and fantastic to alarm her into being again submissive.

She begged him, not because she was afraid she would weaken, but because it was such an effort to keep her attention that she felt as if she would faint unless he went away. 'You must go. Can't you see that there's nothing else for it but that you should go? Don't you see that I'm telling you to go although I'm not angry with you, although I'm quite calm, which shows I really mean it?' Her voice was becoming flatter and flatter with tedium.

His mouth opened slowly. Now that fastidiousness and argument-ativeness were not incessantly arranging and rearranging his features she found it difficult to recognise them. They were so curiously marked with a sense of failure, which it was hard to reconcile with the facts of his life. For this was not a new experience caused by his loss of her; he was so passionately refusing to admit he had lost her that he could not let the thought of it affect his face. Almost as much as if he were dead, the moment was not leaving its mark, was letting appear the sum of judgments of each and every day since he was born on whether that birth had been worthwhile. And surely since that sum was what it was it could not be that there had come quite easily to him riches and fame and power. It would have seemed more likely that he had spent his whole life trying to make a small shop pay and failing in the end.

A little dazed with pity, she moved closer to him; and that made it queerer still that again he should raise his voice, not as if he were angry with her, but as if she were going away from him. He shouted quite loudly, 'Yes, you can go to another paymaster!'

As he spoke his hand went up in the air. The moment she had feared for years had come at last. He was going to strike her.

She could not move out of the way, because her mind was swinging like a pendulum between two aspects of his misery. There was the absurd injustice of what he was saying, which showed how far spent he was; he had now cast truth from him, as a man lost in the desert past hope of rescue strips off his clothing and wanders naked. There was also the absurd way in which he had said it, using words that might have come out of a bad play; even he had cast his own fineness from him, which had been his ultimate pride. Both these losses were so touching that not to become wholly absorbed in each of them seemed callous, so that she was already confused by a sense of conflicting duties and a slow mournfulness that was not compatible with rapid movement, when she saw that what she had long feared more than her own death was happening. There was nothing to do but shut her eyes and wait until his fist came down on her breast.

She had been right in fearing this moment as long as she had. This was the most horrible thing that had ever happened to her, that can ever have happened to anybody since the world began. Not because he had hurt her, but because he had not. He had not even made her sway on her feet. He was not as strong as she was. And that was shame, shame and ruin for them both.

She opened her eyes and saw that he was going to strike her again. He was raising his arm with a curious artificial movement, a trick to achieve strength, like the overarm stroke in swimming. Her heart bled with love for him, for she saw that he was trying to save her world for her; since indeed everything she felt about life depended on men being in some ways stronger than women. She tried to help him in putting it all right by lurching backwards under his blow, but when it came it was so weak that it gave her no help, so that she simply stepped backwards. From a cat-like crinkling of his eyes and a greyness that spread round his mouth, she knew that he had seen what she had been trying to do and seen too why she had failed. She cried into her hands.

When she looked up again he was kneeling beside one of the armchairs at the other end of the room, burying his face in a cushion.

She went and leaned over him, muttering, 'I'll make you some coffee . . .'

He sat back on his heels and turned his face away from her. 'No, no. I must go now. I can't stay after this.' He tried to pull himself on to his feet, and could not manage it. She bent down and helped him. When he was up he cried loudly and disagreeably, 'Think what you must have done to me to get me to the point of striking you!'

She opened her mouth to answer, but stammered because there were two answers she felt inclined to give. She wanted to tell him that he need not reproach himself so greatly for having struck her since he had not hurt her; and she wanted to plead that she had done nothing she had not a right to do, she had only begged him to leave her house because he came there not in love but in hate. But before she had made up her mind which to say it came to her that he had cried out this complaint simply because the strength of her arms when she raised him to his feet had reminded him of the awful thing that had happened. She followed him across the room out into the hall and stood beside him while he put on his coat, biting her lip, looking downwards. Separation was a myth. They were not separate. His shame was hers.

Petulantly he muttered, 'Gloves gone.'

They had slipped down beside the cabinet. Stooping for them, she saw herself clearly reflected in the polished wood, as if the fine furniture were ironically holding a mirror to her flushed human face. She wished that she was one of the things that have no will but only use. She wished that she were a stream which lets land-beasts drink, and water-beasts live, and men and women bathe, and does not flow uphill. She gave him his gloves and as his coat-collar was turned up put out her hand to arrange it. But with a look of fear in his eyes he waved her away from him, further and further, so that she had to mount the lowest step of the staircase, or seem disrespectful of his physical force.

He did not bother about his coat-collar, though he was the tidiest of men. Instead he pulled out his key-ring and was taking from it the key of her house. He had great difficulty in doing it because all his movements were slow and clumsy as if he were a little drunk. She stood and watched him, understanding the fact that he had always been afraid of her and that all his contempt had only been a disguise for fear, and wondering why he should feel like that for her, who had meant nothing but kindness to him. It was a mystery. And now she did not intend to solve it. He had tired her out. Also, at the back of her mind was a feeling that there was some other thing she had to do.

The telephone bell in her bedroom began to ring. Their eyes met. He stopped fumbling with the keys. They both threw their heads back and looked up the staircase, listening.

He made a queer, coarse, hacking noise in his throat. Their eyes met again. His hand gestured upwards, as if to tell her to go up and answer it.

She shook her head.

He said huskily, 'Answer it.'

She shook her head, as if it did not matter.

He looked at her steadily. His glance was vacant. She had a feeling that he was rapidly considering whether to fill its blankness with rebuke, with anger, with forgiveness, with repentance, and that his intellect was coldly telling him that he might look in vain for any apposite emotion, for it was the essence of the moment that no emotion could be apposite to it. It was as if he had been one of those chemists who insist on trying to explode the atom in spite of the risk that if they succeed the whole universe may explode at the same time. He had exploded an integral part of their relationship and the whole universe they lived in was destroyed. It was true that they could not be separated, that though they might remove their bodies far apart their spirits would remain mingled. But they hung locked together in the midst of nothingness.

Dropping the empty look, drooping his head, he went back to the business of freeing her latchkey. At last it came clear. He put out his hand to give it to her. She put out her hand to take it. It was enormously heavy, so that the effort of holding it shook the breath out of their bodies.

'Goodbye, Sunflower.'

'Goodbye, dear.'

They were whispering like two ghosts. The telephone bell whirred, real, robust.

She let the key fall from her hand on the staircase, as if it would not ever be needed again.

He squared his shoulders, shook them, and let them drop again, muttering to some invisible person who stood beside him in the hall and urged him to assert his rights and stop, 'No. No. Can't stay after this. Must go. Dear Sunflower.' Slowly, stupidly, he began to open the door.

Overhead, the telephone stopped ringing. Because his back was turned she pressed her hands to her breast and dropped them as he turned and looked at her.

He got the door to open, stepped outside and weakly drew it to after him. For a long time he held it just two or three inches ajar. She could see his face, again still as a china figure's and scarred by lifelong failure as by old cuts, looking at her through the crack. Their pulses beat on the empty house, the silent night, as on a drum.

Overhead, the telephone began to ring again. Instantly he flung the door wide open and stood on the threshold with his arms stretched out, as if he were going to rush in and do violence to the house, to her. She walked backwards up another stair, putting out her hand in front of her to defend herself. But suddenly he banged the door. One moment she was facing his sour and vehement stare, the next she was confronted with blank black wood.

She heard his footsteps scuffle down the steps into the street, and turned and ran upstairs. She reached her bedroom, she flung herself down on her knees by the telephone.

'Hello . . . Hello.'

'Hello. My God, Sunflower, I thought I was never going to get you. Am I too late? Were you asleep?'

'No. Oh, no.' She began to weep.

'Here, what's this? Sunflower, is that you crying?'

'Yes. Oh, Francis. Essington has just . . . gone away.'

'What do you mean?'

236

'He's gone. We've parted. And, oh, it's dreadful when you think how we used to care for each other. And he's so sweet and good.'

Her sobs stilled. But she heard nothing. She cried into the darkness. 'Can't you hear me? Essington and I have parted!'

'Yes, I hear you. But something went wrong with this telephone. Sunflower, is all this definite and final?'

'Yes. Yes. It's all over.'

'Sunflower, are you quite sure? Essington loves you very dearly.'

'Yes, but it's over. I can't tell you how it happened. You see, there was something dreadful . . . Oh, Francis, Francis, have you read something awful in a horrid paper about me?'

'I have not. I would not. And if it were forced on me I should forget it.'

'Oh, you are kind, you are . . . right. But oh, he was queer, and it was all horrid. Yet he is so sweet. And ten years, ten years! Oh, Francis, what am I to do?' She began to sob again. There appeared before her mind's eye, very clear and bright, a picture of her latchkey lying on the staircarpet. She must go down later and pick it up.

'Sunflower, I want to see you.' She bent down to the telephone as if its black mouth were the trumpet of a flower, and there were honey there. 'But . . .'

Nothing came out of the darkness for a minute.

'. . . the devil of it is that I can't. Something's happened. I won't be free all day tomorrow.'

She stopped sobbing. She arranged her long, shaking breaths. 'Oh, very well,' she said. 'Good-night.'

'No, hold on. Sunflower. Hold on. Hold on.'

'I'm holding on.'

'Hold on. Hold on. There's something . . . I tell you there is something wrong with this telephone . . .'

Suddenly she heard his chuckle. His voice sounded gruff and strong as if he were standing in the room beside her. His charm scented the world, warmed her flesh, nourished her. 'This is the devil! I have business with relatives of Hurrell. They will be with me all day. Seeing him and talking over his affairs with me. And I can't even come to you after the theatre, for I've been let in to giving a party. As a matter of fact I consented to give it because I thought you and Essington might come and that it would cheer us all up. Will you come to that party by yourself? Sunflower?'

'I might.'

237

'Do come to my party. I would be grateful. I am sad enough when I do not see you, Sunflower. And maybe we'll be able to slip away from the others and talk this thing over. Will you come?'

'I think . . . I might . . . I'll come . . .'

'And Sunflower . . .' He brought her name down like a hammer. 'Yes?'

'I am glad you have left Essington. I am damned glad you have left Essington.'

She murmured, 'Oh, but he was so dear and wonderful, you don't know . . .'

He cut in inexorably, 'Good-night to you.'

She breathed, feeling passive, feeling faint with pleasure, 'Good-night.'

V

THIS was the best awakening of all her life. Yesterday had been a dreadful morning, though she had remembered as soon as her eyes were open that she had had her last quarrel with Essington, that he had gone away forever, that she was free. But she had not wanted to be free. What good was that? It had made her feel lonely and unreal. If nobody was fond of you, you wouldn't quite exist. With tears she remembered something that Essington had once told her, of how wise men debated whether a storm out at sea where there was no human being to behold it could truly be said to exist, since thunder was thunder only because an ear heard its roll, and lightning was lightning only because an eye was dazzled by it, and waves immense only because a mind measured them. She had rolled over and buried her face in the pillow, feeling as if she was already beginning to exist less definitely, as if presently she would fall through the bed because she was not solid enough to be borne by its solidity, and seep through it like a mist. She could not be sure, she could not be sure . . .

But this morning, when she awoke, she felt more real than she had ever done before. For one thing, she had not at any time known a feeling as strong as this happiness. Why, it was like clear music

239

bubbling on and on, it was like bright sunshine, surely anyone coming into the room would hear it and see it! It was as amazing to find that she could be so immensely happy with so little previous training as it would have been to find that she had a magnificent singing voice; for this happiness was not just a judgment her mind was passing on what had happened to her, it was an achievement, it was something produced, it jetted out of her. But this was only one of the new things that were going on in her because she was now sure. Because she knew he set a high value upon her, she felt infinitely precious. She passed her hands over her face and under the bedclothes down her body, over her round breasts, down the strong hoops of her ribs, down her flanks, admitting their beauty as honestly as if they were in marble and no concern of hers, feeling such joy as one might feel who being seized by the madness of giving finds in that same moment a treasure in his lap. Yet she cried out aloud and most despairingly, 'Oh, dear, I wish my nose was really straight!' She felt about herself that mixture of severe vanity and carping self-dislike which she had noticed in great actors and great actresses, that was written all over Dusa, with her rounded shoulders and her cherishing arms holding motherwise nothing but her own self, as if to say, 'I find myself dear to myself as other women find their children,' and her face scared with disgust, as if to say, 'Oh, God, when can I die so that I may lose this I?' Ah, but Francis Pitt had made her as great as Dusa! When you came down to it all that made Dusa great was that she knew what she wanted to do. That she thought her parts completely into existence so that she knew what they would do in every conceivable circumstance, and no moment of the play found her at a loss for a perfect characteristic gesture. Now Francis Pitt had thought her completely into existence. When she had gone to his house after the theatre the night before, he had come out into the hall to meet her, and had given the footman a grave nod which made him go and warned him as he went that he must take no liberty of smiles and suspicions. They had stood in the shadows for a moment, while through the door that he had left ajar behind him sounded music and gay yet temperate laughter as of those who had not spoiled the pleasures of dancing and laughing by practising them too much. Then he had taken her right hand in both of his and said, 'At last my Sunflower has come,' and from the way he spoke she had learned that he had thought of her long and passionately, especially in those hours of trance, just before one sleeps, or after one wakes, or during the visit of a bore, when the image of a beloved person is not merely held in the mind but comes to motion, performing acts a little more fantastical than those of common life but illuminating them and explaining them. He had a complete conception of her. She knew that if anyone had come to him and said, 'A thousand miles away, Sunflower is coming out of a church into sunlight,' he would continue, his voice shaking deeply with delight, 'Yes, and as she crossed the threshold she looked up at the sun and her brows frowned but her mouth smiled, and as she went down the steps she turned aside once to give a coin to a beggar.' Because she loved him she would always do according to his imagination. Surely a man who loved one like that was God to one, for he made one. He gave one life. For how could one live unless somebody one cared about wanted one to live in a certain way? Otherwise one just flopped about. And a man who loved like that did not only make one, he made one after a beautiful image. He gave one not only life but salvation. Therefore one would worship him with one's body and soul until one died.

Of course Dusa had done all this by herself, separate, alone. She had been the thinker and that which was thought into being real. Sunflower supposed that was really more wonderful. But who wants to do anything by themselves? Who wants to be separate? Who wants to be alone? Luxuriously she rolled from side to side in her bed, laughing at the dissolving terror of loneliness, who would never be alone again! The bright spaces of her room, which were lit by the morning sunshine and her happiness as by a lamp with a double wick, pleased her as being just right for what she felt. It was because she had hoped that she would wake up one day feeling like this that she made them do the walls like that, pale green, and faintly streaked in the lower half with very fine gold lines, fine as the lines on the petal of a crocus, and pointed upwards so that they had an air of growing. They looked very fresh and clean, as well they might, for they were washed all over every Monday, and she saw that it was done properly too. Oh, she was sorry for Dusa, for anyone whose greatness bound them to theatre! She had always loathed the theatre itself, the actual place where she had to act. That was partly because she disliked all buildings which were not made for people to live in: churches, railway stations, factories, offices, warehouses, seemed to her like the money she had to pay over in income tax, necessary, no doubt, for the community, but somehow also wasted. She liked farms, blacksmiths' forges, shops in the villages and little country towns and the browner parts of London, where people could work alongside of their lives, where their children could come in and tell them that their meals were ready. But her loathing came even more from the feeling one had in every one of them that since the day it was built nobody had swept in all the corners, that those bare boards behind the stage weren't ever scrubbed by anybody who had a nice enough home to realise what being clean is, and that however nice one's dressing-room there were certain to be other ones on the floor above or the floor below where cracked hand basins were supported on awful pipes that looked like the bones of people who had not washed when they were alive. Oh, it was lovely to have one's happiness coming to one here, in one's own place, which one had taken trouble to keep right! And it was lovely to have it strong in the morning, when one always felt at one's best and wanted to do things but if they weren't important didn't dare to because one had to save up one's strength for the evening, as one had to work then, though of course one would have liked just to have dinner and dance or talk a bit and go to bed! But now her life was going to be lived in the right places, at the right hours! But in the very moment when she knew the joy of extrication from the theatre she felt an emotion which she had believed peculiar to the theatre, the feeling one had on first nights of an impatient desire for the curtain to go up and the performance to begin. She wished to proceed at once with her new and magnificent destiny. She threw out her hand and struck the bell that would bring her breakfast, that would start her splendid day. Then shy because it seemed to her that anybody who had seen her make the movement must have known that she was extravagantly loved and loved her lover back again as extravagantly and without shame, she rolled over in bed and drew the sheets tight over her like the wrappings of a mummy and pretended to be half-asleep.

Martyn set down the breakfast tray just as it ought to be set down: not quite silently, for if she had done that you might have gone to sleep again and let the tea get cold, but not so noisily that you woke up feeling cross, and she said, 'Good morning' just right, so that you knew there was someone human about, but not so that you felt you had to do anything about it. She hadn't been much when she came. It was all a matter of training them, of pretending that you weren't frightened of them and sort of suggesting to them what you wanted over and over again. Cook knew how to set a breakfast tray very nicely now. The stone-coloured linen tray-cloth, the Lowestoft china, its flowers painted a little brighter than nature but not out of contempt, rather as if the painter expected to go out into the country the next

242

day and was looking forward to it so much that he was nourishing the absurdest hopes regarding everything that happens in the fields; the brown egg cosy in its cup; the three curled shavings of toast, the shells of butter on a wet leaf, the handful of raspberries on another; the single rose in the candy-striped Nailsea glass jar; it was all prettily done. In Sunflower's house all things were done prettily. In any house she might own she would be able to contrive that they were done prettily. She saw all sorts of houses in her mind's eye . . . Big houses in London, big enough to hold a great man's importance, which must have the guilt of their bigness lifted from them by careful plans to make them warm as a little house. One would have to face the problem that arose all the time if one was rich, of how to make the difference on the nights when one had people in, which, if one were poor, one would make quite easily by having chicken. But it could be done. You'd have lovely things to eat and the place pretty and make everybody feel at home, and the women would go home feeling as if their automobiles were velvet-lined caskets and themselves jewels, the younger men would walk back, halting on the bridge over the Serpentine if the house were in Portman Square, or on the Embankment if it were one of those funny eighteen-eightyish castles at the foot of Tite Street, watching lights that waver on water like exhorting forefingers and discussing weighty matters with flushed sententiousness. The party would not stop, and would in a sense go on forever, the women would always remember the night when they had been so beautiful and charming and take it as their standard. The men would have been so carefully picked and the talk so good that something would remain the next morning, there would be be a trace of it in *The Times* a week later, in the speech in the House of Commons a month later. It would all redound to the greatness of Francis Pitt. It would all make a delightful world into which to introduce young people. (She compressed her lips and reflected that Canterton must go.) There would be furnished homes one would take just for the summer. Green lawns that the sea-air cropped as close as sheep, and wild-haired hedges of tamarisk, broken where the path led down the cliff between changing cornices of sand to a yellow shore; and in the house lots of very big chairs, which one would probably have to bring oneself, for there were never enough, and scones and strawberry jam for tea, which everyone likes when they are on a holiday, and great fireplaces where as soon as evening fell one would light a wood fire and throw handfuls of lavender on it. The East Coast would be good for that, if one could find a place where the bathing was safe. Oh God! One must be quite sure that the bathing was safe. And perhaps there would be a country house where one lived all the year round, where things would be pleasant and would not change. An old house, that had gone on and on. One would not alter the garden very much, one would have the same herbaceous borders year after year, so that they should be loved and remembered and expected. One would not change the servants; one could always keep them if one was sensible. There would be a paddock for the old ponies. One would go to church every Sunday, not that one gets much out of it, but it is good to get into the habit of doing anything every Sunday. If a person was brought up in a settled home like that, and could always come back to it, surely they wouldn't get puzzled and upset about things as other people did. She would be able to arrange all these things. None of them would be beyond her powers. It was strange to think that she had sat here and cried because her house, being beautiful and smoothly run, was of no use to Essington, who simply did not notice whatever was agreeable and afforded no relief to his pricking need to complain; that when she was giving her morning orders to the servants she had sometimes shivered, feeling herself like a crazy ageing childless woman who perpetually sews baby clothes and lays them by in a drawer. She had thought her housewifeliness waste, whereas she had been learning her life like an art, practising against the time of the performance of her love.

Nothing in her life had been wasted. Someone must have been planning it and loving her all the time while they planned, for it could not be by accident that everything which had ever happened to her had worked towards rounding the perfection of this moment. It had seemed utter waste for her to be an actress, to spend her days being rehearsed in theatres that were dark when outside it was light by clever people who became mosquito-like with irritation, and her nights in doing the wrong thing before audiences which always included enough people who didn't know she was wrong to commit her to being engaged but which also included just enough people who knew she was awful for it to get about the world and spoil her peace. Yet being an actress had given her Francis Pitt. He had first seen her on the stage, wearing a silver cloak and speaking other people's words. She had been able to show him her beauty without her stupidity. And now he was hers. Smiling cunningly, she was even glad that she had played leads, although always before she had wished she could have played minor parts and had fewer great moments to fail in, for that way she had got him by another of his foolish forelocks, by the childish pride he felt in being able to keep company with famous people. To get him through his funny little weaknesses was not disgraceful to her love; there is comedy as well as tragedy. But she was distressed to find herself passing from this thought, which after all struck her as a little too aggressive for this time when blessing had been given gently into her hands and all her future life was to be gentleness, into another one more predatory still. Before she knew what she had done she had said to herself, her hands gripping the sheet over her like claws, that she did not even mind the scandal about herself since what it meant was that when people heard her name they thought of Essington and then of love, and if in following that common process Francis Pitt had thought of love in connection with her sooner or more vividly than he would otherwise have done, why, she was glad of it. That was detestable. By making Francis Pitt profit by the world's mauling of her name it put him in the position of a man whose wife goes on the streets to earn his bread. But the force in her that was inexorable so far as he was concerned said harshly, 'Well, would you not, if he had no bread?'

Oh God, but why should she think of ugly things? Everything was good, everything was simple. Francis Pitt was a man; men found love-making easy and delicious, beauty was the source of its ease and delight, and she had beauty. What could be simpler? She flung back the sheet and lay in her nightgown with her arms stretched wide across the bed, joy like a wild dancer springing and whirling in her body, because it certainly had beauty, and because it had already felt his great mouth at several places, on her throat, on her shoulders, in the crook of her left elbow, where he had halted at the little tangle of blue veins, which he had claimed, in a whisper that was low as if he prayed but shook with laughter, to be his monogram. Oh, making love to somebody one really loved was so interesting! She blessed her beauty, she laid her lips to her arms in gratitude, she drew her long yellow hair across her mouth and kissed it. No, nothing in her life had been wasted, not even her beauty, which had sometimes seemed to be wasteful in its essence, to be as fruitless as it was prodigious. The idea had come to her quite terrifyingly one afternoon, when she was sitting in the darkness that was as unrestful as hard daylight because the people who arranged it stood about breathing hard and anxiously, of a spring opening at one of the big dressmakers'. Across the lighted stage had passed the lovely mannequins, slim and polished like Malacca

245

canes, with smooth heads which shone as the top of a cane where it is rubbed by the palm, and delicate plucked eyebrows which made it seem as if an artist sitting at a table in a sunlit garden had spent the time while the coffee dripped down into the glass from the silver strainer in changing his friends' canes to pretty women with a pencil-point, yet with something ardent and moist like sap about their eyes and lips, as if the wood of which these canes were cut was remembering that it had had a habit of coming to flower about this time of year. What they were doing was not as good as what they were. The clothes they were showing were horrid. Like so many English dresses they demonstrated the real disposition of life to take away as much as it gives, for one felt that the designer would never have reached his present position had he not been brought up in the stern nursery of English provincial life, which had taught him habits of diligence and punctuality, but had also unfitted him to make full use of that position since it had left him with a sense that the highest possible destiny for a dress is to be worn on Sunday or at high teas. She had shuddered because life was never easy for anybody, and because these girls were wasting their youth and sweetness on futility, and had sat back in her chair and distracted her thoughts by looking about her and trying to put names to the vague shapes she saw about her in the darkness. That was certainly Germaine Peyton just in front of her. Even in the dim light one could immediately recognise that broad, offering blandness that was like a shallow saucer of thick cream. She had wondered why nearly all actresses, including herself, were so naturally recognisable. It wasn't that they were chosen for that, because they didn't have that quality at the start. It grew on them in the course of their careers, and there was something forced and uneasy about it, as if their appearances were struggling to make as clear a statement of themselves as possible. It was, she supposed, because nearly all actresses were bad actresses, having been chosen to practise an art because of physical qualifications that have nothing to do with that or any other art; and it is the way of the inferior artist to make a bid for personal conspicuousness; the Montparnasse painter with his velvet coat and his coloured scarf; the mediocre pianist with his long hair; the second-rate prima donna with the exaggerated set back of her shoulders. There was something piteous about it. It was a throwing up of the hands and a lifting of the voice of someone who has been swept away from the shores of normal life into a rough sea and finds he cannot swim. 'What I am doing with my art is not noticeable! I must be noticed or I must die, being

246

human! But surely this thing I am doing with myself is noticeable!'
Again she shuddered, and looked away, at a woman who sat on her
right. It was Mina Victoria, the Duke's third wife. She was a lively
little thing, but she did look silly. All the society women looked silly
nowadays because all of them that were at all in the running as
beauties had adopted two fashions that really didn't go together. First,
about ten years ago, they all began dropping their jaws and pushing
their chins as far back as possible, because Lady Artemis Merals did
that to fix attention on the marvellous purity of her brows, the
mermaid blankness of her eyes. Then about five years later they had
all wanted to look like Corton, the great Parisian cocotte and
dressmaker, and because she wore a small hat that covered her forehead
and shadowed her eyes in order to hide an expression of financial genius
that would otherwise have made the men she met climb trees, they all
did the same. To stylise their beauty in the manner of one woman they
had got rid of their chins, to stylise it in the manner of another they
had got rid of their foreheads and their eyes, so now there was nothing
left of them except their noses and sleek mouths, except lovely little
snouts. They looked like a lot of silly animals. And since they looked
like that they behaved like that. If one made a gesture expressive of an
emotion one felt that emotion; she knew that from her acting. The
Duchess of Victoria had acted like a greedy little fool when she
divorced the Duke. Beauty had put her in the way of doing that, and
beauty had placed Germaine Peyton and herself and God knows how
many other women in the ridiculous position of bad actresses. And
beauty had set the mannequins ambling in these clumsy clothes. She
had clenched her hands and muttered aloud, 'Charlock! Charlock!'
There had come to her the memory of something that had happened
long ago, when she and her sister Lily had gone down to stay for a
fortnight after measles with a cousin of her mother's who had married
a stationmaster in a Devonshire village. One afternoon he had taken
them for a walk up a lane that wound higher and higher between tall
hedges until there was a gate and they stepped out on to a heathy
moor and saw half of the countryside lying beneath them, checkered
out over its hills and valleys with different coloured fields that were like
a patchwork quilt stretched over the limbs of a sleeper. She and her
sister had cried out at the sight, and then again, because these were
more beautiful than any others, being bright. 'Oh! Look at that pretty
yellow stuff!' they had squealed, running along the hilltop ridge with
their long hair and their pinafores blowing round them in the upland

wind. And from behind them had come the soft voice of the old man, seeing the catch in things as grown up people do: 'Why, that's charlock, the nasty stuff. Nothing won't grow where charlock is, it kills all good growing.' That had brought her to a standstill. Surely it was sign of something like being naughty in the universe that anything so beautiful should not be useful! Well, it might be that the universe had been naughty in a more fundamental point than that. Beauty, the nasty stuff! 1Nothing won't grow where beauty is, it kills all good growing. The thought khad haunted her. Once, lying half-asleep in Essington's arms, she had moaned aloud, 'Charlock, charlock!' and he had cried in fury, 'Oh God, Sunflower! The mess your mind is in! The ragbag of meaningless bits and scraps! Imagine interrupting me with imbecile mutterings of "charlock, charlock", when I was thinking out proportional representation!'

But beauty was not a weed, it was not waste. It had made Francis Pitt say those things when she had turned her face to him in the moonlight, it had brought her life with Francis Pitt. She was not a field cursed with charlock, she was good pastureland. Lying there, she fell into a dream of how it would feel to be a meadow, to have a body of smooth wet earth pricked upwards with a million blades of growing grass. Someone would open a gate, there would run in a flock of young lambs, they would pound the wet earth with their strong little hooves, they would drop their little twitching muzzles to the grass and tug it up by the roots. Smiling and murmuring with pleasure, she took her own arms to her bosom and laid her lips to her own hands. They were like satin. He had thought so too the night before when he had laid his lips to them. For a moment he had stopped kissing them to murmur deeply to himself, 'So soft, so soft!' Oh, what a blessing her career had been to her, making her ready for him, lifting her out of her first ugly circumstances! She looked back at herself as she had been in 69 Tyndrum Road, getting up on a winter morning, washing at a deal wash-stand in cold water that left her hands all rough and red, not powdering her face or her body, not smoothing her elbows and her knees with lotion to make them ivory like the rest of her flesh; putting on coarse underclothes that left red marks on her with their thick armholes, creaking stays with high husks that rubbed her in between her breasts, black woollen stockings, and a rough serge dress that would not have been nice for a lover to touch and was not very clean, because one could not send it to the cleaners very often; brushing one's hair not enough to burnish it because one had to be at the Jennings' shop on time, and anyway the brush was cheap and had no grip; calling downstairs to warn Mum one was ready for breakfast in a Cockney whine. She lay breathless, panting thanks to God who had thrust on her, against her silly will, in spite of her stupid incapacity to imagine how gorgeous life might be, the gift of being fit to give herself to Francis Pitt. But her heart contracted suddenly, and she cried out, 'But I am not young! I am thirty! He is only having the fag-end of my beauty! Why did he not come to me when I was nineteen!' She sat up in bed and sobbed, having to make to herself the admission that however good her life was it still was not quite so good as it might have been, which was somehow frightful, like having to admit one's Mother hadn't loved you very much and hadn't done her best for you. A protective power had failed. But she cried out in answer to herself, 'Ah, now that I am going to be happy I shall keep young! I shall not grow old for ever so long!' She looked sharply about her, at the cupboards which were full of dresses which would still make people think of fine tincture and bright colours when she came by even if her skin and hair lost theirs, which would give her beauty form and style even if middle age confused the definite image she now presented; and at the bathroom door which was ajar and showed the tall mirror held by golden eagles where the light was strongest, so that she should see the first calamities immediately they befell, and the blue and green marbled shelves where the bubble-tinted Venetian jars and bowls held the balms and astringents she had not yet begun to use. Her career had given her full command over the second chance that a rich woman can give her beauty. Nevertheless she felt a wild impatience to get on with the story of her happiness at once. Her hand fluttered towards the telephone, though she knew it was utterly the wrong hour to find Mr Isaacson and ask him if her understudy could play tonight; he would have left his house at Walton Heath and not yet arrived at the office. She made herself lie down again, and closed her eyes, and thought how pleasant it would be to be a meadow, to feel the hooves of the young lambs kick on one's body and the little muzzles tug the grass by its roots.

Mr Isaacson would let her do it. He might reasonably say that though the management wanted to see the Manbury girl play the part they ought to have had longer notice, but he would not stick to that if she spoke with any of the urgency she felt. She did like Mr Isaacson. He was always the same, sitting at his desk, very slim, very rigid, very calm, with his long, white fingers crooked stiffly round the telephone, the thick discs of his strong glasses giving back the light steadily in front of his blindish, melancholy black eyes, his hair very smooth with brilliantine and his linen discreetly perfect, his skin preserving unflushed the strange discoloured pallor of the Northern Jew, which looks as if the race had daubed itself with the juice of a dark berry for disguise and now that happier circumstances have come were letting it wear off. When he spoke of his wife and his children he became more rigid, more calm than ever. Only one saw rise suddenly in front of the Walton Heath villa the immensely high and thick secretive and defensive walls of an oriental city. In a sentimental world he was a realist. He did not believe that this is particularly delicious, but he knew that if one does not eat one starves, and if one is not clothed one is cold, and if one does not marry and have children one is desolate. He did not believe that it is particularly agreeable to spend all one's money on keeping a family, but he knew that if men did not do these things the bottom would fall out of life. Of course he would let Sunflower off if she gave him the slightest hint of where she was going. When he heard definitely he would congratulate her in formal and unexcited phrases, but his eyes would glow with a sombre and splendid fantaticism, seeing a woman whom he liked passing behind those walls within which is protection and honour and increase. It was a pity he was not quite happy. You could tell that he wasn't from looking at him as he sat at his desk. There was a kind of strain across his shoulders as if he held his head high only by an effort. Of course he hated being subordinate to men so greatly inferior to him as Guggenheim, who was not a Jew but a Yid, and Madison, that fat old dandy with his tight clothes and his unshaded leer which looked as if his lashes had been burned off when some girl upset the lamp in the struggle. But it could not be helped. There was some weakness in Mr Isaacson which, beasts though they were, the other two had not got; when he said, 'Go,' nobody went. So he reconciled himself to the position, sat at his desk, and dealt justly with his work, his clever sensitive head inclined to droop, but his backbone forbidding that.

When one came to think of it, all the people one liked fell into that attitude sooner or later. Mum had done it all the time, working about the house. She'd never had enough fun, and she did so love a good laugh. (Oh, if only Mum had been alive to know how happy she was going to be!) Maxine had sat like that every night at Ciro's and the Embassy in the dreadful time after Jerry, her face emptied of all blood, her eyes emptied of all meaning, but her body bravely braced in her lovely, carefully worn clothes, offering her beauty silently and passively to the love of men as a target offers itself to the arrow. It was funny to think that if she had given up and taken to going home early there would never have been that baby. (She must tell Maxine all about it the minute all the arrangements were made.) And years ago, at Tyndrum Road when Aunt Clara was so bad with pneumonia, Aunt Emma, who drank, begged so hard to be allowed to sit up with her one night that they let her; and when they took a cup of tea to her in the early morning they found her sitting in the basket-chair by the bed in just that pose. Her face, bruised with drunkenness, though she had not touched a drop since her sister got ill, had fallen forward so that her pointed chin dug into her bosom; but her eyes blinked vigilantly among the rheum and turkeyish red ruffles of flesh, and her shrivelled little body was held like a ramrod as if she were a little girl who wanted to show that though she was naughty sometimes she could be good when it was necessary. Poor Aunt Emma, dear Aunt Emma. It was a sign she was really nice that whenever she had one of her bad times one of the first things she did was to go off and buy people presents. And that was the way the nice old stage-door keeper at the Palladium used to sit. The one who was so kind to all the girls, who interpreted everything that happened in a lovely well-bred way, and with such silvery definiteness and precision that his interpretation became the truth, since everybody acted on it; and who went home one day to die quietly of a cancer that must have torn him for years. Oh, human beings were splendid things! And this pose was a symbol of their splendour, of their mad bravery when the odds were against them. The head, which was clever, which knew too well what was happening to it, hung down; but the spine, which was stupid, which only knew it had to go on living, bent only for a moment, and then stiffened straighter than it was before its bending. It was as if a link in a chain should be struck again and again by a vast hammer and doubly resolved, 'I will not break, the chain's the thing, the chain must hold, I will not break!' It was lovely that at the party last night there had been only that kind of person, nobody like Billie Murphy or Lord Canterton, only people who did good work without being News: Farquharson, the little Australian cartoonist, who held his mousy head on one side all the time to make sure he was seeing things all right, because one must tell the truth, and Mackinnon, who went humbly, with an air of raising his hand and coughing behind it, into the furthest and most perilous places of the earth, their nice dowdy wives who smiled at one irrelevantly just to show they liked one, and a lot of young people who worked in Francis Pitt's office. (But he did not seem to have made it up with poor young Mr Harrop and Miss Wycherley. There was not a sign of them.) They were having all sorts of nice feelings about the occasion that made a lovely atmosphere in which to be happy. For they were clever enough to see how funny the musty mid-Victorian house and furnishings were, to look up and laugh at the preposterous mouldings and copings and cosy corners of soap-cornered timber carved into a confused richness like that of pickles seen through the glass jar; and they were simple enough to enjoy the champagne and the very good dance music, and to be a little impressed because they had been asked out by the little man about whom there hung this heavy scent of greatness; and they were so good, with such gestures, as of those who checked themselves perpetually lest they should make some promise they could not perform, lest they should break any growing thing. It was marvellous to feel that though one was about to enjoy the most extravagant delights of love, that though henceforth one's life was going to be saturated with pleasure, one was not going out into any desert of dissipation but would therefore range oneself forever with these sober people. For it was with their rhythm that he had moved when he laid his hand on her arm as they were watching the dear clumsy dancers, and had looked into her eyes so steadily, and spoken so solemnly, irrevocably committing himself to his question, and her to her answer.

'Will you come with me and see the statue at the end of my chestnut alley? I told you, it is a statue of love.'

Remembering the words made her feel exactly as hearing them had done: as if a little silver hammer had struck her nerves and shattered them into a thousand splinters of ecstasy. She wanted to hear his voice now, and be disintegrated by the shock of her love for him, and come together again so that she might again be disintegrated, and so on forever. She wondered how soon he would telephone her. It occurred to her, and her breath stopped with panic, that he might call her up when she was speaking to Mr Isaacson. She must make that call at once. Picking up the receiver, she said, 'Gerrard 773612.' Her eyes moved about the room. That slit of sea-coloured bathroom visible through the open door. She had a nice house. Below was the Chinese room, that cube of perfection. Above were the servants' rooms, which were really quite pretty; that unpolished oak furniture looked so clean, and the sheets were linen though she had bought them unbleached and lavender-scented. Outside the house was London; outside London

252

was England. The fine setting for the fine play. All the colours in the world seemed to have grown much brighter. It was as if someone had passed a silk handkerchief over the surface of the globe.

*

Parkyns said, 'Please madam, there's something in the garden that Cook thought you might like to see.'

She dropped the pen with which she had been writing a letter to her sister Lily. She had felt like writing to her this morning, though for some years there hadn't been much between them except at Christmas and the children's birthdays, all that about Essington making it so difficult; and now she had fixed it up with Mr Isaacson that she need not play tonight there wasn't anything to do but wait.

She put her face against the window-pane. 'I don't see nothing, anything.'

'It's ever so small,' said Parkyns, smiling.

'Oh, it isn't a kitten, is it?'

'It isn't a kitten' said Parkyns. 'I don't remember ever having seen one of what it is before.'

Sunflower opened the French window and ran down the iron steps into the garden. It wasn't such a bad place. She had done what she could with it by paving a good deal of it, and having just four big flower-beds, with all sorts of old-fashioned sweet-smelling herbs round the edge of them, because people always liked to touch the green stuff if you took them out there after dinner, and they seemed specially pleased when they found lavender and rosemary and southernwood on their hands.

Cook and Martyn were leaning out of the kitchen window, resting their busts on their folded arms, smiling at the thought of the surprise they had found for her. But she could not see anything. The beds were full of dwarf snapdragon, that flower which always looks furry and red-blooded, like a plump, bustling, high-coloured little woman, the sort who wears plain dresses that button tightly down the front but has her warm, romantic moments; the widow who inherits the public house and runs it herself, and is liked by all the men and suspected by all their wives, with much reason. But otherwise there was nothing.

'It's here, Madam!' said Cook. 'Just in front of us.'

There, on the paving-stones, lay a loosely assembled collection of knitting needles, making feeble gestures of rejection, like an old man who has no longer the strength to be as disagreeable as he once was refusing to be introduced to somebody.

'Oh!' cried Sunflower. 'It's a hedgehog! Isn't London a funny country sort of place!'

'We thought you'd like to have a look at it,' said Cook importantly.

'Of course I do! Oh, thank you ever so much for telling me! Oh, what a funny little thing. Who found it?'

'Martyn did,' said Cook.

'Yes, madam, I found it when I was putting out the white brocade bag to air after I'd washed it with petrol.' She giggled. 'Thought of keeping it to myself and slipping it into Cook's bed for a surprise.'

Cook's elbow nudged her in the ribs. 'You'd have found something in your soup that would have surprised you!'

There were more giggles. Those two were good friends; but Parkyns always seemed a bit out of it. That was the worst of keeping three. It was apt to happen that way, not that any of them meant to be unkind. She beckoned Parkyns to come closer to her.

'How do you suppose it ever got here? From one of the parks? Oh, look, look, you can see little winking eyes!'

The door between the front and the back garden slammed. It was Harrowby. He took off his coat and grunted some salutation and propped himself against the wall by the acacia tree. As always now, he looked terribly ill.

She called out to him, 'Good morning, Harrowby! Look, we've got a visitor!'

His eyes went to it, but disregarding it and what she said he asked gruffly, 'When will you be wanting me?'

That was surly, but you couldn't blame him when he felt as bad as he evidently did. 'Oh, Harrowby, not till tonight. I want to be up at Mr Pitt's at eight.' She was a little confused. Surely her happiness must be written all over her, they were all looking at her with a certain interested fixity, Parkyns, the two at the window, Harrowby with his cap half across his face. She bent over the hedgehog and cried out, in animation that was not feigned, because now the whole of life was so lovely to her that she had only to bend her attention to any part of it to become immediately enchanted. 'Isn't it silly to stick out its quills like that, when we don't mean it any harm? Oh, I wish it was more like a kitten or puppy, and one could pick it up and make a fuss of it! Aren't you silly to have a lot of quills instead of nice soft fur or a nice short coat! Oh, Parkyns, aren't its little eyes funny?'

Parkyns, at her elbow, murmured benignantly, 'They are indeed, madam.'

She appealed to Cook and Martyn. 'Can't we give it something to eat? Perhaps it'll stay then. What does a hedgehog like to eat?'

They looked doubtful, indisposed to make suggestions. The initial discovery of the animal had put them in a strong position, they did not want to weaken it by any confession of ignorance about its diet.

'There's always lettuce leaves,' said Parkyns, timidly.

'It doesn't look very vegetarian to me,' said Cook coldly.

Harrowby spoke suddenly. 'We had a lot of them at home, down at Warleigh, where my father is head keeper. We don't think anything of them there.' He said it sourly and desperately, and added contemptuously, 'But them that take any notice of them give them milk.'

Illness took people such different ways. 'Milk? Oh, thank you, Harrowby,' said Sunflower. 'Cook, give me some milk, please.'

Cook turned away. The white 'X' drawn on her broad flowered back by her apron straps showed for a minute in the interior dusk. Sunflower went to the window and laid her fingers on the ledge, doing a dance step to pass the time and singing over her shoulder to the knitting needles, 'Oh, Mr Hereward, don't run away!' Parkyns and Martyn laughed slowly, happily, fondly.

'Mind you don't mess your dress, Madam,' said Cook indulgently. 'I've filled the saucer rather full.'

Sunflower set it down on the stones. 'No, that isn't what he wants. He isn't taking a bit of notice. Oh, yes, he is. Harrowby, you were quite right. What lots of things you must know, being brought up in the country. Oh, look how he's drinking it up. The poor thing must have been hungry. Now he's put down all his quills. You'd hardly know he had any. I wonder whether you could ever make him fond of you if you gave him milk regularly, and if he would ever let you pick him up. Oh, look at the funny, funny way his nose works when he drinks.'

It was queer to be living life in two parallel columns, to be bending over the hedgehog and seeing that like anybody else it was divided and distraught, acting far more grown-up and self-possessed than it felt inside itself. For though in what it did with its quills it was like a testy old man, its winking eyes showed it piteous and playful as little animals are; and at the same time remembering with all one's mind and one's flesh what had happened beside the statue at the end of the chestnut alley.

When they had gone out of the house the night had seemed like a great, stirring snake, because of a young moon behind quick clouds, which perpetually cast on the earth faint, gleaming, changing patterns of black and white. All, all was movement, though it was very still. They did not speak a word, yet they were travelling fast as falling stars into a new relationship. When they came to the place where the path rose in steep steps between high walls of shrubs he put his hand on her arm to guide her, pressing his fingers into her flesh, not violently but gently, generously, dependently, to fuse the warmth that was in both their bodies, to share with her what he had that was good, to beg from her what she had that was good. From sheer habit she steeled herself against this delight, and leaned away from him. His fingers stiffened, he was hurt. Then she remembered she was free and moved back close to him, letting her body droop and her breath come softly, so that through the darkness he could feel her submission. His hand was contented again, closed on her arm, ran down it, made a bracelet round her wrist. She had never known him so utterly without laughter. That must mean that at last he felt safe, for his humour was a kind of knuckleduster he carried about with him, a method of defence. Gravity was his tonight, and an immense pride which towered above him like a strong pillar. When they were passing through the dark places in the chestnut alley, where two lines of trees made a tunnel, he was like her breathing hardly at all, moving as if his body were steeped in tenderness as in a softening fluid; but when they stepped into the bright places where there were no trees on the south side, and the moon watched them and the house looked up from the hollow with lighted windows, he walked like a very tall man. Twice his fingers tightened on her wrist and he stood still, drawing her towards him so that they looked into each other's faces. Then it was as if she were bearing the weight of his soul on hers. There was no thought in that moment, and no feeling. Afterwards, she did not know whether she had been able to see his face through the dusk. All she had known was that he was giving himself to her, and she was taking him. The second time he did this it was as if he had said to himself that it could not really have happened the first time, he seemed to be standing a little way back from the experience in a verifying wonder. Then he pointed to the half-seen whiteness ahead of them and muttered urgently, 'The statue! The statue!' and hurried her on, as if since they had done so much they must do more.

On a square pedestal, shoulder-high, stood a boy with wings. He was a child, so that his limbs were round; but he was grown enough to have a hollow back and proudly carried loins. A cloud dressed him in their darkness.

She murmured, 'Oh . . . I thought there was a fountain here.'

He answered, 'No. Only this statue. Of love.'

He had loosened his hold of her. She was not sure if she could stand alone. Swaying, she looked up at the boy and her head fell back on her throat. She stretched up her arms and moulded in the air the childish roundness of his limbs, whispering, 'I would like to be a sculptor . . . I would like to make figures out of wet clay . . .'

Francis Pitt struck down her hands, not cruelly, not kindly. Simply he wanted them for himself, to fold in his, to put to his great mouth. Then, as if he were making an immense trial of strength, he stepped backwards and stood apart from her, and shook himself, and made a soft, roaring noise of triumph, because though they were separate they were still as linked as if the same blood were flowing by some canal through both their hearts. And solemnly he said, 'Sunflower, I love you very, very much.'

Remembering this, she felt again that silver hammer strike her nerves and shatter them into a thousand splinters of ecstasy. She drowned in a deep sea, and in the depths was given back her life, and slowly floated up, and up, and up, into the light, into the sunshine of the garden, into the sunshine where the hedgehog was wriggling its nose on the bottom of the saucer and making it jump on its base, and the three women in the print dresses smiled at her with their nice country faces, and poor Harrowby leaned against the wall, turning his head towards his own shadow, as if he found the noon brightness a little trying. She had never really been away from these things, she had been looking down at the saucer, at the diminishing circle of milk and thinking, 'Now that's too yellow for nature, yellow down to the last drop, country milk's whiter, but there, what are you to do, all London milk is dyed with that annatto stuff, and it's no use changing the dairy, for they all belong to the same combine and one's the same as another.' Yet at the same time she had been with Francis out in the night that was like a stirring snake, she had felt him give her his soul and herself take it, she had heard him say, 'Sunflower, I love you very, very much.' She supposed that it would always be so now. That beside the plain buff surface of life there would be the golden stripe of what happened to her with him, and she could always put out her hand from any dreary place where she might be and touch it with her memory and relive its loveliness. It was a pity she did not go to church now, for she could think of him during the sermon. There was nothing he was not doing for her, he was putting her on a ledge in the universe where she would never be fatigued or bored, he was making her, he was saving her.

She wondered if the others had noticed how far away she had gone that minute. She glanced shyly from face to face. Harrowby had seen nothing. He looked as if he were blind with a sick headache. But the three women were smiling at her with a hushed, steady kindliness. She was afraid they noticed she was very happy. It was nice of them to be glad. They must like her! But it made her feel confused, that they should have seen signs of this most private thing. She smiled back at them partly out of gratitude, partly to hide her embarrassment, and tried to think of some remark that would shift their attention from herself. She looked behind her at the garden and thought that the streaked dark red snapdragons were just the same colour as the juice on one's plate when one had eaten damson tart and cream, and was not sure she really liked lavender, you felt it was aware that it was plain but very fragrant, and had the same acid sense of superiority over mere flowers that character actresses of ability have over all actresses, able or not, who play straight parts. That was no use, she turned round and looked up at the house: her house, that was at last free of Essington, in which she no longer needed to sit despondently like the stupid pupil of an irascible tutor, in which she could now lead her own life and do all the silly, funny things she wanted.

She called out, 'I think I shall buy a dog!'

All three exclaimed, 'Ooh yes!' and Cook said handsomely, as if giving her full permission, 'Yes, we'd like a bow-wow in the house again.'

'You mustn't steal him though!' she warned them. 'I don't ever see Pussy, he's always in the kitchen with you!'

At that moment, as if he had heard himself being spoken of, and wanted to see that no liberties were taken, Sambo thrust his three-cornered black velvet nose between the two print elbows on the window-ledge, closed his eyes as if to announce that he saw nothing worth seeing, let the exquisite moulding of his muzzle be delicately severed in two by a yawn, waved a pink strip of tongue, closed up all with a snap, and then did a brief, derisive, twitching dance with his ears, as if to make it quite plain that that had indeed been all he thought of the matter.

'Oh, you know, he's rude!' exclaimed Sunflower.

'Bless his Almightiness,' said Cook, giving him a pat which he accepted with the tolerance of a young man who has married for money, and found that there is quite a lot of money. 'He knows who his friends are.'

Parkyns said, in rather a low tone, so as to make the other two feel out of it, 'What breed were you thinking of having, Madam?'

'Oh, let's have another peke!' said Martyn.

Sunflower shook her head. She had cried so when she had had to give up Li Hung Chang. 'A terrier would be nice . . . a Sealyham . . .'

She stopped. She had remembered that Francis Pitt had promised her one of the borzoi pups.

The night before drew her back to itself. There they had stood, and he had said those words about loving her. The cloud had travelled past the moon and as it passed unwound the veil of darkness from the statue, as if it were a scarf that had trailed from its hand. A rack of it remained for a little about the child's right shoulder, and right arm, then he gleamed wholly white and dominant, the governor of this clearing. Putting her palms together under her chin, she answered, 'Francis, I love you very, very much.'

He had held up his hand with one of his queer, pompous, great actor gestures. Heavily and conscientiously, like a rich merchant sitting in his office behind a vast mahogany desk and explaining the terms of a contract to one about to sign it whom he wished not to deceive, both because of his sense of honour and a matter of liking, he said: 'Sunflower, I do not mean I love you as a friend. I do love my friends, I am loyal to my friends. But you, Sunflower, I love as a man loves a woman.'

His voice sounded false, it was so deep and laboured. She smiled to herself in the dark at this seeming falseness, it was so strangely at variance with his impassioned honesty, and it sprang from so dear a cause. For he was forcing his voice down as low as it could go, down far below where he could manage it, so that he should sound male.

Lifting her chin, she answered, 'I love you as a woman loves a man.'

He made a growling sound of delight, his hands fluttered in front of him, but still he held himself back. Bringing his chin down on his poutering shirt-front and bending forward his broad shoulders till they were curved like a prie-dieu, he went on in this heavy, scrupulous, explanatory way. 'You understand, Sunflower, I want you to give me your whole life? Would you do that for me?'

259

She asked, amazed, 'Why, what else would I want to do with it?'

Again he made that growling sound. He jerked his head about, as if there were a bit in his mouth and he thought he could break it, and muttered drunkenly, 'Sunflower, Sunflower . . .' A questing, formless bulk, he thrust himself against her without moving his arms from his side. Softly, like somebody encouraging a child to walk, she said, 'Kiss me, kiss me.' Slowly his short, strong arms struggled free of his side, as if there were bands to be broken. When they gripped her he swayed clumsily, as if he were indeed a lion walking on its hind legs. She whispered, 'Kiss me, oh, kiss me!' His great head dropped forward into the hollow between her shoulder and her neck. He sighed deeply, and rolled it from side to side. Then he lifted it, and his mouth came down on hers like a blow.

Again the silver hammer struck her nerves, again she drowned in a deep sea, again she slowly rose into the sunshine of her garden. She was saying, 'I've always thought I'd like an Aberdeen. I do think it's funny the way they look so like Scotch people . . .' That sounded all right. It was the kind of thing they printed in interviews with her, and there wasn't any trouble unless Essington happened to see them. Shyly she glanced from face to face to see if any of them had noticed how far she had been away, but as before Harrowby was resting cheek by cheek with his own shadow on the wall, and the three women in the printed dresses were still smiling into the sunshine with a benignity that was as likely as not caused by the sunshine and nothing else. For it was a lovely day. Surely it was a specially lovely day. The few clouds were so thin they were no more than whorls in a glass bowl where the blower's breath faltered, the unveiled sun softened the day with an apricot down and made all things wish not to move quickly, not to move at all, so that it was like the round cheek of a sunburned, sleeping child. Also everything seemed to be falling into a rhythm, into a pattern. In an infatuated search for the last drop the hedgehog was beating its little nose on the bottom of the saucer so that it spun on the stone like a top, and the two plump women leaning on the window-sill, the thin one standing alone, kept time in their lazy laughter. Looking about her, she saw for the first time that the three trees at the end of the garden grew like trees in a holy picture, as if their trunks had heard of the trinity and brought forth three branches apiece to its glory, as if the little twigs knew of other doctrines and busily sprouted this way and that to tell of them, like lesser brothers in a monastery bustling

260

here and there on minor duties. She would not have been surprised if the dark houses behind them had been changed to the blue mountains that are seen in the country dreamed about by piety, blue as distance might be if it were ascetic, exalted but without the virility of rock, and if their leaves had become a golden treasury. She would not have been surprised if the falling acacia flowers had been supported before they reached the ground by a wind of intention and carried to her breast, where they would form a sign; or if the city thrushes, which were making short, circumscribed flights above her that were more like human aviation than the long surrenders to the air and victories over it which birds make in country skies, had suddenly flown down, slowly and straightly, and come to rest on her shoulders and her head. She stopped talking, she did not feel the need of keeping appearances going, she felt that if she trusted herself to this sunlit hour she would be all right.

It was lovely, just standing there in the brightness. It would not be so bad to be an image of a saint that stood for ever out of doors, in a shrine at the turn of the road above a valley, watching the sun burn the green corn to brown usefulness, watching the spears of rain strike down into the earth, which they do not kill but make more living since they change dust to wet mould, until that day when lightning flashes, and mountains are cleaved to their stony roots, and all images become flesh. During one's waiting one would give hospitality to little creatures. Within the hollows of one's gilt diadem a bird might build its nest, and soon short flights of nestlings would proceed from one's head like rays; and she had heard of a wayside Madonna, creviced by weather within whom wild bees had made their honey. That pleased her. She became quite still, enacting to herself how it would be to stand in rain and shine with full wooden skirts about one, while in a hollow of one's body dark buzzing principles of life built up cell upon cell of golden, feeding sweetness; and on her face she felt the sweet smile all images of holy women wear.

But Harrowby was saying something. She looked at him and was appalled. He had stepped clear of the wall and had one arm flung out. For a second she thought he was going to give her notice in some very insulting way, like the chauffeur before him, who had seemed so nice and jolly and devoted, but who had got terribly gloomy and taken to getting drunk, and when she went to discharge him had shouted at her that he would be glad to leave her and go into the service of respectable married people, and had flung his month's money on the floor.

Whatever had given her that idea? His arm was flung out simply because he was pointing to the library window and all he was saying, and that quite without rudeness, indeed with the flattest lack of any emotion, was, 'The telephone is ringing, Madam.'

It was Francis Pitt. She knew that at once.

She cried, 'Oh!' and looked up at the house as if she expected to see him tapping on the glass and beckoning her. Then she began to run towards the iron steps, but stopped herself at once. This time, surely, she had given herself away! When she glanced round at the three women in print dresses they were all paying attention to other things in the way that was a little too good to be true, like the way people unanimously pretend not to have heard when you have said something stupid so that you know they all have. Cook and Martyn had developed a sudden interest in the cat, which was twitching its ears in annoyance at being abruptly patted from both sides at once; and Parkyns was trying to suggest by angular movements that she well knew her duty was to answer the telephone but that her mistress seemed to want to answer it herself, and anyway she was absorbed in the hedgehog.

She said, 'Parkyns, please . . .'

But it occurred to her that it would be dreadful when Parkyns came to the window and said, 'Mr Pitt to speak to you, Madam.'. Then she would look so that they would all be certain. She said, 'No . . . No . . . I'll go . . . It may be . . . those photographs . . .' and ran up the stairs.

At the top she halted. She wanted everyone, everything to be happy. 'Look after the hedgehog! Put a box over it or something. We'd better take care of it for a few days. It did seem so hungry . . .' They called up to her reassuring things, promises to do what they could. There was a special significant cordiality in their voices, as if they were trying to wish her good luck without saying the words. That made her feel shy, but all the same it was sweet of them to want her to be happy; and anyway they would all have to know quite soon. Probably she would be able to tell them herself, to put it into words. Surely he had meant that. She must see to it that they did not waste their money buying her wedding presents.

She had been quite right. It was one of the sleek-headed young secretaries saying, 'Mr Francis Pitt would like to speak to Miss Fassendyll.' Her voice went husky as she answered, 'It's me, speaking.'

She had to sit down while she waited, her heart was beating so. She smiled to see how the whole of her life was subordinated to her love. Henceforward she would think of the telephone in a specialised sense, just as something that Francis Pitt rang her up on.

'At last,' he spoke gruffly, softly. 'Is that you, Sunflower?'

She knew just how it was with him. He too was shaking so that speech was difficult. She murmured, 'Good morning, dear.'

There was a long silence. Then he said, 'About that little party of ours tonight . . .'

She realised there was someone sitting at his elbow. She laughed shyly at the way he had had to put it.

'Do you mind coming late? I find I cannot get away as early as I thought.'

Caressingly she asked, 'How late, my dear? Half past eight?'

'Yes. No, later than that. A quarter to nine.'

She had to smile at him. He was being so discreet, yet the sound of his voice which was rolling and echoing with emotion must have given away his secret to the stranger sitting by him. 'Very well, I'll come at a quarter to nine. Goodbye. And, Francis, I love you.'

She hung up the receiver and went to the window. They were all still there, the sun had cleared the trees on its way up to noon, the unshadowed snapdragons glowed like jewels. Parkyns's skirts gleamed like an angel's robes. She would have liked to go out and see what they were doing with the hedgehog, but she was afraid she looked too happy. To make sure she went over to the mirror, and had to cry out, 'Oh, it isn't decent!' There was the letter to Lily still lying on the writing desk, but she thought it would be better to leave it till tomorrow. Then she could tell her everything. But she felt too restless to sit down and do nothing. She would go upstairs and choose her dress for tonight.

They had drawn down the blinds in her bedroom and uncovered the two jars of potpourri, so it was nice in there. She went to the big cupboard where her evening dresses were kept, and looked at them hanging in their black silk bags, feeling very fortunate because there were such a lot of them and they were all so beautiful. She sat down on the floor of the cupboard and with her back to the dresses and her chin cupped in her hands, thought them over one by one. 'Nothing too fancy,' she told herself solemnly. And she must not wear the green and gold, though she looked better in that than anything, because it made her look very tall, and he was much shorter than her anyway. The pale green chiffon from Chanel, the Molyneux gold lace, the flesh-coloured satin from Nicole Groult. They would be all right. She turned to find them, to try them on to make a choice. But her hand dropped from the silk it grasped, her lip began to tremble. It had occurred to her that these and all her other dresses had the grave fault that she had worn them before.

This thing had not come to her quite perfectly. That it had come at all was a blessed miracle. But all the same it had not come quite perfectly. It had been bad last night when he had repeated, 'I do not mind at all, Sunflower, I swear I do not mind,' and her hands, travelling up to hold his face so that she could kiss it gratefully, stiffened and slid down to his sides, because they found that even as he was saying he was not jealous, the sweat of jealousy was drenching his brow. Of course he had been sweet when she had whispered, 'I knew that you would mind, I knew you could not help it,' and had taken her to him; and surely she had put it all right when at last he had stuttered, 'But it is true I do not mind, it is only that sometimes I thought I would go mad when you and he went home together and I was left here . . .' For then she had wound her arms tightly round his neck and pressed her mouth close to his ear, because it was an awful thing to talk about, and told him he need not feel bad about that, since lately Essington had been very good to her in that way. Even on those weekends he had not seemed to want anything of her except to lie in her arms. Sometimes she had thought this was not just because she was very tired but because he was very kind, for he had a way just now of lying in bed as still as if he were asleep but with his eyes staring in front of him and his mouth a little open, as he used to when he was in the Cabinet and there was something difficult to be thought out. She had to tell this to Francis Pitt, so that he would realise what an exceptionally fine nature Essington had, and that was dreadful because he kept on not being able to hear and making her repeat it. At last he said, 'I will not mind at all when nobody has been more to you than I have . . .' And that would be tonight. She would not have to worry about this at all after tonight. But all the same, this thing had not come to her quite perfectly.

She rose and shut the cupboard door on all the dresses and stood for a time in the dusk, pressing her forehead against the cool wood. She would go down into the garden and see what they were doing for the hedgehog. And after lunch she would go out and buy a new white dress.

It would not have surprised her if there had been angels hovering over Hanover Square, one at each corner, blowing trumpets, as they do on old maps, that show coronations and royal weddings winding their pomp round cities. Really, there was something strangely appropriate to her happiness about the place. It was square, you know, square. Her happiness was foursquare. Built foursquare to the elements. And the sparrows fluttering dust through their feathers as ill-bred little boys like to blow imaginary bubbles through protruded lips made one remember that not a sparrow falls. And the taxi-drivers lounging against the railings, not of the same species as the sparrows but of the same class, told as plainly that the harsher laws of life were only illusions and did not really operate. They lived by getting fares, you would think it would be terrible for them unless they got fares, and yet there they were without any fares and yet they didn't look as if anything so terrible was happening, showing that their condition was not so hard-pressed as one had thought it, that possibly nothing was ever hard-pressed, if one only knew. Everything was all right, and the frame of everything matched it, for the afternoon was very hot and clear. The powers had pushed back awning after awning in the upper air, and had reached the topmost one of all which is faded to the palest blue because it is so near the sun. Wonderful strong stuff it must be, never for all the wear it has had to split and let through the dazzling white nothingness. Because of these things she smiled blindly at the taxi-driver as if he were Harrowby, left him skimmingly, and was inside Maribonne's saying, as if it were a prayer, 'Surely he will let me buy a model straight off the mannequin, he has before, he is so keen that I should stop going to Paris and get my things from him,' before the commissionaire touched her on the arm and asked her if she wanted the taxi to wait.

Blushing and smiling, as if this were a grave mistake but it would all work out for the best, she fled upwards to the driver, 'I thought it was my own car.'

'Anyone would, wouldn't they, miss!' That fetched him out of his seat. He had the door open, he was patting the upholstery as if it were the hide of a pet he had raised by hand. It appeared that this was the first day he had had it out, that this was the first day in his whole life he had worked as his own master.

More than a fortunate coincidence, an omen.

'Fresh flowers in the 'older,' he recited, prodding them.

'I noticed that! I noticed that!' she assured him. She wished someone would come along the pavement now, to sell her flowers, to be overpaid. Was there nothing she could do for this nice man? People wanted her to write testimonials to face-creams and powders, couldn't she write a testimonial to a taxi-cab? But it would be difficult to find anything to say. About powders one said, 'I find nothing gives the skin such a velvety surface,' but one couldn't do any good by saying a taxi ran in a velvety way, for that would give credit to the kind it was, not to that particular one. And this poor man wouldn't be able to afford to put an advertisement in the papers, anyway. Really there wasn't anything one could do for him. But she need not worry, because he would be sure to do well since they had met on this day. Beaming with confidence in both their futures, she disengaged herself from him, because there were stirring in her mind imperative commands about the dress she must buy for that night. It must be of white satin, because that is the one white stuff which does not seem poor when one thinks of real things. White velvet is like snow lying under a sober sky, but not so good, and all the white crêpes are like sunlit snow crisped by winds of different forces, but none of them so good, and the thinner weaves are not so white and fine as the filaments of frost. But white satin is a human idea, a human triumph. There is nothing like it in nature save the contented face of the cream in its broad bowl on the dairy shelf, and that is not so beautiful, for it looks not quite right, as it tastes not quite right, because of the greasiness which reminds you that the cow is a bit of a silly and does not answer as a horse does when you speak to it over the gate. Thick white satin is like light made solid for a woman's wearing when she wants to think of nothing but pure light, when colours are all wrong because they are stains which refer to passing moods, and there is nothing now on hand but a feeling that is going on for the rest of one's life. It should be simply made, for light takes simple forms, the path of the moon on the water is quite straight, the lightning through the cloud traces a pattern simpler than a branch. It was lovely that there were artists who attended to such things, who would make her a dress for tonight.

*

It held her body closely, brightly, borrowing from the greenness of her

266

dressing-room, and its image in the triple mirror gave green reflections such as one sees in blocks of ice, with which it snarled in the hollow between her breasts, streaked the long tapering of her waist beneath them. Her body was nice enough, that was all right, but her face looked so queer. She had gone white, with the dead whiteness of a white flower in shadow, and her lips, which until now she had hardly ever needed to rouge off the stage, were very pale pink, like pink roses ruined by the rain. And there was something new about her expression.

AFTERWORD

THIS unfinished novel, written in the mid-1920s, is a study in frustration – for its readers, in that the problems it poses remain unresolved, and for Sunflower and her creator in that it is about the unsatisfied physical desire of a woman for a man, unusual for the period and unusual for Rebecca West.

No one will be surprised to learn that *Sunflower* is autobiographical, though Sunflower as a woman may not be most people's idea of the author. Rebecca West is projecting an alternative self: tall, blonde, exquisitely beautiful, non-intellectual, in fact 'stupid'. The difficulty with Sunflower's alleged stupidity and inarticulacy is that her creator cannot, as it were, live down to it: Sunflower's perceptions, and the vivid savagery of her imaginations, are pure Rebecca.

Sunflower the actress is a more credible alternative self. Rebecca West had trained for the stage before she became a writer; she saw life, as in this novel, in terms of scenes, performances and rôle-playing. Around the time she began *Sunflower* she wrote, 'I wish to heaven I had succeeded in getting on the stage. I believe it would have suited me far better.' As a notoriously outspoken journalist, she knew like Sunflower the loneliness and alienation that being a celebrity brings,

268

and she knew too the social embarrassment of being stared at as the mistress of a famous man.

Rebecca West was a powerful public personality, and a radical feminist. Yet what Sunflower wants is 'to marry someone really nice', to pack in her career and be cherished. The imagery at the beginning of the book all relates to feelings of being starved and trapped; to be loved by Francis Pitt, Sunflower imagines, would be like being fed and satisfied. Sunflower longs to be passive, part of nature and the process of birth and death; she wants to be pure earthy femininity, 'one of the things that have no will and only use'. In Francis Pitt, Sunflower feels she has found the primitive male animal, the neolithic hunter whose strength will allow her to luxuriate in her femaleness. Sunflower wants anonymous domestic bliss, like the transforming love of the garage man and his plain wife.

If this does not sound like Rebecca West as judged from her public writings, her tragedy was that this is the way she often felt inside. She was, like Sunflower, a person who felt, rather than a rational person, and by the 1920s she was tired of fending for herself, tired of the ambivalence of her situation with H.G. Wells, whose mistress she had been for ten years. Her own performance as an independent woman no longer convinced her. Yet all around her were men who were less strong than she.

Rebecca remarked to her sister that although men 'gaze at me with adoration at parties' they rarely wanted anything more from her. 'It's obvious that men are terrified of me. I can't imagine why.' Her predicament was that of attractive, strong, achieving women the world over. Men admired and desired her, but did not want to spend their lives with someone who had star quality and who gave her own destiny the same significance as her husband's. Which is why women's magazines urged women to 'keep their femininity' by submitting, conciliating, concealing their expertise and opinions, in order to boost their man's ever-threatened ego – and keep his love. Rebecca West, simply by being as she was, was fighting a battle for sexual parity that is still not wholly resolved. The insecurity of men made Rebecca insecure as a woman.

In the scenes with Essington, Rebecca gives an accurate picture of her life with Wells, whom she had loved. 'Though she rebelled against him, she was a part of him. How could she leave him?' But 'Oh, why couldn't Essington have married her?' She gives a physical portrait of him, ageing now, but still 'like some great cat, with delicate bones, a puma or a cheetah' – or a jaguar, which was her name for Wells. She is at her best in the scenes which show their harmony wrecked by his bullying manipulation of her, and her own emotional exhaustion.

But we already know a lot about Rebecca West and H.G. Wells. More interesting is Rebecca's fictional account of her passion for another man – the 'mighty little gnome' as she calls him here, in the guise of her fictional Francis Pitt.

Rebecca broke off her relationship with Wells in autumn 1923 by going to America to give a series of lectures. They had been getting on badly for a long time, and both had tried to end the affair; this break was to be definitive. What Wells did not know was that for some time Rebecca had been fascinated by another man. At Christmas 1923, in New York, this new affair came to a head, and to an end. Rebecca was disturbed by this failure for years, and began to write *Sunflower* as a way of getting it out of her system.

Sunflower is about herself and Lord Beaverbrook, who is Francis Pitt in the novel. In 1923 he traced Rebecca to her New York hotel, and they spent Christmas together. Rebecca believed that this was the beginning of a permanent relationship, and that they would be married. She was wretchedly mistaken.

William Maxwell Aitken, Lord Beaverbrook, known as Max, was the son of a Scotch Presbyterian minister who emigrated to Canada, where young Max made his first fortune; in the novel, she makes him an Australian who has made good in California. Max Aitken was already a millionaire when he came to London in 1910, at the age of thirty-one.

He made a sensational entry into the British political and social scene. He gained control of Rolls-Royce, made a friend of Rudyard Kipling and a closer one of Bonar Law, who became leader of the Conservative and Unionist party in 1911. Law, a quiet and unglamorous politician, was Max's hero; according to his biographer A.J.P. Taylor, Max said he loved Law 'more than any human being'. Law is depicted as Hurrell in *Sunflower*, with his political allegiance changed to the Liberal party. 'I admire him more than any other living man', Francis Pitt says of Hurrell.

Max Aitken was given a knighthood in 1911, allegedly to persuade him not to return to Canada, and also no doubt in return for contributions to party funds. He was briefly an MP, but his ambition was not to hold office; what he enjoyed was political influence. His heart was in business. He bought a bank, and a chain of cinemas, and in 1916 gained control of the *Daily Express*. By 1923 he also had an interest in the *Daily Mail* and the London *Evening Standard* , and it is as a newspaper tycoon that he is remembered.

In 1916 he was given a peerage, and became Lord Beaverbrook. He was a tough, dynamic, amusing and generous man, with a genius for publicity; he was also highly strung and hypochondriacal, and suffered from asthma. A lover of women, he had no obvious physical graces. He was small, with a heavy torso and short legs, a puckish urchin face and a wide mouth that was a gift to caricaturists. Rebecca describes him in *Sunflower* as 'a little man with hair the colour of a fox and a very big mouth', a child-like, kind little Napoleon, 'the most self-possessed and male person she had ever met'.

There was also Lady Beaverbrook, whom he had married in Canada when they were both very young. She was by all accounts a fine person. She did not share his political and social life in London, and when Rebecca first knew them their relationship was not unlike that between H.G. Wells and Jane, as conveyed graphically in *Sunflower* in the attitude of Essington to his wife Mabel. (Rebecca does not give Francis Pitt a wife, only a sister.) Beaverbrook was like Wells in other ways – in his smallness, his male energy, his driving egotism, his anxiety about his health.

Rebecca first met Beaverbrook in 1918, when he was Minister of Information and Wells was also involved in wartime propaganda. Subsequently she and Wells sometimes dined with Beaverbrook, as Essington and Sunflower do in the novel. Beaverbrook's house, however, was not at all like Pitt's Hampstead mansion. He had a small Tudor house in Fulham called The Vineyard, where he gave exclusive parties – there was no space for big ones, though the garden was large, with a tennis court. After her first visit in 1920, Rebecca wrote to a friend that she still preferred Wells to all other men, but had this to say about their host: 'I found him one of the most fascinating talkers I've ever met, and full of the real vitality – the genius kind that exists mystically apart from all physical conditions, just as it does with H.G.'

In the summer of 1923, when she was in the process of separating from Wells, she wrote to the same friend: 'I had dinner with Beaverbrook and his wife last Thursday. It was so funny. I must tell you about it.' One wishes she had told about it in the letter. What happened between the Beaverbrooks and Rebecca before she left for America is a mystery. Rebecca in her old age concealed the identity of the man she had loved after Wells, but talked and wrote about the affair as a terrible tragedy. She told Gordon Ray, when he was writing his *H.G. Wells and Rebecca West*, that before she left England the man's wife had told her that she and her husband were going to be divorced and that he intended then to marry Rebecca. This is not likely. Lady Beaverbrook may have conveyed to Rebecca that she was unhappy, and was going to travel abroad, as she did. When Rebecca and Beaverbrook met in New York, she told Professor Ray in the 1970s, 'it was on the understanding that they were in love'. But during the next fortnight it became apparent that 'they were completely unsuited to be husband and wife'. She meant that sexual relations between them had been a disastrous failure.

1923 had been a bad year for Beaverbrook. Bonar Law was dying of cancer of the throat – in the novel, Hurrell is dying of tuberculosis – and though Rebecca believed she had been of some comfort to Beaverbrook in his grief and anxiety, the haemorrhage scene in the novel is fictional. In *Sunflower*, Pitt brings the two political enemies, Essington and Hurrell, together at Hurrell's death-bed; in real life, it was Lloyd George whom Beaverbrook reconciled with the dying Bonar Law. When Law died, soon after Rebecca had left for America, Beaverbrook lost not only his best friend but his place at the centre of political life. According to his biographer, he destroyed a lot of his correspondence for 1923, including his letters from Rebecca. Nor did she keep any of his from this period.

Commonsense would suggest that what Beaverbrook wanted from Rebecca was her amusing companionship and, perhaps, casual sex. I do not believe it entered his head to divorce his wife and marry her. She was by no means the only woman to whom he was paying marked attention at this time. But at Christmas 1923 Rebecca – strong-minded, single-hearted, in love, and longing for the stability of marriage – understood nothing of this.

Her confidante in New York was the American novelist Fannie Hurst, to whom she wrote that Beaverbrook said they ought to 'reconcile ourselves to the fact that life together in London is impossible and it was torturing for him to see me'. She wished he had never come, 'the poor old donkey'. But Rebecca was far more damaged by this episode than her note to Fannie would suggest. She remained obsessed by Beaverbrook for years. In London the following summer she wrote to Fannie a letter which provides the only evidence of what had happened. Beaverbrook called at her flat in Queen's Gate Terrace and took her to lunch at The Vineyard:

We were alone. That was a queer thing, for nearly always he had a crowd round him. We had lunch, and we walked round the garden for a time. He then talked quite lightly of our past infatuation as if it were a tremendous joke. He laughed about it. I suddenly realised that he was physically quite indifferent to me. Fannie, I'm not telling you the truth. I'm leaving out the point. He casually implied in a phrase that when he had made love to me in London he had been drunk, and that it had been very awkward for him when he found I took it seriously. New York he didn't explain at all.

This has the ring of cruel truth about it. By the end of the letter she was facing the fact that 'the New York business was I suppose a panic-stricken response to what he realised was my clinging to the idea that he loved me'.

She soon came to believe that it was Beaverbrook's impotence that had been the trouble, rather than his disinclination to involve himself in so purposeful and permanent a relationship as the one she assumed. This may have been indirectly true, in that 'her own inexorable intentions towards him', to quote *Sunflower*, could have seemed alarming to a casual philanderer. 'You are so terrible as an army with banners, Sunflower,' says Francis Pitt. The impotence theory, based on a more general proposition that modern life forced men to abdicate from their primitive maleness, to some extent salved Rebecca's self-esteem. But it left her with the more insidious terror that there was something repellent about her as a woman which made men impotent.

She began writing *Sunflower* in 1925; the following summer she met Beaverbrook's latest protégé William Gerhardie in the south of France, who was also writing a novel about Beaverbrook. Gerhardie reported to Beaverbrook that Rebecca was writing about him too, and Beaverbrook sent a disagreeable message. This was the first check. In 1927, Rebecca determined to discover 'the mental cause in me' that spoiled all her sexual relationships, and went into psychoanalysis. Since her analysis focused on the same problems as her novel in progress, the two got rather mixed up, and Rebecca was writing out her dreams and making notes of her analysis in the back of her *Sunflower* manuscript book.

In 1928, when she was putting together the essays and reviews that made up *The Strange Necessity*, she still had every intention of completing *Sunflower*, though she had made up her mind that it could not be published for years. She knew Francis Pitt would be immediately identifiable as Beaverbrook, and feared he would 'wreak some awful vengeance on me'. Her friend G.B. Stern, who had read the unfinished manuscript, applauded her decision not to publish straight-away: 'I've been terrified for years over what might fall on you, when you published it.'

There are a few more pages of *Sunflower*, in addition to what is printed here, drafted in Rebecca West's small round handwriting, but she was working tentatively, and it peters out. One section should see the light of day: in the dress shop, Sunflower feels oppressed by the presence of one of those 'high-nosed women who talk not of their daughters but of their gehls' – one of the arrogant Englishwomen of the upper class whom Rebecca West loathed, feeling that they despised her, and feeling too that they had no right to their arrogance since they had neither brains nor beauty, neither talent nor achievement, but only snobbish complacency, money, and a resonant family name.

This was the sort of Englishwoman she was to make savage fun of in *The Thinking Reed*; and she uses such a woman in the last unpublished pages of *Sunflower* in a brilliant passage about names and naming, just as apt for today – with its fashionable reliance on logos, designer labels, buzz-words, 'in' places and 'in' people – as it was in the 1920s. Stupid rich people, wrote Rebecca, were only conscious of things that were named, and could experience or discover nothing for themselves. This particular woman was going to travel:

She had looked up at a railway poster and seen a woman sitting on the deck of a steamer with a rug wrapped round her under a sky on which letters wrote a name she had heard from the lips of people whom she regarded as her equals or her superiors in this business of assimilating named things. Therefore she had gone to a named travel agency and booked her ticket, reserving rooms at a hotel she had seen named in the Continental *Daily Mail*, where she would find lots of people whose names are printed under photographs showing them sitting in tweeds on camp stools at the Fuffshire Point to Point or driving a golf ball, which surely itself would have a name, from the first tee at Le Touquet; and at the appointed time she would shut up the country house she and her husband had first seen in a photograph under the name of a reliable estate agent in the front pages of *Country Life* and the flat that had been offered under an equally reliable name on the back page of the *Observer*, and would pass across Europe, looking up at times and naming places, till she settled herself on the deck of a steamer, wrapped in a rug she had seen named in the advertisement in the *Sketch* or the *Tatler*, at which point an artist would see her and realise how perfectly she expressed an ideal of foreign travel and would be inspired to paint a poster in which a woman would sit on the deck of a steamer under a sky inscribed with the name of a place, at which other women would look up.

Yet there is an irony here since, when Sunflower fantasises about her future life with Francis Pitt, it is precisely those named accoutrements of the conventional good life that she yearns for. When 'practising the performance of her love', the imagined setting is a big London house on Portman Square or on Tite Street, or an old country house where nothing changed. Rebecca was uncomfortably ambivalent about where she wanted to belong in the traditional class-and-wealth structure of English life for she belonged nowhere, and anywhere. When she married Harry Andrews, two years after abandoning the manuscript of *Sunflower*, she actually *did* have a flat on Portman Square, and an old country house with all the trimmings, where she embarked on a new 'performance' as a country lady and landowner, becoming quite capable of outdoing 'the high-nosed women' at their own game and on their own territory.

Rebecca West made extensive notes for *Sunflower*, but the manuscript she did complete departs considerably from her original plan. She abandoned it without reaching either climax or anti-climax, which gives it a peculiar tension. She abandoned it when the narrative demanded a major sexual confrontation between Sunflower and Pitt – and this, since it involved problems that she had not solved, may have been more than she could cope with, even fictionally.

The tryst with Pitt was to prove bitterly disillusioning, since there was a crowd around him, he paid her no special attention, and did not even like her new white dress. Sunflower was to escape to America and work as a waitress, trying to find ordinary love with a poor man. After proposals both honourable and dishonourable, she was finally to flee from a kindly lover on learning that he was the 'great man' of the town. The point of the novel was to be that great men – such as Wells or Beaverbrook – spelled death to a woman's sexual and domestic happiness and personal autonomy – another reason maybe why Rebecca decided, with more head than heart, to marry Henry Andrews.

'The Theme of the Book is,' she wrote in her notes:

I. Women have remained close to the primitive type because doing the same job – wifehood and motherhood. Men have departed from the primitive type because they are doing utterly different jobs.

II. The type of civilisation men have produced demands great men – greatness that presses too hardly on the men. They are bound to buckle under the strain.

In Rebecca's thesis, that is, men become inhuman, and sexually impotent. But what about the great women, who 'depart from the primitive type' of wife and mother and do 'utterly different jobs'? They too can buckle under the strain, though Rebecca does not say as much, and though Sunflower was an actress against all her overwhelmingly domestic and maternal instincts. And Rebecca West? She was a mother; and, like most of us, she wanted everything – her work, her personal freedom, her traditional woman's role, a stable marriage. She was a flux of alternative selves, and sometimes a more frightened woman than the world that knew the equally authentic, confident and stellar Rebecca West could well imagine. As a journalist wrote in 1928, naming her beneath a dazzling photograph by Lenare, she was

the owner of the wittiest tongue in London, and the most gentle brown eyes . . . a woman deeply imaginative enough to have discarded more black and vivid fears than most people in this life. Therefore today she stands more cleanly and shiningly free of them than anyone I have ever met.

Is it a mistake to publish *Sunflower*, which blurs that fearless image, and which Rebecca West did not even choose to finish? I do not think so, because there is always something to be learned about history, society, and ourselves from the work, the life, and even the confusions and failures of a great woman.

Victoria Glendinning, London 1985